STUDIES IN ROMANCE LANGUAGES: 6

Editor

JOHN E. KELLER

Associate Editor for French

L. CLARK KEATING

Editorial Board

French

WILLIAM C. CALIN
ROBERT CHAMPIGNY
LESTER G. CROCKER
J. H. MATTHEWS
MICHAEL RIFFATERRE

Italian

GLAUCO CAMBON
WILLIAM DESUA

Portuguese

EDWARD GLASER
GERALD MOSER

Spanish

JOSÉ J. ARROM
JUAN BAUTISTA AVALLE-ARCE
OTIS H. GREEN
KARL-LUDWIG SELIG

Translated by

RAYMOND C. AND VIRGINIA A. LA CHARITÉ

NOVEL PASTIMES AND
MERRY TALES

BONAVENTURE DES PÉRIERS'S

NOVEL PASTIMES
AND
MERRY TALES

Translated
with an Introduction and Notes by

RAYMOND C. LA CHARITÉ
AND
VIRGINIA A. LA CHARITÉ

ISBN: 0-8131-1279-6

LIBRARY OF CONGRESS CATALOG CARD NUMBER: 70-190532

A statewide cooperative scholarly publishing agency serving Berea College, Centre College of Kentucky, Eastern Kentucky University, Kentucky Historical Society, Kentucky State University, Morehead State University, Murray State University, University of Kentucky, University of Louisville, and Western Kentucky University

EDITORIAL AND SALES OFFICES: LEXINGTON, KENTUCKY 40506

PRINTED IN SPAIN

DEPÓSITO LEGAL: V. 4.367 - 1972

ARTES GRÁFICAS SOLER, S. A. — JÁVEA, 28 — VALENCIA (8) — 1972

for
KITTY *and* DON

TABLE OF CONTENTS

PART TWO

(Tales attributed to Des Périers)

INTRODUCTION

POET, HUMANIST, GRAMMARIAN, SATIRIST, SECRETARY, THINKER—Bonaventure des Périers was all that and more, for, with the sole exception of his brilliant contemporary, Rabelais, Des Périers was also the most powerful, resourceful, and original of the sixteenth-century *conteurs*. Yet, much of this versatile and controversial figure's life and an important segment of his work remain enigmatic and shrouded in mystery. Misunderstood and maligned in his own time, he fared no better at the hands of posterity. The pace of revaluation has been halting, but today, thanks to painstaking and penetrating research, Des Périers has been restored to his rightful place as one of the most imaginative and gifted prose writers of the French Renaissance.

Little is known of his life and career with any degree of certainty, and, although he was intimately involved in the intellectual, religious, and artistic developments of his day, hard biographical evidence as well as contemporary accounts of his activities are excruciatingly scarce when not altogether suspect. His origins are obscure. We know nothing at all of his family, his birth, and his early years; speculation has centered primarily on his possible illegitimacy and his noble provenience. His date of birth is no less conjectural; for a long time, it was thought to be toward the end of the XVth century. Today, it is generally agreed that Des Périers was born ca. 1510-15, probably in the province of Burgundy. Although the names of several towns have been suggested, most students of Des Périers favor the small town of Arnay-le-Duc, near Beaune. At any rate, the townspeople of Arnay-le-Duc are convinced; one of their structures bears a commemorative plaque, which reads: "In this house Bonaventure was born in 1498."

By all accounts, Des Périers was formally educated at the College d'Autun, part of the Abbey of Saint Martin, where he remained from the late 1520s to approximately 1532. The rector, Robert Hurault, was a Protestant sympathizer, and he undoubtedly exercised a strong and lasting influence on his young protégé. Moreover, Des Périers acquired a remarkable grasp of Greek and Latin and, through the comparative study of ancient languages, he became well steeped in the literature of Antiquity. When not studying, Des Périers worked at eking out a modest existence, most likely by tutoring.

After Autun, Des Périers travelled a good deal, leading a somewhat vagabond existence, but spending considerable time in Lyons, the heart of much of Renaissance France. His humanist training and interest attracted the attention of Robert Olivétan, Calvin's cousin, and during 1533-34 the two men collaborated on the Waldensian Bible, a translation into French, which was published in June, 1535. The Old Testament was translated from the Hebrew and the New Testament from the Greek; however, most of the New Testament translation was lifted from Jacques Lefèvre d'Etaples's own translation. Des Périers's participation was by no means negligible, but it does appear that he was Olivétan's helper rather than his partner. Specifically, Des Périers established the Index of proper names and an extensive Table of Contents, and he quite probably contributed other details of a general nature.

By 1534, Des Périers had acquired a reputation, however slight, among his fellow humanists and was in some demand within the publishing circles of Lyons as a philologist, copyist, and corrector. In 1535, he collaborated with Estienne Dolet, editing the great humanist's *Commentaries on the Latin Language* and correcting the proofs.

Des Périers was obviously at home in Lyons; he enjoyed its heady and inspiring atmosphere as well as the opportunity to hobnob with the literary greats of the day, Marot, Scève, Rabelais, to mention only a few.

Menial tasks and artistic ventures took up most of Des Périers's time, whether in Lyons or elsewhere. During 1535-36, he was busily trying his hand at poetry. His main inspiration was the reigning poet of France, the beguiling and ever-controversial Clément Marot. Des Périers considered Marot the Prince of French poets, an "immortel poète," and he fondly and respectfully referred to him as "mon père." It is not surprising that Des Périers was the first to come to his defense when Sagon maliciously attacked Marot, who, in the aftermath of the infamous *affaire des Placards* (1534), had taken refuge in Ferrara. François Sagon, a mediocre poet and a crass opportunist, wrote an artless and vituperative tract to the King, accusing Marot of hypocrisy, debauchery, and heresy. Sagon was undoubtedly coveting Marot's post as court poet, and the absent Marot was hardly in a position to defend himself. Des Périers launched the counterattack in his "Pour Marot, absent, contre Sagon," a subtle appeal to Francis I for understanding and forgiveness and a call to other Marotic poets to speak their piece. The ensuing debacle, which lasted a few months, is one of the most hilarious fights in all of French literary history. Sagon was decidedly the loser.

The year 1536 was a crucial one for Des Périers. Talented, restless, courageous, and evangelical in matters religious, he had already thrown in his lot with the moderate reformists, whom he had befriended and whose doctrines, in the main, he had adopted. The anti-reformist trend had now set in, and the pursuit of heretics was intensifying; nearly four hundred victims were put to death at the stake in 1535 alone. Des Périers was definitely a reformist, and his evangelical turn of mind was being sorely tried. Burgeoning skepticism, disillusionment, and anger were certainly smoldering beneath the surface; the eruption would soon make itself heard in the *Cymbalum Mundi*. Meanwhile, it was inevitable that Des Périers should meet Marguerite of Navarre although the circumstances of their meeting are anything but clear. At all events, Queen Marguerite, a humanist in every sense of the term, was an unflagging supporter of evangelism and its many adepts, and Des Périers, like so many other reform-minded individuals, was to benefit financially as well as intellectually from his association with the illustrious and committed Queen.

Des Périers probably met Marguerite of Navarre in Lyons in the late spring or early summer of 1536; by the end of the year, he had entered her service as a secretary, and shortly thereafter he became Marguerite's *valet de chambre*. Des Périers performed all sorts of odds and ends for his protectress. A superb grammarian and fine copyist, he transcribed some of Marguerite's work and may even have edited somewhat both her spelling and her language. Marguerite took him under her wing and even took care of him when he was sick in August and September of 1537. Des Périers travelled extensively with Marguerite's retinue, and through court circles he met artists, writers, and other important and well-known people. Two in particular stand out, the very beautiful Jacqueline de Stuard and Claude de Bectone, a very respected abbess, both of whom replied in verse to his amatory overtures. However, allegations of affairs with both women are fanciful and unproved. Des Périers's association with Claude, for example, was a literary match, typical of the period.

The next few years were to bring Des Périers notoriety, sickness, and debts. It was during this period that he composed his now celebrated *Nouvelles Récréations et Joyeux Devis*, although these sparkling tales were not published until after his death.

In 1537, Des Périers published a *Prognostication des prognostications*, a satirical work in verse against astrologers. But his satirical, skeptical, and Lucianic vein fairly burst in the composition and publication of his allegorical *Cymbalum Mundi* toward the end of the same year; the work bristled with contempt for Protestants and Catholics alike, and both camps were quick to retaliate. Calvin's friendship for Des Périers came to an abrupt end, and the Sorbonne soon condemned the book and shortly thereafter ordered its destruction. Although both editions of the *Cymbalum Mundi* were published anonymously—the first in Paris, 1537 and the second in Lyons, 1538—it is almost certain that Des Périers was identified as the author; at any rate, Des Périers was fortunate in that he does not seem to have been pursued legally.

It is highly probable that from 1538 on Des Périers was a controversial figure. Yet, friends and acquaintances, as well as foes, were remarkably wary of saying much of anything about him; one can only surmise that everyone considered discretion the better course. Hence, Des Périers's last years are no less obscure than the first. He was still in Marguerite's employ in October, 1541, which does indicate that he had not fallen into disfavor with her over the publication of the *Cymbalum Mundi*. Nevertheless, he was undoubtedly unhappy, lonely, and surely impoverished, and although we do not know exactly where and when he died—we do know that he died prior to August 31, 1544—there is no reason to doubt a contemporary account of his suicide. According to Henri Estienne, Des Périers put an end to his life by throwing himself on his sword. In all probability, Des Périers was about thirty-two at the time of his death.

There is every likelihood that some portion of Des Périers's literary production has been lost. Conversely, many works were erroneously attributed to Des Périers, and the authorship of the *Nouvelles Récréations et Joyeux Devis* was already being contested in the XVIth century. Obviously, the posthumous publication of much of Des Périers's work has been at the center of the controversy.

On the other hand, there is no reason whatever to question the authenticity of the *Recueil des œuvres de feu Bonaventure des Périers* which was published in Lyons in 1544 by Jean de Tournes. Dated 31 August 1544, it is dedicated by Antoine du Moulin, Des Périers's friend, to Marguerite of Navarre; it appears that, as a filial gesture of affection and gratitude, Des Périers wanted Marguerite to inherit the little that he possessed.

In addition to an excellent prose translation into French of Plato's *Lysis*, the *Recueil* contains most of Des Périers's extant poetry. As a poet, he *marotizes*, that is he skillfully displays wit, elegance, and charm—and at times with a pessimistic note—in the manner of Marot, whom he so frequently imitates. Moreover, he does not shun the linguistic complexities of the Rhétoriqueur poets. Although not a great poet, he shows considerable talent in the handling of such traditional themes as the flight of time and the fragility of the rose.

Much of Des Périers's poetry is circumstantial: for example, he writes an epitaph for Francis I's son, who was poisoned by a page in August, 1536. Like Marot, he writes epistles, rondeaux, and paraphrases homilies from the Bible. On the other hand, the platonist and evangelical bent of many of his poems can only come from his close association and collaboration with Marguerite of Navarre. Des Périers addressed several of his poems to her, and this may account, in part, for the religious inspiration of these texts.

As a humanist and thinker, Des Périers expresses himself through deft and biting satire. The *Prognostication des prognostications* (1537), also a part of the *Recueil*, is an attack on divination and its practitioners as well as on man's inanity and overriding urge to seek out constantly and indiscriminately what is new and different.

The Protestant and evangelical feeling which the *Prognostication* already exudes will increase manifestly in the *Cymbalum Mundi*.

The *Cymbalum Mundi* was published separately in 1537. It was not included by Antoine du Moulin in the *Recueil des œuvres de feu Bonaventure des Périers* (1544). As far as known records show, the *Cymbalum Mundi* was attributed to Des Périers for the first time in 1566 by Henri Estienne in his *Apologie pour Hérodote*. Although there are one or two exceptions, most scholars believe that Des Périers's authorship is now firmly established. However, the major problem has been the elucidation of the meaning of the work.

Proceedings against the enigmatic and Lucianic *Cymbalum Mundi* began almost immediately, and, by July, 1537, the Sorbonne had reached its verdict; although the work did not contain "express errors in the matter of faith," it was, nevertheless, a "pernicious" book. As a result, the *Cymbalum Mundi* was condemned and publicly burned by the executioner. Protestants and Catholics alike rejected it, although the Protestants attacked it more vociferously than the Catholics.

The *Cymbalum Mundi* is a sequence of four short and seemingly unrelated dialogues. In the first one, Mercury, who has been sent to earth to have Jupiter's Book of Immortality rebound, is shortchanged by two conniving thieves who substitute a worthless book for the one he has brought. In the second dialogue, Mercury looks on mischievously while three "philosophers" indulge in endless prattle over who has found the true fragments of the Philosopher's Stone. An important shift takes place in the third dialogue: although Mercury is still present, Cupid and the subject of love come to the fore; indeed, Phlegon, a talking horse, pleads for the privilege of mounting a mare whenever the urge overtakes him. The fourth dialogue is devoted to two talking dogs who discuss man's insatiable curiosity.

In a brief preamble, Thomas du Clevier—doubting Thomas—informs his friend Pierre Tryocan—Peter the *croyant*, the believer—that he has finally gotten around to translating into French the Latin *Cymbalum Mundi* he had found in an old library. Hence, the work is basically skeptical in nature, and, although it unfolds with considerable alacrity and in a sprightly manner, it casts its sarcasm and animosity unsparingly. In general, the *Cymbalum Mundi* has been viewed as the venomous pamphlet of a polemical atheist; however, internal evidence points to the pessimism and disillusionment of a man who has lost his belief in man, not in God.

The whole of the *Cymbalum Mundi* seems to revolve around the second dialogue and its allegory of the Philosopher's Stone. The Stone, a symbol of Faith, has been so misinterpreted, misrepresented, and falsified that one can no longer recognize the original. Through ceaseless commentary and constant chicanery, self-serving moralists have hidden God's Truth from man.

Des Périers excoriates man in a fervent and ardent tone; the *Cymbalum Mundi* vibrates with a great depth of thought and feeling. Although the exact meaning, or more specifically the positive message, of the work is still a matter for debate, most critics believe that the *Cymbalum Mundi* is a plea for the strict respect of the Gospel and a return to the evangelical and Pauline notion of pure Love.

Whereas the *Cymbalum Mundi* satirizes man's presumptuousness and marvels at his inanity, the *Nouvelles Récréations et Joyeux Devis* revel in the diversity of human characters and, in a consistently humorous style, reveal a strong affirmation of life. The *editio princeps* of the *Nouvelles Récréations et Joyeux Devis* was published posthumously by Robert Granjon in Lyons in early 1558; the printer's foreword is dated 25 January 1558. This edition and the subsequent re-edition of 1561 contain 2 sonnets and 90 *nouvelles* or tales. However, a re-edition of 1568 added 39 new tales and the question of Des Périers's authorship was further complicated; in fact, a considerable number of the additional 39 tales come from Henri Estienne's *Apologie pour Hérodote* (1566).

Who wrote what first? Moreover, how could Des Périers, who presumably died no later than 1544, make reference to events that took place after that date? Hence, the authorship of even the first 90 tales has been debated since almost the very beginning. In 1584, the bibliographer La Croix du Maine wrote that only a few tales were original with Des Périers and that most had been written by Jacques Peletier and Nicolas Denisot. Tabourot des Accords, who wrote on all sorts of odds and ends, said more or less the same thing in his *Bigarrures*, but Estienne Pasquier, a critic of considerable learning and subtlety, flatly denied it and unreservedly attributed the composition of the initial tales to Des Périers. In the early XVIIIth century, La Monnaye, in an edition of the *Nouvelles Récréations et Joyeux Devis*, concluded that La Croix du Maine was the author, and his contention was sustained as late as 1895 by Gaston Paris. Today, in line with the early twentieth-century studies of Ph. A. Becker, Lazare Sainéan, and Jean Plattard, scholars agree that the first 90 tales are definitely Des Périers's and that the last 39 are not. As for the post-1544 allusions in the original text, they are few and insignificant and were probably interpolated by an editor.

The *Nouvelles Récréations et Joyeux Devis* is a conglomerate of 90 light, good-natured, and amusing tales. They do not elicit the boisterous laughter usually associated with the Rabelaisian tale, nor do they normally call forth the broad chuckle emitted by the reader of Noël du Fail's stories. Rather, Des Périers's tales summon up a wry grin of approval, for the reader is constantly drawn into the tale, and through his act of participation and witness he cannot help but be awed by the finesse of the storyteller's craftsmanship; this is all the more true in that several of Des Périers's subjects are not inherently comic.

One is immediately struck by the great diversity of stories as well as of characters; indeed, diversity and variety are key features of the work. In addition to well-constructed tales and anecdotes, there are narratives which consist of humorous pranks and escapades as well as plays on words normally emanating from confusions and misunderstandings. Many stories deal with waggish remarks about outlandish human beings, nimble and quick-witted purse snatchers, or feminine wiles and intrigues. Moreover, throughout all of the tales there is a great deal of slapstick. The choice of development from one tale to the next appears haphazard and impulsive, and this accounts to a great extent for the fluidity of the work.

Although the *Nouvelles Récréations et Joyeux Devis* is a composite rather than a unified whole, the stories are loosely grouped in clusters of two and three around a similar theme, type, or regional area. Hence, the narrator, who is moved by the inspiration of the moment, creates spontaneity and an oral atmosphere, the principal elements which tie this work together. Moreover, because Des Périers does not adopt an artificial setting or fixed cadre for his tales, he is not hampered by the necessity of returning to a convention, and, hence, the work takes on even more flexibility.

The opening and closing sonnets and the very jovial, pacesetting, and perambulating "First tale, by way of preamble" consist of a combination of appeals to good fun and laughter and a concern for escape and illusion. All the other tales exhibit these qualities to a greater or lesser degree. The narrator frequently stresses the medicinal properties of his stories; indeed, tale 89 relates the cure of a man by means of laughter. Throughout the *Nouvelles Récréations et Joyeux Devis* one is reminded that this is a world of cares and that one must escape it from time to time. In several tales, one senses a longing for the good old days, for their simplicity and tranquillity, and for a return to normalcy.

The narrative *persona* exudes a distinctly Rabelaisian quality. He is a saucy, naughty, playful and beguiling male raconteur who loves to cajole, tease, harangue, and mystify his audience. Through constant and sly interventions, he draws the reader's attention to specific details, heightens his sense of irony, and generally maintains an aura of free and easy camaraderie with his reader/listener. By means of asides and mischievous winks, the devil-may-care narrator makes of the reader an intimate and sympathetic friend.

As the narrator makes clear in the first tale, he does not want to be pinned down to anything. Whether he discusses extra-curricular sexual activity—and always in a charming and delicate way unlike the robust and earthy Rabelais—indulges in verbal play, tells a bawdy story, or humorously illustrates the pitfalls of learning and its misapplication, the narrator insists that he does not follow any set pattern and that he gets his material where he can. On the whole, his subject matter is contemporary or from a very recent past, and, although one or two tales deal with Italians, one never leaves French soil. Hence, the human types and social classes that parade through the *Nouvelles Récréations et Joyeux Devis* are typically French.

While most tales average no more than one or two pages, several run to three and four pages and a great number consist of a mere paragraph or two. Approximately one fourth of the constructed tales begin *in medias res*; a majority of the others begin with the descriptive statement "there once was" or "so-and-so did the following" or "such and such a thing happened." Some of the better stories list the difficulties encountered by a protagonist who finally comes up with a solution. Several contain little or no action: the high point of the story is frequently a comparison, a bon mot, or the like. Often the tale appears to be the development and illustration of a possibly humorous situation; for instance, how might a cantor compare a group of canons to their stew (tale 3)? In some narratives, the interest of the story lies in the subtle analysis of character and the reversal of roles (41).

Relatively few stories lack humor (13, 90). Des Périers seems to be at his best in terms of storytelling in tales like "the lawyer who spoke Latin to his chambermaid and the clerk who was the go-between" (14) and "the professor who fought a fishwife from the Petit Pont with fine insults" (63). Indeed, tale 63 may very well be the most hilarious and rollicking one of the lot. As in tale 14, it relies on strong emotions and a great deal of invective, and the hurled epithet becomes a constant source of comic renewal. Like Rabelais, Des Périers excels at linguistic humor, and these confrontations afford him the multivocal and dramatic emotional range which he seems to prefer.

There is no specific pattern to Des Périers's narrative conclusions although he is very fond of the flippant finale. On the other hand, the comic and sprightly mood of some stories recedes toward the end in favor of a serious, reflective, even thought-provoking, conclusion (44, 53). Yet, in others, the closing remark, often in the form of a last anecdote, introduces obliquely and with great subtlety a scene whose comic visualization the reader cannot escape (60).

In general, the telling of the tale is the element which brings it to life and, in keeping with the oral and dramatic ambiance of the work, speed and shifts in pace and timing characteristically propel the tale forward. Des Périers suppresses unnecessary detail and gets right to the point. Although his narrative style is accumulative and meandering, he also proceeds elliptically, relying on a tightly-knit, sparse, and effervescent style. He accelerates or decelerates the pace of the narrative through the use or lack of narrative infinitives, conjunctions, and adverbs. Frequently, the quick and hurried narrative pace goes hand in hand with the finesse and agility of the characters in the tale. In general, short and simple sentences contribute to the fast clip of these tales.

Des Périers has a great deal of flair for theater. In fact, the structure of a number of his tales reminds one of a skillful playwright. The dramatic quality of his work owes much to his frequent and remarkably ingenious use of dialogue. He writes very few tales in which he does not combine direct dialogue with narration. Hence, there is a lot of conversation in Des Périers's lively world. However, in the interest of speed and drama, dialogue is usually staccato-like and more in the nature of repartee. Des Périers usually dramatizes the *scène à faire*, and the fast and witty dialogue which ensues creates hilarious and memorable scenes. The highly oral and dramatic aspect of these tales is also heightened by the occasional use of sub-narrators (6); these stories-within-a-story create an interior audience wherein bystanders listen, laugh at, and comment on the protagonists. Like Rabelais, Des Périers favors live situations for live people.

Exasperation and vengeance is the motif and compelling force of many of the tales: it transforms naïve and average men into resourceful rascals. It is axiomatic of Des Périers's narrative technique that the ingenuity of the protagonist's invention is what creates the comic effect. Thus, invention and ingenuity are recurrent motifs. In fact, Des Périers's love of cunning and resourcefulness has no limits; he applauds it in thieves and animals as well as in cantors.

One of the more remarkable aspects of Des Périers's creativity is the great quantity and diversity of characters who people the *Nouvelles Récréations et Joyeux Devis*. Indeed, his tales give us a social tapestry of the times: king, court, pages, counselors, lawyers, judges, doctors, scholars, and students. He puts us in the street and marketplace with hawkers, cattle, valets, whores, and thieves. The entire hierarchy of the Church passes in review and comes in for a considerable share of the spoofing. Although clerics do carry on promiscuously, it is their gluttonous nature and niggardliness that are usually emphasized. For the most part, they are knaves and hypocrites, and they are sadly lacking in manners. All of them are good eaters, and they live the good life; in fact, many tales revolve around the dinner table, so to speak.

Country people, field hands, and the provincial aristocracy in particular are frequently on stage. Apothecaries and doctors and their slipshod practices receive a fair portion of satirical review. The legal profession is depicted as a devious group, while professors and students with little learning constantly misapply it. Pomposity is the standard target, and Des Périers seeks to deflate pompous asses wherever he finds them.

The repertoire of characters and professions also includes various kinds of artisans, pranksters, thieves, fools, drunkards, animals, and all sorts of women. But, above all, Des Périers seems to prize the bad lot, the bandit, the mouthy student, the joker, and the smart aleck. In several tales, one encounters genuine affection and admiration for the pickpocket who lives by his wits and whose dangerous and adventurous life is a daily gamble. These pint-sized Panurges strut and sway, and through their flouting of norms and values and bedevilment of their fellowmen they emerge as a fascinatingly rich, colorful, and varied collection of scalawags.

Some characters have names, others do not; it is all a matter of the greater or lesser degree of individuation Des Périers wants to impart to them. Although characterization in Des Périers rarely goes beyond the basic necessities, his characters are not mere stock figures, devoid of personality. He gives them a psychology, but he does not seek to analyze. Through recapitulation, repetition, and the ingenious selection of appropriate details, Des Périers accentuates a telling characteristic and subtly suggests the mood, temperament, and situation. He uncannily grasps the pertinent gesture that reveals more than mere words, and, while he fits the language to each character, he rarely depicts physiques; he is content to sketch them in. He does not pay much attention to decor and physical settings. On the other hand, he is an astute observer of clothing, regional customs, dialects, food and drink.

In the main, the comic mode prevails throughout the *Nouvelles Récréations et Joyeux Devis*, and it runs the gamut from the most traditional forms to the sheer love of words and verbal fantasy that stamps Des Périers's tales with his particular originality. Des Périers is a witty, insouciant, and debonnaire laughing philosopher. He loves life, but he has no illusions about it. He shows us the world as it is; he depicts man's weakness, foibles, and even misfortunes in a light vein, constantly stressing the humorous side of things.

Des Périers does not wish to commit himself; he does not allow his emotions to intervene. One is struck by the author's great detachment. He refuses to comment on portentous events and issues of the day and prefers to tread lightly rather than get involved. On the whole, he adopts a conciliatory attitude towards men and events.

Des Périers subscribes to Rabelais's philosophy of Pantagruelism or stoic epicureanism. Resignation and patience born of good common sense combine with laughter as man's only sensible way of coping with the world. It is no small measure of Des Périers's stature that Rabelais and Montaigne, the two greatest French prose writers of the century, immediately come to mind when one seeks a comparative appreciation of Des Périers. Like Montaigne, Des Périers does not want man to take himself too seriously. If there is a lesson in the *Nouvelles Récréations et Joyeux Devis*, it is that man must learn to live with what he is, be able to laugh at himself, and accept himself.

The *Nouvelles Récréations et Joyeux Devis* were very popular in France throughout the XVIth century and during the very early XVIIth century; a dozen editions, as well as a frequently reprinted anthology which included some of Des Périers's tales, attest to the widespread renown of the work. However, Des Périers's fame underwent a considerable decline in the XVIIth century, and it was not until Charles Nodier's sensitive and forceful reconsideration (1841) that Des Périers began anew to be appreciated and finally studied and ranked as one of France's foremost storytellers.

To this day, Des Périers remains relatively unknown outside of France. There has been only one attempt at translating a reasonable portion of his tales into English. In 1583, *The Mirrour of Mirth and Pleasant Conceits* was published anonymously in London. The translator, known only by his initials, T. D., "englished" 39 tales; ten years later, in 1592, *The Mirrour* was reprinted, but in an abbreviated and slightly edited form.

The Mirrour fared no better than the *Nouvelles Récréations et Joyeux Devis*, and it has remained almost totally unknown. Although T. D.'s Elizabethan English is usually chipper and still charming today, his translation, without ever distorting anything, is frequently too free. He omits whole sentences within tales, and he even deletes the concluding remarks of several stories. Moreover, T. D. does not proceed sequentially nor systematically; rather, he skips about and chooses those tales which, for one reason or another, appeal to him.

In addition to *The Mirrour of Mirth and Pleasant Conceits*, there have been two other translations of two tales; in 1764, Horace Walpole versified tale 87 and more recently John A. Rea translated tale 32 ("Cock of the Walk") for *Playboy* magazine (6: 63, 1959).

We have chosen to translate all 129 tales. Although scholars now agree that the last 39 tales were not written by Des Périers, modern editors continue to publish them along with the original 90. In the absence of conclusive attribution for the last 39 tales, the *Nouvelles Récréations et Joyeux Devis* will surely continue to be reproduced as a compendium of 129 tales, and we thought it wisest to translate the lot.

In our translation, we have endeavored to retain the texture of the original and to render its liveliness and ebullience. Mindful of the need to be both faithful and inventively flexible, we have tried to recreate Des Périers in English, to preserve the spirit of his work, not just the literal meaning.

NOVEL PASTIMES AND MERRY TALES

by the late

Bonaventure des Périers

Valet to the Queen of Navarre

Ex aequitate et prudentia bonos.[1]

---

[1] From moderation and wisdom, good.

FROM THE PRINTER TO THE READER
GREETINGS

Gluttonous time, devourer of human excellence, has the habit very often (so much is it our enemy) of suffocating the budding glory of many noble minds or of burying with ungrateful forgetfulness their exquisite works; if knowledge of them were permitted us, O benevolent God, what advancement to learning this would be. Of this wrong, bygone centuries and even our own times give us more than ample proof. And I even venture to persuade you (friendly reader) that the same thing would have happened to the present volume, and we would still be deprived of it, were it not for the diligence of a worthy person who did not want this wrong to be done to us and the memory of the late Bonaventure des Périers, a great poet, be denied the fame it deserves. Therefore, having snatched it from the greedy hand of that unwelcome reaper, I present it to you with the same eloquence that everyone knows characterizes his other works. Of one thing I am sure, the envious can bark at it as much as they wish, but bite it, they cannot. Moreover, the frowning forehead will find here something with which to unwrinkle its severity and laugh for a change, so delightful is our author's charm in handling his merry remarks. Sad and anguished persons will also be able to find amusement in them and easily destroy their troubles. As for those who are free from sorrow and want to have fun with them, they will notice their pleasure growing to such an extent that cruel anxiety will not dare intrude upon their happiness. These tales will act as a rampart against all sinister annoyances. I have considered it suitable to offer our generation such an enchanting thing, especially in these very calamitous and troubled times. Your service (gentle reader) will be to receive it in a friendly way and be grateful to us for our work; if it is well received, we will be encouraged to continue in such a praiseworthy endeavor in order to let you enjoy more difficult and serious things Farewell. At Lyons, this the 25th of January, 1558.

SONNET

Pensive men, I will not let you peruse
My tales unless you hold in somehow
The haughty mien upon your sullen brow:
My only purpose here is to amuse.

Set aside your sorrow, your anger forswear
And your careful words so long ago thought.
At another time well will you be taught.
In writing this, I have taken much care.

I have forgotten my sad afflictions,
I have suspended my occupations.
Let us give, let us give some room to folly,

So that we may have fun despite our plight,
And in a day full of melancholy
Let's mix in at least an hour of delight.

First tale, by way of preamble

I was keeping these merry remarks for you for the time when there would be peace so that you might have something to rejoice about publicly and privately and in every way; but when I saw that the broom of peace was missing its handle and that people didn't know how to hold on to it,[1] I decided to go ahead and give you a way to outfox time, sprinkling merriment upon your anxieties, until such time as peace might be made by the will of God. And so I came to the conclusion that now was truly the time to give them to you, for it is the sick who need doctoring; and you can be sure that this is no little thing that I'm doing for you by giving you something to cheer you up, which is the best thing that man can do. The best prescription for life is *Bene vivere et laetari*.[2] Some will tell you that it's very important to keep your anger in check; others that it's to say little, others to heed advice, others soberness, others friendship. Agreed! That's just fine! But you can study all you want, you won't find anything as good as this: Enjoy life and be merry. Too much worrying is wearing you out; a little silence torments you; a piece of advice leads you astray; a diet dries you out; a friend abandons you. And for all that, must you despair? Isn't it better to be merry while waiting for something better than to be irked by something which is beyond our control? "Yes, but," you will say, "how will I be merry if there aren't any opportunities?" My friend, get used to it; take things as they come; let the more bothersome ones go by; don't be distressed by something which is beyond remedy: that only heaps ill upon ill. Believe me and you

---

[1] Allusion to the treaty made at Nice in 1538 between Francis I and Charles V and the resumption of hostilities in 1542 which annulled it.

[2] Lead a pleasant life and be joyful.

will be the better for it, for well have I experienced that a hundred francs' worth of melancholy won't pay for a hundred sous' worth of debts. But let's drop these lovely lessons. Ye gods and little fishes! Let's laugh. And how? With the mouth, the nose, the chin, the throat, and with all of our five natural senses. But it isn't worth anything if you don't laugh from the heart; and in order to help you along, I'm giving you these amusing tales; and then we will dream up some more serious ones for you when the time is ripe.[3] But do you know what kind I'm giving you? I promise you I don't intend evil or malice in them; there is no allegorical, mystical, or fantastical meaning in them. You won't be troubled with having to ask what does this mean, what does that mean; you don't need any glossary or commentary: take them as you see them. Open the book: if one tale doesn't please you, rush to another! There are all kinds, all shapes, all sizes, of every price and every proportion, except to make you cry. And don't come and ask me what order I've followed, for what order is necessary in matters of laughter? And let's not have anyone come and quibble with me either: "Oh! he wasn't the one who did that. Oh! this wasn't done in that district. I'd already heard it! That was done in our region." Just laugh and don't fret over whether it was Gautier or Garguille.[4] Don't worry about whether it was at Tours in Berry or at Bourges in Touraine.[5] You'd be worrying for nothing, for just as the years exist only to make us pay taxes, so too names exist only to make men argue. I leave them to the contract-makers and to the suitfilers. If they mistake one for the other, it's their loss; as for me, I'm not that scrupulous. And moreover, I faked a few names on purpose just to show you that you mustn't cry over all I'm telling you, for perhaps it isn't true. What do I care, provided it is true that you enjoy them? And too, I didn't go get my tales in Constantinople, in Florence, or in Venice, or even as far away as that. After all, if they are as I wish them to be, that is for your entertainment, didn't I do better by taking the subjects that we have at our door rather than go borrow them from so far away? And as the good fellow used to say when the cham-

---

[3] Perhaps an allusion to the *Cymbalum Mundi*.

[4] Proverbial names for clowns or bumpkins. The actor Hugues Guéru became famous at the Hôtel de Bourgogne in the role of Gautier Garguille.

[5] Comic inversion in frequent use. Rabelais situates London in Cahors and Bordeaux in Brie, *Gargantua*, chapter 19.

bermaid, who was beautiful and gay, brought him messages from her mistress: "Why should I go to Rome? Indulgences are available here." [6] Tales which come from such distant lands either deteriorate as saffran does or grow dearer like silk brocade, or like spices half is lost or like wines they turn, or they're faked like precious stones, or completely altered before they make their way home. In short, they are exposed to a thousand mishaps unless you want to tell me that stories are not like merchandise and that they are sold for the price they cost. And really that's fine with me. Anyway I prefer to take them from nearby, since there is nothing to gain. Ha! Ha! Enough talk! Please laugh, otherwise you're playing a dirty trick on me. Read confidently, ladies and maidens, there is nothing indecent here. But if perchance there are some among you who are too sensitive and are afraid of stumbling upon some overly spicy passages, I recommend that you have your brothers or your cousins sample them for you first so that you won't have too much of what is too appetizing: "Brother, check those which aren't proper and mark them with a cross." "Cousin, is this one suitable?" "Yes." "And this one?" "Yes." Ah! my little maids, don't trust them; they will mislead you, they will make you read a *quid pro quod!* [7] Take it from me! Read everything; read, read! You're really being narrow-minded. So don't read them. We will see presently if you don't do what you're forbidden. Oh, how many ladies will water at the mouth when they hear of the clever tricks that their friends have played and how they will marvel that they don't stop halfway! But I don't mind their pretending in front of people that they are sewing or spinning, provided that while they turn aside their eyes they open up their ears and hold back from laughing until they are alone. Oh! my lord, you really tell some good ones when you women or you girls are alone! What a great pity! Mustn't we laugh? Let me tell you that I don't believe what they say about Socrates, that he was without passions. Not even Plato nor Xenophon could make me believe it. And even if it were true, do you think I'd praise that great severity, rusticity, grumpiness, seriousness? I would praise a

---

[6]. Both Protestants and Catholics mocked the sale of indulgences. The point here is that there is no need to look for pleasures elsewhere since they are available at home.

[7] quid pro quo.

lot more a man of our day who was called the joker [8] because he
was so jolly in life. This attitude was so natural and peculiar to
him that at the very hour of his death, even though everyone present
was grieving over him, nobody got upset because he died so jokingly. His bed had been placed by the fire, on the cement part of the
hearth, so that he would be warmer. When he was asked, "Now then,
my friend, where does it hurt?" he answered very weakly, having
but heart and speech left, "It's got me," he said, "between the bench
and the fire," which meant that he was in a bad way all over. When
it came time to give him extreme unction, he drew his feet up under
him and the priest said, "I don't know where his feet are." "Just
look," he said, "at the end of my legs, you'll find them!" "Now,
my friend, don't fool around," he was told; "commend yourself to
God." "And who's going there?" he asked. "My friend, you'll go today, if it's God's will." "I'd certainly like to be sure," he said, "of
being able to be there tomorrow and thereafter." "Commend yourself to Him, and you'll be there today." "Well then!" he said, "so
long as I'm there, I'll make my own recommendations." What
greater simplicity could you ask for? What greater bliss? Surely
all the greater in that it is bestowed upon so few men.

---

[8] Probably Triboulet, famous court fool during the reigns of Louis XII
and Francis I; he appears again in the second tale.

Tale 2

OF THE THREE FOOLS, CAILLETTE, TRIBOULET, AND POLITE [1]

Some pageboys had fastened Caillette's ear to a post with a nail,
and poor Caillette stood there without saying a word, for his only
thought was that he would be confined there for the rest of his
life. Along came one of the lords of the court; as soon as he saw
him in counsel with the pillar, he had him released and inquired
specifically who had done it and put him there. What do you expect?

---

[1] All three were famous court fools in the early sixteenth century; Polite
belonged to the abbot of Bourgueil, and Caillette succeeded Triboulet at the
court of Francis I.

An ass put him there. When he was asked, "Was it the pageboys," Caillette naturally answered in his own way, "Yes, yes, it was the pages." "Could you recognize who it was?" "Yes, yes," Caillette said, "I sure know who it was." The squire, by order of his lord, had all his worthy pages appear before this wise fellow Caillette, and he asked each one of them in turn, "Come on, was it you?" And, as bold as Saint Peter, the page denied it: "No, sir, I wasn't the one." "And you?" "Nor I." "And you?" "Me neither." I say, just you try to get a pageboy to say "yes" when a whipping is in the offing. Caillette was there in front saying in his own way, "It wasn't me either." And seeing that they all said "no," Caillette said "no" when he was asked "wasn't it this one?" "And how about this one?" "No." And as they answered "no," the squire made them step aside, until there was only one left, and he wasn't about to say "yes" after so many honest young fellows had all said "no." And so he said like the others, "No, sir, I wasn't there." Caillette stood there and thought that they should also ask him if he hadn't been the one, for he no longer remembered that they were talking about his ear. So, when he saw that he was the only one left, he went about saying, "I wasn't there either." And he went back among the pageboys so that he might have his other ear sewed to the first pillar they found.

At Rouen's entrance, I'm not saying that Rouen entered, but the royal entrance was taking place at Rouen, Triboulet was sent ahead to say "here they come." Wearing his most festive cap and bells and mounted on a beautiful horse, decked out in his colors, he was the proudest man in the world. He spurred, he rode, he went at it only too well. His master was with him to guide him. And that poor master! He had his work cut out for him. The whole thing was enough to turn him into a Triboulet. His master said to him, "Are you going to stop, you rascal? If I catch you...Will you stop it?..." Triboulet dreaded his master's blows (he did give some occasionally) and wanted to stop his horse; but the horse was feeling the effects of what he was carrying, for Triboulet was spurring him energetically, pulling the bridle, shaking it violently. And the horse kept going. "You wretch, aren't you going to stop?" his master said. "For crissake," Triboulet said (for he swore like a man), "I'm spurring this goddamn horse as much as I can, but he won't stop!" What can you say, except that nature wants to amuse herself whenever she sets about making these lovely male specimens. They ought to be happy, but they are too unwittingly amusing and can't recognize that they are happy, which is the most unfortunate thing in the world.

There was another fool named Polite, who belonged to an abbot from Bourgueil. One day, one morning, one evening, I don't know exactly when, the abbot had a lovely wench, hot to trot, stretched out beside him. Polite came to see him in bed and put his arm between the sheets at the foot of the bed. He immediately found a human foot and he asked the abbot, "Abbot, whose foot is this?" "It's mine," the abbot said. "And this one?" "It's mine too." And as he grabbed the feet, he pushed them to one side and held them down with one hand, and with the other hand he grabbed another one and asked, "And this one, whose is it?" "Mine," the abbot said. "Aha," Polite said, "and this one?" Get lost, you're just a fool," the abbot said, "it's also mine." "The devil take the monk!" said Polite, "he has four feet like a horse." And yet for all that, he's the right sort of fool. But Triboulet and Caillette were twenty-five carat fools, when twenty-four are enough. Now then, the fools have made their entrance, but what fools! I the very first for telling you these silly things, and you the second for listening to me, and that one the third, and the other the fourth. Oh! there are so many! I could never finish counting them. Let's leave them here and go find the wise ones. Give me a good light, I can't see a thing here.

Tale 3

OF THE CANTOR OF SAINT HILARY IN POITIERS WHO COMPARED THE CANONS TO THEIR STEWS

In the church of Saint Hilary in Poitiers there once was a cantor with a deep bass voice and, because he was a jolly fellow and loved to drink (as such people do), he was welcome among the canons, who often invited him for dinner and supper, and, because of the friendship they showed him, it seemed to him that there wasn't one among them who did not desire his advancement. It was for this reason that he often said to one and then another:

"Sir, you know how long I've been serving in this church; it would now seem time that I be provided for: please bring up the matter to the chapter. I'm not asking much: you gentlemen have so many benefices: I'll be content with one of the least." His request was well received and listened to, and each one of them in private gave him a favorable answer, saying that it was a reasonable thing. Each one said to him, "And should the chapter not have the means to reward you, I will give you some of mine instead." In short, he was always there at all the comings and goings of the chapter in assembly in order to be remembered by the gentlemen, each of whom said to him, "Wait just a little longer, the chapter won't forget you, you will get the first one to become vacant." But when it came down to brass tacks, there was always some excuse: either the benefice was too big but, nevertheless, one of the gentlemen had gotten it; or it was too small and they didn't want to make him a gift of such a trifling thing; or they had been obliged to give it to one of their brothers' nephews,[1] but he would without fail get the first vacancy. And with these fine words they entertained the bass in such a way that time went by, and he kept on serving without getting anything. In the meantime, according to his humble means, he continued to give presents to those among them whom he knew to have more say in the matter. The poor cantor bought fresh fruit, chickens, squabs, partridges, according to the season, at the cut-rate market or at the bargain shop, and he let them think that it didn't cost him anything. And they always accepted. Finally, when he saw that he was no better off and that on the contrary he was wasting his time, his money, and his effort, the bass resolved not to expect anything any longer; but he determined to show them what he thought of them, and, in order to do this, he managed to put four or five crowns together, and, while he was saving them up (for it took time), he began to take greater notice of these gentlemen than he used to and to exercise greater discretion. When his chance came, he went to the leading ones among them and asked them one after another to be so good as to do him the honor of having dinner in his home the following Sunday; he told them that inasmuch as he had been in their service nine or ten years the least he could do was to have them to dinner once and he would entertain them, not as was their due, but as best he possibly could, and all the while he used such expressions of respect. They promised to come;

---

[1] Euphemism for their own illegitimate offspring.

but when the appointed day arrived, they weren't so careless as to forget to have their usual fare prepared, each in his own house, for fear of being poorly fed by this bass, trusting his voice more than his cuisine. At dinner time, each sent his usual fare to the cantor's, and in turn he would say to the valet who brought it, "Why does your master slight me this way, my friend? Is he so afraid of being poorly treated? He didn't have to send anything." And yet he accepted everything, and as the stews got there he put them all together in a big pot he had purposely made ready in a kitchen corner. Along came the gentlemen for dinner, and they all sat according to their indignity. The cantor immediately offered them the mixture of stews from the pot, and God knows how lovely it was: for one had sent a capon cooked with leeks, another had sent one with saffron; another had a piece of beef sprinkled with turnips, another a chicken cooked with herbs, another a boiled one, the other a roasted one. When they saw this beautiful course, they didn't have the heart to eat, and each waited for his stew to come, without noticing that it was already in front of him. The cantor, who went back and forth acting very occupied in serving them, kept looking at their expressions at the table. Because the course was a little long, they were unable to refrain from saying to him, "Take these stews away, cantor, and bring us our own." "They are yours," he said. "Ours! No, they aren't." "Indeed they are," he said. To one, he said, "There are your turnips"; to the other, "There's your cabbage"; to the other, "There are your leeks." Then each one of them began to recognize his own dish and they looked at one another. "Really!" they said, "we've been tricked. Is this the way you treat your canons, cantor?" "I'll be damned! Didn't I say this fool would deceive us," one said; "I had the best stew I've eaten this year." Another said, "And I had such a good dinner prepared! I knew it would have been better to eat it at home." After the cantor had heard them out, he said, "Gentlemen, if all your stews were so good, how could they have gotten worse so quickly? I had them kept well-covered by the fire; it seems to me I couldn't have done better." "Yes, but," they said, "who taught you to put them all together like that? Didn't you know that they wouldn't be worth anything that way? "And so," he said, "what is good by itself is not so good when put together? Really, I believe you, and that's the way it is with you gentlemen. When each of you is by himself, there's

no one worthier than you; you promise the moon and stars, you
make everyone rich with your fine words; but when you are together in your chapter, you resemble your stews." They then understood exactly what he meant. "Aha! " they said, "so that's what you
had in store for us! Really, you're right, you know! Meanwhile,
aren't we going to have dinner?" "Yes, indeed, of course," he said,
"better than you deserve." And he brought them what he had had
prepared for them. They ate very well and went away content, and
together they resolved at once that he would be provided for,
which they did. Thus his invention with the stews gained him more
than all his requests and entreaties of the past.

Tale 4

OF THE BASS OF RHEIMS, CANTOR, NATIVE OF PICARDY
AND MASTER OF ARTS

A cantor from Our Lady of Rheims in Champagne had a particularly good bass voice, but he was the most difficult man in the
world to keep in check, and a day didn't go by that he didn't do
something foolish: he'd strike one man, he'd beat another, he played
cards and dice, he was always in the tavern or after wenches. Complaints were lodged at all hours with the gentlemen of the chapter,
and they frequently scolded this bass for it, threatening him in
private and in public. They often made him promise to be a good
fellow, but as soon as he was out of their sight, Master John Wine
would send him on a toot again, and this always made him revert
to his fine habits. Nevertheless, they were forced to put up with it
for two reasons: for one, he sang extremely well; for another, they
had obtained him through an archdeacon whom they respected and
they didn't want to reproach him about the man's follies, thinking
that he knew them as well as they did and that he must have reprimanded him for it, as he did indeed when he was informed of
it. But he didn't know the half of it. It happened one day that the
cantor acted so scandalously that the canons were forced for once
to mention it to the archdeacon. They explained to the archdeacon
that it was only because of their regard for him that they had put

up with the man's insolences for a long time. However, now that they saw he was incorrigible and that he was only getting worse, they could no longer keep silent about it. "Last night," they said, "he beat a priest so badly that he won't be able to say mass for at least two months. If it hadn't been for your sake, we would have dismissed him a long time ago. Now that there's no other way out, we hope you won't take offence at our telling you what is going on." The archdeacon replied that they were right and that he would take care of it, and, as a matter of fact, he immediately sent for this bass, who guessed that it wasn't to give him a benefice. Nevertheless, he went. He had no sooner entered than the archdeacon began to sing him a lesson that wasn't matins. "Come here," he said; "you know how long the people in this church have been putting up with you and how much I've been reproached for your existence. You know what is in store for you? Go away, and don't ever let me see you again. I don't want to be blamed any longer for a man like you. You're just a fool. If I did my duty, I'd have you put on bread and water for a whole year." You needn't wonder whether the cantor was crestfallen. Still, he was not so stunned that he wasn't able to answer. "Sir," he replied, "you understand people so well, why are you surprised to find out I'm a fool? I'm a cantor, I'm a native of Picardy[1] and a master of arts." When he heard the answer, the archdeacon didn't know whether to be angry or to laugh. But he took it in the right way and calmed down a bit, for he had no choice but to do as the bishop in *The Courtier*[2] who forgave the priest who had gotten five young nuns, his spiritual daughters, pregnant because of the unexpected answer he gave him: *Domine, quinque talenta tradidisti mihi, ecce alia quinque superlucratus sum.*[3] A native of Picardy is hot-headed, a cantor always has a few half notes in his head, a master of arts is so full of *ergo*'s that you couldn't put up with him. And really, when these three fine qualities come together in one individual, we shouldn't wonder if he is a little bit scatterbrained. On the contrary, we would be much more amazed if he were not.

---

[1] The inhabitants of Picardy had the reputation of being awkward.

[2] Balthasar Castiglione's *Il Cortegiano* (1528).

[3] Lord, thou deliveredst unto me five talents: behold, I have gained beside them five talents more. Matthew 25:20.

Tale 5

OF THE THREE NEWLY WED SISTERS AND HOW EACH
ANSWERED HER HUSBAND CLEVERLY ON HER WEDDING NIGHT

In the province of Anjou there once was a gentleman who was rich and of good family, but who was rather fond of his pleasures. He had three beautiful and charming daughters and of such an age that the youngest would have been ready for the rough-and-tumble of love. They had been without a mother for some time now; and because the father was still in the prime of life, he continued to indulge in his habit, which was to receive at home all fun-loving groups, and the customary thing was to dance, frolic, and enjoy all sorts of sumptuous foods. And because he was by nature indulgent, easy-going, and rather carefree about the running of his house, his daughters had ample freedom to chat with the young gentlemen, who generally don't talk about the rising cost of food or about the government of the commonwealth. Besides, the father himself made love like the others, which made the young girls bolder about letting themselves be loved and, consequently, about loving in return; and since their hearts were in the right place and they were of good family, they considered it wrong and selfish to be loved and not to love in return. For all of these reasons and because each of them was prized, caressed and pursued every day and at any and all hours, they let themselves be caught up in love, had pity on their fellow-creatures and began playing the two-by-two pastime each in her own corner. They were so successful at this game that their winnings began to show. The eldest, who was full and ripe, didn't guard against her belly rising up, and this bothered her a little, for it was impossible to keep it hidden, especially in a place where there are no mothers; they usually take care that their daughters are not led astray too early, or else they know how to cope with difficulties when something unexpected happens to them. And because the daughter had neither intention nor means of slipping away without her father's permission, he just had to know about it.

When he heard the news, he was angry at first; but, otherwise, he didn't give way to despair, particularly since he was one of those good people who don't take matters to heart too much. And, as a matter of fact, what's the use of worrying about something once it's done, except to make it worse? He quickly sent his eldest daughter two or three leagues away to one of their aunts, under the pretext that according to the doctors she needed a change of air; and this is what was done while waiting for the little feet to come out. However, since it never rains but it pours, the second daughter was getting herself into trouble just as the first one was getting out of it, perhaps by divine permission because in her heart she'd made fun of her older sister, and God wished to punish her. To cut it short, she noticed that she had something this side of her back, indeed in her belly, and her father found it out too. "Well," he said, "the saints be praised! The population is increasing: that's the way we were made." Fearing the worst, he immediately went to see the youngest, who wasn't yet pregnant, but she was doing her best. "And you, my daughter, how are you? Are you sure you didn't follow in your older sisters' footsteps?" The daughter, who was quite young, couldn't help blushing, and the father took it as a confession. "Well then," he said, "may God look favorably upon you and keep us from greater fortune!" And so, he decided that it was time he took care of his affairs. He also realized that the best thing to do was to marry off his three daughters, but he found it somewhat difficult since he knew only too well that to give them to his neighbors was out of the question because the goings-on at his house were known or at the least very much suspected. On the other hand, he couldn't very easily force them on the men who had made them, for it was possible that there was more than one and that one had made the feet and the other the ears and yet another one the nose. Who knows how the things of this world work? And besides, even if there had only been one for each girl, a man doesn't readily trust a girl who has given him a taste of it beforehand. And so the father thought it more practical to go look for his sons-in-law some distance away. And because men of merry disposition and good cheer hardly ever come to a bad end, he didn't fail to find what he needed. He went to the province of Brittany where he was well known as much for his family name as for the property he had in that region, not very far from the city of Nantes, and he was easily able to justify his trip on that basis alone. In short, when he got there, he not only personally proposed his daughters' marriages but used intermediaries as well. The Bretons quickly pricked up their ears, and

he was able to choose at will. However, he was particularly pleased
with a noble and wealthy Breton family in which there were three
handsome sons of the right age, good passepied and three-step
dancers, good wrestlers who feared no man in a tussle. The girls'
father was delighted and, since time was of the essence, he promptly concluded his business with the father and the three sons. They
agreed that they would marry his three daughters and that they
would even hold three weddings in one, that is, they would all three
get married on the same day. And in order to bring this about, the
three brothers got ready in a hurry and left their home to go to
Anjou with the father of the three girls. Now there wasn't one of
the three who wasn't well experienced, for although they were
Bretons they weren't bumpkins, and they had taken a hand in some
good bouts with those Breton gals, who are willing enough, as the
saying goes, every time they are pinned. When they arrived in the
gentleman's home, each one began to look over his bride-to-be, and
they found all three of them beautiful, fit, and pert; to top it all, they
looked wise and well-behaved. The weddings were arranged, the
preparations were made; they got their marriage licenses and their
pews from the bishop. The night before the weddings, the father
called his three daughters aside in a room and said to them as
follows: "Come here. All three of you know the mistake you made
and the trouble you caused me. If I were a harsh father, I would
have disowned you as my daughters and you would never inherit
my estate; but I preferred taking the trouble once and for all to
mend things rather than drive all three of you to despair and me
into perpetual regret for your folly. I've brought a husband here
for each one of you: make up your minds to make them welcome.
Cheer up, it won't kill you. If they get wind of something, that's
their tough luck! Why did they come here? I had to go get them.
When you were playing around, you weren't thinking of them, were
you?" All three answered (smiling) that they had not. "Well then,"
the father said, "you haven't done them wrong yet. But in the future
don't get me into anymore trouble through your misconduct; don't
you dare. And you can be sure that I'm determined to forget all the
mistakes of the past. Moreover (in order to give you greater encour-
agement), I promise that I'll give an extra two hundred crowns to
whichever one of you gives the wittiest answer to your husband the
first night that you spend with him. Now, go and consider the

matter well." After this sound advice he went to bed, and so did the daughters, each one of them wondering in her heart what witty remark she could make on the night of the tussle in order to get those two hundred crowns; but in the end each one decided to wait for the bout, hoping that the good Lord would tell her at the proper moment what she ought to say. The weddings took place the following day: they get married, they live it up, they dance; what more could you wish for! The beds are made ready, the three maidens go to bed, and their husbands after them. The eldest's husband, while caressing her, put his hand on her stomach and all around and quickly realized that it was a little wrinkled underneath, and it was crystal clear to him that he'd been had. "Oho!" he said, "the birds have flown the coop." The young lady, very pleased with herself, answered: "Stick to the nest." And one down! The second one's husband, while fondling her, noticed that her stomach was a little round. "Why!" he said, "the barn is full!" "Beat on the door," she answered him. And that makes two! The third one's husband, while playing his hand, realized at once that he didn't hold the trump card. "This is a beaten path," he said. The young girl told him: "You won't lose your way as easily." And that's three! The night went by and the following day they went to their father, and each one reported to him what had happened to her and what she had answered. *Queritur*: [1] to which of the three should the father give the two hundred crowns? Think about it and I wonder if you won't agree with me that all three should share the two hundred crowns, or else each one should have two hundred, *propter mille rationes, quarum ego dicam tantum unam brevitatis causa:* [2] the fact of the matter is that all three had good intentions; every good intention is accepted as the act itself: *ergo in tantum consequentia est in Barbara,* [3] or elsewhere. But in the meantime, if you have no objection, how would you like to deal with this question: which would you rather be, a budding cuckold or a ripe one? And don't

---

[1] Traditional formula for posing a problem in scholastic philosophy.

[2] on account of a thousand reasons, of which I will mention only one for the sake of brevity.

[3] therefore, the reward is based only on that according to Barbara. Parody of the scholastic formula used to conclude an argument. Des Périer's syllogism is in fact in Barbara (universal affirmatives) although he comically feigns to take it as the name of an author.

answer too quickly that it's better to have been a green one than
a ripe one, for you know what a rare and gratifying thing it is to
marry a virgin. Well then, even if she later makes you a cuckold,
the pleasure is still yours, I don't mean of being cuckolded, I mean
of having deflowered her. And besides you obtain a thousand favors,
a thousand advantages from her. Pantagruel says so; [4] but I don't
want to argue the reasons pro and con, I'll let you think about it
at your leisure; then you'll know how to answer me.

------

[4] A reference to Rabelais's *Tiers Livre*, chapter 28. Since the *Tiers Livre*
was published in 1546 after Des Périers's death, the reference to Pantagruel
must have been added by an editor.

Tale 6

OF THE HUSBAND FROM PICARDY WHO DREW HIS WIFE AWAY FROM WANTON LOVE BY UPBRAIDING HER IN THE PRESENCE OF HER PARENTS

There once was a king of France, whose name is not exactly
known insofar as this matter I want to talk about is concerned, but
the fact remains that he was a good king and worthy of his crown.
He was very affable with everyone, and he was all the better for
it, for he learned the truth about things, and that doesn't happen
when you don't listen. But to get to the point of my tale, this good
king used to travel throughout the provinces of his kingdom, and
he even went through towns at times dressed in disguise in order
to get at the truth more easily in all kinds of matters. One day he
decided to visit his region of Picardy as his Royal Highness, but,
still, he kept his accustomed familiarity. While in Soissons, he sent
for the most notable people in town and, as a friendly gesture, he
had them sit at his table and urged and encouraged them to tell
him all kinds of stories, humorous as well as serious, as the subject
came up. Among others there was a man who began to tell the king
the following story: "Sire," he said, "it happened not long ago, in
one of your towns in Picardy, that a man of the courts, who is still
living, lost his wife after having been with her for a very long time.
Since he had been very satisfied with her, he decided to marry again

and he chose a girl who was beautiful, young, and from a good background. She wasn't his equal in wealth, however, and even less in other things, for he had already lived more than half his life, and she was in the prime of hers and playful to boot, so much so that he wasn't equipped to satisfy the wench. When she began to have a little taste of the joys of this world, she realized that her husband was only whetting her appetite, and although he dressed her well, wined and dined her and spoke kindly and lovingly to her, still this only served to add fuel to the fire. So she took a fancy to look elsewhere for what she didn't have to her liking at home. She found a friend with whom she carried on for a while; then, not satisfied with him alone, she found another, and then another, so that in no time at all their number was so great that they hindered one another. They entered the house at any and all hours for the young woman's favors, for she had already set aside the thought of her honor in order to give herself up completely to pleasure. Her husband knew nothing of it, or, if by chance he did, he put up with it, thinking to himself that he had to pay for having been so foolish as to marry such a young girl in his advancing years. This state of affairs lasted and went on for so long that the townspeople talked about it, and this greatly angered the husband's relatives. One of them, who was no longer able to contain it, went to talk to him about it and told him of the rumors that were circulating and that if he didn't do something about it he would create the impression that he was spineless and eventually all his relatives and all decent people would abandon him. When he heard these words, he pretended for the benefit of the man who had spoken to him that the matter displeased and angered him no end, and he promised him that he would set his house in order by every means available to him. But when he was alone, he saw clearly that, no matter how hard he tried to clean up the mess, he wouldn't be able to keep the stains from showing forever or at least for a long time. He felt that his wife should be guided by respect for virtue and fear of dishonor; otherwise, all the walls in the world wouldn't be able to stop her from pulling one of her tricks. Moreover, because he was a man of good sense, he reasoned that a man's honor wasn't much of anything if it depended on the acts of a woman. This kept him from going too far into the matter. Nevertheless, in order not to appear unconcerned about his domestic mishap, which most men considered so dishonor-

able, he thought of a way which he felt was the only practical one
in such a case. He bought a house which adjoined his at the back
and made one out of both of them, saying that he wanted to provide
himself with a front and back entrance on both sides. This was
carried out promptly, and a back door was installed in the most
convenient place that could be devised. He had a half-dozen keys
made, and he didn't forget to have a very convenient gallery built
for those who came and went. When it was all ready, he chose a
suitable day to invite his wife's close relatives to dinner; however,
this time he didn't invite his side of the family. He entertained and
fed everybody well. After dinner and before anyone could leave the
table, he started telling them the following in his wife's presence:
"Ladies and Gentlemen, you know how long it's been since I married
your relative here. I've had time to realize that I wasn't the one she
should have married, particularly since she and I were not alike.
Nevertheless, when you can't undo what's been done, you have to
see it to the end." Then, turning towards his wife, he said to her:
"My dear, I've just recently been reproached about your conduct,
and it displeases me immensely. I've been told that young men
come to see you here at all hours of the day, and that dishonors both
you and me greatly. If I had known it earlier, I would've seen to it
earlier and better. Still, better late than never. I want you to tell
those who visit you that from now on the're to be more discreet
when they come to see you. And that won't be difficult because
I've had a back door built for them. Here are a half-dozen keys
that you can have in order to give each one his own; and if there
aren't enough, I'll have others made, since the locksmith is at
my disposal. And tell them to find the most profitable way of working out their time with you: if you don't want to refrain from
doing wrong, the least you can do is do it secretly in order to stop
people from talking about you and me." When the young woman
heard these remarks from her husband and in the presence of her
relatives, she began to be ashamed of her actions, and she saw the
wrong and dishonor she was doing to her husband, to her relatives
and to herself, and she was so filled with remorse that from that
moment on she closed the door on all her lovers and her dissolute
pleasures, and from then on she lived with her husband as a virtuous
and honorable wife." The king, when he heard the tale, wished to
know who the man was: "By the word of a gentleman!" he said,

"that man is one of the calmest and most patient men in my kingdom. He would certainly be useful since he knows so well how to be patient." And then and there he gave him the position of attorney general in the province of Picardy. For my part, if I knew the name of that worthy man, I would want to honor him with immortality. But time has done him the wrong of obliterating his name, which rightly deserved to be chronicled, indeed canonized: for he was a true martyr in this world, and I believe that he is now very happy in the next. May you follow suit. *Amen*, for a priest isn't worth anything without a deacon.

Tale 7

OF THE NORMAN WHO PICKED UP SOME LATIN IN ORDER TO GO SEE THE HOLY FATHER IN ROME AND HOW HE USED IT

A Norman, seeing that priests had the best time in the world, decided after his wife died to become a man of the Church; but he could barely read or write. Nevertheless, having heard that money talks and considering himself as capable a man as many priests in his parish, he spoke to one of his friends. He told him what he wanted to do, and he asked his advice as to how he ought to conduct himself in this matter. After much debate both pro and con, his friend cheered him up and told him that if he wanted to be successful in his enterprise he would have to go to Rome and that only with great difficulty would he get permission from his bishop, who was particular about admitting priests and giving the *a quocunque*,[1] but that the Pope, who was busy with so many other things, would not look him over too closely and would accept him at once. Moreover, if he did that he would see the country, and when he returned, having been ordained a priest by the hand of the Pope, everyone would do him honor and in no time at all he would get a benefice and become an important man. The man found these remarks very much to his liking; but he still had this qualm on

---

[1] Dimissory letters from a pope, bishop, abbot, or other high ecclesiastical official authorizing the ordination of the bearer were officially styled *facultas de promovendo a quocunque*.

his conscience concerning the matter of Latin, and he mentioned it to his counselor, saying to him: "Yes, but when I'm in front of the Pope, what language am I going to speak? He doesn't understand Norman, nor I Latin, what shall I do?" "You mustn't let that hold you back," the other said, "because to be a priest, all you need to know is your Requiem mass, the Beata mass, and the mass of the Holy Spirit,[2] and you'll learn them soon enough after you get back. But to speak to the Pope, I'll teach you three Latin phrases that are so good that when you say them in front of him he'll believe you're the greatest scholar in the world." The man was very pleased and wanted to know those three phrases right away. "My friend (the other said to him), as soon as you're in front of the Pope, you'll fall on your knees and say to him: *Salve Sancte Pater.*[3] Then he'll ask you in Latin: *Unde es tu*? that is: Where are you from? You'll answer: *De Normania.* Then he'll ask you: *Ubi sunt litterae tuae*?[4] You'll tell him: *In manica mea.*[5] And right away, without further delay, he'll order that you be ordained. Then you'll return." The Norman was never happier, and he stayed fifteen or twenty days with his friend in order to put those three Latin phrases into his head. When he thought he knew them well, he got ready to take the road for Rome, and on the way he said nothing else but his Latin: *Salve Sancte Pater. De Normania. In manica mea.* But he must have said them over and over so often and with such ardor that he forgot that noble first phrase, *Salve Sancte Pater*, and unfortunately he was already well on his way. You needn't wonder whether the Norman was angry. He didn't know to which saint he should pray in order to remember his phrase and he felt that to present himself to the Pope without it was like going fishing without bait, and yet he didn't believe that it would be possible to find a man who would be as good a teacher and could instruct him as well as the one in his parish who had taught it to him. Never was a man so distressed, until one Saturday morning he entered one of the chur-

---

[2] The *de Beata* mass in honor of the Virgin Mary is said nearly every Saturday of the year. It is also the second mass a priest says after ordination, the first being that of the Holy Spirit. The *Requiem* mass for the repose of departed souls is commonly sung at funerals and on All Souls' Day.

[3] Hail, O holy Father.

[4] Where are your letters?

[5] In my sleeve.

ches in the town where he happened to be, and while waiting for the
grace of God, he heard them beginning the mass of Our Lady
intoning: *Salve sancta parens.* [6] And the Norman pricked up his
ears: "Praise be to God and to Our Lady!" he said. He was so
overjoyed that he was sure he had returned to the living from the
dead. He immediately had a cleric who was there repeat those words
for him, and he didn't forget *Salve sancta parens* again as he
continued his journey with his Latin. You can imagine how
delighted he was to have been born. At length he travelled so far that
he reached Rome. And you must remember that in those days it
wasn't as difficult to speak to the popes as it is now. He was ushered
in before the Pope, and he didn't forget to bow before him, saying
to him very devoutly: "*Salve sancta parens.*" The Pope said to him:
"*Ego non sum mater Christi.*" [7] The Norman answered him: "*De
Normania.*" The Pope looked at him and said: "*Daemonium ha-
bes?*" [8] "*In manica mea,*" the Norman replied. And when he said that,
he put his hand in his sleeve in order to pull out his letters. The
Pope was a little surprised, thinking that he was going to pull a
goblin out of his sleeve. But when he saw that they were letters, he
was reassured and he asked him again in Latin: "*Quid petis?*" [9] But
the Norman was at the end of his lesson, and he never answered
anything again to the questions that were put to him. Finally, after
some of his countrymen had heard him speak the Caux dialect, they
began questioning him, and he soon gave them to understand that
he had learned the little Latin he knew in his village and that he
knew it well but didn't know how to use it.

---

[6] *Hail, O holy Mother,* first words of the Introit to the *de Beata* mass.
[7] I am not the mother of Christ.
[8] Are you possessed of the devil?
[9] What do you want?

Tale 8

OF THE ATTORNEY WHO SENT TO THE VILLAGE FOR A YOUNG WENCH
TO PLAY WITH AND HOW HIS CLERK TRIED HER OUT FOR HIM

A High Court attorney, who wasn't forty yet, had been left a
widower. He had always been a gay dog and still was. In fact, he

couldn't do without the female sex, and it annoyed him to have lost
his wife so soon when she still had some good stuff left in her.
Nevertheless, he put up with it and found ways of supplying himself as best he could by doing charitable works; to wit: loving his
neighbor's wife as though she were his own, sometimes reviewing
the cases of widows and others who came to his house on business.
In short he took it where he could find it and he banged away like
a madman. But after carrying on this way for some time, he found
it a little troublesome, for he couldn't easily take the trouble to be on
the lookout for opportunity to knock, as young men do; he couldn't
go to his neighbors without raising suspicion because he hadn't
been in the habit of doing it. Moreover, it pained him to have to
pay for an assignation. So, he decided to find one of his own. And
he remembered that in Argueil, where he had some vineyards, he
had seen a young wench of sixteen or seventeen, named Gillette, who
was the daughter of a poor woman who earned her living spinning
wool. But this wench was still unsophisticated and inexperienced
although her face was pretty enough. In any case, the attorney
thought that she would fill the bill, having once heard the proverb:
Wise man and foolish girl. For it never pays to deal with too sharp
a gal; she always plays a trick of her trade on you; she is forever
snitching money from your wallet; either she wants to be too
elegant, or she makes you wear horns, or both. To make a long
story short, one fine grape season the attorney went to Argueil and
asked the mother for the young wench as a chambermaid. He told
her that he didn't have one and couldn't do without one and that
he would treat her well and marry her off when the proper time
came. Although the old woman knew exactly what those words
meant, nevertheless, she pretended not to understand because of her
poverty, and she readily agreed to give him her daughter, promising
to send her to him the following Sunday, and she did. When the
young wench arrived in the city, she was amazed to see so many
people because until then she had seen only cows. And so the
attorney didn't take anything up with her for a while and kept on
going out for his adventures, letting her build up her confidence.
And, moreover, he wanted to have some clothes made for her so
that she might be more willing to do well. Now then, he had a clerk
in his house who wasn't that considerate, and two or three days
later, while the attorney was out having dinner in town, the clerk,

who had realized how inexperienced the wench was, began to carry on with her, asking her where she was from and where she liked it better, in the fields or in town. "My dear," he said, "don't you worry about a thing; you couldn't have latched on to a better place, and you won't have a hard time; the master's a fine man, and you'll be well off with him." He went on: "Now then, my dear, hasn't he told you yet why he brought you here?" "Not at all," she said, "but my mother told me to serve him well and to remember what I was told, and I'd gain a great deal from it." "My dear," the clerk said, "your mother did indeed tell you the truth. And because she knew that the clerk would explain all of your responsibilities to you, she didn't say anything more about it to you. My dear, when a young girl comes to town to work for an attorney, she must let the clerk do everything he wants; on the other hand, the clerk is obliged to teach her the customs of the town and the moods of his master so that she'll know how to serve him; otherwise, the poor girls would never learn anything, and their masters would never welcome them and would send them back to the village." And the clerk said it so forcefully that the poor wench didn't dare disbelieve him when she heard him talk about the need to learn how to serve her master. And she answered the clerk in a half-hesitating way and with a completely ignorant look: "I'd be most grateful to you," she said. The clerk, judging by the wench's expression that his case was coming along all right, begins to play with her; he fondles her, he kisses her. To be sure, she exclaimed, "Oh! my mother didn't tell me about that." But anyhow, the clerk kisses her, and she let him because she was so stupid that she thought it was the custom and the fashion of the city. He turns her up, all aglow, upon a trunk. I'll be hanged if he wasn't in seventh heaven! And from then on they continued their business together every time the clerk found his opportunity. While the attorney waited for the wench to lose her naïveté, his clerk was taking this responsibility without power of attorney. The young girl, who was now completely dressed by the attorney, was getting better looking every day, partly because of the good treatment and because nice feathers make for good-looking birds, and partly because her lower region was getting polished. After a few days, the attorney had a fancy to find out if she would let him sit in the saddle, and so one morning he sent his clerk, who by chance had just grabbed a piece on the fly with Gillette, to town to deliver a parcel. After the clerk had left, the attorney began to play around with her, putting his hand on her tits, then under her skirt. She giggled, of course, because she'd already learned that there was nothing to cry about; but, nevertheless, she was still timid with a country-like sense of shame she hadn't lost yet, particularly in front of her master. The attorney pressed her against the bed, and because he was getting ready to do the same thing as the clerk when he kissed her, squeezing her tightly, the wench (oh! how stupid she was!) said to him, "Oh! no, thank you, Sir; the clerk and I have just done it." The attorney, whose fly was taut, made a bull's-eye all the same; but he was very crestfallen, realizing that his clerk had already started to initiate her for him. You can imagine that, at the very least, the clerk was fired.

Tale 9

OF THE MAN WHO FINISHED THE BABY'S EAR FOR HIS NEIGHBOR'S WIFE

You mustn't be amazed if country girls aren't very smart; after all, city ones sometimes let themselves be taken in very easily. Of course, it doesn't happen to them often because it's in the cities that women pull off the best tricks. Damn! that's right, and I want to tell you that in the city of Lyons there was a very beautiful young woman who was married to a rather prosperous merchant. But they hadn't been married for more than three or four months when he had to go out of town on business. She was only three weeks pregnant when he left and she knew she was because of the fact that she swooned sometimes and had other reactions that pregnant women have.

As soon as he had gone, one of his neighbors, named Mister André, came to see the young woman as he did regularly because they were neighbors, and he began to banter with her, asking her how she was getting along in her married life. She answered that she was doing fairly well but that she thought she was pregnant. "Is that possible?" he said; "your husband couldn't have had the opportunity to get you pregnant in the short time that you've been together." "Yes, indeed, I am," she said; "Mrs. Toiny told me that she reacted the same way with her first child." "Now," Mister André told her, never thinking mischief or that what happened would happen to him, believe me, I know all about that, and just looking at you, I suspect that your husband hasn't made the entire child and that there are still some ears to make. Take my word for it, you'd better be careful. I've known many women who met with grief and several others who were wiser and had their children finished during their husband's absence for fear of misfortune. So, as soon as my buddy gets back, have him finish it." "What!" the young woman said, "he went to Burgundy; he won't be back for another month at the earliest." "My dear," he said, "you're in bad shape then; your child will only have one ear, and you're also running the risk that the others to come will only have one too because when some defect comes about in women who are pregnant with their first child, the next ones are apt to have the same thing." When she heard that, the young wife became the most distressed woman in the world: "I'm amazed that he didn't think to do a thorough job before he left." "I can tell you (Mister André said) that there's a cure for everything, except death. For your sake, really, I'll be glad to finish it for you, and I wouldn't do that for anybody else because I have my hands full with my own; but I wouldn't want such a misfortune to happen to you for lack of help." Because she trusted him, she thought that what he was telling her was true, for he spoke brusquely as if he wanted her to understand that he was doing a lot for her and that it was just sheer drudgery for him. Conclusion: she had her child finished for her, a task which Mister André carried out nicely, not only on that occasion, but fairly often thereafter. And on one of these occasions the young woman said to him, "Yes, but what if you're making four or five ears? Stop, it'll be a bad job." "No, no," Mister André said, "I'll only make one; but do you think it can be done that quickly? Just think how long it took your husband to make what he did! And besides, I can easily do less, but I can't do more: after all, when a thing's finished, it doesn't need anything else." And under those circumstances the ear was finished. When the husband returned, his wife said to him that night, while romping about: "You know something, you're a fine baby-maker! You made me one who would have had only one ear because you left without finishing the job." "Come, come," he said, "how silly can you get! Are children made without ears? "That's right, they are made that way," she said, "ask Mister André; he told me he saw more than twenty who had only one because they hadn't been finished and that a child's ear is the most difficult thing to make; and if he hadn't finished it for me, just think what a lovely child I would have produced! " The husband wasn't too happy when he heard that. "What do you mean, finished," he said. "What did he do to you to finish it?" "You're asking me?" she said; "he did to me what you do." "Aha! " the husband said, "is that so? So you pulled that one on me?" And God knows he didn't sleep a wink thinking about it! And since he was an irascible man, he imagined, while thinking about that ear being finished, that he knifed the finisher a hundred times over; and throughout the night, which seemed to last more than a thousand years, he had nothing but thoughts of his revenge. And, in point of fact, the first thing he did when he got up was to go see that Mister André, and he insulted him a thousand times and threatened that he would make him regret the dirty trick he had played on him. Nevertheless, his threats were all for nought: for when he was through belching fire and smoke, he was forced to calm down because of a Barcelona rug Mister André gave him, but on condition, nevertheless, that he would no longer take a hand in making his children's ears, for he could make them without his help.

Tale 10

OF FOUQUET, WHO MADE HIS MASTER, AN ATTORNEY AT THE CHÂTELET, BELIEVE THAT A MAN WAS DEAF, AND MADE THE MAN BELIEVE THAT THE ATTORNEY WAS, AND HOW THE ATTORNEY AVENGED HIMSELF ON FOUQUET

An attorney at the Châtelet [1] had two or three clerks under him, and one of them was an apprentice who was the son of a fairly wealthy man from the city of Paris itself and who had been sent to this attorney to learn the legal profession. The young son's name was Fouquet; he was between sixteen and seventeen, was very prankish and was always playing tricks. Now, according to the custom of law firms, Fouquet did all the irksome tasks, one of

---

[1] Central criminal court in Paris.

which was that he had to open the door when someone knocked in order to greet the parties his master was helping and to find out what they wanted so that he could tell him. There was a man from Bagneux who was pleading in court and had taken Fouquet's master as his attorney; he often came to consult him and, in order to be better taken care of, he always brought him capons, woodcocks, young rabbits; he usually came a little past noon, just as the clerks were having their meal or finishing it, and Fouquet had to let him in; but he didn't enjoy doing it at such an hour, for it took a good deal of his time because the man would set out to chatter with him, and Fouquet frequently had to go talk to his master and bring the answer back to him, which meant that he didn't eat very much at times. And his master, on the other hand, didn't have much consideration for him because he would send him to town at all hours of the day, twenty or a hundred times, I don't know how many, and this annoyed him no end. On one of these occasions, the man from Bagneux came to the door at the usual hour, and Fouquet easily recognized him by his knock. When he had knocked two or three times, Fouquet went to let him in and, on the way, took it into his head to play a cute trick on the man and on his master as well. He opened the door and said, "Well then, my good man, what can I do for you?" "I should like to speak to my attorney," he said, "about my case." "Well!" Fouquet said, "tell me what it is, and I'll tell him." "Oh!" the man said, "I must speak to him myself; it wouldn't be any good without me." "Very well then," Fouquet said, "I'll go tell him that you're here." Fouquet went to his master and said, "It's that man from Bagneux and he wants to speak to you." "Have him come in," the attorney said. "Sir," Fouquet said, "he has become completely deaf; at least, he's very hard of hearing. You will have to speak very loudly if you want him to hear you." "Well," the attorney said, "I'll speak quite loudly." Fouquet returned to the man and said to him: "My friend, go speak to my master, but something's happened, you know. He's had an ear infection and is almost deaf. When you speak to him, yell out loud; otherwise, he won't hear you." With that out of the way, Fouquet went to see if he could finish his dinner, and on the way he said to himself, "In a minute our friends won't be speaking discreetly." The client entered the room where the attorney was and greeted him saying "Good day, Sir" so loudly that he could be heard throughout the house. The attorney said to him even more loudly, "Welcome, my friend. What can I do for you?" As they talked about the case, both of them began to yell as though they were in the woods. When they had finished shouting, the man took leave of his attorney and left. Within a few days the man returned, but it was at an hour when, by chance, Fouquet had gone to town where his master had sent him on business. The man entered and, after having greeted his attorney, asked him how he was. He answered that he was fine. "Well, Sir!" the man said, "praise be to God! you're no longer deaf, I hope? The last time I was here, I had to speak very loudly; but now you hear well, thank God." The attorney was quite surprised. "But you, my friend," he said, "have you recovered from your ear trouble? You were the one who was deaf." The man answered him that he hadn't been afflicted that way and that he had always heard well, thanks be to God. The attorney realized immediately that this was one of Fouquet's pranks. But he found a way to get even with him. One day, when he had sent him to town, Fouquet didn't miss going out on a tennis court not very far from the house, as he frequently did when he was sent somewhere; his master was very well aware of this and had even seen him there a few times while passing by. Knowing full well that he was there, he sent word to one of his friends, a barber who lived nearby, to have a nice new broom ready for him and told him what he needed it for. When he was certain that Fouquet was probably hot and sweaty from hitting the ball, he went to the tennis court and called Fouquet, who had already bandied his share of two dozen balls and was playing the deciding set. When he saw him so flushed, he said, "Hey! my friend, you're wearing yourself out; you'll get sick, and then your father will lay the blame on me." And as soon as he came off the tennis court, he made him go into the barber's, and he said, "My friend, please lend me a shirt for this young man who's dripping with perspiration and have him rubbed down a bit." "God!" the barber said, "he really needs it; otherwise, he'll run the risk of pleurisy." They made Fouquet go into the back of the shop and had him undress by the fire which they had lighted to keep up the pretense. And meanwhile the rods were being readied for poor Fouquet, who would have gladly done without a clean shirt. When he was undressed, they took those damn rods, and they thrashed him front and back and all about. And while they were whipping him, his master said, "Yes, indeed, Fouquet, I was deaf the other day; and you, you've lost your taste now, haven't you? How does the broom taste?" And God knows the blows rained down upon his back! And so the good Fouquet had time to learn that it isn't wise to trifle with one's master.

Tale 11

OF A PROFESSOR OF CANON LAW WHO WAS SO BADLY HURT BY AN OX THAT HE DID NOT KNOW IN WHICH LEG

A professor of canon law, who was on his way to his classroom lectures, met a herd of oxen (or the herd of oxen met him) that a butcher's groom was driving ahead of him. As the professor was going by on his mule, one of the oxen brushed a bit against his robe, and he immediately began to shout, "Help! oh, that vicious ox! he's killed me! I'm dead!" When they heard the shouting, many people gathered about because he was well-known and hadn't budged from Paris for thirty or forty years. When they heard him yell, they thought he was seriously wounded. One man held him up on one side, and another on the other, for fear he might fall off his mule. In the midst of his loud cries, he said to his servant, whose name was Corneille, "Come here. Oh! my God! Go to the university and tell them I'm dead and that an ox has killed me, that I'm just not able to go give my lecture and that it'll have to be some other time." The students, and also the gentlemen on the faculty, were very upset at the news, and immediately some of them were delegated to go see him. They found him stretched out on a bed and round him the surgeon, who had bandages, oils, ointments, egg whites and all the instruments necessary in such a case. The professor was moaning so loudly about his right leg that he couldn't stand to have his stocking removed, so they had to rip it off. When the doctor saw the bare leg, he found no cuts or bruises, nor any semblance of a wound although the professor was still shouting, "I'm dead, my friend! I'm dead." And when the doctor went to touch it with his hand, he yelled louder yet, "Oh! you're killing me! I'm dead!" "And where does it hurt you the most, Sir?" said the doctor. "Why, don't you see it?" he said. "An ox killed me, and he asks me where he's hurt me! Hey! I am dead!" The doctor asked him, "Is it there, Sir?" "Not at all." "And there?" "Not at all." In short, it could not be found. "Hey! Good lord! What is this? These people can't find where I'm hurt. Isn't it swollen?" he said to the doctor. "Not in the least." "Well then," said the professor, "it must be in the other leg because I know very well that the ox ran into me." They had to take off the stocking on the other leg, but it was wounded like the other one. "Hell! this doctor doesn't know anything: go get me another one." They did. He came, and he didn't find anything. "Hey! my lord," the professor said, "this is a strange one! Could an ox have struck me this way without hurting me? Come here, Corneille; when the ox hurt me, in what direction was he going? Wasn't it towards the wall?" "Yes, Sir," the servant said, "it must be in this leg then." "I've told them so from the beginning, but they think I'm fooling them." When the doctor saw that the man was only suffering from apprehension, he put a light ointment on his leg in order to satisfy him and bandaged it, telling him that that would do for the first dressing. "And then," he said, "my good Sir, when you've figured out which leg hurts you, I'll do something else for it."

Tale 12

COMPARISON OF ALCHEMISTS TO THE GOOD WOMAN WHO WAS TAKING A JUG FULL OF MILK TO MARKET

Everyone knows that alchemists are all agreed that they look forward to a world of riches and that they know secrets of nature that all men put together don't know; but in the end their whole case goes up in smoke, so much so that their alchemy might be more properly defined: *Art which undermines*, or *Art which is not*. [1] In fact, you couldn't do better than to compare them to a good woman who was taking a jug full of milk to market and who reckoned as follows: she would sell it for two liards; with these two liards she would buy a dozen eggs and give them to a hen to brood and she'd end up with a dozen chicks; these chicks would grow

---

[1] The French reads: *Art qui mine*, ou *Art qui n'est mie*, a play on the earlier form of alchemy, *arquemie*.

up and she'd have them caponized; the capons would be worth five
sous each: that would mean a crown or more; with that she would
buy two pigs, male and female; they would grow up and make
a dozen more, and she'd sell them for twenty sous each after having
fed them for a while: this would mean twelve francs, and she could
buy a mare, which would have a fine colt, which would grow and
become so nice: he would gambol about and go "neigh." The good
woman was so pleased with her calculation that when she said
"neigh," she started to buck as her colt would, and in doing so her
jug full of milk fell and spilled all over. And there went her eggs,
her chicks, her capons, her pigs, her mare and her colt, all on the
ground. And so it is with alchemists; after they've heated, blackened,
daubed, cooled, distilled, oxidized, congealed, molded, liquefied,
vitrified, and putrefied everything, the mere breaking of an alembic
puts them in the same boat with the good woman.

Tale 13

OF KING SOLOMON, WHO MADE THE PHILOSOPHER'S STONE, AND THE REASON WHY ALCHEMISTS CANNOT SUCCEED IN THEIR PURPOSE

Not everyone is aware of the reason why alchemists cannot succeed in their undertakings; but Mary the prophetess [1] explains it
very well, pertinently, and at length in a book which she did on the
great excellence of the art, exhorting the philosophers and en-
couraging them not to despair and saying that the philosopher's
stone is so worthy and so precious that, among its admirable virtues
and properties, it has the power to command spirits and that whoever has it can conjure them up, anathematize them, tie them, bind
them, abuse them, torment them, imprison them, torture them,
martyr them. In short, he who owns it does as he pleases and can
do anything he wants if he knows how to use his fortune well. It
so happens, she says, that Solomon perfected this stone and thus
knew through divine inspiration its great and marvelous property,

---

[1] Miriam, the sister of Moses and Aaron. It was she who watched Moses
in the ark of bulrushes. She is called "the prophetess." The work in question
is apocryphal.

which was to command demons, as I've said. Therefore, as soon as
he fashioned it, he decided to have them come; but first he had a
wondrously large copper cauldron made, for it was no smaller than
the entire circumference of the woods of Vincennes, except that it
was short a half a foot or so, but it makes no difference: we mustn't
insist on a trifling matter. It's true that it was rounder, and it had to
be that big in order to do what he wanted to do with it; and in the
same way he had a lid made, the best fitting possible. At the same
time he also had a pit dug in the ground, large enough to bury the
cauldron, and he had it dug as deep as he could. When he saw that
everything was ready, he called forth, by virtue of the holy stone,
all the spirits here below, great and small, beginning with the four
emperors from the four corners of the earth; then he summoned
kings, dukes, counts, barons, colonels, captains, corporals, lance
corporals, foot and horse soldiers, and everybody else there was.
And, at that rate, there wasn't a single one left to do the cooking.
When they got there, Solomon ordered them all, by the above
mentioned virtue, to get into the cauldron, which was sunk in the
hole in the ground. The spirits were unable to refuse to get in, and
you can imagine that it was much to their regret and that there
were some who made horrible faces. As soon as he got the devils
inside, Solomon had the cover put on and had it tightly sealed, *cum
luto sapientiae*, [2] and lastly he had the cauldron covered with dirt
until the pit was filled. His entire purpose in this was that the world
no longer be infected with those evil and execrable vermin and that
men from then on should live in love and peace and that all virtue
and happiness might reign on earth. And, in point of fact, immediately thereafter men were joyful, content, sound, gay, friendly, strong,
lively, cheerful, jolly, high-spirited, jovial, sprightly, nice, frisky,
gentle, kind, alert. Oh! They were so well off! Oh! Everything went
so well! The earth brought forth all kinds of fruit without the help
of man; wolves didn't eat livestock; lions, bears, tigers, wild boars
were as gentle as lambs. In short, the whole earth seemed to be a
paradise while those no-good devils were in the bottom of the pit.
But what happened? After a long period of time, just as kingdoms
change and cities are destroyed and others are built, so there was a

---

[2] With the cement of wisdom; according to the alchemists, this substance
was a hermetic sealer.

king who had a fancy to build a city. Chance so ordained that he undertook to build it in the very place where these devils were buried. I guess Solomon failed to force into it a little devil who hid under a lump of earth when his companions went into it, and that certain little devil put it in the king's head to build his city on that spot so that his companions would be freed. So, the king put people to work building this city, and he wanted it to be magnificent, strong, and impregnable; and to this end, fantastic foundations were necessary for the walls, so much so that the excavators dug so deep that one of them ahead of the rest discovered the cauldron where those devils were. When he bumped into it and his companions noticed it, they all thought they were rich and that there was a priceless treasure in it. Alas! what a fortune it was! Oh, lord! it certainly was a misfortune! Oh! how the heavens must have then been envious of the earth! Oh! how the gods were angry with the poor human race! Where is the pen that could write, where is the tongue that could call down enough curses against that horrible and unfortunate discovery? That's what avarice does, that's what ambition does when, unable to stand its well-being, it digs the ground all the way to Hell to find its misfortune. But let's get back to our cauldron and our devils. The story says that it wasn't within the power of those diggers to open it immediately because, besides its size, it was correspondingly thick. Hence, it was imperative to inform the king, and when he saw it he thought just as the excavators had. After all, who would have imagined that there might be devils in it when it was now thought that there weren't any in the world, considering how long it had been since anyone had heard of them? The king remembered only too well that his royal predecessors had been infinitely rich, and the only thing he could figure was that they had hidden and buried there an incredible treasure and that destiny had ordained that he be the possessor of such wealth in order to be the greatest king on earth. Conclusion: he used as many people as there were around the cauldron. And while they were working, those devils kept their ears open and really didn't know what to think, except that they were being taken out in order to be hanged and that their case had been tried while they were inside. Now, the laborers pounded so much on the cauldron that they wrenched it open, and at the same time they finally removed a large part of the cover and opened the way. You can be sure that the devils fought and crowded to get out of there, and they yelled so on leaving that they terrified the king and all his people so much that they fell on the spot as though they were dead. And the devils got to their feet and away they went, throughout the world, each one to his own home, except that by chance there were a few who were quite astonished to see that the regions and countries had changed since their imprisonment. For this reason they roamed about the world for some time, not knowing what country they came from, no longer seeing the steeples of their parishes. But everywhere they went, they did so much harm that it would be too horrible to relate. Instead of the one mischief they used to do in the past in order to torment the world, they invented some brand new ones. They killed, they lashed out, they stormed, they turned everything topsy-turvy. The people spent money hand over fist, but that was also the devils' doing. In those days there were many philosophers (for alchemists are called philosophers *par excellence*), particularly because Solomon made an art of creating the holy stone and left it all in writing; classes were held as with grammar and many learned how to do it, especially since the vermin couldn't trouble their minds because they were in prison. However, the devils resented the dirty trick Solomon had played on them with that stone and, as soon as they were free, the first thing they did was to go to the philosophers' furnaces and break them to pieces. And they even found ways to erase, scratch, tear apart and falsify all the books they could find on the science; in fact, they rendered it so obscure and so difficult that men no longer know what they're looking for, and the devils would have gladly abolished it completely; but God didn't give them the power to do it. However, they had permission to go back and forth in order to stop the most learned from doing their jobs, and when an alchemist took the right path to success and at last was nearly within a hair's breadth of hitting the mark, a little devil came along and broke an alembic, which was full of precious matter, and destroyed in an hour's time all the effort that the poor philosopher had put into it for ten or twelve years, so that it had to be done all over again. It isn't the swine which root through the fields, but the devils, who are worse. That's the reason why today you see so few alchemists who succeed in their undertakings; it isn't that this science is not as true as it ever was, but rather that the devils are enemies of this gift from God. And because it may be that someday someone will receive the blessing to do it as well as Solomon did, I'd like to plead with him here and now, in case he should come in our time, that he not forget to conjure, adjure, excommunicate, anathematize, exorcise, cabalize, ruin, exterminate, confound, and destroy those evil goblins and vermin, enemies of nature and of all good things, who hinder poor alchemists, as well as all men, and women too, of course, for they make them play hard to get and, in fact, they even enter the heads of old hags and make perfect she-devils of them. That's the reason why it is said of a wicked woman that she's gone to the devil.

Tale 14

OF THE LAWYER WHO SPOKE LATIN TO HIS CHAMBERMAID AND THE CLERK WHO WAS THE GO-BETWEEN

Twenty-five or forty years ago in the city of Le Mans, there was a lawyer whose name was La Roche Thomas. He was one of the most renowned lawyers in the city, even though there were many good ones at that time; in fact, people even came from the University of Angers to seek advice in Le Mans. This Mister La Roche was a merry man, and he easily reconciled relaxation with serious things; he lived well in his house, and, when he was in a good mood, which was quite often, he latinized French and frenchified Latin, and he enjoyed it so that he spoke half Latin to his valet as well as to his chambermaid, whom he called Pedissèque. [1] And when she didn't understand what he said to her, she didn't dare ask him to interpret his words because La Roche Thomas always said to her: "You big Arcadian numbskull, don't you understand my idiom?" The poor chambermaid was completely dumbfounded by these words, and she thought it was the greatest malediction in the world. And to tell the truth, his language was so rough at times that the chickens would have gotten up from their perch. But she found a way to cope with it; she got together with one of his clerks, who was perhaps putting knowledge of those words in her head from down below, and he

---

[1] From the Latin *pedisequa*, a follower, servant in attendance, waiting-woman.

shook her, I mean succoured her, when necessary. Whenever her master said something to her, she went right away to her go-between, and he explained it to her. One day a venison pâté was given to La Roche Thomas and, after having eaten sparingly two or three thin slices of it with those who dined with him, he said to his chambermaid, as she was clearing the table: "Pedissèque, *serve* this *ferine* forcemeat, and don't let it get *famulied*."[2] The chambermaid understood well enough that he was talking to her about a pâté because she had heard him use the word *forcemeat* once before, and besides he was pointing to it; but she didn't know yet the meaning of the word *famulied*, and she kept it in mind while hastening to listen. She took the pâté and, pretending to have understood it all, said: "Very good, Sir." And she went to the clerk when they were left alone to ask him to explain this word *famulied*, and by chance he had been present when his master gave his instructions. But, unfortunately, he wasn't loyal to her this time, and he said to her: "My dear, he told you to give some of this pâté to the clerks and then put the rest away." The chambermaid believed him because she'd never gone wrong on the information he had given her. She put the pâté in front of the clerks, and they didn't spare it the way the others had at the first sitting, and they grabbed so much of it that it showed. The following day La Roche Thomas invited to dinner the most prominent people from the castle of Le Mans (which was just called the hall at that time) and bragged to them about his pâté, thinking that it was still in good condition. They came, they sat down at the table. When it was time to present the pâté, it was easy to see that it had been in good hands. It would be hard to say whether Pedissèque was bawled out more by her master for having let that forcemeat be famulied, or whether the aforesaid master was laughed at more by those he had invited for having spoken Latin to his chambermaid when giving her charge of a delicious pâté, or whether the chambermaid was put out the most with the clerk who had tricked her; but, at the very least, the first two didn't last as long as the third, for she growled at the clerk for more than a day and a night, and she vigorously threatened him that she'd never lend him anything she had again. But when she thought better of it

---

[2] Take care (Lat. *servare*) of this venison (Lat. *ferina*, game) pâté for me and don't let the servants (Lat. *famulus*) get their hands on it.

and realized that she couldn't do without him, she was forced to come to terms on Sunday morning when everyone, except the two of them, was attending high mass, and they ate together what was left over from Thursday and went back to fiddling together like good friends. There came another day when La Roche Thomas had gone to town to dine with one of his friends; it has always been customary in those neighborhoods to eat with one another and to bring one's dinner and supper so that the host doesn't have to put himself out, except to set the table. La Roche Thomas wasn't married at the time, and he had ordered only a roast chicken for his dinner, which his chambermaid brought him between two plates. He said to her quite joyfully: "What are you *adferring* [3] me there, Pedissèque?" She answered him: "Sir, it's a chicken." He had wanted to show off, and he didn't think her answer was a good one. He remembered it until he got home, and then he called his chambermaid very angrily, "Pedissèque! " She understood from her master's tone of voice that she was going to get a lecture, and she immediately went to get her go-between to attend the lecture so that he could explain what her master would tell her because he very often scolded in Latin and everything else. When she appeared, La Roche Thomas said to her: "Come here, you big thick clod, you idiot, stupid, *insulse, nugigerulle, imperite,* and all the terms of the Donat. [4] When I dine in town and I ask you what you're adferring me, who taught you to answer a chicken? Next time, speak in the pluries number, [5] you big quadruped, speak in the pluries number. A chicken! That's a fine dinner for a man like La Roche Thomas! " Pedissèque had never been treated to that word *pluries number,* so she had it explained to her by his clerk, who said to her: "You know what it is? He's angry because when you brought him his dinner today and he asked you what it was you were bringing him you answered a chicken, and he wants you to say chickens, and not a chicken. That's what he means by pluries number, do you understand?" Pedissèque remembered it well. A few days later when La Roche Thomas went out again to dine with one of his neighbors

---

[3] Bringing me (Lat. *adferre,* to bring).

[4] *Insulsus,* insipid; *nugigerulus,* one who talks a lot of nonsense; *imperitus,* ignorant. The Donat, from Aelius Donatus, a fourth-century Latin grammarian, was widely used in the sixteenth century.

[5] In the plural.

(I don't know if it was the same one as the other day), his chamber-maid brought him his dinner. La Roche Thomas asked her, as usual, what she was adferring. She remembered her lesson well, and she immediately answered, "Sir, cows and lambs." Her reply made everyone present laugh, particularly when they heard he was teaching his chambermaid to speak in the pluries number.

Tale 15

OF THE CARDINAL OF LUXEMBOURG AND THE GOOD WOMAN WHO WANTED TO MAKE A PRIEST OUT OF HER SON WHO DID NOT HAVE TESTES, AND HOW THE AFORESAID CARDINAL NAMED HIMSELF PHELIPPOT

In the days of King Louis XII there was a cardinal of the House of Luxembourg who was bishop of Le Mans [1] and who normally stayed in his manor; he was a man who lived magnificently and he was loved and honored, as the prince that he was, by the people of his diocese. Magnificence and all, he still had a certain friend-liness which made him even more appreciated by everyone, and he was even witty when the occasion called for it; and although he loved to tease, he didn't object to being made fun of. One day a country woman came before him, since he was willing to listen to anyone, and after she had kneeled before him and received his bles-sing, as they did very religiously in those days, she said to him, "Sir, by your leave, may it please your Grace to hear me out. I have a son who's already over twenty, your reverence! and he is quite big; he's already been teaching in the schools of our parish for a year: I'd really like to make him a priest if it's God's will." "Indeed, yes," said the cardinal, "that would be a good thing to do, my dear woman, we must make him one." "Yes, Sir, but," said the good woman, "there's something which keeps him from it; but I've been told that you could easily recompense him." (The good woman meant dispense). The cardinal was enjoying the good woman's sim-plicity and he said to her, "And what is it, my dear?" "Sir, you see, he doesn't have …" "What doesn't he have?" he said. "Well! Sir,"

---

[1] He died in 1519. He wrote several mediocre devotional works.

she said, "he doesn't have...; I don't dare tell you, and you know what I mean, what men have." The cardinal, who understood her well, said to her: "And what do men have? Doesn't he have long hose?" "No! No! That's not what I mean, Sir; he doesn't have any doodads." The cardinal was a long time sparring with her in order to see if he could get her to speak good French; but he couldn't do it and she kept on saying to him, "Oh! Sir, you know what I mean, why do you make me waste my time this way?" Nevertheless, she finally said to him, "Look, Sir, when he was little he fell off the top of a ladder and got such a hernia that he had to be felled (to fell in that part of the country is to castrate), and if it hadn't been for that I would have married him off because he's the biggest of all my kids." The cardinal said to her, "Believe me, my dear, that won't stop him from being a priest, provided he receives dispensation, of course. I wish to God all the priests of my diocese didn't have any more than he does!" "Oh! Sir," she said, "thank you very much; he'll be bound to pray to God for you and for your departed friends. But, Sir, there's something else I'd like to tell you, if you don't mind." "And what is it, my dear?" "Oh! Listen! Sir, I'd like to ask you, I was told that bishops can change people's names. I have another boy, and people do nothing but laugh at him. His name is Phelippes (may it please your Grace); my impression is that when he has another name, I'll be happier about it. They yell after him Phelippot! Phelippot! and you know, Sir, how irritating it is for people when others make fun of them. I'd very much like for him to have another name, if it were your pleasure." Now it so happened that the right reverend's name was Phelippes. "Why, of course, my dear," he said, "it's wrong for them to call your son Phelippot that way, we must do something about it. But you know, my dear, I won't take the name of Phelippes away from him because I want him to keep it for my sake: my name is Phelippes, my dear, do you understand? I shall give him my name and take his; his name will be Phelippes and my name will be Phelippot; and if someone calls him anything other than Phelippes, come and tell me, and I'll give you permission to take ecclesiastical action against them. How's that, my dear? You won't be displeased to have your son bear my name?" "Honestly, Sir," she said, "you do us more honor than we deserve; I pray God that by His grace He grant you a long and happy life and Heaven at the end." The good woman went away very happy to have received such a good answer from her bishop, and she told everyone in her village what the bishop had told her. And from then on the bishop, who gladly repeated such stories, called himself Phelippot by way of fun and said that he would no longer be called Phelippes. And thereafter he was often called Phelippot, which only made him laugh. Augustus Caesar too joked willingly and didn't mind having fun poked at him. Witness the well-known anecdote about him and a young man who came to Rome and looked so much like Augustus that one could hardly distinguish between them in terms of facial features, and he was stared at throughout the city like some sort of oddity because of the great resemblance between the emperor and himself. Augustus, who was aware of this, said to him one day, "Tell me, my friend, was your mother ever in this city?" The young man, who understood what Augustus meant, said, "Sire, not my mother, she was never here as far as I know, but my father was quite a few times." And in that way he turned on Augustus what Augustus had wanted to pull on him, for it was no more impossible for the young man's father to have known Augustus' mother than for the emperor to have known the young man's mother. Neither did the same emperor take offense when Virgil called him a baker's son because when he first knew him the only presents he gave him were loaves of bread; but afterwards he gave him many other great gifts.

Tale 16

OF THE MAN FROM PARIS WHO WAS NEWLY MARRIED AND BEAUFORT, WHO FOUND A WAY TO MAKE LOVE TO HIS WIFE, NOTWITHSTANDING MADAM PERNETTE'S CAREFUL WATCHING

After having attended universities at home and abroad, a young man, born in Paris, returned to his city, where he was for a time without getting married, enjoying himself, having no lack of any kind of pleasure he wanted, and also women, although there aren't many to be had in Paris, unfortunately! Having gotten acquainted with their tricks and subtleties in so many countries and having used them himself for his own benefit, he wasn't too interested in getting

married. He feared that accursed and common evil of being cuckolded, and if it hadn't been for his desire to see himself a father
and have an heir, he would have gladly remained a perennial bach-
elor. But because he was an intelligent man, he thought it best to
go through with it (I mean get married) and that it was just as well
to go into it early as wait until later, realizing that you mustn't hold
off from taking a wife until you're all worn out because nothing
opens the door to cuckoldry like a husband's impotence. And, besides, he remembered and had written down the more common ruses
which women invent in order to have their pleasure. He was aware
of the comings and goings of wives from house to house under the
guise of bringing thread, linen, fancywork, little dogs. He knew how
women pretend to be sick, how they go out to gather grapes, how
they speak to their lovers who come in disguise, how they help one
another out under the pretext of being related. And to boot he had
read Boccaccio and the *Celestina*. [1] And he resolved to beware of all
these things, thinking to himself: I shall do the best I can not to wear
horns. For the rest, what will be will be. And he immediately crossed
himself with his right hand, commending himself to God's good
graces. So among the Paris girls who were his to choose from he
found one to his liking who had the best background, the best mind,
and the best shape. And he very nearly got it all, for he got one that
was young, beautiful, rich, and well-connected; so he married her
and brought her to his family home. Now there lived with him a
rather elderly woman, named Madam Pernette, a wary and wily
woman who had been his nurse and had always lived in the house.
He introduced her to his young wife, who was just setting up house-
keeping, saying to her, "My dear, I'm very attached to this woman,
she was my nurse; she's rendered many services to my mother and
father and to me after them. I'm giving her to you to keep you company, she's a good and respectable woman: you'll be pleased with
her." Then in private he instructed Madam Pernette to stay close
to his wife and not to leave her, no matter where she went, or she
would pay for it dearly. She promised him faithfully that she would

---

[1] Giovanni Boccaccio, Italian writer born in Paris (1313-1375), author of
the famous and very influential *Decameron,* a collection of ribald tales and
amorous ruses. *La Celestina,* well-known tragicomedy about a procuress and
the tricks of the trade by the Spanish author Fernando de Rojas (*ca.* 1465-
1541).

do it. And here let me say in passing that there's a wicked proverb, I don't know who invented it, but it's well-known: *Casta quam nemo rogavit*. [2] I'm not saying that it's true, I'll let it speak for itself; but I dare say that there isn't a beautiful woman who hasn't been asked or who won't be sooner or later. "Ah! Aren't I beautiful?" this one will say. "And I?" that one will say. Well, then, I'm satisfied, I don't want an argument. The fact remains that a smart woman takes care not to say that she's been asked, particularly to her husband, because if he's shrewd, he will realize that his wife wouldn't have been sought if she hadn't given cause and listened. But to get back to my story, it happened that among those who habitually went to this married man's house (don't expect me to give you his name) there was a young lawyer, called Lord Beaufort, who was from the province of Berry and who frequented the bar in order to use and practice what he had learned in his studies. The married man was very friendly with him and welcomed him because they had known one another in the universities and had even been comrades in arms on many a caper.

This Beaufort was well named, for he was goodlooking, adroit, and graceful. And, therefore, the young lady looked upon him favorably, as he did her, and in no time at all, by frequent visual messages, they gave one another signs of their desires. Now the husband, who knew what life was all about, didn't seem to be perturbed, even with the newness of it all; he wasn't overly distrustful of his wife's great youth, or of the integrity of his friend, and was content with the sharp lookout Madam Pernette kept. Beaufort, for his part, knew what made the world go round, and he saw the very friendly way in which the husband treated him and the hearty welcome which the young woman accorded him, and with a warmth of affection (it seemed to him) not lavished upon others. That was indeed the case, and he easily found the opportunity, while talking to her, of getting around to the subject of love, particularly because she'd been raised in a business family and could follow and entertain all kinds of topics. Little by little, Beaufort began to tell her such things as, "My dear lady, it's easy enough for intelligent and virtuous women to know a man's good will because they always have our hearts,

---

[2] Ovid, *Amores*, I, 8, 43. The correct quotation is *casta est quam nemo rogavit*: Chaste means never asked.

even when they don't want them. Therefore, I don't have to tell you
any more expressly the affection and esteem I have for your infinite
charms, and they're accompanied by such nobility of mind that no
man who isn't well-born and whose heart isn't in the right place
would dare aspire to them. After all, precious things are desired only
by gentle and noble minds, and I have every reason to praise fortune,
which has been so favorable as to offer me such a worthy and
virtuous subject so that I might have the means of demonstrating
the inclination I have toward precious and worthy things. And although I may be one of the least of those whose service you deserve,
I feel sure, nevertheless, that your great perfections, which I admire,
will be the cause of increasing in me those things which are necessary for true service. As for my heart, it couldn't be any more en-
raptured and in love with you than it is, and I hope to show you
this so clearly that you'll never regret having given me the opportunity to remain your servant forever." When she heard these words
of affection, the young woman, who was pretty and wordlywise,
wished it were as easily done as said. For her age (when women
normally display fear and modesty), she was both coy and forward and she answered him as follows: "Sir, even if I wanted
to look elsewhere, I wouldn't have had time yet to think of taking
a lover other than the one I married because he loves me so much
and treats me so well that he keeps me from thinking of anyone
but him. Moreover, even if fortune ordained that my heart be
divided in two, I am sure that your virtue and good faith are such
that you wouldn't want to be the principal cause of making me do
something which would be to my disadvantage. As for the charms
you attribute to me, I leave that aside, not recognizing them in me,
and return them where they came from, that is, to you. But, to
defend myself in another way, would you want to do this wrong
to the one who trusts you so, who behaves in such a friendly fashion
towards you? It seems to me that a noble heart like yours would
not harbor such an intention as that one. And besides, you can see
that the inconveniences are great enough to dissuade you from such
an undertaking, even if it were within your grasp. I'm always accompanied by a guardian, and she keeps such constant watch over
me that, even if I wanted to do wrong, I wouldn't be able to hide
anything from her." Beaufort was very pleased when he heard this
answer, and particularly when he felt that the lady based herself

on reasons of which the first ones were a little strong, but as for
the last ones the young woman minimized them herself. Beaufort
summarily dealt with them: "I had indeed foreseen and weighed
seriously the three points you allege, Madam; but you know that
the first two depend on your good will, and the third lies in diligence
and good advice. As for the first one, since love is a virtue which
seeks hearts and minds of a noble nature, you must realize that
sooner or later someday you will love; and since this will eventually happen, it's better that you obtain as soon as possible the service
of a man who loves you as dearly as his own life rather than wait
any longer to obey the Lord, who has the power to make you pay
interest on the past and put you into the hands of some hypocritical
man who won't take good care of your honor as it deserves. As
for the second, that point was resolved a long time ago by those
who know what it is to love: because of the affection I have for
you, far be it from me to wrong the man you married, and rather
I honor him when I love so much what he loves. There is no greater
sign that two hearts are in perfect harmony than when they love
the same thing. You know perfectly well that if he and I were
enemies, or if we didn't have any friendship for one another, I
wouldn't have the opportunity to see you, or to speak with you
so often. So, since the good will I have for him is the cause of the
great love I have for you, it mustn't be the cause of your letting
me die for loving you. As for the third one, Madam, you know
that nothing is impossible for a valiant heart. Imagine what could
burst forth from two hearts controlled by Cupid, a lord who brings
out the best in his subjects!" To cut it short, Beaufort stated his
case to her so honestly that she honestly could not refuse him.
And the matter progressed to such a point that the young woman
gave in willingly, and the only thing left to do was to find some
nice opportunity to carry out their venture. They considered every
means possible; but when it came time to make them work,
Madam Pernette spoiled everything, for she had two eyes which
were certainly worth all those of Inachos' daughter's guardian. [3]
Of course, they couldn't use the tricks Beaufort had engineered

---

[3] Io, daughter of Inachus, was loved by Zeus and was changed into a
heifer by jealous Hera or, in some tales, by Zeus, to protect her: she was
watched by hundred-eyed Argus.

in the past because the husband knew them all by heart. Nevertheless, he so exercised his wits that the thought of one which seemed
to him rather good: because he knew all too well that in all good
love affairs a third party is necessary, he disclosed his secret to
one of his friends, a young silk merchant who was still unmarried
and who lived in a house his father had left him long ago at the
end of Notre-Dame bridge; he also knew the husband well. One
All Saints' day, as agreed upon by the parties involved, the young
woman, led by the god of love, left her house at sermon time to
go hear a theologian who was preaching at St. John's on the Strand
and who had a large crowd; [4] and the husband stayed home for some
business of his. As the lady was passing in front of Mister Henry's
house (for that was the merchant's name), a full pail of water was
suddenly thrown at her (according to the plan which had been
devised), and it drenched her completely, and it was thrown so
deftly that all those who saw it thought it was done by accident.
"Oh! alas," she said, "Madam Pernette, I'm a mess! What am I
going to do?" The quickest was for her to step into Mister Henry's
house, and she said to Madam Pernette, "My dear, run home quickly and get me my Persian lamb robe; I'll wait for you here at
Mister Henry's." The old woman left, and the young woman went
upstairs, where she found a very nice fire her lover had had
prepared for her; he didn't give her time to get undressed, but
threw her on a bed which was near the fire, and you can imagine
they didn't waste time, and they had ample time to do it well
before the old woman could return and bring her dress and all
the other accessories. The husband, who was at home, heard
Madam Pernette in the front bedroom going about her business
without telling him anything about it for fear that he might get
angry. By chance, he went and found the good Pernette, and he
immediately said to her, "What are you doing here? Where's my
wife?" Madam Pernette told him what happened and that she had
come to get some clothes for her. "Oh! I'll be damned!" he said,
making a face, "that's a cunning trick which wasn't in my book;
I knew them all, except that one. I've really been had! It only
takes one lousy hour to make a man a cuckold! Get back to her,

---

[4] St. John's stood near the site of the present Hôtel de Ville in the Place
de Grève, now called the Place de l'Hôtel-de-Ville.

dammit! I'll have the servant bring her the rest." Madam Pernette returned, but it was too late. Beaufort had finished his business and fled through a back door in accordance with the warning he received from his friend who was on watch to see Madam Pernette coming. When she arrived, she didn't notice anything because even though the young woman had taken on a little color, she thought it was from the heat of the fire. And so it was, but it was from a fire which water from the river can't extinguish.

Tale 17

OF THE HIGH COURT LAWYER WHO HAD HIS BEARD TAKEN OFF
TIT FOR TAT AND THE DINNER HE GAVE FOR HIS FRIENDS

A High Court lawyer, who was a run-of-the-mill fellow, was pleading a case before President Lizet, [1] who died not long ago as abbot of Saint-Victor's *prope muros*; and because it was a case of some importance, he was arguing earnestly; in such cases, lawyers always feel that they cannot speak too expressly for the benefit of their clients and for their own glory. Therefore, he repeated by chance a point which had already been alleged, fearing perhaps that it hadn't been caught by the court (which you needn't doubt in Paris), and, in fact, the president was leaving to go into counsel. The lawyer had the matter at heart and he said, "Mister President, just one more word." The president didn't hear him because he was listening to the opinions of the members of the Council. The lawyer, who was excited, said, "Mister President, a word with you. Hey! a word with you, and I'll match you tit for tat." When the president heard him say *tit* (for which you shouldn't honestly refuse yourself anything), he willingly lingered to listen to the lawyer in order to make him understand that he'd be glad to tat his wife's tits for him, and there was much laughter; and

---

[1] Pierre Lizet (1482-1554), first president of the Parlement de Paris, who spent the last years of his life at St. Victor's Abbey, but he never became its abbot. Des Périers alludes to the title of Théodore de Bèze's spirited attack against Lizet: *Responsio ad commissionem sibi datam a venerabili domino Petro Lizeto, nuper curiae Parisiensis praesidente, nunc abbate Sancti Victoris prope muros.*

God knows he wanted to hang onto them! Nevertheless, he said what he wanted to say: the story doesn't mention whether he won or lost tit for tat, but it does say that the lawyer in question sported a long beard, something which was no longer a novelty, for many others had them, even lawyers; nevertheless, it displeased Lizet because the beard ordinance[2] had been promulgated during his term of office, even though it wasn't enforced very long because court fashion was followed and everyone wore his beard as he pleased. According to the story, it happened that some days later the same lawyer argued another case (the aforesaid lord president was then in a good mood). When it came time to pronounce the verdict, the judge added on to it, saying, "And while you're at it, Jacquelot, shave off that beard." And, after a little pause, he said, "Tit for tat." There was even more laughter at this than there had been the first time because this tit for tat business was still fresh in their minds. He was forced to cut off his beard; otherwise, he never would have been tolerated by the president, to whom he owed this tit for tat. At about the same time, Jacquelot happened to be one of six guests and men of good cheer in abbot De Chatelus's home, and they had a rather meager lunch, perhaps because the meat wasn't ready on time and because they were all friends whom Chatelus treated in a free and easy manner in private. When he left, Jacquelot invited them to dinner and added a few other friends, and they all dined together informally. And among them there was a man[3] whose name is well-known in France, for his distinguished title as much as for his knowledge, and he had also been at Chatelus's luncheon. And I'm sure that for his part he was very content with the entertainment of both hosts because men of importance notice the hospitality of people more than the quality of their food. Nevertheless, for fun he made up an epigram about them:

> To six guests Chatelus gives lunch
> For less than the cost of a cent,
> And Jacquelot has a larger bunch
> For less to a dinner event.
> After these disorderly meals,
> Each one departs in rosy glows.

---

[2] Fictitious edict, but Francis I is generally credited with having brought in the fashion of wearing beards.

[3] Mellin de Saint-Gelais (1491-1558), well-known French poet and abbot.

Who misses me at Chatelus's deals
Need not look for me at Jacquelot's. [4]

---

[4] Saint-Gelais, II, p. 243.

Tale 18

OF GILLET THE JOINER AND HOW HE HAD HIS REVENGE ON THE GREYHOUND THAT ALWAYS CAME AND ATE HIS DINNER

A joiner from Poitiers, named Gillet, worked to earn his living as best he could; although he had lost his wife, he still had a nine or ten-year old daughter whose service pleased him so that he had no other valet or chambermaid. Every Saturday he brought in the food he needed for the week, and early every morning he placed his little potful on the fire, and his daughter cooked it. And he was just as happy with his little fare as a richer man with his. Now it is commonly said that it's not good to have a neighbor who is either too poor or too rich because, if he's poor, he'll always be asking you for something without ever being able to help you in any way; if he's too rich, he'll keep you down and you'll have to put up with him and not dare borrow anything from him. This joiner had as a neighbor a city gentleman, who was a little too much of a lord for him and who had a whole slew of valets and comers and goers. And because he loved to hunt so much, he kept dogs in his house and didn't have to go far outside the city in order to amuse himself rabbit hunting. Among his dogs there was a very mischievous greyhound which went in everywhere and nothing was ever too hot or too heavy for him: bread, meat, cheese, everything was game for him, and the poor joiner was the most afflicted of them all, for between him and the gentleman there was but a wall over which the greyhound went to his place at all hours and carried away everything he found. And, in fact, the greyhound was so smart that with his paw he toppled the pot boiling on the fire, took the meat out, and ran off with everything so that very often poor Gillet didn't have much to eat, and this angered him no end because, after having worked all morning, his table was cleared before he could sit down to eat. And the worst of it was that he didn't dare complain about it; but he vowed to get his revenge, no matter what might come of it. One day when he saw the greyhound going after his prize, he followed him without making much noise with a thick square plank in his hand, and he found him near his pot pulling out the meat which was inside. He deliberately closed the door and caught the greyhound, and he swatted his haunches in a flash five or six times with the plank, and he laid it on vigorously. And all of a sudden he dropped his plank and picked up a riding switch no bigger than his finger, about a yard or so long, and opened the door for the greyhound, who was yelping his head off, like the whipped dog that he was. The joiner ran after him with his switch and, hitting him with it constantly, chased him right into the street, saying, "Get out of here, mister hound! Don't you come back! How dare you come here to eat my dinner!" Meanwhile, he pretended that he had only hit him with the switch. But he had thrashed the greyhound so soundly with a switch as supple as the leg of a chair that the gentleman was never able to eat his dog's booty again.

Tale 19

OF THE COBBLER BLONDEAU, WHO WAS NEVER MELANCHOLY BUT TWICE IN HIS LIFE AND HOW HE TOOK CARE OF IT, AND HIS EPITAPH

In Paris on the Seine there are three boats; [1] but there was also a cobbler, named Blondeau, who had a shop near the Cross of Trahoir [2] where he repaired shoes and earned his living happily. But he loved good wine above all and talked about it readily to people who came in; and if there was any at all in the whole district, he had to taste it, and he was delighted to have more, especially when it was good. All day long he sang and made the entire neighborhood happy. No one ever saw him sad but twice in his life: once, when he found in an old wall an iron pot in which there was a

---

[1] First line of an old French song, "A Paris il y a trois bateaux sur la Seine," which alludes to the three boats on the city's coat of arms and which also implies here that the Seine is teeming with vessels.

[2] At the intersection of Saint-Honoré and l'Arbre-Sec streets.

great quantity of very old coins, some of silver, others of alloy, whose value he didn't know. Then he started to become pensive. He no longer sang, he no longer thought of anything but this pot of ironmongery. He thought to himself: "The money is no longer in use; I couldn't get bread or wine with it. If I show it to the goldsmiths, they'll expose me, or they'll want to have their share of it and won't give me half of what it's worth." At times he worried that he hadn't hidden the pot well enough and that it might be stolen from him. At all hours he left his booth to go move it. He was as troubled as you could be; but in the end he pulled himself together, saying to himself, "What! I'm only thinking of my pot! People can tell by the way I act that there's something different about me. Phooey! To hell with the pot! It's bringing me bad luck." In point of fact, he gingerly went and got it and threw it in the river and drowned all his melancholy with the pot. Another time, he got angry with a man who lived right next to his little shop; at least, his shop was right next to the man's place, and this certain man had a monkey which pulled a thousand tricks on poor Blondeau. The monkey used to watch him from a high window when he was cutting out his leather, and he noticed how he did it; and as soon as Blondeau had gone out to dinner or somewhere about his business, the monkey came down and went into Blondeau's shop, took his paring knife and cut up Blondeau's leather as he had seen him do; and he made a habit of it everytime Blondeau slipped out. And so, the poor man didn't dare go out of his shop for quite a while to drink or eat without putting his leather away. And if sometimes he forgot to lock it up, the monkey didn't forget to cut it up into pieces for him, and this made him very angry, but he didn't dare harm the monkey for fear of his master. When he got thoroughly annoyed with it, he determined to get even with him. He had become well aware of the monkey's habit, which was to do exactly as he saw him do: if Blondeau sharpened his paring knife, the monkey sharpened after him; if he dipped thread in pitch, the monkey did too; if he sewed a new sole, the monkey came and worked his elbows as he had seen him do. On one of these occasions, Blondeau wheted a paring knife and made it as sharp as a razor, and then, when he saw the monkey on the lookout, he placed the paring knife against his throat and moved it back and forth as if he wanted to slit his throat. And when he had done that long enough for the monkey to have picked it up, he left the shop and went to eat. The monkey didn't fail to come down right away because he wanted to amuse himself with this new pastime which he hadn't seen before. He came and took the paring knife and straightaway put it against his throat, drawing it back and forth as he had seen Blondeau do. But he brought it too near and, carelessly raking it against his neck, he cut his throat with the paring knife, which was really sharp, and he died before the hour was out. And so Blondeau was safely avenged of his monkey, and he went back to his old habit of singing and making merry, which lasted until his death. And in memory of the happy life he had led, the following epitaph was written about him:

> In this tomb there lies below
> A cobbler who was named Blondeau,
> Who while alive gathered nothing at all,
> And then later he passed beyond recall.
> His neighbors were filled with sorrowful signs,
> For he used to point out the finer wines.

Tale 20

OF THREE BROTHERS WHO NARROWLY MISSED BEING HANGED BECAUSE OF THEIR LATIN

Three brothers from a good family had lived in Paris for a long time, but they had wasted all their time gadding about, playing around and chasing women. It happened that their father sent for all three to come home, which surprised them very much because they didn't know a single word of Latin; but they conspired to learn each a word for their need. To wit, the eldest learned to say *Nos tres clerici*; [1] the second took his theme from money and learned *Pro bursa et pecunia*; [2] the third, while passing by a church, overheard from the high mass the phrase *Dignum et justum est*. [3] And so, prepared as they were, they left Paris to go see their father; and together they agreed that wherever they would be and to all

---

[1] We three clerics.
[2] For purse and money.
[3] "It is meet and right so to do," one of the responses in the mass.

kinds of people they would speak nothing else but their Latin, hoping that way to have themselves considered the greatest clerks in the whole country. Now, while they were on their way through the woods, it happened that thieves had slit a man's throat and left him there after having robbed him. The sheriff was after them with his men when he found these three fellows close to where the murder was committed and where the dead body lay. "Come here," he said to them. "Who killed this man?" Right away the eldest, who claimed the honor of speaking first, said "Nos tres clerici." "Oh! Oh!" said the sheriff. "And why did you do it?" "Pro bursa et pecunia," said the second. "Well then!" said the sheriff, "you will hang for it." "Dignum et justum est," said the third. And the poor guys would have been hanged without grounds if it hadn't been for the fact that, when they saw it was in earnest, they began to speak their mother's Latin and to say who they were. The sheriff, who saw they were young and not very smart, realized that they weren't the ones and let them go and set out in pursuit of the thieves who had committed the murder. But did he find them? "And how should I know, my friend? I wasn't there."

Tale 21

OF THE YOUNG MAN WHO MADE THE MOST OF THE FINE LATIN HIS PARISH PRIEST HAD TAUGHT HIM

A rich farmer, who had supported his son for a few years in Paris, sent for him on the advice of his parish priest. When he arrived, the father, who was already old, was glad to see him and didn't fail to send right away for the priest to come to dinner in order to show off his son to him. The priest came, saw the young man, and said to him, "Welcome home, my friend; I'm so pleased to see you. Now then, let's have dinner, and then we'll talk." They dined very well. After dinner, the father said to the priest, "Father, you see this boy; I sent for him from Paris, as you advised me. He went there three years ago this Candlemas. I'd certainly like to know if he has profited, but I'm very much afraid that he doesn't want to amount to anything. I hoped to make a priest out of him. Please, Father, question him a little in order to find out how he's used his time." "Yes, of course, my friend," said the priest, "I'll do it for your sake." And on the spot and in the presence of the good man, he had the young man come forward. "Now then," he said, "your teachers in Paris are great latinists; let me see what they've taught you. I am very pleased that your father wants to make a priest out of you; but tell me now, what is a priest in Latin; surely you must know that." The young man answered him, "Sacerdos." "Well!" said the priest. "that isn't too bad, for it is written, *Ecce sacerdos magnus:* [1] but *prestolus* [2] is much more elegant and more proper; after all, you know very well that a priest wears a stole. Now then, what is a cat in Latin (the priest could see the cat near the fire)?" The boy answered, "catus, felis, murilegus." [3] The priest, in order to have the father believe that he knew much more than they did in Paris, said to the young man, "My friend, I'm sure that your teachers taught you that; but there's a better word: it's *mitis,* [4] and you know that there's nothing as meek as a cat; and even the tail, which is so soft when you touch it, is called *suavis.* Now then, what is fire in Latin?" The boy answered, "ignis." "No, no," the priest said: "it's *gaudium* because fire gladdens. Don't you see how comfortable we are here near the fire? Now then, water, what is that called in Latin?" The boy said, "aqua." "It's much better to say *abundantia,*" the priest said, "you know there's nothing more abundant than water. Now then, a bed?" The boy said, "lectus." "Lectus?" said the priest. "You speak only the most vulgar Latin: there isn't a child who couldn't say as much. Don't you know any other?" The boy answered, "thorus." "You still don't have it right," the priest said. "Don't you know any other?" The boy said, "cubile." "That still isn't it." Finally, when the boy had nothing more to say to him, the priest said: "The Latin for bed, why, I'll tell you what it is; it's *requies,* my friend, because you sleep in it and you take your rest in it." While the priest was questioning him that way with his *Now then*'s, the boy's father didn't look very cheerful

---

[1] Behold, a great priest; the words of the Introit when a bishop is celebrating pontifically.

[2] Pejorative diminutive (a sorry priest), but in no way connected with the stole, a vestment.

[3] *Cattus* is a late Latin form, and *murilegus* is a normal medieval Latin word for cat.

[4] Soft, gentle; comic etymology, just as later the Latin *suavis* has nothing to do with tail.

and would have gladly beaten his son because he thought that he had wasted his money. But the priest, when he saw that he was angry, said to him, "No, no, no, friend, he has profited all right; I know he was taught to say just as he does. He doesn't answer too poorly, but hell! there's Latin and then there's Latin. I know words they've never heard of in Paris. Send him to me often, I'll teach him things he doesn't know yet; and you'll see that within three months I'll turn him into something far different from what he is." Meanwhile, the young boy didn't dare answer back because he was fearful and ashamed; but, nevertheless, he thought about it all the more. A few days later, the priest had a fat hog slaughtered and asked the father to come to dinner to share grilled meat and pudding with him and told him not to forget to bring his son. They came and dined. The young son, who hadn't forgotten the Latin the priest had taught him and who had already thought of a way to put it into practice, left the table early, went quietly and got the cat, and, after tying a wisp of straw to its tail, put fire to the straw with a match and let the cat go, which took off as though its ass were on fire. The first place it went and hid itself was under the priest's bed, which promptly caught fire. When the young man saw that it was time to put his Latin to work, he quickly ran up to the priest and said to him, "Prestole, mitis habet gaudium in suavi: quod si abundantia non est, tu amittis tuum requies."[5] It was the priest's turn to run when he saw that the fire was already blazing; and in this way the young man put to use the Latin that the priest had taught him in order to teach him not to disgrace him any more in front of his father.

---

[5] In the priest's own macaronic Latin: "Father, the cat's tail is on fire, but there is no water and you're losing your bed."

Tale 22

OF A PRIEST WHO DID NOT SAY ANYTHING BUT *Jesus* IN HIS GOSPEL

In a parish in the diocese of Le Mans, called St. George's, there was a priest who had once been married. When his wife died, he decided to become a priest in order to fulfill better his duty of praying to God for her and also to gain the money she had left in her will for the saying of masses in the parish church. And although he knew just enough Latin to get by, and not much at that, still he did like the others and managed to finish his masses as best he could. One fine feast day a gentleman came to St. George's for some business he had there, and he arrived in between masses; and because he just didn't have the time to wait for high mass, he wanted to have a low one said, and he ordered his man to find him a priest to say it for him. His man spoke to this priest I've been talking about and he was more than willing. And although he only knew his Requiem, Our Lady and Holy Ghost masses well, nevertheless, he never let on about it, for fear of losing his thirty deniers. [1] He put on his vestments, he began his mass, he raced through the Introit, even though it was an effort for him, and the Epistle, which was even harder. But the gentleman didn't notice it, because he was busy saying his prayers, until it came time for the Gospel. The priest wasn't very familiar with it because he'd only said it three or four times; for that reason, he was very upset, knowing full well that his fear made his tongue slip even more. He read the Gospel with great difficulty, and he found in it so many new and very long words to pronounce that he was obliged to omit half of them, and so he said *Jesus* every time, even though it wasn't there. Finally, he made his way through the mass somehow and finished it as best he could. The gentleman, who had noted this good chaplain's ability, had him paid for his mass and told his man to have him come to the pastor's house for dinner when high mass was over. The priest did it gladly, for anyone who gives a man thirty deniers and then gives him a good dinner actually contributes a good five sous to his budget. At dinner, the gentleman started to talk about the mass and the service of the day and he finally said, "Father John, today's Gospel was very reverent: there were many Jesuses in it." Then Father John, who was somewhat cheered up by the gentleman's friendliness as well as by the good food he had had, said to him, "I already know what you're trying to get at, Sir; but let me tell you, Sir, I've only been a priest for three years, Sir; I'm not as used to it yet, Sir, as those who have been priests for twenty

---

[1] The price of a mass.

or thirty years, Sir. To tell the truth, Sir, I had only seen today's Gospel, Sir, three or four times before. There are many others in the missal, Sir, which are a little difficult, Sir; so when I say mass, Sir, before the good people, Sir, and there are some of those difficult words to read in the Gospel, Sir, I skip over them, Sir, for fear of making the mass too long, Sir; and I say *Jesus* instead, which is better, Sir." "Really, Father John," the gentleman said, "you are probably quite right. Whenever I come here, I will always want to hear your mass. I'll drink to you on that." "Thank you very much," Father John said, "*et ego cum vos.* [2] To your health, Sir. Whenever you need me, Sir, I will serve you as well as any priest, Sir, in this parish." And so he took his leave, as happy as a lark.

------

[2] and I to you.

Tale 23

OF MASTER PETER FAIFEU, WHO GOT BOOTS WHICH DID NOT COST HIM ANYTHING, AND THE SCOFFERS [1] OF LA FLÈCHE IN ANJOU

Not long ago there lived in the town of Angers a fine trouble-maker named Master Peter Faifeu. He was a man full of wit and clever tricks who didn't do any serious harm, except that sometimes he played Villon-like pranks, for

> As a clever man trying to possess
> The goods of others plus his own pile,
> And leave them completely penniless,
> Master Peter did it in fine style.

In fact, he thought it was a good proverb which says that all goods are common property and that only the way of getting them is different. The truth is that he did it so dexterously and in such a cute way that no one could be annoyed with him about it; they could only laugh, yet all the while keeping up their guard against him as

------

[1] It was customary at the time for the inhabitants of many towns to have nicknames.

well as they could. It would take too long to relate all the fine tricks
he played in his lifetime, but I'll tell you one of them, which isn't
bad at all, so that you can judge what the others must have been
worth. Once upon a time he was in such a hurry to leave the town
of Angers that he didn't have time to take his boots. What! boots?
he didn't even have time to have his horse saddled because the
townspeople were following rather closely on his heels. But he was
so wily and so full of tricks that as soon as he was well out of
bowshot of the town, he managed to get a mare from a poor man
who was going back to his village, and he told him that he was
going that way and that he would leave it with his wife on his way
through. And because the weather was a bit stormy, he went into
a barn and, in great haste, he made himself some nice new boots
out of hay and got on his mare and spurred it or, at léast, dug his
heels into it, and at last he got to La Flèche completely soaked and
in very bad shape, which was not the way he liked to be, and so
he was very crestfallen. Moreover, to make matters worse, everybody in town as usual knew him, and the scoffers of Angers (they've
been called that way because of their teasing) began to jeer at him
good-naturedly as he was riding through. "Master Peter," they said,
"now's a good time to talk to you! You're certainly sober for being
so soused." Another said, "You look like Saint George on a mare."
But, above all, the shoemakers made fun of his boots. "Ah! really,"
they said, "it'll be great for us: horses are going to eat their masters'
boots." Master Peter was hooted exuberantly and they teased him
all the more readily in that he was the one who made fun of others.
He accepted it calmly and fled into the inn to have himself looked
after. When he had recovered somewhat near the fire, he began to
think of how he would avenge himself on those jokers who had
welcomed him in such a way. And he thought of a good way which
time and necessity presented him in order to revenge himself on the
shoemakers; as for the others, he'd have to wait until God gave
him some help. Since he needed leather boots, he conceived of a
trick to have himself supplied with boots by the shoemakers at their
expense. He asked the innkeeper (as if he hardly knew the town at
all) if there was a shoemaker nearby, and he led him to believe
that he'd left Angers in a hurry on business and that he hadn't had
time to put on his boots or spurs. The innkeeper told him that there
were shoemakers to choose from. "Great," Master Peter said, "get

me one, my good man." And he did. The man who came was, by chance, one of those who had taunted him a great deal on his arrival. "My friend," said Master Peter, "could you make me a good pair of boots by tomorrow morning?" "Yes, indeed, Sir" the shoemaker said. "But I'd like to have them an hour before daylight." "You'll have them then, Sir, and earlier if you wish." "Well, my friend, please rush them for me; I'll pay you whatever you ask." The shoemaker took his measurements and left. As soon as he had gone, Master Peter had another servant go get him another shoemaker, pretending he hadn't been able to come to terms with the first one. The shoemaker came, and he asked him, just as he had the other, to have a pair of boots ready for an hour before dawn the following day, and he told him he didn't care how much they cost, provided he didn't let him down and that they were made of good cowhide, and he told him the precise style he wanted, exactly as he had told the other. The shoemaker took his measurements and left. And the two shoemakers worked all night on the boots, neither one knowing anything about the other. The following morning, at the appointed hour, Master Peter sent for the first shoemaker, and he brought the boots. Master Peter put on the one for the right foot, and it fit him like a glove or as though it had been moulded in wax, or as you wish, for boots made of wax wouldn't be any good. Rest assured that it fit him very well; but, when it came to putting on the one for the left leg, he pretended to have a sore leg. "Oh! my friend, you're hurting me! This leg is a little swollen from some dampness which came over it, and I forgot to tell you about it. The boot is too narrow, but there's a way to fix it, my friend. Go put it back on the boot tree, and I'll wait another hour for it." As soon as the shoemaker left, Master Peter hurriedly took off the right boot and sent for the other shoemaker, and, in the meantime, he had his horse saddled and readied and his bill added up and paid. Now the second shoemaker came with his boots. Master Peter put on the one for the left foot, and it was a marvelous fit; but when it came to the one for the right foot, he pulled the same trick he had on the other shoemaker and sent the right boot back to be stretched. As soon as the shoemaker left, Master Peter picked up the boot for his right foot, mounted his mare and took off with his boots and the spurs he'd bought (he hadn't had time to deceive so many people at one time) and away he galloped! He was already a good league away when the two shoemakers arrived at the inn, each with a boot in his hand, and they asked one another who the boot was for. One said, "it's for Master Peter Faifeu; he had me stretch it because it hurt him." "What!" said the other, "I stretched this one for him." "You're wrong, you haven't been working for him." "Yes, indeed, yes, indeed," he said; "I spoke to him, didn't I? You think I don't know him?" While they were arguing over the matter, the innkeeper came and asked them what they were waiting for. "It's a boot for Master Peter Faifeu, and I'm bringing it back to him," one of them said. And the other said the same thing. "You'll have to wait then until he comes this way again," the innkeeper said, "because he's a long way from here if he's still riding." God knows how nonplussed the two shoemakers were! "And what will we do with our boots?" they said to each other. They decided to play cards for them because they were both of the same style. And Master Peter, who was a little better off in attire than the day before, escaped light-heartedly.

Tale 24

OF MASTER ARNAUD, WHO TOOK AN ITALIAN'S HACKNEY TO LORRAINE AND RETURNED IT NINE MONTHS LATER

There was in Avignon a very sly fellow. I don't know if Master Peter Faifeu and he had gone to the same school together; but the fact remains that one played as many good tricks as the other, and also they weren't far apart in time. The one in this story was called Master Arnaud, and he used in Avignon the same means of getting boots as I've just talked about, and yet he wasn't in the same hurry to leave as Master Peter. Anyway, one day he decided to take a trip to Lorraine, and he mentioned it to everyone. And because he never kept himself supplied with anything, relying on his tricks, they thought he was joking. When he found a coat, they asked him where he was going to get his boots; when he got boots, they asked him where he was going to find a hat. And then they asked him about money, which was the key to the whole thing. Still, he kept looking and, slowly but surely, he found everything he needed for his trip to Lorraine, except a horse. But he was sure that God wouldn't forget him in need, and he constantly kept himself shod like a messenger, walking here and there, pretending to say good-bye to his friends. He was on the lookout for his prey, and he hoped to get a horse by some stroke of luck. Those who knew him said to him, laughing, "Now then, Master Arnaud, you'll go to Lorraine when you have a horse; you're only wearing boots to sleep in this town." "Well, then! well!" he said, "never mind, I'll leave when it's time." Our man thought just the opposite of the people; what they thought would be the most difficult for him to get he considered the easiest, and he had no trouble proving it. When he saw his chance, around nine o'clock in the morning, he went to the front of the palace where a few gentlemen had gone in the morning on business for the legation; most of them were Italian, and some were on hackneys and others on mules, particularly the old people, for the young can do without. Now there's always one which isn't closely guarded; after all, the lackeys tie them to any buckle on the wall and go off to play or drink until it's time to get their masters. So, around nine o'clock, Master Arnaud saw a few mounts, and among them there was a very pretty hackney which he preferred to all the others and which belonged to an Italian whom he knew to be a good person. And when he saw that the lackey wasn't around, he drew near the hackney, untied it, and asked it if it wanted to go to Lorraine. The hackney didn't say a word and let itself be untied. And our man, who was a legist, turned to his advantage the legal dictum: *Qui tacet, consentire videtur.* [1] And he began to lead his hackney by the bridle out of the palace square and headed towards the bridge where *j'ouis chanter la belle.* [2]

When he saw that the people who had watched him take it could no longer see him, he got on it nimbly and went towards Villeneuve, which was outside the Pope's jurisdiction, and from there he rode as straight as he could down the road to Lorraine. After days of travelling, he arrived three happy and healthy and stayed eight or nine months without sending news of himself to Signore Julliano. The Italian had been very surprised to find his hackney missing when he left the palace, and he was even more puzzled not to hear any news about it for a day, two days, a month, two months, three

---

[1] Silence gives consent.

[2] A quotation from the famous song about the bridge at Avignon: "Sur le pont d'Avignon j'ouis chanter la belle! Qui en son chant disait une chanson nouvelle."

months; finally he was forced to buy a mule because he was old and not very strong. And, in the meantime, Master Arnaud took care of his hackney for him and made it earn its oats. By the end of the term for pregnant women, Master Arnaud had cleared up his business in Lorraine, and he returned to Avignon on the same hackney. However, instead of entering the city, he watched and waited for the exact hour that it had been when he took the hackney, and so he tarried a little while in Villeneuve to drink a nip. At the stroke of nine, he was in front of the palace and he gingerly tied his hackney to the same buckle from which he had taken it and went to town. And, by chance, *il Magnifico Signore* was at the palace that morning, and he came out shortly afterwards. And as he was about to get on his mule, he glanced at this hackney, which was rather easy to recognize. And he thought to himself that it greatly resembled the one he had lost the previous year in color, in size and even by its harness, which Master Arnaud hadn't changed. It's true that it wasn't as new as when he had taken it because he'd made use of it for three-fourths of a year, but the Italian didn't dare be certain of it right off, seeing how long it had been since he had lost sight of it. He called his boy, whose name was Torneto: *"Ven qua: vede che questo mi par'esser il cavallo ch'io perdi l'an passato."* [3] The groom looked at the hackney and found it exactly the same, except that it wasn't in such good condition; but he really didn't know what to answer because they both imagined that it must belong to another gentleman. Nevertheless, the more they looked at it, the more certain they became that it was the one, and both of them stayed there until eleven o'clock and beyond, and, by constantly reasoning together about the hackney and seeing that no one took it, they assured themselves that it was the same one; Signore Julliano ordered Torneto to take it and lead it to his stable, and it settled in as snugly as if it had never budged from there. He had it brought back the next day to the same place to see if someone would claim it; but no one came, which surprised him a great deal, and he thought that some spirit had brought it back. Some time later Master Arnaud went to Signore Julliano, whom he found mounted on his hackney, and said to him, "Sir, I'm very pleased to know that this hackney is yours, and you can rest assured that

---

[3] Come here: take a look, this seems to me like the horse I lost last year.

it's a good one: I tried it out. I found it about a year ago near the Rhone bridge where it was going along by itself, and a boy was trying to take it; and when I realized by his behavior that it wasn't his, I took it away from him and kept it a day or two without being able to find out who owned it; the third day I led it as far as Villeneuve, where I heard that a French gentleman was looking for it and that he'd been told that someone had seen it being led away by a boy on the road to Paris. The gentleman was going after it, and so I rode after him in order to give it back to him; but I was never able to catch up to him because he was going at a fast clip in order to overtake his thief, and I went so far while looking for him that I wound up in Lorraine. And because I didn't hear anything about this gentleman, I kept the hackney for a long time, and I finally came back to this city where I had taken it, and among some of my friends I found one who did remember having seen it in this city in the past, but he didn't know who owned it, except perhaps one of you gentlemen of the legation. When I learned that, I had it taken to the palace square so that the man to whom it belonged could see it; and, in the meantime, I went from here to Nîmes, and I returned two days ago. But praise be to God that it has found its master again because I was very worried about it." The Italian listened to all of Master Arnaud's lovely harangue and finally thanked him, saying to him: "*O valente huomo, io vi ringratio; io faceva conto de l'aver persa, ma Iddio hà voluto che sia casca in buona man. Se voi avete bisogno di cosa che sia ne la possenza mia, io son tutto vostro.*" [4] Master Arnaud thanked him in turn and thereafter he often went to see the Italian. And you can imagine that it wasn't without always playing one of his proper tricks on him, and I'd gladly tell you about them, if I knew them, in order to please you; but I'll tell you some others to make up for it.

---

[4] O excellent man, I thank you; I figured I had lost it, but God willed it should fall into good hands. If you want anything that is within my power, I am entirely at your disposal.

Tale 25

OF THE COUNSELOR AND HIS STABLEBOY, WHO GAVE HIM BACK HIS OLD
MULE, PASSING IT OFF AS A YOUNG ONE

A counselor in the law courts had kept a mule for twenty-five years or so and among his servants he had a stableboy, named Didier, who had looked after this mule for ten or twelve years. After having served him for a rather long time, he asked him to be relieved of his duties, and with his kind consent he became a horse dealer. Nevertheless, he continued to frequent his master's house, and he offered to serve him just as though he were still his servant. Some time later, the counselor noticed that his mule was getting old, and he said to Didier, "Come here; you know my mule well; it has carried me marvelously well; I'm sorry that it's getting so old because it will be very difficult to find another one like it. But please, keep an eye out to get me one. I don't have to tell you anything: you know exactly what I need." Didier said to him, "Sir, I have one in the stable which seems to me to be very good: I'll let you have it for a while. If you find it to your liking, we'll come to some agreement about it; if not, I'll take it back." "All right," the counselor said. He had this mule brought to him, and, in the meantime, he gave his old one to Didier in order to get rid of it. Didier immediately filed its teeth, rubbed it down, curried it, and treated it so well that it looked as though it were still a good animal. In the meantime, his master was using the one he had given him, but he didn't find it to his liking, and he said to Didier, "The mule you gave me isn't right for me; it's too temperamental. Won't you find me another one?" "Sir," the horse dealer said, "you asked me just at the right time. It so happens that within the last two or three days I found one that I've known for a long time. It will be just the thing for you, and when you've tried it out, if it isn't right for you, you can blame me for it." Didier brought him this beautifully rejuvenated mule, and it was a delight to behold. The counselor took it, got on it, and found it as gentle as could be; he praised it highly and marveled at how well attuned it was to his hand: it was as easy to mount as could be. In short, he found in it all the dispositions of his first one, and since it was also of the same size and color he motioned to the horse dealer: "Come here, Didier. Where did you get this mule? It looks exactly like the one I gave you and behaves the same way." "I assure you, Sir," he said, "when I saw that it was the same color and size as yours, I thought it might have the same qualities or that you could very easily teach them to it; and so I bought it, hoping that you would be satisfied with it." "Really," the counselor said, "I'm very grateful to you; but how much will you sell it to me for?" "Sir," he said, "you know that I and everything I have are at your service. If it were someone else, he wouldn't get it for forty crowns; I'll let you have it for thirty." The counselor agreed and spent thirty crowns for what was his and wasn't worth ten.

Tale 26

OF THE SCOFFERS OF LA FLÈCHE IN ANJOU AND HOW THEY WERE TRICKED BY PICQUET WITH A LAMPREY

I spoke here earlier of the scoffers of La Flèche, who are said to have been such great mockers that no man ever went through there who wasn't taunted. I don't know if they still go in for that, but I can tell you that once upon a time a great lord attempted to pass through there without being mocked, and he thought he would get there so late and leave so early in the morning that there wouldn't be anyone who could make fun of him. And, in fact, he so paced out his trip for his arrival that it was completely dark when he got there. Therefore, since everyone had gone to bed, he found neither man nor woman to say anything worse to him than his name. And when he arrived at the inn, he pretended to be a little under the weather and retired to his room, where he was served by his attendants, and the night passed without incident. But in the evening he ordered his house steward to have everyone ready to leave in the morning two hours before sunrise, and they did just that; and he himself was the first one up since he hadn't been able to sleep because his desire to pass without being mocked was so great. He mounted his horse as soon as dawn began to appear and when no one was up and around yet in the town. He rode as far as the last houses of La Flèche and thought he had avoided all the dangers, and he was very pleased with himself; but now there was an old woman squatting at the corner of a wall who came to make sport of him, saying to him in her oldster's language, "Getting up early to beat the flies?" Never was a man more disgruntled to be so laughed at unawares, and by an old woman at that. And had he been a king, as they say he was, I believe he would have knocked the old hag about; but the sounder believe he wasn't a king although the people from La Flèche brag that he was. Now, whoever he was, he was laughed at like the rest. But as they say in a familiar proverb, mockers are often mocked, and those of La Flèche had some good jokes played on them at times, like the one I told about Master Peter Faifeu, and another good one was played on them by a man named Picquet. He bought a lamprey in Durtal and put it in a cloth sack which he carried behind him on his saddle bow; he tied the lamprey very tightly through one of the holes near the gills with a string so that it couldn't slip out of the bag; however, he did let its tail show on the outside. When he was near La Flèche, the lamprey, which was very much alive, kept on wagging its tail so that while passing through town the jokers noticed that in wriggling about it increasingly appeared a little bit more out of the bag: and these people waited on tenterhooks for it to fall out! And Picquet rode very leisurely through town, as though he weren't in any great hurry, in order to attract more scoffers, and they came out of their houses and followed him in order to catch the lamprey when it fell. Among them there were four or five of the most discriminating eaters, and they were looking forward to it as they did their Easter eggs, saying to each other, "I'll have it for dinner, I'll have it for dinner." And Picquet pretended not to see them, except at times when, as though his horse weren't well girthed, he looked sideways at these lackeys who were following him. When he was out of town, he started to ride a little faster, and our jokers went after him, thinking it wouldn't be long before it fell because it seemed to be almost completely out. He led them a scant quarter of a league after the lamprey. But there were two of them who got tired of trotting because they were a little loaded down with fat. The other two held on and were very pleased that the first two had quit, and they said to each other, "Fools, there'll be more for us." When Picquet realized that he had only two lackeys left—and they were in pretty good physical form—he started to ride a little faster, and faster yet; and our two jokers kept on after him, so much so that they followed him for more than a good half league, still running after him, thinking they'd at least get the lamprey for their trouble; and Picquet kept pricking his horse, but the lamprey didn't fall, and it began to make them angry. Moreover, Picquet was having such a good time that he burst out laughing so loud at times that they noticed it, and they realized that they'd been had. Nevertheless, to put up a good front, one of them shouted to Picquet, "Ho there! Sir, your lamprey's going to fall." Picquet turned towards them, saying to them, "Aha! you need the lamprey? Come on, come on, you'll get it: it'll soon fall." Our fellows were quite embarrassed and said, "To hell with the lamprey!" Then, when they returned, God knows how they were laughed at by the people in town who had heard of the trick and who asked them what kind of sauce they wanted with it. Thus jokes sometimes turn against the jokers.

Tale 27

OF THE SKITTISH ASS WHICH WAS FRIGHTENED WHENEVER A MAN
TOOK OFF HIS CAP AND SAINT-CHELAUT AND CROISÉ, WHO
PUT ON EACH OTHER'S BREECHES

Many have heard the name of Sir René du Bellay, who died recently as bishop of Le Mans [1] and who used to stay in his manor, studying things of nature, especially agriculture, herbs, and gardening. In his home at Tourvoye, he had a horse farm of brood mares and he took delight in having colts of good breeding. He had a house steward who took pains to keep up what he liked; one of his friends gave him an ass, which, by some great oddity, was so beautiful and so big that it was always taken for a mule, and it even had the same kind of coat; to top it all, it ambled as well as a mule. So, since the steward knew how good the ass was, he frequently gave it to one of the officers, whose pace it followed just as well, although the aforesaid gentleman rode unlike any of the others. And finally the ass was left to one of the almoners, who was called Saint-

---

[1] He died in 1556. He was the brother of Guillaume du Bellay, diplomat, general, and historian; of Cardinal Jean du Bellay; of Martin du Bellay, bishop of Paris. He was the cousin of the well-known poet Joachim du Bellay.

Chelaut. I don't know if that was his name, or if it had been given to him as a nickname, or if it was some benefice he had received from his master. Now, because there's nothing so excellent that it doesn't have some imperfection, this ass was a bit skittish. What am I saying, a bit? I mean a bit much, for at the least stirring that it felt, it leaped, it jumped; and the man who failed to hang on tightly was thrown to the ground. For that reason, Saint-Chelaut, who wasn't one of the ablest riders in the world, had become a horseman on this ass because of all the thumps. When on a curve he saw a stump lying in the road, or when a man came up to him unexpectedly, or when Saint-Chelaut's breviary fell from his sleeve, the noise alone made the ass jump about until he sent our almoner to the ground. But, above all, the ass got angry when he saw a cap being taken off; when somebody greeted the gentleman from Le Mans along the roads—and such persons are hailed by everyone—the ass went wild when the hats were raised. It ran through the countryside as if the devil were after it, and it didn't fail to toss poor Saint-Chelaut in a ditch or in some mudhole. Therefore, he was obliged to remain behind and travel alone in order to avoid the mishaps that the greetings caused. And if by chance he met someone he knew coming towards him on the road, he yelled to him from a distance, "Sir, please, don't greet me! don't greet me!" But very often, in order to have fun with him, greeters were sent to him to make great curtsies and bows before him in order to see the ass in its idiosyncrasy perform its antics. Sometimes Saint-Chelaut rode on ahead, which was far better for him: first of all, to avoid the above mentioned danger; secondly, to go have a few drinks for the road, particularly in the afternoons when he didn't have to wait for his master to say mass for him. Anyway, one day, smack in the middle of summer, damn, on a very hot afternoon while his master was waiting for the heat to pass, Saint-Chelaut rode on ahead with a man named Croisé, who was the aforesaid lord's representative. And because the journey wasn't too long, they reached the house early, and they refreshed themselves by drinking and drank while refreshing themselves, and, while waiting for the retinue to arrive, they ordered supper. But when they realized that their master wouldn't arrive anytime soon, they just began to eat whatever they wanted; and, moreover, when they saw that no one was coming, they turned everything over to the innkeeper and to the

cook, who had come at the same time as they had, and they too
had come at the same time as the cook; and they asked for a little
room worthy of a Jacobin, and they went to bed quite comfortably
and very nicely and began to snore. By and by, the lord arrived; and
when his attendants learned that our two fellows were in bed, they
left them alone until after supper. Then, two or three of them, without making any noise, found a way of entering the room where they
were staying and found them fast asleep. Now it is necessary to
note that Saint-Chelaut was so thin that he was nothing but skin
and bones; but Croisé certainly did as much honor to the man who
fed him as Saint-Chelaut did him dishonor, for he was so fat and
plump that a fish bone would have made him burst. What did these
attendants do? They took the two sleepers' breeches and ripped
them in half and mixed them up together, resewing one's right with
the other's left, and the left with the right as neatly as they could,
and they put them back in their place and let these two pilgrims
sleep until early the next morning when their master was ready
to mount his horse, since he wanted to go while it was still cool.
And at this point, one of the pages, who knew all about the prank
—such people are never far away from all good adventures—,
knocked impatiently at the door of the room where they were sleeping, saying, "Mister Croisé, Mister Saint-Chelaut, the lord is already
on his horse! Aren't you going to get up?" The two fellows woke
up with a start and grabbed their clothes in a hurry. Saint-Chelaut
came out much better than Mister Croisé because, thin as he was,
he got into Croisé's breeches as easily as married couples who've
been doing it for a year. He put on the breeches, got dressed, and
was ready as quickly as a dog could have jumped a fence. He mounted his ass and away he went! But, by chance, Croisé put on the right
pant leg first; when it came to Saint-Chelaut's, there was the devil
to pay; it was so narrow he could hardly have put his arm in it.
He pulled and pulled, but the devil was still at it; and besides he
didn't dream that the pant leg wasn't his; he never would have
thought of such things, and besides he wasn't wide awake yet, just
like fat people who've had a feast at night. In the end, by dint of
pulling, he split everything, and it made him wake up and fly into
a rage. "What the devil is this?" he said. He looked at the matter
more closely and realized that it wasn't his pant leg and that he
could never get into it unless he put his whole leg and thigh through

the rip he had made so that at least his behind would remain
covered until he was able to remedy his situation; and, on that
side, he put his boot on his bare leg and mounted his horse and
galloped after his lord, who was already a league away. And God
knows how the others laughed at their prank! Later, when they
were at dinner, and by chance there were no menders or tailors
because it was in a gentleman's house which was a little out of the
way, they saw the thing clearly as it had happened. They returned
their pant legs to one another and went about mending and putting
them back on while the others were eating, for they had eaten so
well that night. It wasn't difficult for Mister Croisé because the diet
could only do him good. But poor Saint-Chelaut had a hard time of
it because he didn't need that; and besides Croisé had ripped his
whole pant leg. Thus, bad luck never comes alone, but in twos or
threes, Sir. Yes, yes, that's in Marot.[2] Some recommended I say that
this happened in winter in order to make the most of the story;
but since I know very well that it happened in summer, I didn't wish
to lie: besides the fact that a cold story isn't considered as good,
I'd be damned or at the very least I'd have to do penance for it.
Nevertheless, those who will tell it after me will be free to say that
it was in winter in order to enrich the subject. I leave it up to you.
As for me, I'm going on.

---

[2] Clément Marot (1496-1544), famous French poet, in his poem "Au roi,
pour avoir été dérobé" (1531): "On dit bien vrai: la mauvaise fortune / Ne
vient jamais qu'elle n'en apporte une, / Ou deux, ou trois avecques elle, Sire."

Tale 28

OF PROVOST COQUILLAIRE, WHO HAD POOR EYESIGHT AND WAS MADE TO BELIEVE BY DOCTORS THAT HE COULD SEE

In the same country of Maine there once was a magistrate of
the Provost Marshal whose name was Coquillaire; he was a man
who knew how to judge a case and who was well acquainted with
magistrate Maillard's[1] ruse: one day, Maillard got his hands on a

---

[1] Gilles Maillard, indefatigable and harsh public prosecutor during the
reign of Francis I.

man who had committed more than enough felonies but who alleged
that he was a priest, and so he let him cool off a while in prison;
then, at a set hour, he had him brought before him and began to
be friendly with him. "Really," he said, "So-and-So," and he called
him by his name, "it's only right that you should be sent back to
your bishop. I don't want to deprive you of your privilege, but, on
the contrary, I would insist on informing you of it even if you didn't
think of it; but I advise you from now on to confine yourself to
places where honorable acts are done. You're a handsome and
valiant individual; you should go serve the king; you would make
yourself known immediately and you'd live to hold responsibility and
become great instead of amusing yourself in towns and on the highways and putting your life in danger and dishonoring yourself forever." Immediately, the crafty fellow, who thought he was being
praised, said, "Sir, I don't need to learn now how to serve the king.
I was under the command of Captain Lorge[2] at Pavia when it was
taken, and since then I've been with Lord Lautrec[3] in Milan and
in the kingdom of Naples." Immediately, Maillard dispatched his
case and had him hanged high and quickly, tonsure and all, and he
taught him what it was to serve the king. Coquillaire knew how to
do that and similar things and could see clearly enough through a
legal pouch with the eyes of his mind; but with the eyes in his head
he couldn't see the length of his nose, and he needn't have been
asked which he would rather have, his nose as long as his sight or
his sight as long as his nose, for there wasn't much difference between the two. It happened one day that the bishop of Le Mans,
who was visiting around his diocese, decided to see him while passing through because he knew him to be a good judge and because
his journey took him that way; he found him in bed, suffering
from a humor which had affected his poor eyes. "Well! Mister Provost," the bishop said, "how are you?" "Sir," he said, "I've been
in bed for more than a month." "Your eyes are still bothering you,"
the bishop said. "How are you getting along?" "Sir," Coquillaire
said, "I hope that I'll improve. The doctor has told me that I do
see." You can imagine that he was a very wise man to rely on the

---

[2] Jacques de Lorge, captain of Francis I's Scotch Guard and father of
Gabriel de Lorge, Count de Montgomery, who accidentally but mortally
wounded Henry II in a tourney.

[3] Odet de Foix, Lord de Lautrec, who died at the siege of Naples in 1528.

doctor as to whether he saw or not; but he didn't put his faith in the prisoners' accounts of their own cases as readily as he did in the doctor about his own.

Tale 29

OF THE TRICKS AND MEMORABLE ACTS OF A FOX THAT BELONGED TO THE SHERIFF OF MAYENNE-LA-JUHÉE

In the city of Mayenne-la-Juhée, in the low country of Maine, which is at the border of that good country of Cydnus,[1] there was a sheriff who was a man of good cheer after the fashion of that country; he took delight in many tricks and had in his house a few tame animals, among which there was a fox he had raised from a cub, and, because his tail had been cut off, he was called Bobtail. This fox was crafty by nature; but he had gone even beyond nature by associating with men, and he had such a good foxy mind that, had he been able to speak, he would have shown a lot of people that they were nothing but animals. And certainly it seemed by his look that at times he tried to speak in his delightful foxese which he gibbered. And when he was with the valet of the house or with the chambermaid, who treated him well in the kitchen, you would have said that he wanted to call them by name. Likewise, he knew when the sheriff was going to give a banquet just by seeing all the house staff working away and particularly the cook. He went to the henhouses and didn't fail to bring back rabbits, capons, pigeons, partridges, hares, according to the houses, and he took them so cunningly that he was never caught in the act, and thus he supplied his master's kitchen marvelously well. Nevertheless, he went back and forth on these misdeeds so often that he began to be known by the poulterers and others from whom he stole game; but for all that he didn't worry about it. He always found new tricks, constantly stealing more and more from them, so that finally they conspired to kill him. But they didn't dare do it openly for fear of his master, who was the principal gentleman in the town, but each on his own determined to catch him by surprise at night. Now this bobtail,

---

[1] According to tradition, the early settlers of Maine were called Ceno-manians, after a certain Cydnus, son of Ligur.

when he wanted to go collecting, entered sometimes through the cellar window, sometimes through a low window, sometimes through a skylight; sometimes he waited until they came to the door without a candle, and he entered furtively like a rat. And if he had ways of getting in, he had just as many for getting out with his prey. Oh! how many times the poulterers talked about killing him while he was right there listening to the conspiracy, thinking to himself, "You're not getting hold of me!" They set a trap for him with some game worth the taking and a poulterer watched over it with a taut crossbow and an arrow on it to kill him. But this fox could smell that as though it were the smoke from a roast, and he never came near while they were on the lookout; but no sooner would the man close his eyes to sleep than the bobtail would snatch his game, and away he went! If they set some deadfalls or spring traps for him, he knew how to beware of them as if he had put them up himself, so that they could never be wary enough to be able to catch him, and they found no other means except to keep their game locked up where the bobtail couldn't get to it; yet, for all that he didn't fail to find some along the way, but it wasn't very often. So, he began to get angry, partly because he no longer had such ready means of doing the cook a service, partly also because he wasn't as well off personally as he used to be. And so, since he was already getting on in years, he became distrustful, and he decided that they no longer cared for him, and perhaps also they didn't pet him as much as usual, for it is a great pity to grow old. And, for these reasons, he started to become wickedly crafty and began to eat the fowl from his master's house; and, when everybody was in bed, he went to the henroost and took at times a capon, at times a chicken. And no one suspected him; they thought it was the weasel or the marten. But in the end, as all knavery is discovered, he went there so often that a little wench who was sleeping in the woodshed for the glory of God noticed him and disclosed everything. And, from then on, great misfortune fell upon the bobtail because it was reported to the sheriff that the bobtail was eating the fowl. Now this fox was everywhere listening to what they were saying about him, and he was in the habit of hardly ever missing his master's dinner and supper because he greeted him affectionately and loved him and always gave him a piece of roast. But after he heard that he was eating the house's fowl, he changed his attitude towards him, so that one time, while eating, when the bobtail was there on the sly behind the attendants, the sheriff said, "What do you think of my bobtail who eats my hens? I'll deal with him accordingly within the next three days." When the bobtail heard that, he realized that it was no longer healthy for him in town, and he didn't wait for the three days to go by but banished himself and fled to the fields with the other foxes. You can be sure that it wasn't without picking up the last good thing he could. But the poor bobtail had a hard time getting along with them: while he was in town, he had learned the ways of dogs and how to speak good dog talk too, and he went hunting with them, and, under the cloak of friendship, he deceived the poor wild foxes and led them into the jaws of the dogs; the foxes remembered this and didn't want to take him with them and didn't trust him. But he used rhetoric and excused himself in part and in part too asked for their forgiveness; and then he gave them to understand that he had the means of making them live as comfortably as kings, especially since he knew the best henhouses in the area and the hours when they should go there; so, in the end they believed his fine words and made him their captain. This gave them cause for satisfaction for a time because he led them to the right places, and they found plenty of booty. But the trouble was that he tried to accustom them too much to city and companionable life, making them roam the fields and live off what they lifted, so that the people in the area, when they saw them in packs that way, set the dogs after them, and one of our foxy friends was always taken. But meanwhile, the bobtail was always on his guard and he stayed at the rear; and while the dogs were after the first ones, he had time to escape. Besides, he never went into the den, except in the company of other foxes; and when the dogs got there, he bit his companions and forced them to get out so that the dogs would run after them and he could escape. But the poor bobtail wasn't able to shift so well as not to get caught in the end: since the people in the area knew very well that he was the cause of all the mischief that was being done around there, they sought only him and bore a grudge only against him, and they all swore they would get him once and for all. And, in order to do this, all of the surrounding parishes gathered together, and each appointed a churchwarden to go ask for help from the gentlemen in the area; they asked each of them, for the good of the community, to lend a few dogs in order to free the country of this mischievous rogue of a fox. The gentlemen readily agreed and gave a favorable answer to the ambassadors; and, in fact, most of them had been looking for him for their sport for a long time without much success. In short, they set so many dogs after him that there were enough for him and for his companions, and he bit and hurried them in vain because when they were taken he was also caught, no matter how quick he was. He was taken alive and was brought to bay and dragged out by dint of trenching and digging; the dogs just couldn't get him to come out of the hole, either because he always outfoxed them, or, and this is easier to believe, because he spoke to them in good dog talk and made up with them, and so they had to get to him by other means. Now the poor bobtail was taken and was led or carried alive to the city of Mayenne, where he was prosecuted and publicly sacrificed for the robberies, thefts, lootings, misappropriations, treacheries, deceptions, slayings and other heinous and cruel acts he had committed and perpetrated; and he was executed before a large gathering since everybody ran to it as to a fire because he was known for ten leagues around as the worst rascal of a fox that the earth had ever borne. But, for all that, I hear that several kind-hearted people were sorry for him because he had done so many good tricks and so skillfully, and they thought it was a pity that a fox of such good intelligence should die; but in the end they had no control over it even though they laid their hands on their weapons in order to save his life, for he was hanged and strangled at the castle of Mayenne. Now you see that there is no trick or knavery which isn't punished in the long run.

Tale 30

OF MASTER JOHN PONTALAIS AND HOW HE PULLED A GOOD ONE ON THE BATHHOUSE BARBER WHO WAS A BRAGGART

Nowadays, there are very few people who haven't heard of Master John Pontalais, [1] who is still vividly remembered, or of the

---

[1] Master Jean de l'Epine du Pont-Alais, famous in Paris at the time of Francis I for his stage productions of morality plays and farces.

jests, gibes and merry words he did and said, or of the good tricks
he played, or how he put his hump against a cardinal's showing
him that two mountains can meet in spite of the common proverb.
But why do I mention that one when he did a million better ones?
But I can still tell one or two more. There was a bathhouse barber
who was very conceited, and he was sure that there wasn't a man
in Paris who surpassed him in wit and skill. Even when he was
stark-naked in his bathhouse (as poor as Friar Croiset who said
mass in his nightshirt), with only his razor in his hand, he said to
those he was rubbing down and shaving, "You see, Sir, what comes
from having brains. What do you think of me? Just as you see
me, I got ahead on my own. No relative or friend I've ever had
helped me with anything. If I'd been a fool, I wouldn't be where
I am." And if he was pleased with himself, he wanted others to
have even greater regard for him. Master John Pontalais knew this
and profited by it, using him at all times for his pranks and jests,
and he availed himself of him whenever he wished: he simply told
him that there wasn't a man in Paris who knew how to play a role
better than he. "And I'm never praised," Pontalais said, "except
when you're playing. And then I'm asked, 'Who was that who was
playing such and such a part? Oh, how well he played it!' Then
I tell everybody your name in order to make you known. My friend,
you will be quite amazed when the king wants to see you: it only
takes one lucky break." You needn't ask if the barber was in his
glory. And, in fact, he became so conceited that no man could
enjoy him any longer. And, indeed, he said one day to Master John
Pontalais: "You know what, Pontalais? I'm not going to have you
putting me on every day from now on, and I don't want to play
anymore unless it's in some good morality play in which there are
great characters, such as kings, princes, lords. And also, I always
want the best part there is." "Really," said Master John Pontalais,
"you're right, and you deserve it; but why didn't you tell me about
it sooner? I don't know where my head was that I didn't think of it
myself; but I have plenty to satisfy you with from now on because
I've got some of the finest subjects in the world, and I'll have you
play the best part on the stage. And to begin with, make sure you're
with me next Sunday when I'm to put on a very good mystery play
in which I have a king of the East Indies speak. You'll play the role,
how's that?" "Yes, yes," said the barber, "and who would play it

if I didn't? Just give me my script." Pontalais gave it to him the
very next day. When the day of the performance came, the barber
appeared on his throne with his scepter, playing the best royal
majesty a barber ever did play. In the meantime, Master John
Pontalais had made his preparations to flout the barber. And
because he himself gladly did the prologue for the plays he produced, he was the last to come onto the stage when the company
gathered together but he was the first to speak, and he said:

> Of the lowliest I am the least,
> And I haven't a crown, alas;
> But the king of the Indies East
> Has frequently shaved my bare ass.

And he said this with just the right amount of grace to insinuate
the boastfulness of the shaver. And also he had produced his play
in such a way that the king of the Indies didn't have much to say;
all he had to do was put on a good show and so, had the barber
been offended, the play wouldn't have suffered any from it. And
God knows how he taught Mister Barber to play the king and how
he wished he were heating his bathhouse. I've heard another story
about this same Pontalais, but some people attribute it to somebody
else; anyway, whoever the man is, it's a fairly jolly one. There was
a parish priest who ascended the pulpit one feast day to preach,
and he was very busy saying little of anything good; indeed, when
he strayed from his subject (which was fairly often), he fell into
some of the finest digressions in the world. "And what do you think
of me?" he said. "There are few men who are worthy of ascending
the pulpit because, although they may be learned, they don't have
the knack of preaching. But God has blessed me with both of them;
and I also know all there is to know about all the fields of learning."
And raising his finger to his forehead, he said, "My friend, if you
want grammar, there is some in here; if you want rhetoric, there
is some in here; if you want philosophy, there is some in here;
theology, I don't fear any doctor in the Sorbonne; and yet only
three years ago I knew nothing, and, nevertheless, you see how I
preach; but God gives His blessings to whom He pleases." Now it so
happens that Master John Pontalais, who had something good to
put on that afternoon and who knew this preacher fairly well for
what he was, was parading through town, and by chance he had

to pass in front of the church where this preacher was. Master John Pontalais, as usual, beat his drum at the intersection, which was right next to the church, and beat it very loud and long on purpose in order to silence the preacher so that the people would come to his performances. But it was just the reverse because the more noise he made the louder the preacher shouted; and they fought, Pontalais and he, or he and Pontalais (so as not to err), as to who would have the last word. The preacher got angry and said at the top of his lungs with the authority of a preaching friar, "Somebody go make that drummer stop." But for all that nobody went, except that when people left, it was to go see Master John Pontalais, who was beating his drum louder and louder. When the preacher saw that he wasn't quietening down and no one was coming back to give him an answer, he said, "Really, I'll go myself." And he came down from the pulpit, saying, "Nobody move; I'll be right back." When he was in the street, all in a huff, he said to Pontalais, "Hey! where do you get the nerve to play the drum while I'm preaching?" Pontalais looked at him and said, "Hey! where do you get the nerve to preach while I'm playing the drum?" So the preacher, angrier than ever, took a knife from his servant, who was next to him, and made a large slash in the drum with his knife; and he went back to the church to finish his sermon. Pontalais took his drum and ran after the preacher and set it on his head, as though it were a high-crowned Albanian hat, putting it on him through the side that was torn. And then the preacher, still in that particular state, wanted to ascend the pulpit again in order to point out the wrong which had been done to him and how the word of God was degraded. But the people were laughing so loud, seeing him with that drum on his head, that he wasn't able to make himself heard that day and was obliged to leave and to hold his peace because he was chided that to argue with a fool wasn't the act of a wise man.

Tale 31

OF MISTRESS CAVERNOUS, WHO LODGED A GENTLEMAN ROOMILY

Not too long ago there was a willing woman who was called Mistress Cavernous and who sometimes followed the Court when her husband was on duty. But most of the time she was in Paris, and she liked it there, especially as it is paradise for women, hell for mules, and purgatory for petitioners. One day when she happened to be at the door of the house where she stayed in Paris, a gentleman went by there, accompanied by a friend of his, and he said to him in a loud voice as they passed the lady, so that she could hear, "God," he said, "if I had a mount like that for tonight, I'd do a lot of travelling between now and tomorrow morning." Mistress Cavernous heard the gentleman's remark, and she found him to her liking because he was well built; so she said to a little budding procurer she had with her, "Go follow that gentleman you see in those clothes, and don't lose him without finding out where he enters; and see to it that you speak to him and tell him that the lady he saw just now at the door of a particular house commends herself to his good graces and that, if he wants to come and see her this evening, she'll give him a snack between eight and nine o'clock." The gentleman accepted the message and conveyed his compliments; he also sent word to the lady that he'd be there at the appointed hour. And you have to understand that the two houses weren't far apart. The gentleman didn't miss the assignation and found Mistress Cavernous waiting for him. She received him graciously and regaled him with candy. They talked about the weather; it was getting late, and, in the meantime, the chambermaid readied the bed properly, as she was trained to do; the gentleman went to bed according to the agreement both parties had reached, and Mistress Cavernous was right next to him. The gentleman mounted up, and he began to ride and then ride again. But altogether he was never able to run more than three races from night until morning; and he got up rather early to get on his way, and left his mount in the stable. The next day, or a few days later, Mistress Cavernous, who always had some errand in town, encountered the gentleman, and she greeted him, saying, "Good day, Mister Deuce-Ace." [1] The gentleman paused and, looking straight at her, said, "By golly, lady, if the board had been good, I would have rolled a pair of threes." And since he'd learned her name the day before (for she was a well-known woman), he said to her, "Mistress Cavernous, you put me up very roomily the other night."

---

[1] In backgammon, a dice throw of two and one.

"That's true Sir (she said), but I didn't know you had so little baggage." Well attacked, well defended.

Tale 32

OF THE GENTLEMAN WHO HAD RIDDEN POST-HASTE AND THE ROOSTER WHO COULD NOT TREAD THE HENS

A gentleman, who was a great lord, had been absent from his house for some time; so he took the time to go see his wife, who was young, beautiful and in good shape. And to be there sooner, he began to make haste some two days' journey from his house, and he arrived late when his wife had already gone to bed. He got in next to her. She was immediately awake, very glad to have company, hoping that she'd get her little bit at the very least. But her joy was short-lived, for the husband was so weary and worn out from his run that, no matter how much she caressed him, he wasn't able to set about doing it and fell asleep without doing anything; but he apologized to her: "My dear," he said, "the great love I have for you made me hasten to come see you, and I rode hard all along the way; please excuse me this time." The lady didn't find that very much to her liking; in fact, they say that there's nothing a woman dislikes more, and not without reason, than when her husband whets her appetite without satisfying her. And it has often been seen by experience that a lover who pursues a lady for a long time and is then so surprised — when it happens that she's suddenly prepared to accept him — that he becomes impotent either through too much longing or through fear or through some other misfortune will never get it again, except through great luck. Nevertheless, the lady was patient, primarily because she had to, and she didn't get anything else from him that night. In the morning she left her husband's side and let him rest. When he got up an hour or two later, he went, while dressing, to a window that overlooked the barnyard and his wife was beside him. He caught a glimpse of a rooster making love to a hen; he'd let her go, then he'd return to caress her many times, but he didn't do anything else. The husband, who was looking on, became angry and said, "Look at that wretched rooster, how slow he is! He's been making love to that hen for an hour, and he can't do anything for her: he's worthless; take him away and get me another one." The lady answered him, "Oh! Sir, forgive him: maybe he's ridden post-haste all night." Her husband kept quiet at that and spoke no more of it, knowing full well that it was to him that those words were addressed.

Tale 33

OF THE PRIEST OF BROU AND THE GOOD TRICKS HE PLAYED DURING HIS LIFETIME

The parish priest of Brou, who's been called the priest of Brionne in many places, did so many memorable acts in his lifetime that whoever would like to write them down would create a legend greater than that of a Lancelot or of a Tristan. And there's been so much talk about him that, when a priest has done something worthy of remembrance, it's attributed to the priest of Brou. The people of Limoges have wanted to usurp that honor for their priest at Pierre-Buffière; but the priest of Brou won out by more votes, and I'll relate here a few of his noble deeds and leave the rest for those who may someday want to practice their style by describing them at greater length. You have to know that this priest did one thing and another on the basis of his own individual judgment and didn't approve of everything that had been introduced by his predecessors, such as the antiphons, the responses, the *Kyries*, the *Sanctus*, the *Agnus Dei*. He often sang them in his own style; but, above all, he disliked the manner of saying the Passion in the way it is customarily said throughout the churches, and he sang it just the opposite: when our Lord said something to the Jews or to Pilate, he made him speak loud and clear so that everyone could hear it. And when it was the Jews or someone else, he spoke so softly that he could hardly be heard. It happened that a lady of fame and power was making her way to Châteaudun to do her Easter duty there, and she passed through Brou on Good Friday around ten o'clock in the morning. She decided to hear the service, and she went to the church where the priest was saying it. When it came to the Passion, he said it in his style, and he made the church reverberate when he said:

"*Quem quaeritis?*" [1] But when it came to say *Jesum Nazarenum*, he spoke as softly as he could. And in this manner he went on with his Passion. This lady, who was very devout and, for a woman, well versed in the Holy Scripture and a close observer of ecclesiastical ceremonies, was scandalized at this manner of singing and would have liked not to be there; but she decided to speak to the priest about it and tell him what she thought about it. She sent for him after the service was over to come speak to her. When he came, she said to him, "Father, I don't know where you learned to conduct the service for a day like today when the people should be in complete humility. The way you say the mass, there isn't a prayer which isn't wasted." "How's that, Milady?" said the priest. "Why! " she said, "you've read a Passion that is all wrong. When Our Lord speaks, you shout as though you were in a market place and when it's Caiaphas or Pilate or the Jews, you speak softly like a bride. Is that the way to do it? Should you be a priest? If someone complained about you, you'd be deprived of your benefice, and you'd be made to acknowledge your error." When the priest had heard her out, he said, "Is that what you wanted to tell me, Milady? Upon my soul, what is commonly said is very true, there are many people who talk about things they don't understand. Milady, I think I know the service as well as anyone else, and I want everybody to know that God is as well served in this parish according to His rank as in any place for a hundred leagues around. I know full well that other priests sing the Passion very differently. I could sing it as they do if I wanted to; but they don't know the least thing about it. After all, is it fitting for those Jewish rascals to speak as loud as Our Lord? No, no, Milady, you can be sure that in my parish I want God to be the master, and He will be that as long as I live; and let the others do in their parishes as they please." When this good lady recognized the man's temper, she left him with his extraordinary opinions and said to him only, "Really, Father, you are a smart man; I had been told just that, but I wouldn't have believed it if I hadn't seen it."

---

[1] Whom do you seek?

Tale 34

OF THE SAME PRIEST, HIS CHAMBERMAID, THE WASHING HE DID, AND HOW
HE ENTERTAINED HIS BISHOP, HIS HORSES, AND HIS ENTIRE RETINUE

This same priest had a twenty-five year old chambermaid, who served him night and day, the poor wench! Because of this, he was frequently summoned before the ecclesiastical court and was fined for it; but for all that his bishop could not prevail over him. Once he forbade him to have maids who weren't at least fifty years old. The priest got one who was twenty years old and another who was thirty. The bishop, when he saw that it was an error *pejor priore*, [1] forbade him to have any at all; the priest was forced to obey, at least he pretended to. And because he was a jolly fellow and of good cheer, he always found means to appease his bishop, who frequently went by his place, because he gave him good wine and sometimes provided him with wenches. One day the bishop sent word to him that he wanted to go have supper with him the next day but that he only wanted light meats because he hadn't been well the past few days and the doctors had prescribed them for him in order to re- store his stomach. The priest sent him word that he'd be welcome, and he immediately went to buy several calf and sheep innards; he put them all to boil in a large pot, and he was determined to entertain his bishop with them. Now he didn't have a maid then because it had been forbidden him. So what did he do? While his bishop's supper was being prepared and at about the time he knew the bishop was to come, he took off his breeches and shoes and went and carried a load of linen to a small stream which was on the road along which the bishop had to pass, and he got into the water up to his knees, with a stool, holding a paddle in his hand, and he vigorously washed his clothes; and his head and ass bobbed back and forth like a crow knocking down nuts. Along came the bishop; the people in his retinue who were riding ahead saw from a distance the priest of Brou washing his clothes and, raising his ass, sometimes showing all he had. They pointed him out to the bishop: "Sir, do you want to see the priest of Brou washing linen?" The bishop, when

---

[1] Worse than the first.

he saw him, was greatly appalled and didn't know whether he ought to laugh or be angry about it. He drew near the priest, who was still beating with all his might, pretending not to see anything: "Hey there, my dear priest; what are you doing here?" The priest, as though he were surprised, said to him: "Sir, you see, I'm doing my wash." "You're doing your wash?" the bishop said. "Have you become a launderer? Is that the role of a priest? Ah! I'll make you drink a cupful of water in my prisons and take your benefice away from you." "And why, Sir?" the priest said. "You've forbidden me to have a maid, so I have to wait on myself because I don't have any more clean linen." "Oh, you miserable priest!" the bishop said. "Come, come, you can have one; but what will we have for supper?" "Sir, you'll have a good supper, God willing; don't worry, you'll have light meats." When suppertime came, the priest served the bishop, and the only first course he presented him consisted of these boiled innards. The bishop said, "What is this you're giving me? Are you making fun of me?" "Sir," he said, "you sent word to me yesterday that I should prepare only light meats for you: I tried all kinds of meats; but when it was time to prepare them, they all went to the bottom of the pot, except that in the end I found these innards, which stayed on top of the water: they're the lightest of all." "You've never been worth anything in your life," the bishop said, "and you never will be. You know very well what tricks you've played on me. Well, I'll teach you to know who you're dealing with." Nevertheless, the priest had had a very fine supper prepared, with meats of another kind which were brought forth, and he graciously entertained his bishop, who was quite pleased. After supper, it was a matter of playing cards for an hour, and then the bishop decided to retire. The priest, who knew his disposition, had provided a dainty maiden as his bedtime wine and a partner for each of his men as well: in fact, it was their usual when they came to his place. The bishop, while going to bed, said to him: "All right, you may go, Father; I'm fairly well satisfied with you this time. But do you know what? I have a groom who's nothing but a drunkard: I want my horses to be treated like myself, be sure you see to it." The priest didn't forget those words; he took leave of his bishop until the following morning, and he immediately sent throughout his parish to borrow a great many mares; within a short time, he found as many as he needed, and he put them in the stable next to the bishop's horses. And the horses whinnied, kicked, and carried on around these mares; it was a joy to hear them. The groom, who had gone to curry his two-legged mount, trusting the priest for the care of his horses, heard this lovely racket going on in the stable and went there as quickly as he could in order to settle things. But he couldn't get there soon enough to keep the bishop from hearing the noise. The following morning, the bishop wanted to know why his horses had carried on like that all night. The groom wanted to pass it off as nothing, but there was no keeping it from the bishop: "Sir," the groom said, "there were mares with the horses." The bishop was sure that this was one of the priest's tricks, and so he sent for him and called him a thousand names. "You miserable wretch, are you always going to play tricks on me? You've spoiled my horses; don't you worry, I'll! ..." The priest answered him, "Sir, didn't you tell me last night that your horses were to be treated like yourself? I did the best I could for them. They had hay and oats; they were in straw up to their bellies; the only thing left was a female for each, and I sent to get them for them: didn't you and your men each have one of your own?" "To hell with the wretched priest! " the bishop said. "That's a likely story. Hold your tongue, we'll settle together and I'll pay you for the good treatment you gave me." But in the end he found no other remedy for it but to go away until some other time. I wonder if it wasn't Bishop Miles,[2] who had a million lawsuits and used to say that it was his exercise; and he took pleasure in seeing them multiply, just as merchants are glad to see their wares increase. And they say that one day the king decided to settle them for him; but the bishop wasn't happy about that and didn't want to hear of it, and he said to the king that, if he took his lawsuits away from him, he'd be taking his life away. Nevertheless, by dint of remonstrances and fair words, for one had to go at it in that fashion, the king made him agree to his decrees. So, in no time at all two or three hundred of them were resolved, or reconciled, or squelched. When the bishop saw that his lawsuits were thus going to nought, he went to the king and implored him with clasped hands that he not take them all away from him, but that he kindly leave him at least a dozen of the nicest and the best in order to while away the time in fun and merriment.

---

[2] Miles d'Illiers, bishop of Chartres; he was very fond of lawsuits, and he died while still involved in one in 1493.

Tale 35

OF THE SAME PRIEST AND THE CARP HE BOUGHT FOR HIS DINNER

To get back to our priest of Brou, he was walking around his gardens one Sunday morning on a feast day when he saw a man carrying a beautiful carp. He remembered that the next day was a fast day, perhaps a Rogation day, and so he bargained for the carp and paid for it. And because he was alone, he took the carp and tied it to the aiguillette of his doublet and covered it with his cassock, and in this state he went to church, where his parishioners were waiting for him to say mass. When it came to the offertory, the priest turned toward his people with the paten in order to receive the offerings. The carp, which was alive, wriggled its tail from time to time and made the priest's amice rise, but he wasn't aware of it. However, the women certainly noticed it, and they looked at one another and hid their eyes behind parted fingers. They laughed and made a thousand different faces. And, in the meantime, the priest stood there waiting for them. But there wasn't one who dared go first: they all imagined that the carp was that very pleasant thing grown by God. No matter how much the priest and his assistant shouted: "Come to the offering, ladies, if you wish to do your devotions!" they didn't go. When he saw that they were laughing that way and making so many faces, he realized that something was up, and finally he noticed the carp moving its tail. "Ha! ha!" he said, "my lady parishioners, I was very puzzled by what was making you laugh so: no, no, it isn't what you think it is; it's a carp I bought this morning for dinner tomorrow." And when he said it, he pulled up his chasuble and his amice and his cassock to show them the carp: otherwise, they would never have come to the offering. The good old priest was concerned about the following day, notwithstanding the word of the Gospel, *Nolite solliciti esse de crastino,*[1] which he, nevertheless, interpreted nicely to his advantage. When someone said to him, "Why, Father! God has forbidden you to worry about tomorrow, and yet you've bought a carp for your provision,"

---

[1] Matthew 6:34. The correct quotation is *Nolite ergo solliciti esse in crastinum*: Take therefore no thought for the morrow.

he said, "It's to fulfill the precept of the Gospel; when I'm well provided for, I don't worry about tomorrow." Some people maintain that it was a monk who had hidden a pâté up his sleeve while dining at a certain banquet. But it all amounts to the same thing. They also tell many other very pleasant things about this priest of Brou, such as, among others, the one which follows.

Tale 36

OF THE SAME PRIEST, WHO EXCOMMUNICATED EVERYBODY IN THE HOLE

One solemn feast Sunday and at sermon time, the priest of Brou ascended the pulpit, which was near a pillar, as they normally are, in order to preach to his parishioners. While he was preaching, the cleric from the rectory came to him and presented him some notes having to do with complaints according to the custom of announcing them on Sundays. The priest took these notes and put them in a hole which was in the pillar on purpose for such cases, that is, for the stashing of all the notes brought to him during the sermon. When he got to the end of his sermon, he wanted to get those notes back, and he put his finger in the hole; but they were somewhat farther in because, while putting them in, he was perhaps engrossed in explaining some difficult point of the Gospel. He pulled, he wiggled his finger, he did everything he could; he just couldn't get to them, and instead of pulling them out he was pushing them in. When he had struggled sufficiently with it and realized that there was no sense to it, he said, "My parishioners, I put some papers in there which I cannot get out; but I am excommunicating everybody in that hole." [1]

Some attribute that to another priest and say that it was a city priest. And, in fact, it's very likely because in villages there are ordinarily no pulpits for delivering sermons; but I let the matter speak for itself. If whoever it is claims that I've done him wrong by taking this honor away from him and giving it to the priest of Brou, he need only inform me; I'll be glad to put his name to it.

---

[1] i.e., all those whose names appear in the notes.

At the worst, he must realize that the same thing was done with Jupiters and Herculeses, for what many have done is attributed to one in order to get it over with more quickly, especially since the ones with those names were excellent and valiant. Therefore, there would be no objection to calling "priest of Brou" any priest, curate, canon, monk and chaplain who might do such virtuous acts as he did.

Tale 37

OF TEIRAN, WHO COULD NOT BE SEEN ABOVE THE POMMEL OF THE SADDLE WHEN HE WAS ON HIS MULE

In the city of Montpellier, there once was a young man who was called the prior of Teiran; he was a man of good family and rather well learned, but he had an awkward shape. He had a hump on his back and another on his stomach, and this gave him a poor carriage in the saddle and had so stunted his growth that he was no taller than a foot and a half. Wait, wait, I mean from the waist up. One day, he went to Toulouse from Montpellier accompanied by some of his friends from Montpellier; they stopped in Saint-Thiberi for one of their meals, and because it was summer and the days were long his companions weren't in much of a hurry to leave after dinner. They were waiting for the heat to go down, and also some of them wanted to go to sleep. But Teiran didn't approve of it, and so he had his mule bridled in a huff (don't take it to mean that his mule was angry: it was he) and mounted it, saying, "Now sleep all you want; I'm leaving." And he rode on alone as fast as he could. When his companions saw him going, they hurried after him because they didn't want to leave him. But Teiran was already very far away. Now, in order to ward off the sun, he wore one of those big Spanish sombreros, which almost covered him and his mule, but you can, however, knock off what seems reasonable. Those who were going after him saw a local man in a field not far from the road, and they asked him, "My friend, have you seen anything of a man on horseback along here who was riding straight to Narbonne?" The fellow answered them: "Not at all," he said, "I didn't see anybody; but I did see a gray mule which had a big felt hat on its saddle and was running at top speed." The men began to laugh because they realized full well that it was their man, and he was riding with such a passion that they were never able to catch up to him until they got to Narbonne. Some have argued that the mule wasn't gray, but black. But there are some people who have contrariness in their bones; and whosoever would want to argue with them, it would never be settled.

Tale 38

OF THE THEOLOGIAN WHO CONDEMNED DANCING, THE LADY WHO DEFENDED IT, AND THE REASONS PUT FORTH BY BOTH SIDES

In the city of Le Mans there once was a doctor of theology, named Mister d'Argentré, who had a doctoral prebend; he was a man of vast learning and upright conduct, but he wasn't so scholarly that he wasn't well acquainted with civility and social behavior, and this made him welcome among all good and honest company. One day, when he was having dinner with a group of leading citizens of the city, there was by chance dancing after dinner; after watching it for a time, he began to speak with a very good-looking lady, the sheriff of Sillé's wife, a woman who, because of her virtue, good looks and good mind, was very welcome among honorable company; she was graceful in everything she did, and especially in dancing in which she took a very great delight. Now, while talking about one thing and another, they began to discuss dancing, and the theologian said that, of all the acts of recreation, there wasn't another that set off the individual to such poor advantage. The sheriff's wife told him that, on the contrary, nothing roused the mind better than dancing and that the beat and the rhythm would never enter the mind of a lout, which is evidence that a dancer is nimble and temperate in his thoughts and deeds. "There are also," she said, "young people who are so clumsy that you could teach an ox to amble sooner than you could teach them to dance; but you also see what kind of mind they have. Dancing gives pleasure to those who dance and to those who watch it, and I'm also of the opinion that, if you dared tell the truth, you yourself take great pleasure in watching it: after all, there is no one, no matter how serious and awkward he may be, who isn't delighted to see people moving so well and so gracefully." The theologian listened to her but dropped the subject of dancing temporarily; however, he kept on talking to this lady about a number of other things, but they weren't so far afield that he couldn't pick up dancing again when he wished. After a short time, when he thought it apropos, he asked the sheriff's wife: "If you were," he said, "at a window or on a gallery and you saw at a distance on some large square one or two dozen people holding hands and jumping, turning about, back and forth, wouldn't you think they were crazy?" "Yes, of course," she said, "if they weren't keeping time." "I'll even grant them rhythm," he said, "provided there be no drum or flute." "I admit," she said, "that that could look outlandish." "Well, then," the theologian said, "can a hollow piece of wood and a pail stopped up at both ends with parchment have so much power as to make you approve of something which in and of itself smacks of madness?" "And why not?" she said. "Don't you know the power of music? The sound of the instruments enters a person's mind, and then the mind commands the body; all it does is show by signs and movements the disposition of the soul toward joy or sadness. You know that unhappy men show a different face than do gay and happy ones. Moreover, in all cases one must consider the circumstances, as you yourself preach every day. A minstrel who played the flute by himself would be the same as a preacher who went into the pulpit without an audience. Dancing without an instrument or without songs would be like people in a gathering place without an orator. Anyway, you condemn our dancing in vain because you'd have to take away our ears and feet; and I assure you," she said, "that if I were dead and heard a violin I'd get up to dance. People who play tennis exert themselves a great deal more running after a small fuzzy leather ball, and they go at it with such enthusiasm that sometimes it looks as though they're going to kill themselves, and yet they have no musical instrument as dancers do, but it doesn't keep them from finding marvelous recreation in it. Do you want to take away the pleasures of this world? When you preach against pleasures, if you wanted to tell the truth, it isn't to abolish them, except the bad ones; you know very well that it's impossible for this world to endure without enjoyment; on the contrary, it's to stop us from having too much." The theologian wanted to reply, but he was surrounded by women, and he decided to keep quiet, fearing that in case of need they might take him to dance; and God knows how well that would have suited him.

Tale 39

OF THE SCOT AND HIS WIFE, WHO CARRIED ON
A LITTLE TOO EXPERTLY

A Scot, who had followed the Court for a while, aspired to a post as yeoman of the Guard; that's as high as they wish to go when they begin to serve in France, and then they all consider themselves to be cousins of the king of Scotland. In order to reach this high rank, the Scot had performed a great number of services for which, among other favors, he obtained this one: he married a girl who was rather young and the lady-in-waiting of a very great lady. She was no sooner married than she remembered the commandments that are given to young brides: first, that at night they hold their kerchief tightly with both hands, for fear their husbands might remove their head-dress; that they squeeze their legs like a man who goes down a well without a rope; that they be a little unruly, and for each stroke they get give two in return. This young lady began to observe early these fine and holy teachings one after another until she mastered them, and she then used them all at the same time; the Scot wasn't too happy about it, especially about the last point; and when he saw that she knew how to make use of them so early the poor man thought that she'd learned these contorsions from some other teacher, and so he glared at her intently, saying to her, "Ah! you screw," and he never slept soundly after that. And then, whenever he was with her, he said to her, "Ah! you screw, ah! you screw, she's a whore that screws." And he was so sure of it that he couldn't look at his wife favorably, nor did he embrace her wholeheartedly at night. For her part, she withdrew little by little and was careful from then on not to be too frisky. And when she saw that the Scot was still jealous and sore and that he was still pouting, she became very melancholy and pensive. Her mistress noticed it, and she often asked her, "What is the matter, my dear? Are you pregnant?" "No, Milady," she said. "What is it then? Something is the matter." She pressed her so that there was no keeping from her what it was all about. Women want to know everything. I can say this here because I know full well that they won't read this passage. She told her about the problem; the lady heard her out and then she said, "And is that all there is to it? Keep quiet; don't you worry, I'm going to speak to him," and she did promptly. She called the Scot aside and began to ask him if he was satisfied with his wife. "Milady," he said, "I am satisfied, thank you." "Yes, but your wife is very upset; what have you done to her?" "I haven't done anything, Milady; I don't know why she's so glum." "Well, I know why," she said, "because she's told me everything. You know what's the matter, my friend? I want you to treat her well and not be ridiculous. How can you be so naïve as to think that women aren't supposed to have their pleasure like men? Do you think you have to go to school to learn it? Nature teaches it very well. And how can you think that your wife shouldn't stir any more than a tree stump! Now then," she said, "don't let me hear of it again, and treat her kindly." The Scot was satisfied, partly out of necessity and partly out of love, and right away the lady let the young lady know what she'd said to the Scot; and it may very well be that the young lady herself was in the closet listening without the Scot knowing anything about it. But she didn't let on to her husband that she knew anything about it, and she still acted annoyed night and day, and she no longer revenged herself of the strokes she received, until one night he said to her, while stroking her: "Screw, screw, Milady wants it so." She let herself be persuaded for it a bit; but in the end she became sociable again, and the Scot was never so unpleasant again.

Tale 40

OF THE PRIEST AND THE MASON WHO CONFESSED HIS SINS TO HIM

There was a village priest who was very proud of having seen a little more than his Cato.[1] In fact, he had read *De syntaxi*[2] and

---

[1] The *Distichs* of Dionysius Cato, fourth-century grammarian; the work was a standard text until the seventeenth century.

[2] Jean Despautère's Latin *Syntax* was published in 1513.

his *Fauste precor gelida*. [3] And because of that, he thought a great deal of himself and he bragged a lot and used words which were mouthfuls in order to have himself considered a great scholar. And even when he heard confession he used terms that astonished the poor people. One day, he was confessing a poor workman, and he asked him, "Now then, my friend, aren't you ambitious?" The poor man said no because he thought that the word belonged to the great lords, and he was almost sorry for having come to confession to this priest. He had heard that he was very learned and spoke so loftily that you couldn't understand anything. The word *ambitious* proved it to him because although he might have perhaps heard the word before still he didn't know what it meant. The priest then asked him: "Aren't you a fornicator?" "No." "Aren't you a glutton?" "No." "Aren't you vain?" He kept on saying "no." "Aren't you irascible?" "Even less." The priest, when he saw that he was still saying no, was completely amazed. "Aren't you concupiscent?" "Not at all." "Well what are you?" said the priest. "I'm a mason," he said. "Here's my trowel." There was another one who answered in like manner to his confessor, but he seemed to be a little craftier. He was a shepherd, and the priest asked him, "Now then, my friend, have you kept the commandments of God?" "Not at all," the shepherd said. "That was bad. And the commandments of the Church?" "No." "Well," the priest said, "what have you kept?" "I've kept nothing but my sheep," the shepherd said.

There's another one as old as an ink pot; but it may be that it's new for someone. It's about a man who was asked by the priest, after he had told his whole story, "Well then! my friend, what else do you have on your conscience?" He answered that there was nothing left, except that he remembered having stolen a halter. "Well then! my friend," the priest said, "stealing a halter isn't very serious, you can easily make restitution for that." "Yes," the other said, "but there was a mare at the end of it." "Aha!" the priest said, "that's another matter. There's a big difference between a mare and a halter. Therefore, you must return the mare, and then, the first time you come back to me for confession, I'll give you absolution for the halter."

---

[3] Opening words of Battista Mantuanus's first eclogue, famous Latin poet of the fifteenth century; *Fauste, precor, gelida quando pecus omne sub umbra ruminat*: Faustus, I pray, since all the herd is grazing in the cool shade.

Tale 41

OF THE GENTLEMAN WHO CALLED OUT TO HIS BIRDS AT NIGHT AND THE WAGONER WHO WHIPPED HIS HORSES

There's a kind of people who have choleric or melancholic or flegmatic humors (it has to be one of these three because sanguine humor is always good, so they say); their vapors go up to their brains and make them fantastic, lunatic, erratic, fanatic, schismatic, and all the atics you could name, and there's no cure, no matter what purgative you give them. Therefore, since I want to help these poor people and please their wives, relatives, friends, benefactors, and all those whom it may concern, I'm going to demonstrate here with a brief example which happened how they're to act when they have someone thus afflicted, particularly by nocturnal reveries: after all, it's a considerable inconvenience to rest neither night nor day. In the region of Provence, there was a fairly rich gentleman of some years; a man of leisure, he loved hunting a great deal and took such pleasure in it during the day that at night he got up in his sleep; he'd then call out to his birds just as he did in the daytime, and this displeased him no end and his friends too. No one who was in the house where he slept could rest, and he frequently awakened his neighbors because he called out to his birds so loud and so long. Otherwise, he was a good sort and was well known, as much for his graciousness as for this rather annoying imperfection he had, and so everyone called him the birdcaller. One day, while following his birds, he found himself in an isolated area when night overtook him without his knowing where to seek shelter; he twisted and turned so much in the woods and mountains that he finally came upon a house which stood by itself on the highway; the owner sometimes put up people who were about at night because there was no other lodging nearby. When he arrived, the owner was in bed; he got him up and asked him if he'd kindly give him shelter for that night because the weather was cold and dreary. The owner let him in and put his horse in the cattle shed and showed him to a bed on the ground floor as there was no room upstairs. Now there was a wagoner in there who had come from the fair at Pézenas, and he was lying in another bed nearby; he woke up at the gentleman's arrival, and this annoyed him a great deal because he was tired and he had just begun to sleep; and, besides, such people are by nature seldom gracious. So, suddenly awakened, he said to this gentleman, "What the hell brings you so late?" The gentleman, alone and in an unknown place, spoke as courteously as he could: "My friend," he said, "I dragged myself here following some of my birds; allow me to take cover here until morning." The wagoner woke up a bit more and took a good look at the gentleman; he recognized him immediately because he'd seen him often enough at Aix-en-Provence and had often heard what a sleeper he was. The gentleman didn't know him, but, while undressing, he said to him, "My friend, I beg of you, don't get angry with me for this one night; I have a habit of calling out to my birds at night. I love to hunt, and all night long I think I'm doing it." "Oh! oh!" the wagoner said, swearing, "Jesus! the same thing happens to me. It seems to me that throughout the night I'm driving my horses, and I can't help it." "Well," the gentleman said, "one night is soon over; we'll put up with one another." He went to bed, but he wasn't far into his first sleep before he jumped out of bed and began to yell around the place, "Whoop, whoop, whoop!" When he heard this, the wagoner woke up and took his whip, which he had next to him, and let it go here and there where he thought the gentleman was, saying, "Gee, haw, gee, haw." He lashed the poor gentleman, as you can well imagine. He woke up in a hurry with these whip lashes and changed his tune. Instead of yelling whoop, he began to shout for help and scream bloody murder; but the wagoner kept on whipping, and the poor gentleman was finally forced to throw himself under the table without saying another word and wait for the wagoner's fury to subside: when the wagoner realized that the gentleman had taken refuge, he went back to bed and pretended to snore. The owner got up, struck a light, and found the gentleman hidden under a bench which was so small that it could have been put in a small purse; his legs were full of welts and his body was bruised by the whip lashes; this certainly worked a great miracle because he never called out to his birds again while sleeping, and this later amazed those who knew him; but he told them what had happened to him. Never was a man more beholden to another than the gentleman to the wagoner for having thus cured him of such a sickness as that one, as they say that the sick of St. John were cured in the past.[1] And for stubborn horses, they say that you need only hang a cat on their tails, and it will so scratch them from behind that they'll have to run, by Heaven or Hell; and they'll lose their stubbornness by keeping it up for three hundred and seventy-seven times and a half and half of a third:[2] if that's the case, how much do seventeen sous and one onzain plus twenty-five sous minus one trezain add up to?[3]

---

[1] Epileptics, supposedly cured by the intercession of Saint John the Baptist.

[2] Or 377 1/6. This probably means once a day for a year; the French reads: "trois cent soixante et dix-sept fois et demie et la mioté d'un tiers"; if this means that 17 1/2 is to be divided by 3, the result is 5 5/6, or 365 5/6 days.

[3] The answer is 41 sous 10 deniers, but what it all means is anybody's guess.

Tale 42

OF THE GOOD WIDOW WHO HAD A PETITION TO SUBMIT AND
HOW SHE GAVE IT TO A PLAIN COUNSELOR

A good widow had a suit in Paris, and she had gone to look after it; she worked very diligently at it although she hardly understood her case; but she trusted that the lords of the High Court would make allowances for her age, her widowhood, and her just cause. One morning, early before dawn, earlier than usual, she didn't go into her garden to gather violets, but picked up her petition, which dealt with the matter of certain excesses which had been committed against her late husband. She went to the palace for the arrival of the lords and went up to the first counselor she saw coming and gave him her petition to submit. He took it, and, while the woman was giving it to him, she made her complaints to him so that he'd clearly understand her case. When the counselor, who by chance dealt with ecclesiastical matters, heard her speak of crimes, he said to the good woman, "My dear, it isn't up to me to present your petition, it has to be a plain lay counselor who submits it." The good woman, not knowing what a plain lay counselor was, thought that it must be a plain-looking counselor because she saw that that one by chance was a good-looking and well-built man. She began to look closely at the counselors who were entering to see if they were handsome or plain, and this task kept her very busy. At last along came one who wasn't among the best looking men in the world, at least to the good woman's mind, because (perhaps) he wore a long beard and his hair was clipped. The good woman was sure she had found her man; she gave him her petition and said to him, "Sir, I was told that a very plain counselor must present my petition: I looked closely at all those who went in, but I didn't find any plainer than you; so please present it." The counselor, who well understood what she meant, enjoyed her simplicity and took her petition, and, while submitting it, he didn't fail to relate the story to the men in his Chamber, and they ruled in the good woman's favor.

Tale 43

OF THE YOUNG GIRL WHO DID NOT WANT A PARTICULAR HUSBAND
BECAUSE HE HAD EATEN UP HIS FIRST WIFE'S BACK

With regard to word ambiguity which lies in enunciation, the French have a rather soft pronunciation, so much so that one doesn't hear the last letter of most of their words, and, therefore, words would very often be mistaken for one another were it not for the fact that they can be understood by the meaning of the other words which accompany them. There was in the city of Lyons a young girl, whom her relatives wanted to marry off to a man who had had another wife, who had died on him, with the help of God, a year or two earlier. This particular man had the reputation of being a spendthrift because he'd sold and squandered his first wife's property. When it was time to talk about this marriage, the young girl hid behind a door in order to hear what would be said. They spoke of this man in different ways, and one of them said, "I don't think we ought to give her to him; he's a man of poor conduct: he ate up his first wife's dowry." The young girl heard this remark, but she didn't take it to mean as the other meant it [1] because she was

---

[1] Her confusion comes from the similarity of *le dos*, back, and *la dot*, dowry.

young and hadn't yet heard of the word *dowry,* which they say in certain parts of this kingdom, and particularly around Lyons, instead of *dower*; and she thought they'd said that this man had eaten his wife's back or spine. And the girl, very worried, went pouting to her mother and told her frankly that she didn't want any part of the husband they wanted to give her. Her mother asked her, "And why don't you want him, my dear?" She answered, "Mother, he's a most wicked man; he killed his wife: he ate her back." They laughed a good deal about it when they learned how she'd understood it. But she was in no way wrong not to want him: after all, although a man may not be famished enough to eat a woman's back as though he were eating up her dowry, still, in neither case is he worth anything to her.

Tale 44

OF A GREAT LORD'S BASTARD, WHO WAS LETTING HIMSELF
BE HANGED UNJUSTLY AND WAS ANGRY THAT HE WAS SAVED

There was a great lord's bastard, or, at the least, putative son, who was only wise after a fashion, if that: he felt that everyone should honor him as much as if he were a prince because he was the bastard of such a noble house; furthermore, he thought that everyone was bound to know his rank, his birth, and his name; however, he didn't give people an opportunity to recognize this, for more often than not he wandered about the countryside with a retinue of little worth and joined all sorts of company, good and bad; it was all the same to him. He gambled his horses when he got new ones, as well as his accouterments, in the inns, and he frequently went on foot without a thing. One day, when he had reached a very sorry state, he went through the region of Rouergue on his way to France to get some more horses, and he happened to go through a forest where a few thieves had just killed a man. The provost marshal, who was pursuing the thieves, ran into this bastard, dressed like a ruffian, and he asked him where he was coming from. The bastard answered nothing else, except, "What business is it of yours where I come from?" "Why it certainly is my business," the provost said; "Aren't you one of those who killed this man?" "What man?" he said. "You don't have to ask what man," the provost said; "I'd certainly take you for knowing something about it." He answered, "What are you going to do about it?" The provost took him at his word and by the scruff of his neck, which was much worse, and had him taken away. On the way, the bastard kept on saying, "Ah! so you're accusing me, my Lord Provost? I'll have you taken care of." The provost, thinking that he was threatening him with his partners, was on his guard and led him straight to the next town, where he summarily tried him; but, when he asked him who he was and what his name was, he would only answer, "Ah! so you hang people, huh! You'll find out who I am." Upon these threats, the provost condemned him by his own confession and promptly had him climb up the scaffold. The bastard offered no resistance and never said anything else, except, "Damn, my Lord Provost, you've never hanged a man who'll cost you so much! Ah! you're a hangman!" When he was at the top of the scaffold, there was by chance, as there are so many people at such executions, a native of Rouergue who had been at Court in the past; he knew this bastard well because he'd often seen him at Court and in other places. He recognized him immediately and went even nearer the scaffold so as not to be mistaken, and he was even more convinced that it was he. "My Lord Provost," he said out loud, "what are you trying to do? That's So-and-So. Think twice about what you're going to do." When the bastard heard this man from Rouergue, he said: "Be quiet! be quiet! in the name of the devil, let him alone, it'll teach him not to hang people." The provost, when he heard him mentioned by name, had him quickly brought down, and the bastard said to him again: "Ah! you wanted to hang me! You would have been made to remember it, goddamnit! my Lord Provost. But why didn't you let him do it?" he said angrily to the man from Rouergue. Imagine what great sense he had to let himself be hanged in order that he might be well avenged. But who will believe that he was the son of a great lord or even of a gentleman? The poor fellow wasn't like the man the king wanted to send to the king of England, who at that time was a very bad Frenchman; this gentleman replied to the king: "Sire," he said, "I owe you my life and my possessions, and I'll never create difficulties about risking them for your service and allegiance; but if you send me to England at the present time, I'll never return from there alive; that's going to a slaughter and for a matter which isn't so very pressing that it can't be postponed until some other time when the king of England will have gotten over his anger; incensed as he is now, he'll have my head cut off." "Upon the word of a gentleman!" the king said, "if he did that, it would probably cost me thirty thousand lives for yours, but I'd get my revenge." "Yes, Sire," the gentleman said, "but out of all those heads would there be a single one that would do me any good? It's little comfort to a man to know that his death will be well avenged." It is indeed true that the good man goes to worthy executions with his head bowed without any other reason but the respect of his honor and the service of the Republic.

Tale 45

OF LORD DE RASCHAULT, WHO WENT TO DRAW WINE, AND HOW THE SPIGOT SLIPPED INTO HIS PINT

In the city of Poitiers, there was a good-hearted gentleman from a very wealthy family; he was a man fit for great undertakings, but he had a tremendous physical defect, his tongue; he couldn't say three words without stuttering, and, besides, it took him an hour to utter them, and in the end he couldn't make himself understood. And yet he tossed off very smartly the first word he said, like a *damn it* and a *hang it,* when he was in a temper, which is a sign that such a defect is but the result of a choleric humor, extremely plentiful in man, which prevents him from tempering his speech. I ought to pay a fine to teach me not to philosophize. At any rate, when his father saw that he was afflicted this way, he placed him from his earliest childhood in the care of the curate of Saint Didier, who made him psalmodize in church, chant the *Benedicamus*[1] and lessons at matins and vigils in order to improve his tongue; however, he didn't profit from anything except that, when he sang, he pronounced fairly distinctly his everyday speech, but in speaking he always retained this imperfection. He was married

---

[1] A liturgical versicle: Let us bless the Lord.

off to a young lady from a good family; she was virtuous and wise and knew how to handle him easily. One day, on one of the four great feast days,[2] while everyone was doing his devotions, this good gentleman, having finished his, came home with one of his servants to eat some venison pâté the young lady had made. But when it came to having breakfast, it turned out that she had the key, and this angered him greatly because there was no cause for interrupting the young lady's devotions and having her come from church for a pâté. But since he was hungry, he sent his man here and there to get something for breakfast. However, when he had one thing, he was short of another; butter for frying, an egg to make the sauce; onions, vinegar, mustard; they were both very much at a loss in the absence of women, who understand those things, particularly in homes run by wives, but they, not the homes, but the wives, weren't going to come from church until high mass was over. The gentleman was anxious to ply a trade he didn't understand, and when he saw that his servant wasn't doing his appetite any good he chased him from the house and told him to go to the devil. When he thus saw himself deprived of help, he was very perplexed; nevertheless, he didn't want to lose his breakfast, which was ready, by hook or by crook, except that the word of the Gospel was applicable: *Vinum non habent.*[3] What did he do? He didn't have the key to the cellar, but he went at that lock with a vengeance and completely smashed it with a volley of hammerblows and whatever else he found; and he took a tankard and went to draw wine, but he knew even less about that than about frying: first of all, he forgot to bring a candle; secondly, he didn't know which cask he should draw from; nevertheless, for that reason, he groped so much around the casks that he found one that had a spigot, and he went at it. However, he wasn't careful with the spigot while drawing the wine, and it slipped into the tankard: now he was roundly punished, for the vessel was so narrow that he couldn't put his hand in it, and, besides, perhaps the spigot had fallen on the ground. O poor man! what are you going to do? There was nothing nearby, so he put his finger in the hole in the cask because he didn't want to let his wine go to waste, and he stayed there quite a while;

---

[2] Easter, Whitsunday, All Saints' Day, Christmas.
[3] "They have no wine": the marriage in Cana; John 2:3.

but all the while, he stamped his foot, he gritted his teeth, he snorted, he trampled, he swore vehemently, he cursed Colin Brenot and his receipts. [4] At last, while he was thus putting up with it and getting angrier, along came the young lady from church; she found the doors open, including the one that went to the cellar, its lock and cramps on the ground; she thought then and there that De Raschault had done that fine bit of housework. Presently, she heard him through the cellar vent saying his litanies, and she said to him: "Oh! my God! what are you doing down there, De Raschault?" He answered by swearing, sometimes stammering, sometimes doing both at the same time; and, if he was distressed, so was she: she didn't dare go down to the cellar because she was in her good clothes, and, besides, not understanding what he was saying, she never dreamed that he was thus engaged. At last, seeing that he hadn't come up, she thought that there must be something wrong, and she took it into her head, in order to make him talk, to tell him, "Sing, De Raschault, sing!" Even though he didn't feel up to it, neverthelesss, he preferred doing it to staying there forever. He began to sing that great *Maledicamus* [5] in high key: "Come here, in the name of the devil, come here," he said, "the spigot is in the pint." When the young lady understood him, she sent her chambermaid to release him. But you can just imagine that in a fit of anger Lord De Raschault gave her smacks on the back for her breakfast, even though it wasn't a fish day and there was nothing she could do about it.

---

[4] La Monnaye, seventeenth-century annotator of these tales, states that this is an allusion to a rich swindler who forced his debtors to pay him twice by using on the original receipts an ink which faded away after a few days. However, the context seems to indicate that it is some sort of catchword, perhaps from a song or poem.

[5] The opposite of *Benedicamus*, his earlier exercise, above.

Tale 46

OF THE TAILOR WHO STOLE FROM HIMSELF AND THE GRAY CLOTH THAT HE RETURNED TO HIS CRONY THE HOSIER

A tailor from the same city of Poitiers, named Lyons, was a good workman at his trade and he could very properly outfit a man and a woman and everybody, except that sometimes he'd cut out three quarters for the rear instead of two, or three sleeves in a cloak, but he only sewed on two. After all, men have only two arms; and he was so accustomed to pulling this sleight of hand that he couldn't refrain from doing it in all kinds of cloth and in all colors. Indeed, when he cut out a garment for himself, he would have thought his cloth hadn't been properly used if he hadn't taken off a piece and hidden it in the drawer or in the chest for extras, just like the one who was such a great thief that, when he didn't find anything to take, he got up at night and stole money from his own purse. I don't mean that tailors are thieves, for they only take what they're given, just as millers do, and just as the good chambermaid who said to the one who approved of her, "You see, Madam, I'll serve you well, but..." "But what?" the lady said. "Look here!" the wench said; "my heels are a little round, I flop on my back, I can't help it; but that's my only fault, and in everything else you'll find me as diligent as possible." Likewise, this tailor plied his trade very well, but he had this little fault. Therefore, by golly, he once made a cloak of gray Rouen cloth for a hosier crony of his who wanted to go out of town very soon on some business, and the tailor held back a good quarter of the gray cloth. His crony noticed it, but he didn't particularly want to complain about it because he knew well through his own business that everyone had to live off his own trade. One morning when the hosier was passing in front of the tailor's shop with his cloak on, he stopped to chat with him. The tailor asked him if he wanted to breakfast on a herring, for it was Lent; he was delighted. They went up to cook the herring; the tailor shouted from upstairs to the apprentice, "Bring up that grill." The apprentice thought he was asking for the gray cloth [1] left over from the cloak and that he wanted to return it to his crony the hosier. He took the cloth and brought it upstairs to his master. When the crony saw this great piece of cloth, he said, "Why, that's some of my cloth! And that's all you took? Ah! Dammit, that's not enough." When the tailor saw that he'd been found out, he said to him, "And do you think I'd keep it from you; you're my friend. Don't you see that I had it brought up in order to return it to you?

---

[1] The apprentice understands *le gris* (the piece of gray cloth) instead of *le gril* (grill).

I save your cloth for you, and you say I stole it from you!" The hosier crony was very pleased with this answer; he had breakfast and went off with his gray cloth. But the tailor sermonized the apprentice about his being wiser the next time. The slip came from the fact that the apprentice had always heard grille said in the feminine, and not grill, and that's what exposed the mystery.

Tale 47

OF THE ABBOT OF SAINT AMBROSE, HIS MONKS, AND OTHER ADVENTURES OF THIS ABBOT

Master Jacques Colin,[1] who died not long ago as abbot of Saint Ambrose, was a man of great learning with a good mind, as he amply demonstrated while he lived; he spoke knowledgeably about whatever the subject might be, and his wit was particularly keen; therefore, all his supporters together brought him into the favor of the late King Francis before whom he lectured a long time. They tell a great number of good stories about him and it would take a long time to relate them; but among all of them I'll tell one or two which are delightful and which he told before the aforesaid Lord. He was on bad terms with his monks, who did all the worst things they could to him, and they really reminded him of the common proverb which says: you must beware of the front end of a bull, the rear of a mule and all the sides of a monk. It's true that he did avenge himself, and in every way that he could think of; the most annoying of them for the poor monks was that he made them fast; they didn't take it in good part, however, and complained about it to so many people and in so many places that, by all these means, it finally reached the king's ears; the king wanted to know the truth of the matter, and he said one day to Master Jacques Colin, "Saint Ambrose, your monks are complaining about you, and they say you aren't treating them as their order states and that you're starving them to death." "Is that so, Sire?" replied St. Ambrose; "you chose to make me their abbot, they are my monks, and since

---

[1] Humanist and patron of arts and letters, he became one of the Royal Readers under Francis I.

I represent the person of the founder of their order reason dictates that I make them act according to his will, which was that they live in humility, poverty, chastity, and obedience. I considered and pondered every means possible; but I didn't find any more expedient than temperance: it's the cause of all good, as gluttony is of all evil. I believe that David understood God when he said: *'Si non fuerint saturati, murmurabunt'.*" [2] And he interpreted this statement for the king, in accordance with his office as reader. "And since then," he said, "the New Testament has spoken very frankly about them, for it is written in St. Matthew, chap. XVII, v. 20: *Hoc genus demoniorum non ejicitur, nisi oratione et jejunio.* [3] *Hoc genus demoniorum,*" he said, "means this kind of monk."

Another time, in the days when sentences were handed out in Latin, he lost a suit at court and perhaps it was against those same monks. In accordance with legal procedure, the judgment against him contained this: "*Dicta curia debotavit et debotat dictum Colinum de sua demanda.*" [4] And Saint Ambrose, having received double his sentence from his lawyer, went before the king and told him at the appropriate time, "Sire, I've never received such a great honor as I did three days ago." "And how's that?" the king said. "Sire," he said, "your sovereign court has 'de-booted' me." [5] The king understood how he was being taken in, and he thought it very funny, particularly when he learned of their fine choice of that lovely unfailing Latin. But since then, sentences have been put in good French, [6] and for that reason it is jokingly said that Master Jacques Colin was the cause of it; hence, it could no longer be said that the court took a hand in "de-booting" people, but rather in dismiss-

---

[2] Psalm 58: *Ipsi dispergentur ad manducandum; si vero non fuerint saturati, et murmurabunt*: Let them wander up and down for meat, and grudge if they be not satisfied.

[3] Matthew 17:20. The correct quotation is *Hoc autem genus non ejicitur nisi per orationem et jejunium*: Howbeit this kind goeth not out but by prayer and fasting. The abbot's fabrication (*demoniorum*: of the devil, devilish) creates a play on words in French: *genre de moine* (kind of monk) and *genus de moniorum.*

[4] The said court dismissed and dismisses the said Colin's suit.

[5] Taken off my boots; play on *debotare* (from French *debouter*, to dismiss) and *débotter*, to unboot.

[6] Because of the Villers-Cotterêts ordinance, promulgated in October 1539; Francis I ordered that all official judicial acts and pronouncements be made in French instead of Latin.

ing claims at will, and more than many wanted. Many other witty remarks are attributed to him.

Once, at dinner, a steward, while setting down the dishes, spilled soup on a velvet cloak he was wearing. He found the opportunity of striking up a conversation with a gentleman named Fundulus, [7] who was at the table beside him; Fundulus was a man of learning, but completely emaciated, partly because of his natural constitution and partly because of study. Abbot Saint Ambrose said to him, "Mister Fundulus, you're so thin, you look as though you're not well." "I'm always like this," Fundulus said; "I can never put on any fat." "I'll tell you about a good cure," St. Ambrose said. "You need only speak to the steward here, he'll put fat on you in no time." There are many like this about him, but they all belong to apophthegms.

---

[7] Jerome Fondulo, Italian humanist.

Tale 48

OF THE MAN WHO DISMISSED THE SAME ABBOT WITH A COCKY REMARK

The same man I've been talking about was one of those about whom it is said that they were suckled by a wet-nurse with tough breasts, against which the nose is blunted and becomes flat; but it didn't look bad on him because he was a thick-set man, very stocky, who, in fact, knew how to get around very well. Because of this, he exemplified what a lady said when she compared men to women. "We women," she said, "aren't prized very much, except for our beauty; and, for this reason, we have to keep ourselves up carefully and make the most of ourselves while we have the opportunity because, when our beauty is gone, we're no longer valued. As for men, I don't see any ugly ones, I find them all good-looking." To go on with the story, Saint Ambrose, one day at Fontainebleau with a few of his friends, was leaning out of a gallery, and he noticed in the court below a man whom he thought he knew well and who was all by himself and had the look of a newcomer about him. Saint Ambrose wasn't mistaken, for he had seen him often enough and had even kept company with him in the days when he used to raise hell. "I'll be damned!" he said to those who were with him, "that's So-and-So, that's the fellow. I'm going to give him a little bit of a hard time." He went down to greet the man, but in a different way than in the past: indeed, he put on airs, which courtiers cannot easily disguise anyhow, even when they want to. When the man saw Saint Ambrose's mien, he stood just as fast: although he scarcely frequented the Court, still, he knew its ways rather well. After a few salutations, Saint Ambrose said to him, "Now then, what are you doing in this court? You're not here without a reason." "Upon my word," the other said, "I'm not doing much of anything at the moment; I'm looking to see who has the best looking nose." Master Jacques Colin pointed to the king, who by chance was at a window talking. "Now there," he said, "is the one you're looking for." As a matter of fact, King Francis, besides being regal in every way, had a nose as handsome and long as Master Jacques Colin's was short and pushed in. For that reason, he well understood that those words were addressed to no one else but him. And he was anxious to get away from there in order to go tell the story to those he had left behind, and he said to them, "Damn! my man put me down on the spot. I asked him just what he was doing here; he answered me that he was looking for the one who had the best looking nose." They say that the same character, who is reputed to have been Eloin, the tax collector of Lyons, did the same thing to a cardinal who asked him, "Now then, what are you doing these days? Surely, you have a good iron in the fire." "Upon my word, Sir," he answered, "saving Your Grace, I'm not doing any more than a priest would do."

Tale 49

OF CHICHOUAN THE DRUMMER, WHO HAD HIS FATHER-IN-LAW SUMMONED FOR NOT HAVING DIED, AND THE SENTENCE THAT THE JUDGE HANDED DOWN

Not too long ago, in the city of Amboise, there was a drummer who was named Chichouan; he was a merry man and full of witty remarks, and because of this he was as welcome as his drum in every house. He married the daughter of an old man who lived in his own home within the city of Amboise: a man of good faith, with the integrity of the old days written all over him, he was quite content with not having any other children but this daughter. And because Chichouan had no other means but his drum, he asked this good man for some ready money as a wedding settlement to cover the cost of the new household. But the old man didn't want to give him any, and he said in his defense to Chichouan: "My friend, don't ask me for any money; I can't give you any at this time; but you can see that I have one foot in the grave; I have no other heir but my daughter; you'll get my house and all my furniture: I can't live more than another year or two at the most." The old man gave him so many reasons that he was content with taking his daughter without any money, but he said to him, "Listen, good sir: I'm doing at your word what I wouldn't do for anybody else; but do you indeed assure me of what you're telling me?" "Ahem!" the old man said, "I've never deceived anyone; God forbid that you should be the first." "Well then!" said Chichouan, "I don't want any other contract but your promise." The day of the wedding came; Chichouan left his house and went to get his wife at her father's and led her to church himself with his drum. When she was there, he said, "And that's not all; Chichouan went to get his wife, now he's going to get himself." And he went back to his house. And right away, to the beat of his drum, he led himself back to church, where he married his wife, and then he took her back home; and he was both groom and minstrel and earned his own money. He got along well with her, living very happily. At the end of two years, seeing that his father-in-law hadn't died, he waited another month, then two months; but he went on living. He decided, in order to indulge himself, to have his father-in-law summoned before the court, and, as a matter of fact, he sent a sheriff's officer to him. The old man, who had never had anything to do with the law and who didn't know what a summons meant, was the most astonished man in the world to see himself summoned and even more so at the request of his son-in-law, whom he had seen the previous day and who had said nothing to him about it. He immediately went to Chichouan and complained to him, pointing out that he was very wrong to have had him summoned and that he didn't know why. "No! No!" said Chichouan; "I'll tell you in court." And he wasn't able to get anything else out of him, so he had to go to court. When they were before the judge, Chichouan presented his suit himself. "Sir," he said, "I married this man's daughter, as everyone knows; I received no money from him, he'll not contradict me; but he promised me, when he gave me his daughter, that I'd have his house and all his goods and that he wouldn't live more than a year or two at the most. I've waited two years and more than three extra months; I received neither his house, nor anything else. I request that he die or that he give me his house, as he promised me." The old man had himself defended by his lawyer, who answered what he had to in a brief speech for the defense. Having heard the parties and the arguments on both sides and knowing the joke which Chichouan intended with his suit and the silly summons, the judge condemned him to pay damages and the old man's court costs and, in addition, twenty pounds to the king. Immediately, Chichouan said: "Ah! Sir, Chichouan appeals." "Wait! wait!" the judge said, turning toward Chichouan. "I reduce it," he said, "to one capon and its giblets, and the old man will pay it tomorrow at his house. And you will all go eat your share together, like good friends; and you'll serenade him every year on the first day of the month of May, for as long as he lives. And then after his death, you'll have his house if it hasn't been sold or mortgaged or razed by fire." Thus, the judge's sentence was according to Chichouan's suit, but he had given him a scare in the beginning; however, he reduced his sentence, as a judge can do, provided it be done at once, as noted *In 1. nescio,* ff. *ubi et quando; per Bartholum, Baldum, Paulum, Salicetum, Jasonem, Felinum, et omnes tormentatores juris.* [1]

---

[1] This should read in ff. *1. nescio ubi et quando;* the symbol ff. indicates the *Digest* (the corpus of Roman Law) and the *1 (lex)* stands for the title of the law, which he says he cannot locate in time or place. His authorities are genuine legists, but the final phrase, "and all legal tormentors," is a parody of *commentatores juris.*

Tale 50

OF THE GASCON WHO GAVE HIS FATHER A CHOICE OF EGGS

A Gascon, who had been at war, had returned home to live with his father, who was already an old countryman and who was quite gentle; but his son was a scatterbrain and gave commands in the

house as though he were the master. One Friday, at dinner, he said
to his father: "Dad," he said, "we have enough wine for you and
for me although you don't drink any." He and his father had put
three eggs to cook in the fire; the Gascon took one to cut into and
drew another to his side and left only one on the dish; then he said
to his father, "Choose, Father." His father said: "Why, what do you
want me to choose? There's only one." Then the Gascon said to him,
"Hang it! you still have to choose: take it or leave it." That was
some choice he gave his father. And when his father sneezed, he
said to him, "God help you! Father." And he added, "If He wants to,
for He doesn't do anything under duress." He was as shamefaced
as a sow carrying off leaven, for he didn't dare curse his father, but
he'd say, "a pox on half the people in the world!" And at the same
time he'd say to one of his friends, "Give a dose to the other half, so
that my father will get his share."

Tale 51

OF THE TREASURY CLERK WHOSE TWO DICE FELL FROM HIS
WRITING DESK IN FRONT OF THE KING

King Louis XI was a prince of great deliberation and of like
performance; among his other characteristics, he loved those who
were subtle and answered promptly, and also, so they say, he never
gave as a gift more than one hundred crowns at a time. One day,
among others, when there were some letters to sign and no royal
secretary was present, the king appointed a young treasury clerk
who was there, for there was nothing more to it than that, and,
upon opening his writing desk in order to sign, he dropped on the
table two dice which were in the penholder. "What!" said the king,
"what kind of pill is that? What's it good for?" "*Contra pestem,*[1]
Sire," the clerk said. "*Contra pestem!*" the king said. "You're a
man after my own heart." And he ordered that he be given one
hundred crowns. One day, the Genoese, of whom it is written: *Vane
ligur,*[2] seeing that he was bringing his enemies to heel and hoping

---

[1] Against the plague, infectious disease.
[2] *The Aeneid,* XI, 715 reads *vane Ligus*: Foolish Ligurian.

to obtain his good will, sent him an ambassador; with a lovely harangue, he did his best to make the king think that it was good that his enemies were so ready and willing to obey him and that, willingly and of their own accord, they'd rather give themselves up to him than to any other prince on earth because of the greatness of his name and deeds. "Indeed!" the king said; "the Genoese are giving themselves to me?" "Yes, Sire." "They're then mine without regret?" "Yes, Sire." "And I'll give them," the king said, "to the devil!" He gave a present which was as nice as the one he had received, and he also didn't give anything which wasn't his: after all, it's commonly said that it's better to give than to receive.

Tale 52

OF TWO ARGUMENTS TO MAKE A WOMAN HOLD HER TONGUE

A young man, who was talking to a woman from Paris who boasted that she ruled the roost, said to her, "If I were your husband, I'd stop you from having your own way." "You!" she said; "you'd have to put up with it just like the others." "Indeed!" he said; "you can be sure that I know two arguments to get the better of a woman." "Is that so?" she said. "And what are those two arguments?" The young man closed his hand and said, "There's one of them," then quickly closed his other hand: "And there's the other." This caused much laughter because the woman thought he was going to show her two new arguments to make women toe the mark, taking argument for reason; but by argument he understood fists. And, upon my soul, I believe there's neither fist nor argument that could make a woman wise when she's decided to have her own way.

Tale 53

THE WAY TO BECOME RICH

From small business beginnings, peddling needles, belts, and pins, a man had become so very rich that he bought his neighbors' properties, and he was the talk of the region. Marveling about this, a gentleman who was travelling with him said to him, "Well, come now, So-and-So! " calling him by name, "what did you do to get as rich as you are?" "Sir," he said, "I'll tell you in two words: I worked hard and spent little." There's a good motto; but you still need bread and wine, for there are those who could break their necks without being any the richer for it. At least, his way is more appropriate than that of the man who said that, in order to get rich, one need only turn his back on God for a good five or six years.

Tale 54

OF A LADY FROM ORLEANS WHO LOVED A STUDENT WHO PRETENDED TO
BE A LITTLE DOG AT HER DOOR AND HOW THE BIG DOG CHASED THE
LITTLE ONE AWAY

A lady from Orleans, who was good and kind, albeit contrary, was married to a cloth merchant and had been pursued for a long time by a student, a handsome young man who danced gracefully, for there were at that time dancers from Orleans, flutists from Poitiers, bold fellows from Avignon, students from Toulouse. This student was named Clairet, and the woman, because she was kind and human, was finally seduced by means of the notes, remarks, and messages they addressed to each other, and she bestowed upon him love's reward, which he enjoyed contentedly. Between them, they had little signs of communication which were amusing and which they used in sequence, first one and then another; one of them was that Clairet came about ten o'clock at night to her door and barked like a little dog; the chambermaid was used to it and immediately opened the door without a candle or a lantern, and the whole ritual was acted out without a word. There was another student, who lived right next to the young lady; he was very much in love with her and he would have liked to share her with Clairet, but he wasn't able to bring it about, either because he didn't suit her, or because he didn't know how to go about it, or, and this is easier to believe, because women, who are somewhat shrewd, don't readily give themselves to their neighbors for fear of being discovered too soon. Nevertheless, knowing full well that Clairet went there and having seen him come and go at his games, and among other things having heard him bark and having seen how he was let in, what did he do? Once when the husband was out, and, after having made sure of the time that Clairet arrived, he decided that he had the right voice like Clairet to pretend to be a little dog and that he'd only need to bark in order to catch his prey. Then, a little before ten o'clock, he went and pretended to be a little dog at the lady's door: "Yap! yap!" The maid, who heard him, immediately came to let him in, and he was very happy about it; knowing well the ins and outs of the house, he didn't fail to go straight to bed, next to the young lady, who thought he was Clairet; and you can be sure that he didn't lose any time with her. While he was playing his games, along came Clairet as was his custom, and he began to bark at the door: "Yap! yap!" But no one let him in although the lady began to suspect something or other and chiefly because the one who was with her seemed to have a different manner and a different way of handling her than Clairet had. And for that reason, she decided to get up in order to call her chambermaid to find out what it was. The student wanted to have this night to himself, for he was enjoying it so, and, when he saw her up, he immediately got out of bed and went to the window, even as Clairet was still barking "Yap! yap!" and he answered him with the howl of village hounds: "Woof! woof! woof!" When Clairet heard this voice, he said: "Ah! ah! hang it all! it's only right that the big dog chase the little one away. Farewell, farewell, good evening, and good night"; and he left. The other went back to bed and calmed the lady down as best he could, and she was obliged to bear with it; and since then, he found a way to get along with the little dog; they agreed to go hunting cony each in his turn as good friends and companions.

Tale 55

OF VAUDREY AND THE TRICKS HE PLAYED

It wasn't too long ago that the Lord of Vaudrey [1] was still living; he was very well known by princes and by nearly everyone

---

[1] An old and illustrious family in the province of Franche-Comté.

because of the acts he did during his lifetime with great eccentric-
ity, accompanied by such luck that no one, except him, would have
dared to undertake them, and, as is commonly said, a wise man
would have died a hundred times over. For instance, when he was
in Beauce he wore out a magpie by riding after it so hard that it
finally gave up. Another time he strangled a cat with his teeth, with
both of his hands tied behind him. Once when he wanted to test
a leather neckpiece he had on, or a coat of mail, I don't know which,
he had an unsheathed sword placed against a wall, with the tip
towards him, and he began to run towards the sword with such
force that he pierced himself through and through, and yet he didn't
die from it. It goes without saying that he was touched in the head.
Among all his foolish acts, there's one more worth telling. He rode
over the bridge of Cé near Angers, which is very high off the water
for a wooden bridge, and a young gentleman who was riding on
the saddle behind him said to him laughingly: "Come now, Vaudrey!
Since you have so many clever tricks and know how to play so
many fine pranks, if you now saw that the enemy was waiting for
you at both ends of this bridge, what would you do?" Vaudrey
immediately said, "What would I do? Good heavens! this is what
I'd do." And on saying this, he spurred his horse and made it jump
over the railings into the Loire, and he maneuvered so well that
both he and the horse came through it. If his companion got through
it as he did, he must have been happy as well as wise to say the
least, for it was sheer madness for him to get on a saddle behind
a fool because when a man is one league away from him, he still
isn't far enough away.

Tale 56

OF THE GENTLEMAN WHO CUT OFF A PURSE SNATCHER'S EAR

In the church of Notre-Dame in Paris, a gentleman [1] in the crowd
felt a thief cutting off the gold buttons on the sleeves of his robe,
and, without seeming to take any notice, he drew his dagger and
took the thief's ear and cut it off on the spot; and showing it to

---

[1] According to Henri Estienne in his *Apologie pour Hérodote*, the gentleman
in question is Jean du Bellay.

him, he said: "Look, your ear isn't lost, do you see it here? Give me back my buttons, and I'll give it back to you." It wouldn't have been a bad bargain for him if he could have sewn his ear back on as the gentleman could his buttons.

Tale 57

OF THE MAID FROM TOULOUSE WHO NO LONGER ATE SUPPER AND THE ONE WHO WAS ON A DIET

At harvest time, a maid from Toulouse was in one of her units in the fields, and she had as a neighbor another young lady from the same city; they supervised the making of their wine, and they saw each other often and sometimes ate together. But one of them had taken up the habit of not eating supper, and she said to her neighbor: "My dear, I've seen the time when I was almost always ill until I took up the habit of no longer eating supper and of having only a small snack in the evening." "And what do you snack on, my dear?" the other said. "Do you know," she said, "how I go about it? I roast two quail between good grape leaves (as they prepare them in that region in order to cook them in their own fat, for they are very fatty), and I put a winter pear between two burning coals. (These pears are as large as a fist, and more). I make a snack of that," she said, "and when I've eaten that and drunk a flagon of wine (which is exactly equal to a Parisian pint) with a liard's worth of bread, I'm as well off with that as if I'd eaten all the meat in the world." "My goodness," the other said, "if you're not well with all that, it's the work of the devil." And when the quail season was over, you can imagine that the poor maid was to be pitied over squab, doves, partridges. I'm also fond of the one who said to his valet: "Put in a good word for me with the steward, and tell him I'd like for him to send me just some soup, a piece of veal, a capon wing and a partridge wing, and some other little tidbit, since I don't want to eat much because of my diet." And another man, believing he'd be considered moderate in his request for something to drink, said, after he'd been asked what he wanted: "Give me five or six shots of white wine and then as much of the claret as you please." But he wasn't like the one who complained of her stomach; she said: "I've eaten a lark's thigh, and my stomach is so stuffed I can't stand it." The tip of a bulrush coudn't have gotten in.

Tale 58

OF THE MONK WHO ANSWERED EVERYTHING IN RHYMED MONOSYLLABLES

A monk, travelling through the country, arrived at an inn at suppertime. The innkeeper had him sit with the others who had already begun, and the monk, in order to catch up with them, began to stuff himself greedily as though he hadn't seen bread for three days. The wily fellow had stripped down to his doublet in order to give a better account of himself; when he saw this, one of the men at the table asked him many things, which didn't please him because he was busy filling his paunch. But in order to lose as little time as possible, he answered everything in rhymed monosyllables; and I'm pretty sure he'd learned this language a long time ago because he was very good at it. The questions and answers were as follows. The other asked him: "What habit do you wear?" "Frocks." "How many monks are you?" "Flocks." "What kind of bread do you eat?" "White." "What kind of wine do you drink?" "Light." "What kind of meat do you eat?" "Boar." "How many novices do you have?" "Four." "What do you think of this wine?" "Fun." "Don't you drink any like it?" "None." "And what do you eat on Fridays?" "Skate." "How many do you each have?" "Eight." Thus he didn't lose a mouthful all the while, and he laconically answered the questions. If he made his matins as short, he was a good pillar of the church.

Tale 59

OF THE LAW STUDENT AND THE APOTHECARY WHO TAUGHT HIM MEDICINE

A student, who had lived in Toulouse for a while, went to a small town near Cahors in Quercy named Saint Anthony in order to put his law books to use there; he hadn't gained a great deal from them because he'd always stuck to the humanities, in which he was well versed; but since he'd decided to take up the law profession, he thought he shouldn't go back ignorant and unable to handle himself as well as the others. As soon as he was in Saint Anthony, for in these little towns one is immediately seen and noticed, an apothecary came up and said to him: "Welcome, Sir"; and he began to chat with him, and in the course of the conversation the student slipped in a few words which belonged to the field of medicine, just as a man of learning and judgment always has something to say about every profession. When the apothecary heard him speak, he said to him: "Sir, you're then a doctor from what I can tell?" "No, I'm not," he said; "but I do know something about it." "I'm sure," the apothecary said, "that you don't want to admit it because you haven't thought of settling in this town; but I assure you indeed that you wouldn't do badly. We don't have a doctor at present; the one we had before died worth forty thousand francs. If you decide to stay here, you'll find it a good living; I'll put you up, and you and I shall live well, but let us understand each other well. Come and dine with me." The student listened to the apothecary, who wasn't stupid, for he'd been in the better towns of France in order to learn his trade, and let himself be taken to dinner and thought to himself: "You have to try your luck, and if this man will do what he says, I'll also have a good thing: this is an out-of-the-way place, no one knows me, let's see what will come of it." The apothecary took him home to dine. They kept up their initial conversation throughout dinner, and they quickly became partners. To cut it short, the apothecary made him believe that he was a doctor, and then the student said to him right away: "Well, you know what? I've never yet practiced our art, as you can well imagine; but my intention was to hole up in Paris to study for another year and to go into practice in my hometown; but since I've met you and since we both know that we're right for one another, let's get on with our business; I'm delighted to stay." "Sir," the apothecary said, "don't worry, I'll teach you all about medicine in less than two weeks. I've been with doctors in France and elsewhere for a long time; I know all their ways and prescriptions by heart. Moreover, in this area, you only have to be pleasant and know how to guess, and that makes you the greatest doctor in the world." And from that point on the apothecary began to show him how to write out an ounce, a dram, a scruple, a handful, a fistful, and two days later he taught him the names of the most common drugs, and then to dose, to compound, to mix up, and all such tasks. That easily lasted ten or twelve days, and all the while he kept to his room and had the apothecary say that he was slightly indisposed. The apothecary didn't forget to say throughout the town that this man was the best and most learned doctor who had ever come to Saint Anthony. The townspeople were very pleased about this and began to carry on over him as soon as he left the house, and they fought over who would invite him, and you would have said that they were already anxious to be ill in order to put him to work so that he'd be willing to stay. But the student (what am I saying, student! doctor at the hands of an apothecary) played hard to get, frequented only a few people, looked pleasant, and, above all, he scarcely left the apothecary, who provided him with his oracles in nothing flat. Along came urine samples from all sides. Now, in that area, it was necessary to guess by the urine if the patient was male or female, in what part he felt bad, and how old he was. But this doctor did much more, for he guessed who his father and mother were, if he were married or not, and for how long, and how many children he had. In short, all the way from the old ones down to the very young, he told all there was about them and all with the help of his master the apothecary; when the apothecary saw someone bringing a urine specimen, he went to question him while the doctor was upstairs and asked him from beginning to end all the things mentioned above, and then he made him wait a bit while he went to inform his doctor secretly of all he'd learned from the bearer of urine. As soon as he had it, the doctor looked it up and down, placed his hand between the urinal and daylight, lowered it, and turned it around with the expressions required in such cases; then he said: "It's a woman." "Oh, upon my word! Sir! you're truly speaking the truth!" "She has a severe pain on the left side under her breast," or in her head, or her stomach, according to what the apothecary had told him. "Only three months ago she had a daughter." The bearer was the most astonished person in the world, and he immediately left to tell everywhere what he'd heard from this doctor, so that the rumor spread from mouth to mouth that he was the greatest man in the world. And if by chance his apothecary wasn't there at times, he wormed the secrets out of these Rouergue people by saying in amazement: "Very ill!" And the bearer would im-

mediately answer: "He or she." By this means, he'd look at the urine
for a little while and then say, "Isn't it a man?" "Oh, certainly!
indeed he is a man," the person would say. "Ha! I knew it immediately," the doctor would say. But, when it came to writing prescriptions in front of people, he always stayed near his master, who spoke
to him in medical Latin, which at that time was as fine as sackcloth.
And under that guise the apothecary told him the entire prescription,
pretending to speak of something else; you can imagine how funny
it was to see a doctor prescribing under an apothecary. In fact,
either because of the opinion he generated about himself, or because
of some other reason, the sick got well with his prescriptions, and
there wasn't a mother's son who didn't go to this doctor, and they
convinced themselves that it was good to be sick while he was there
and that, if he left, they'd never find another like him. They sent him
a thousand presents, such as game or bottles of wine, and the
women made him handkerchiefs and shirts. They so fattened his
purse that in less than six or seven months he earned many crowns,
and his apothecary too, because they helped each other; so, he got
ready to leave St. Anthony, pretending to have received from home
letters in which he was sent word that he had to leave, but that he
wouldn't fail to return soon. He went to Paris, where he then studied
medicine and perhaps he was never again as good a doctor as he'd
been in his apprenticeship; I understand he wasn't as successful:
sometimes fortune helps the adventuresome more than the overly
discreet, for the learned man deliberates too much; he thinks about
the circumstances, a fear and a doubt develop and cause men to
mistrust you, and this discourages them from seeking you out; and,
in fact, it is said that it's better to fall into the hands of a happy
doctor than a learned one. An Italian doctor understood that well;
when he had nothing to do, he wrote two or three hundred prescriptions for various illnesses and he took a number of them and put
them in his coat pocket; then, when someone came to him for a
urinalysis, he pulled out one of these prescriptions at random and
gave it to him saying only, "*Dio te la daga buona.*" [1] And, if he got
well, "*In buona hora.*" [2] If he got worse, "*Suo danno.*" [3] So the world
turns.

---

[1] Let us hope for the best.
[2] Well and good!
[3] So much the worse for you.

Tale 60

OF FATHER JOHN, WHO CLIMBED ON THE SMITH THINKING IT WAS HIS WIFE

A smith, who lived in a village which was on the main road, had a fairly beautiful wife, at least in the eyes of a priest who lived very near him; he was called Father John, and he angled so that he reached an agreement with that young woman. In fact, he got on with her so well that, when the smith got up in order to work in his forge — and the priest knew it when he heard him hammering because it was the sign that the smith was there with his helper—, he didn't fail to enter through a back door, for which she'd given him the key, and he got in bed in the smith's place which he found still warm; there he forged for his part on another anvil, but from a distance one couldn't hear him doing his job, and, when he was through, he quietly left through the same door. But they weren't able to carry on their affair so secretly that the smith didn't notice it, or at least have a strong suspicion of it, because he heard this door open and close; so, one day he accused his wife and threatened her and pressed her so and with the anger that such fiery people usually have that she asked his forgiveness and confessed the affair to him and told him how Father John came to bed next to her whenever he heard him hammering. When the smith heard this and after his wife begged for mercy, he had to accept it; but you can be sure that it wasn't without giving her raps and lumps anyway. A few days later, the smith found the priest and said to him: "Father John, you come to see my wife whenever you can." The priest denied it strongly and firmly, telling him that he wouldn't want to play that trick on him and that he'd rather be dead. "You're my friend," the priest said. "Very well, then!" the smith said; "I'll take your word for it; straddle her as you please when you're there; but make sure you don't straddle me, because if it happens, your luck will have run out." The priest knew that the smith was a hothead and so he was on his guard from then on and didn't want to go to the forge anymore; but the smith said to his wife: "You know what you have to do? But be sure you don't pretend you're blind in one eye or lame because you know you won't get off any better. Resume your friendship with Father John and entertain him with words, and

then, one morning, I'll tell you what you have to do." She was very
happy to promise him all he wanted for fear of the consequences.
And you have to understand that she knew how to pound and with
a good beat because she'd learned to pound with the helper in order
to do the job when the smith wasn't there. Accordingly, she began
to be friendly to Father John, as her husband had instructed her,
and she gave him to understand that the smith no longer thought
about it and that it was only a notion which had passed through
his mind, and she reassured him with fine words, saying, "Come,
come, tomorrow morning at the usual time when you hear them
hammering." Father John believed her, the poor man! When
morning came, the smith said to his wife in the presence of his
helper: "Get up, and go hammer in my place; I don't feel well."
She did just that and went to the forge with the helper. As soon as
Father John heard them hammering, he was wide-awake; he got up
in his long nightshirt, went in through the usual door, and got in bed
next to the smith, thinking he was next to his wife; and because he
hadn't had a go at it for a long time, he was more than ready to
perform, and no sooner was he in bed than in one bound he jumped
on top of the smith, but the smith began to squeeze him tightly with
both hands, saying to him, "Hey, for crissake (you can bet it was
with a capital C), Father John, who asked you to come here? I told
you you'd better not straddle me and that I was a mean brute, and
you didn't believe me!" The priest wanted to get free, but the
smith held him with both arms and began to shout for his helper,
who was downstairs and who immediately came up and brought a
light; and God knows how the priest was thrashed with a bullwhip,
which the smith had ready and expressly for whacking on Father
John's back, the smith and his helper relieving one another. And, yet,
he didn't dare shout for help because the smith threatened to put
him in the furnace, and so he preferred to put up with the blows
rather than the fire. Still, he got off cheaply compared to the one
who had both testicles enclosed in a coffer and a fire lit at his rear
so that he was forced to cut them off himself with a razor which had
been placed in his hand.

Tale 61

OF THE SENTENCE HANDED DOWN BY THE PROVOST OF BRITTANY, WHO HAD JOHN TRUBERT AND HIS SON HANGED

In the province of Brittany, there was a man, among others, who wasn't worth much; his name was John Trubert, and he had committed several larcenies, for which he'd been captured frequently and had been flogged on one occasion and thrashed on another, which should have been enough for him to remember. Nevertheless, he was so attracted to it that he couldn't reform; and he even began to teach the trade to his son, who was between fifteen and sixteen years old, and he took him along on his expeditions. There came a day when he and his son stole a mare from a rich farmer, who suspected immediately that it was John Trubert; he didn't fail to make such an investigation that it was ascertained through good witnesses that John Trubert had taken this mare to be sold in a market held the previous Wednesday five or six leagues away. John Trubert and his son were handed over to the provost marshal, who expedited the trial and announced the sentence, which contained these words among others: "*John Trubert, for having seized and stolen a large mare, will be hanged and strangled, the boy along with him*"; and with that he had John Trubert and his son turned over to the high court executioner, to whom he assigned his clerk, who wasn't one of the most learned men in the world. When it was time for the execution, the executioner hanged the father good and high, and then he asked the clerk what he was to do about this young boy. The clerk read the sentence, and, after having closely examined these words, "*the boy along*," he told the executioner to do his duty, which he did, and he strung up that poor boy and strangled him, which was much worse. When the execution was over, the clerk returned to the provost, who asked him, "And what about John Trubert?" "John Trubert," the clerk said, "has been hanged." "And the boy?" the provost said. "You bet! the boy too," the clerk said. "What the devil!" the provost said, "the boy was hanged?" "By golly! yes, the boy," the clerk said. "What!" the provost said, "I didn't order that." And the provost and the clerk argued about that for a long time, the clerk saying that the sentence stated that the boy was to be hanged, and the provost the opposite; after a long argument, the provost said, "Read the sentence. Dammit! I couldn't have meant for the boy to be hanged." The clerk read the sentence with these essential words: "*John Trubert, for having seized and stolen a large mare, will be hanged and strangled, the boy along with him.*" By these words, "*along with him,*" the provost meant that John Trubert would be hanged and that his son would be present to see the execution carried out so that the example of his father would cure him from doing wrong. The provost wanted to explain these words; but it was too late for the poor boy, and the clerk, on the other hand, defended himself, saying that these words, "*along with him,*" meant that the boy was supposed to be hanged with his father. Finally, the provost didn't know what to say except that his clerk was right or had reason to be, and he only said, "*Well, so the boy's hanged. Dammit!*" he said, "we're well rid of a young wolf." That's all the compensation the poor boy received, except that the provost had him taken down for fear the news might spread.

Tale 62

OF THE YOUNG MAN WHO CALLED HIMSELF TOINETTE IN ORDER TO BE
RECEIVED IN A RELIGIOUS ORDER OF NUNS AND HOW HE UPSET THE GLASSES
OF THE ABBESS WHO EXAMINED HIM

There was a young boy between seventeen and eighteen who got into a convent of nuns one feast day and saw four or five of them whom he thought very beautiful; in fact, there wasn't one of them for whom he wouldn't have gladly broken his fast, and they became so much a part of his imagination that he thought about them constantly. One day, when he was speaking about it to a good friend of his, the friend said to him: "You know what you should do? You're a handsome fellow, dress yourself as a girl and present yourself to the abbess; she'll receive you readily; you're not known in this area." As a matter of fact, he was a handyman and travelled all around the country. He quickly accepted this advice, thinking to himself that there was no danger he couldn't easily avoid whenever he chose. He dressed as a poor girl and decided to call himself Toinette. And so, by golly, he went to these nuns' convent, and she found a way of seeing the abbess, who was very old and who very luckily didn't have a chambermaid. Toinette spoke to the abbess and told her about her situation, saying that she was a poor orphan from a nearby village, and she gave her the name. And, in fact, she spoke so humbly that the abbess found her to her liking and, as an expression of charity, decided to give her shelter, telling her that for a few days she could stay there. Toinette acted like a good girl and followed the good abbess, whom she was able to please very well, and at the same time she made all the nuns like her; and, moreover, in no time at all she learned to do needlework (perhaps she already knew something about it), which pleased the abbess so much that she immediately wanted to make her a nun. When she had her habit, which was, of course, what she wanted, she began to get very close to the ones she considered the most beautiful, and, from familiarity to familiarity, she was put to bed with one of them. She didn't wait for the second night to let her companion know, by straightforward and friendly games, that she had a horned belly, giving her to understand that it was through a miracle and the will of God. To make a long story short, she placed her peg in her companion's hole, and they were both satisfied with it; happily, he (I mean she) kept this thing up for a good while, and not only with that one, but also with three or four of the others with whom she became intimate. And when something comes to the attention of three or four people, it's easy for a fifth to know it, and then a sixth; so, among the nuns (there were only a few beautiful ones and the rest were ugly, hence — and one could make many other conjectures — Toinette wasn't as intimate with them as with the others), it was easy for them to think something or other, and they were so much on the watch that they found it out for sure, and they began to whisper about it so that the abbess soon became aware of it; it wasn't that she was told specifically that it was Sister Toinette, for she'd put her there, and, besides, she loved her very much and wouldn't really have believed it; but she was told in veiled terms that she wasn't to trust the habit and that everyone there wasn't as good as she thought and that there was one among them who was dishonoring their religion and spoiling the nuns. But, when she asked who it was and what it was, they answered that, if she wanted to make them undress, she would know. The abbess was astonished at the news and wanted to know the truth as soon as possible, and, in order to do that, she had all the nuns assemble. Sister Toinette, having been warned by her most loved ones of the abbess' intention, which was to see them completely naked, tied her peg on the end with a string which she pulled from behind, and she fixed her little condition so well that she seemed to have a cloven belly like the others to anyone who didnt' look at it very closely, and she thought that the abbess, who didn't see beyond the tip of her nose, would never be able to notice it. All the nuns came. The abbess remonstrated with them and told them why she had assembled them and ordered them to undress completely. She took out her glasses to make her inspection, and, examining them one after the other, she came to the row with Sister Toinette; but when Toinette saw these bare naked nuns, young, fair, trim, and plump, she was unable to control and stop that peg from acting up. When the abbess got as close as she could, the string broke and, springing up suddenly, the peg hit the abbess' glasses and made them fall two good steps away. The poor abbess was so surprised that she cried out: "*Jesu Maria!* Ah! there's no mistake," she said; "you are the one! But who would ever have believed it! How you have deceived me!" Nevertheless, what could she do about it, except remedy it with patience, for she wouldn't have wanted to scandalize the order? Sister Toinette was given leave to go away with the promise that she'd save the nuns' honor.

Tale 63

OF THE PROFESSOR WHO FOUGHT A FISHWIFE FROM THE PETIT PONT WITH FINE INSULTS

One day in Lent, a student went to the Petit Pont[1] and approached a fishwife to haggle over some cod; but, when she asked him for two liards, he offered only one, which angered the fishwife, and she insulted him saying, "Scram, scram, you jerk! Take your liard and shove it." When the student saw himself berated to his face that way, he threatened to report it to his professor. "Go on, squirt!" she said, "go tell him, and just let me see you here again, the two

---

[1] The Petit Pont, between the Quai St. Michel and the Quai de Montebello, leads to the square at the Cathedral of Notre-Dame.

of you!" The student didn't fail to go straight to his professor, who was a fine rascal, and said to him, "*Per diem, Domine!*[2] there's the worst old hag on the Petit Pont; I wanted to buy some cod, and she called me a jerk." "And who is she?" the professor said; "will you point her out to me?" "*Ita, Domine,*"[3] the student said; "and she also told me that, if you went there, she'd send you packing." "Leave it to me," the professor said; "*per Dies!*[4] she'll get hers." The professor thought to himself that, in order to take on such a woman, he mustn't be unprepared and the best supplies he could get would be lovely insults and he'd throw so many at her that he'd leave her *ad metam non loqui;*[5] and he quickly gave the order to gather all the insults that could be thought of; he even engaged his friends, who composed so many of them while drinking that it seemed to them there were enough. The professor wrote them on two large scrolls and learned one by heart; he put the other in his sleeve as a precaution in case the first one was inadequate. When he had thoroughly studied his insults, he called the student to come take him to the Petit Pont and point out the fishwife to him, and he took along with him a few smart alecks, whom, *in primis et ante omnia,*[6] he took to the Mule Tavern[7] for a drink; and when they'd had enough to drink, they set out. They were no sooner on the Petit Pont than the fishwife recognized the student, and, when she saw them grouped together, she realized what they were up to. "Ah! there they are!" she said; "there they are, the loudmouths! School has let out its garbage." The professor went up to her and hit the bucket in which she kept her herring, saying, "And what does this damn old hag need?" "Oh, Mister Know-it-all!" the old woman said; "did you come as soon as you could to quarrel with me?" "Who set this old bawd on me!" the professor said. "By cracky! you're really the one I have it in for." And, on saying that, he stood in front of her as though he wanted to fence with his tongue. The fishwife, seeing that she was challenged, said: "Merciful heavens! so you want

---

[2] *By God, Master*; the student muffles the oath *per deos* with the use of *diem*, day.

[3] Yes, Master.

[4] Like the lawyer La Roche Thomas in tale 14, the professor prefers the plural.

[5] Speechless, dumbfounded.

[6] among the first and before all things.

[7] A tavern in the Latin Quarter.

yours, Mister Dung? Come on, let's take turns, you big ass, and you'll see how I'll fix you. Speak, it's your turn." "You doddering old fool!" the professor said. "You lecher!" "You filthy nag!" "You scum!" As soon as they were in the thick of it, I left because I had business elsewhere. But I've heard it said by those who knew something about it that the two characters fought valiantly and threw at each other a hundred or so good and strong insults without interruption; but the professor happened to say the same one twice, for they say that he called her a "filthy nag" a second time. But the fishwife reminded him of it. "Good heavens!" she said, "you've already said it, you son-of-a-bitch." "Well! well!" the professor said, "aren't you a filthy nag twice over, if not three?" "You're a liar, you slimy toad!" Apparently, the two champions fought each other for a long time so admirably that those who watched them didn't know which of the two would have the upper hand. But, finally the professor reached the end of his first scroll, and so he took the other one out of his sleeve, but he didn't know it by heart as he did the other, and for that reason he got a little flustered, seeing that the fishwife was just getting started, and he began to read what was on it, academic insults, and he wanted to polish them off in one long tirade, thinking he'd overwhelm the old woman by saying to her, "Alecto, Megaera, Tisiphone,[8] detestable, execrable, loathsome, abominable one!" But the fishwife interrupted him: "Ha! merciful heavens!" she said, "you no longer know what you're doing; speak good French, I'll answer you, you big ninny! speak good French. Ah! you carry a scroll! Go study it, you fathead! go on, you don't know your lesson!" And, as in answer to a howling dog, all those fishwives began to hoot at him and to harass him so that the best thing he could do was to flee hurriedly; otherwise, he would have been beaten up, the poor man. And, to be sure, it was felt that, even if he'd had a Calepin,[9] a word list, a dictionary, a promptbook, a thesaurus of insults, he wouldn't have had the last word against that she-devil. So, he fled to safety in the College of Montaigu,[10] running without a break and not looking behind him.

---

[8] The three Erinyes or Furies.

[9] Calepinus' multilingual dictionary was such a standard item that just about any kind of glossary was called a *Calepin*.

[10] Famous for its harsh discipline and dirt.

Tale 64

OF THE YOUTH FROM PARIS WHO PLAYED THE FOOL IN ORDER TO ENJOY A
YOUNG WIDOW, AND HOW, WISHING TO MAKE FUN OF HIM, SHE WAS
PUT TO EVEN GREATER SHAME

A young man from Paris, who was lively, neat-looking, and from a good family, was in love with a very pretty widow, who was very happy to be loved; she constantly revealed new charms to those who gazed at her and she took pleasure in analyzing the hearts of young men. However, she paid attention only to those who appealed to her, and not necessarily the worthiest ones, and, above all, she knew how to lead on this young man I'm talking about to such an extent that she seemed to be willing to do everything for him. He spoke to her in private; he kissed and played with her breasts and he even touched her flesh frequently, but he never got any, and hence he almost died whenever he was with her. He begged her, he implored her, he gave her presents, but he could get nothing from her, except that once, when they were talking together in private and he was earnestly making his appeal, she said to him, "No, nothing doing unless you kiss my behind," and she emphasized the word, thinking to herself he would never do it. The young man was very embarrassed by this condition; nevertheless, he'd tried so many ways that he thought he might as well do that and, besides, no one would know anything about it, and he answered her that, if that was all he had to do in order to please her, he wouldn't object to it. And so, because he took her at her word, she took him up on his and had him kiss her bare behind. But, when it came to the front, there was nothing doing; she only laughed at him and made the greatest fun of him in the world; he gave up hope and left, the angriest man that ever was; nevertheless, he was unable to stay out of her sight, except that he didn't show up for a little while, ashamed of being not only in her presence, but also with other people, as if everyone knew what had happened to him. One day, he spoke to an old woman who knew the young lady well, and, in talking about his problem, he said to her, "Come now. Isn't it possible for me to have that woman? Couldn't you invent a good way to get me out of the agony I'm in? You can be sure that, if you hand her over

to me, I'll give you the best dress you've ever worn in your life."
The old woman reassured him and promised him to do all she could,
telling him that if there was a woman in Paris who could bring it
about it was she. And, in fact, she made a considerable number of
worthy efforts; but the widow, who was clever sensed that it was
for this young man, and she wouldn't hear anything of it at all,
perhaps hoping to marry him, or for some other reason she had
in mind: as you know, the crafty ones have that way of always
keeping one of their suitors on a string in order to cover up the
good time they give others. The fact remains that the old woman
could do nothing about it and she went back to the young man,
telling him that she'd used every possible means, but that there
was no way to bring it about, except that, in her opinion, if he
disguised himself, such as dressing up like a poor man to go beg
for alms at his lady's door, he'd enjoy her favors. He thought that
was feasible. "But how should I go about it?" he said. "You know
what you have to do?" the old woman said; "you have to smear
your face so that she won't recognize you, and then you have to
play the fool because she's wonderfully smart." "And how shall I
play the fool?" the young man said. "How should I know?" she said.
"You must laugh all the time and say the first word that comes to
mind, and say only that, no matter what you're asked." "I'll do just
that." And he and the old woman decided that he would only say
cheese. He dressed like a beggar and went to his lady's door at a
time in the evening when everyone was getting ready to go to bed;
and the weather was rather cold although it was after Easter. When
he was at the door, he began to laugh and shout rather loudly, "Ha!
ha! cheese!" two or three times; he paused a little, and then he
began again his "Ha! ha! cheese!" When the widow, whose room
faced the street, heard him, she sent her chambermaid to find out
who he was and what he wanted; but he never answered, except,
"Ha! ha! cheese!" The chambermaid went back to the lady and
said to her, "My goodness! Madam, it's a poor boy who's crazy; he
only laughs and says cheese." The lady wanted to know what it was
all about and went down and spoke to him: "Who are you, my
friend." And the only thing he said to her was, "Ha! ha! cheese!"
"Do you want some cheese?" she said. "Ha! ha! cheese." "Do you
want some bread?" she said. "Ha! ha! cheese!" "Go away, my
friend; leave." "Ha! ha! cheese!" The lady saw that he was an

idiot and said, "Perrette, he'll die from the cold tonight; have him come in, he'll get warm." "Upon my soul," she said, "that's a good idea, Madam. Come in, my friend, come in; you can get warm." "Ha! ha! cheese!" he said. And with that he went in, laughing inside and out, for he thought that things were beginning to look up. He went to the fire, where he displayed his rear, bare, fleshy, and plump, and the lady and the chambermaid kept peeping at it. They asked him if he wanted to drink or eat; but he said only, "Ha! ha! cheese!" Bedtime came. The lady, while undressing, said to her chambermaid, "Perrette, he's a handsome boy; it's a pity that he's such a fool." "Upon my soul," the wench said, "that's right, Madam; he has rocks in his head." "What if we put him to bed in our bed," the lady said; "what do you think?" The chambermaid began to laugh. "And why not? He can hardly give us away if he doesn't know how to say anything else." In short, they made him undress, and he didn't need a clean shirt, for his wasn't dirty, except perhaps torn, and they made him go to bed nicely between the two of them. And he got on his lady, saying to himself, "Let's go to it, you'll get your fill of it." The chambermaid did get a few strokes; but he showed that it was the lady he was interested in, and yet he never forgot his "Ha! ha! cheese!" The next day, they let him out early in the morning and he went his way; and, thereafter, he continued to go back there frequently for his prize, which pleased him no end, and, on the advice of the old woman, he never revealed his identity. In the daytime, he put his usual attire back on and returned to his lady's company, chatting with her in the accustomed manner, courting her as before, pretending there was nothing new. The month of May came, and the young man decided to wear a green doublet, saying to his lady that it was for love of her, which pleased her, and she told him that, as a return favor, she'd set him up with some ladies the first chance that came along. In this state of affairs, he found himself in the company of ladies, one of whom was his, and there were also other young men; they were in a garden, seated in a circle, each man next to a woman, and this young man was next to his lady. It was suggested that they play games and by the young widow herself; she was a clever and wily woman, and for a long time now she'd thought of how she'd make fun of the young man, whom she thought she had really tricked that other time; and so, she devised a game in which each one had to say a few brief words of love or some other sweet nothing, according to what would suit them best and whatever came to mind, and they all did it in turn. When it was the widow's turn to speak, she said with affected charm what she had already prepared:

> What would you say of a green-clad friend
> Who kissed his lady on her rear end,
>   While trying hard to please?

Everyone stared at the young man because it was easy to see that this was addressed to him, but he wasn't taken aback by it. On the contrary, consumed with poetic fury, he promptly answered the lady:

> What would you say of a green-clad friend
> Who pounded often on your rear end,
>   While saying: Ha! ha! cheese?

You needn't ask if the lady was embarrassed, for, no matter how wily she was, she was forced to change color and expression, and it made her guilty in front of the whole group; the young man got his revenge in one stroke for all the tricks of the past. This example is excellent for women who tease and confidently play hard to get because it nearly always catches up with them to their great shame. For the gods send their help and favor to lovers who are sincere, as you can see with this young man; Phoebus bestowed poetic wit upon him so that, in defending himself, he could reply promptly to the gibe that his lady had so cleverly and deliberately dreamed up against him.

Tale 65

OF THE SCHOOLBOY FROM AVIGNON AND THE OLD WOMAN WHO CHEWED HIM OUT

There was in Avignon a bunch of schoolboys who where playing tennis outside the city walls; one of them, while making his play, failed to lob the ball straight and sent it into a garden. He found a way to jump over the wall to go get it. After he had jumped, he found in the garden an old woman who was planting cabbage and who immediately began to shout at him, "And what the devil are you doing here? You're coming to steal my melons." But the schoolboy didn't heed her and kept on looking for his ball, saying to her only, "Hush, you old witch!" The old woman began to curse him roundly. When the schoolboy saw that she was hurling insults at him, he decided to have some fun with her, and he spoke to her in the first language that came to mind, saying to her, *"Cum animadverterem quam plurimos homines,"* [1] and making threatening signs at her in order to have her do battle all the better. And the old woman shouted, but it was with her Avignon accent, "Oh! you nasty boy, you thief, jumping over walls!" The schoolboy continued to tell her these beautiful precepts from Cato: *"Parentes ama."* [2] "Go to the devil!" the old woman said to the schoolboy; "may lightning strike you!" And the schoolboy answered, *"Cognatos cole."* [3] "Yes, yes, to school with you, damn it all!" And the schoolboy said, *"Cum bonis ambula!"* [4] "Don't bother me with your ball," she said; "the devil take you! You speak Italian, I know what you're saying." "Yes, yes," the schoolboy said, *"Foro te para."* [5] But, even if he had wanted to keep up with her, he would have had to say all his Cato, all his *quos decet,* [6] and he still wouldn't have had the best of her. But he left to finish his game.

---

[1] From Dionysius Cato's *Distichs*; the correct quotation is *Cum animadverterem, quam plurimos graviter in via morum errare*: When I noticed how very many go seriously wrong in their manner of living.

[2] From Cato's *Distichs*: Love thy parents.

[3] From Cato's *Distichs*: Cherish those of kin to thee.

[4] From Cato's *Distichs*: Walk with the upright.

[5] From Cato's *Distichs*; the correct quotation is *Foro parce*: Shun the market place.

[6] for whom it is fitting: first words of a children's poem written by Sulpice de Veroli in the fifteenth century.

Tale 66

OF A JUDGE FROM AIGUE-MORTES, A PASQUINADE, AND THE LATERAN COUNCIL

In the city of Aigue-Mortes, there was a judge named *De Alta domo,* [1] whose brain was made of wax; in his court, he handed down

---

[1] Of noble birth, from a great family.

very strange verdicts, and outside of his court he discoursed in the same manner. It happened one day that he got into an argument over a passage from the Bible with a sanctimonious soul who was pleased to have the judge talk nonsense. The controversy was over whether, of all the animals in the world today, there were two of each on Noah's ark. One said that there were no mice and that they're engendered by filth, as has since been confirmed by Master John Buter, [2] of the order of St. Anthony in Dauphiné, in his treatise *De Arca Noe*. The other said that there was only one hare and that the female got away from Noah and was lost in the water; and that is why the male breeds like the female. One said one thing, the other another. But in the end, the judge, who always wanted to be in the right, got angry because this fine dealer held out so well against him, and he said to him, "You don't know what you're talking about. Where did you see it?" "Where did I see it!" said the other; "it's written in Genesis." "Genesis!" said the judge; "really, you're putting me on! He's a scribbling scribe who lives in Nîmes: I know him well. He doesn't know anything about it, nor do you." And, in fact, there was in Nîmes a clerk named Genesis; and the poor judge thought he was the one whom the other meant. It goes without saying that he knew the whole Bible by heart, except the beginning, the middle, and the end. He was almost like the one of whom it is said that, when he was before King Francis and while everyone was talking about a pasquinade which had recently been posted in Rome, he wanted to speak his mind too, and he said to the king, "Sire, I've seen him, Pasquinade; he's one of the most galant men in the world." At this, the king, who recognized the man's nature, said to him, "You've seen him? Where did you see him?" "Sire," he said, "I saw him recently in Rome and he was in good form. He wore a Spanish cape trimmed with velvet and around his neck a chain worth eighty or a hundred crowns, and he had two valets with him. But he was also the wittiest man in the world, and he was always with those cardinals." "Go on! go on!" the king said, "go get the food; you're going to entertain me." There was another fine man who was produced as a witness in a case concerning a benefice and a certain decision of the Lateran Council. [3] The judge said to this good man,

---

[2] Jean de Bolton, author of several works of questionable scholarship.
[3] The Fifth Council, during which the revocation of the pragmatic sanction was approved (1517).

"Come now, my friend, do you really know what we're talking about?" "Yes, Sir; you're talking about the Lateran Council. I've seen him often enough; he wore a large red hat and always had a sash and a large game bag of crimson velvet. And I've also known his wife, Milady Pragmatic." That's how it seemed to the good man; I don't know if you believe me, but you're not damned if you don't.

Tale 67

OF THE CAVALRYMEN WHO WERE IN THE HOME OF A VILLAGE WOMAN

In the days when soldiers lived off what they got from their countrymen — they also lived off what they got from the women — a troop of them went through a village, where they did no better than those in the proverb which says: "One lawyer in a line, one walnut tree in a vineyard, one pig in a wheat field, one mole in a meadow, and one sargent in a town is enough to ruin everything." They pillaged, they ruined, they destroyed everything. There were two, or three, or four of them, I don't know how many, in a woman's home, and they were cleaning her out; and since they ate her hens, which they'd killed, she was a sorry figure, muttering with clenched teeth. But these cavalrymen mouthed off, saying to the old woman: "Aha! my good lady from Meudon, you're going to die if you keep that up. Are you that sorry about your hens? Come on now, cheer up. Repeat after me: To hell with being stingy! Say it!" Grumbling, the good woman said to him, "To hell with being plundered!" She was quite right, for

> With the warrants now in force,
> Soldiers bringing ills on high,
> Monks travelling forth by horse,
> Everything has gone awry.[1]

---

[1] Frequently quoted in the sixteenth century: see Rabelais, for example, chapter 52, Book IV.

Tale 68

OF MASTER BERTHAUD, WHO WAS MADE TO BELIEVE HE WAS DEAD

There once lived in the city of Rouen, I don't know exactly when it was, a man who provided amusement for all and sundry — when one knew how to manage him, that goes without saying. He went through the streets dressed sometimes like a sailor, sometimes like a schoolmaster, sometimes like a plum picker, but always like a fool; and he was called Master Berthaud. Perhaps he was the one who counted twenty and eleven for thirty-one; he was as proud of that title of Master as a jackass with a new packsaddle; and if a man failed to call him by it, he didn't get any fun out of him; but if you said to him, "Master Berthaud," you could make him crawl through a rat hole. And what made him such a foolish ninny was that a few fine masters in that line had watched over him for eleven nights in a row, sticking big pins in his buttocks in order to keep him from sleeping, which is naturally the best way to drive a man to perfection in the art of folly. It's true that one has to be inclined towards it, as you can imagine that Master Berthaud was. It so happens that one day he fell into the hands of some good people who took him to the fields, and, on the way, they had as much fun with him as they could; they began to make him believe that he was ill and had him confessed by one who played a priest; they had him draw up his will, and finally they gave him to understand that he was dead, and he believed it principally because while burying him they said, "Hey! poor Master Berthaud's dead. We'll never see him; alas! no." And they put him in a cart which was coming back from town and they constantly sang *Libera me domine* [1] over the body of Master Berthaud, and he played dead the best he knew how. But there were some among them who made him feel that he was still alive, for they pricked his buttocks with pins, as I said before; however, he didn't dare notice it for fear of not being dead; and sometimes he even tried to pull his buttocks in when he felt the pinpricks. But finally, one of them pricked him so hard that he

---

[1] Deliver me, O Lord; first words of the Responsory sung after the mass for the dead.

could no longer endure it, and he was forced to raise his head, saying very angrily to the first one he saw, "By God, you miscreant, if I were as alive as I'm dead, I'd kill you right now." And, all of a sudden, he went back to playing dead, and he didn't stir again regardless of what they did to him, until someone said, "Ah! poor Berthaud's dead." Then our man got up. "You're lying," he said; "you didn't call me Master. Now then, I'm not dead out of spite." And that's how Master Berthaud came back to life because he hadn't been called Master.

There's another story about a Master Jourdain, who thought he was a little smarter than the former although it was hard to tell. There was a porter who, while carrying his loads around town, bumped into him rather tactlessly, that is to say rather hard, and then he told him to look out; it should have been earlier or never; Master Jourdain said to him, "Come now, why did you do that, you gallows bird? By God, if I weren't a philosopher, I'd knock your brains in, you big blockhead." Both of them had a claim to that name; indeed, one was a fool and the other a philofool.

Tale 69

OF THE MAN FROM POITOU WHO GIVES DIRECTIONS TO TRAVELLERS

There are many ways of practicing patience, like women who rebuke a valet who chatters, or who grumbles, or who doesn't listen at all, and who brings you slippers when you asked for your sword or your bonnet instead of your belt, and puts a piece of green wood in the fire when you're dying of cold so that you have to burn all the straw from the bed before it catches fire; or it can be a horse which picks up a nail or loses a shoe along the road, or which gets stung at every step, and the other hundred thousand misfortunes that can happen. But those are too exasperating; they're to be wished on your enemies. There are others which aren't so hard to put up with because they don't last as long, and they're even of such a nature that one is then happier for having experienced them and profited from them. Such adventures are good for young people in order to teach them to curb their anger a little. One of them is the encounter of a man from Poitou when you're travelling: for instance, imagine your being in a hurry and that the weather is cold or somehow disagreable; in short, you're frustrated by something or other, and by chance you don't know your way; you start out asking him, "Hey, you! my friend, where's the road to Parthenay?" The plowman, although he hears you, is in no hurry to answer; but he talks to his oxen: "Garea, Frementin, Brichet, Castain, come on, you're just clopping along!" He says this to each ox and lets you shout two or three times good and loud. Then, when he sees that you're angry and that you want to ride straight up to him, he whistles to his oxen to stop them and says to you, "What are you saying?" But it's much more charming in the speech of the region: "Whasay?" You can imagine how pleasant it is for you when you've been there for so long burning up and shouting yourself hoarse and this cowherd asks you what you're saying; so you have to say, "Where's the road to Parthenay?" "Well now! To Parthenay, Mister?" he'll say to you. "Yes, to Parthenay; a pox upon you!" "And where do you come from, Mister?" he'll say. "Either you're out of your mind or you act like it! Where do I come from! Where's the road to Parthenay?" "Do you want to go there, Mister? Now then, be patient." "Yes, my friend, I'm going there. Where's the road?" Then, he'll call another cowherd nearby, and he'll say to him, "Mike, this man is asking about the road to Parthenay; doesn't it go down that way?" The other will answer (if it's God's will), "Oh, it seems to me it's that way!" While the two of them are there arguing about your road, it's your turn to wonder if you'll go crazy or become wise. In the end, after the two men have thoroughly thrashed it out together, one of them will say to you, "When you get to that large cross, turn right and go straight ahead, you can't miss." Do you understand now? Go on confidently, you'll make out all right today; you've been very well directed. Then when you're in the city, if by chance it's market day and you're going to buy something, you'll deal with fine and clever merchants: "My friend, how much for this young goat?" "This goat, Mister?" "Yes." "Do you want it with its mother? Really, this is a good goat!" "Yes, indeed! it's a very good one. How much are you selling it for?" "Think about it, Mister, it has a thick neck." "Yes, but how much?" "Mister, its mother has only had two so far." "Ha! I understand; but how much will it cost me?" "All you want is a word? I know I mustn't try to overcharge you." "But how much shall I give you for it?" "Upon my word! it won't cost you less than five and a half sous." "That's your price?" "Take it or leave it."

Tale 70

OF THE MAN FROM POITOU AND THE OFFICER WHO PUT HIS CART AND OXEN IN THE KING'S HANDS

I'm not going to while away the time at this point telling you other tales about men from Poitou, which are undoubtedly very pleasant; but you'd have to know the dialect of the region in order to enjoy them, and, besides, the greatest charm of all lies in the pronunciation; but I can at least tell you one more while I'm at it. There was a man from Poitou who, because he hadn't paid his taxes, had had his property seized by an officer, who, serving the writ as he'd been ordered, placed the poor man's cart and oxen in the king's hands; the man was rather upset about it, but he had to put up with it. It happened some time later that the king went to Châtellerault. When he found out about it, this fellow, who was from La Tircherie, decided to go there to see the hunt, and he maneuvered so that he saw the king as he was going hunting. As soon as he'd seen him and having nothing else to do at court, the man went back to the village. And, while dining with his fellow cowherds, he said to them, "Holy Mother of God! I was as close to the king as I am to that dog; he has a face like any man; I'm really going to talk to that fine officer who day before yesterday put my cart and oxen in the king's hands. Holy Mother of God! His hands aren't any bigger than mine." This man had the impression that the king was as tall as the steeple at St. Hilary's and that his hands were as large as oaks and his cart and oxen ought to be in them. But why don't I tell you another one?

Tale 71

OF ANOTHER MAN FROM POITOU AND HIS SON MIKE

There was a working man who was rather well off and who had taken his two sons to Poitiers to study at the university with the ignoramuses; they roomed with other fellows from Poitou near the Crowned Ox. The elder was named Michael and the other William. Their father housed them, took note of the place where they were staying, and he left them there. They were there for a rather long time without writing to him, and he was even happy to get news of them from friends and neighbors who sometimes went to Poitiers and through whom he sometimes sent his children cheeses, hams, and well-mended shoes. It happened that both of them got sick, and the younger one died; the elder one, who wasn't well yet, wasn't fit enough to write to his father about his brother's death. A little while later, the father was told that one of his children had died; but they couldn't tell him which one it was. Because he was very frustrated over this, he had the parish curate write a letter, which was addressed: To my son Mike, living at the King of the Oxen, or nearby; and inside the letter there was, among other fine remarks, the following: "Mike, let me know who died, you or your brother Will; I'm very troubled over it. Moreover, I want you to know that our bishop is in Dissai. Go get tonsured there, and have it done good and well so that you won't have to have it done twice." Master Mike was so pleased to have received this letter from his father that he immediately got completely well, and he got up to write his answer, which was full of the rhetoric he'd learned at Poitiers, but I won't render it here for the sake of brevity; but among other things there was this: "Father, I want you to know that I'm not the one who's dead, but my brother Will is; it's quite true that I was sicker than he was; in fact, my skin fell off as it does on a little pig." Wasn't that an excellent answer? Truly, whoever would like to say the opposite would really be out to find fault.

Tale 72

OF THE GENTLEMAN FROM BEAUCE AND HIS DINNER

One of the gentlemen from Beauce — they say that they're two to a horse when they travel through the country, — had dined rather early and very lightly on a certain meat they prepare in that region with flour and a few egg yolks; but, frankly, I couldn't tell you in detail how you make it: the fact remains that it's a sort of stew, and I've heard it called *caudelée*. [1] This gentleman made his dinner out of it. But he ate it so diligently that he didn't have time to lick his lips clean, and small morsels of the *caudelée* remained, and in this state he went to see one of his neighbors, according to the habit they had of visiting in one another's home and of catting around the countryside together. He walked in on his neighbor just as he was getting ready to sit down to eat, and he began to speak spiritedly: "What," he said, "you haven't eaten yet!" "But you," said the other, "have you eaten already?" "Of course, I've eaten!" he said, "yes, and very well; in fact, I made a feast out of a couple of partridges, and there were only my wife and I; I'm sorry you didn't come to eat your share of it." The other, who knew very well what he lived on most of the time, answered him, "You're telling the truth, you've eaten some good partridges, there's still a bit of feather left there," and he pointed to this piece of *caudelée* which had stuck to his beard. The gentleman was quite embarrassed whe he saw that his *caudelée* had exposed his partridges.

---

[1] Modern French *chaudeau* and English *caudle* are fair approximations.

Tale 73

OF THE PRIEST WHO ATE FOR LUNCH THE ENTIRE ALLOWANCE
OF THE MONKS OF BEAULIEU

In the city of Le Mans there was a priest who was called Father John Melaine; he was an excessive eater, and he devoured the portions of at least nine or ten people in one meal. And his youth had been a rather happy one: indeed, up to the age of thirty or thirty-five, he always found people who took pleasure in feeding him, particularly those canons who fought over who would have John Melaine in order to have fun stuffing him. As a result, he sometimes went around for a week having dinner and supper here and there in turn. But, when hard times set in, they began to withdraw, and they let poor Father John Melaine fast; he became as dry as a log and his stomach as hollow as a lantern; and the poor man lived too long, for his thirty deniers [1] weren't enough to buy him the bread he

---

[1] The price of a mass; see tale 22.

ate. However, in the days when things were still going well for him, there was an abbot at Beaulieu who fed him rather often, and on one occasion he set out to have him so filled up that he'd have enough. There was a commemorative service at the abbey, and many priests were there, including Father John Melaine. The abbot said to his cellarer, "You know what we're going to do? Give lunch to Father John, and give him so much to eat that he won't be able to put it all down." And with that he himself said to the priest, "Father John, as soon as you've said mass, go to the larder and ask for lunch, and have a good feed, understand? I told them to give you whatever you wish." "Thank you very much, Father," the priest said. He dashed off his mass, which he said on the fly, because his heart was set on food. He went to the larder, where as a first course he was provided with a large piece of the monks' beef, a huge loaf of coarse bread, and a good quart of wine, as they measure it out in that area. He dispatched that in less time than a clock would have struck ten because all he did was gulp down these pieces. He was brought again as much, and he dispatched that right away. The cellarer, seeing the man's hearty appetite and remembering the abbot's instructions, had two more pieces of beef brought to him at the same time, and he immediately put them in the same bag with the others. In short, he ate everything that had been set out for the monks' dinner: they did what was done at Arras when the King laid siege, [2] they dragged out every last piece, and so they were forced to cook others in a hurry. Meanwhile, the abbot walked in the gardens, waiting for Father John to finish lunch; the latter, having eaten his fill, left to go on his way. The abbot, who saw him leaving, asked him, "Well now, Father John, have you had lunch?" "Yes, Father, my thanks to God and you," the priest said; "I had a bite and drank once while waiting for dinner." In your opinion, how could he expect a good dinner when there was hardly anything left?

Another time on Friday, he was given for lunch a large bowl full of pea stew and enough sop bread for six or seven vineyard workers. But the one who prepared it for him knew the patient, and so he put in the peas two large handfulls of round cod fish bones, called paternosters, with a lot of butter and verjuice, and he presented it

---

[2] Louis XI, in 1477, threw every piece of artillery he had against the fortifications of Arras.

to Father John, who dispatched it without so much as a by-your-leave, and he ate the paternosters and all. And I believe he would have eaten the *Ave Maria* and the *Credo* if they'd been there. Of course, those bones cracked occasionally between his teeth; but they went down just the same. When he was through, he was asked, "Well! Father John, were those peas good?" "Yes, sir, thanks to God and you: but they weren't thoroughly cooked." Didn't this one live well for a priest? God did a lot for us here below by having him in the Church: if he'd been a merchant, he would have starved every road to Paris, Lyons, Flanders, Germany, and Italy. If he'd been a butcher, he would have eaten all his cows and sheep, horns and all. If he'd been a lawyer, he would have eaten papers and scrolls, which wouldn't have been a great pity; he would have done much worse because he would have eaten up his clients although others eat them up just as well. If he'd been a soldier, he would have eaten armor, headpieces, harquebuses, and all the powder kegs. And if he'd been married on top of all that, you can imagine that his poor wife wouldn't have gotten a better bargain from him than the wife of Cambles, [3] King of Lydia, who ate her completely up one night. May God help us, what a king! He surely must have eaten others.

---

[3] Perhaps an allusion to Candaules, eighth century B. C.?

Tale 74

OF JEHAN DOINGÉ, WHO CHANGED HIS NAME ON HIS FATHER'S ORDERS

In the great city of Paris there was a gentleman of note and quality, a man of great learning and judgment, who was called Mister Doingé; [1] but, since it does happen that learned men don't readily produce the brightest children in the world (I believe it's because they leave their minds in their studies when they go to bed with their wives), the one I'm talking about had a son who was already grown, named Jehan Doingé, and the thing in which he resembled his father the least was his mind. One day when his father was busy

---

[1] Anagram of Gédoin. Robert Gédoin was in the service of Louis XI, Charles VIII, Louis XII, and Francis I.

writing or studying, this virtuous son stood there before him like a statue, staring at his father without doing anything but with the appearance of a man who'd gotten his day's pay. Finally, his father became annoyed with this and said to him, "Hey, my friend, what are you doing for the king here? Why don't you go do something?" "Sir," he said to his father, "what would you like for me to do? I don't have anything to do." The father, seeing this good-natured soul, said to him: "You don't know what to do, poor man! Well, go change your name." His father said these words to him as one usually says them to a man who dislikes work, but Master Jehan took them at face value and favorably. And he immediately went and shut himself up in his study in order to turn his name all around. First, he worked out Doingé Jehan, then Jehan Gedoin, then Gedoin Jehan. And then he went to show all these samples of his name to one of his young friends, and he asked him if it was well changed that way; but the other told him that, in order to change his name, it wasn't enough to switch the syllables back and forth, but that he had to mix the letters up and make a good motto out of them. The man immediately returned home to shut himself up, and he began to cut his name up again more than ever; he went at it two or three days and forgot to eat and drink, not daring to appear before his father until that name was changed. Finally, he turned and twisted it so that he came up with two of the most suitable possibilities in the world, and this pleased him so much that he laughed all by himself walking back and forth, and it was like a thousand years to him waiting for the opportunity to tell his father; when he saw his chance, he went to tell him all in a rush, as though he wanted to catch him by surprise: "Sir," he said, "I changed it." His father, who was thinking about everything else but this name change, was astounded, both because he hadn't seen him at all for those two days and also because he now heard him speak meaninglessly. "You've changed it?" he said; "and what did you change?" "Sir, you told me on Monday to go change my name. I've not stopped working on it since; but finally I managed it." "Really! I'm grateful to you," the father said; "so you changed it, and what did you come up with, you poor man?" "Sir," he said, "I changed it many ways, but I only found two good ones. I lit on Janin Godé and Angin d'oye." [2]

---

[2] John the drunkard and Goose tool.

"Really!" his father said, "I'll take your word for it; you certainly didn't waste your time." Now wasn't that a fine son? Gypsies could certainly tell him: Your father is fine and your mother is too, but the child is hardly worth a sou. Someone will tell me: Fine, but we don't write engine with an *a*. No, but what do you want? You want a man to lose a beautiful motto like that for the sake of a single letter?

Tale 75

OF JANIN, WHO WAS NEWLY WED

Janin wanted to get married too, and so he took a wife who played around and who didn't make any secret of it because she didn't want to do any harm to her husband's good name. One day, one of Janin's neighbors asked him some questions, and he gave him the answers in the form of a rather amusing farce. "Say, Janin, are you married?" And Janin replied: "Yes, indeed!" "That's good," the other said. "Not too good, really," Janin said. "And why?" "She's too unruly." "That's bad." "Not too bad, really." "And why?" "And why? She's one of the beauties in our parish." "That's good." "Not too good either." "And why?" "There's a gentleman who comes to see her at all hours." "That's bad." "Not too bad, really." "And why?" "He always gives me something." "That's good." "Not too good either." "And why?" "He always sends me here and there." "That's bad." "Not too bad, really." "And why?" "He gives me money, and I have a good time with it along the roads." "That's good." "Not too good either." "And why?" "I'm out in the rain and wind." "That's bad." "Not too bad, really." "And why?" "I'm very used to it." Finish the rest if you wish; you can stretch this one all you want.

Tale 76

OF THE LAW STUDENT WHO WANTED TO PRATICE LECTURING AND THE SPEECH HE MADE AT HIS FIRST LECTURE

A law student in Poitiers had gained a fair amount from his law studies, and he didn't know too much either; he didn't have much confidence or means of explaining his knowledge. And because he was the son of a lawyer, his father, who had gone through it, told him to start lecturing so that he might improve his memory through practice. In order to obey his father's wish, he decided to lecture at the law school in Poitiers. And, in order to give himself greater confidence, he went every day into a garden which was far from the house and rather secluded and which had big beautiful cabbages. For a long time, as soon as he had studied, he went to give his lecture in front of those cabbages, calling them *domini* and quoting his paragraphs to them, just as though they were a student audience. When he'd prepared himself this way for two or three weeks, he decided it was time to go up to the rostrum, thinking that he'd speak as well before the students as he did before his cabbages. He presented himself and began to give his speech. But, before he could say a dozen words, he was so nonplused that he was at a complete loss, so much so that he was unable to say anything, except *Domini, ego bene video quod non estis caules*, that is to say (for there are those who wish to have theirs translated), "Gentlemen, I see that you are not cabbages." When he was in the garden, he could assume that the cabbages were students; but, when he was on the rostrum, he couldn't assume that the students were cabbages.

Tale 77

OF THE GOOD DRUNKARD JANICOT AND HIS WIFE JANETTE

In Paris, where there are so many kinds of people, there was a tailor named Janicot, who was never avaricious, for all the money he earned was for drinking. He liked this trade so much and got so used to it that he had to give up tailoring because when he returned from the tavern and wanted to get back to work he missed the mark while threading his needle, just as newlyweds do; and he thought that one piece of thread was really two, and he'd just as soon sew a sleeve on the back as on the front: it was all the same to him. Hence, he completely gave up that bothersome tailoring in order to retire to the pleasant trade of drinking, which he kept up valiantly: in fact, from the moment he was within the depths of a tavern, he didn't budge until nighttime, except when his wife occasionally went to get him and subjected him to a thousand insults; but he swallowed them all with a glass of wine. Frequently, he flattered her so much that he got her to sit down next to him, saying to her, "Try a little of this wine, my love: it's the best you've ever had." "I don't need a drink," she said; "you drunk! Are you coming?" "Hey! Janette, you can drink as little as you want." In the end, she gave in, for the good woman said to herself, "I might just as well since I pay for everything; I ought to drink my share." It's true that she was a little more discreet than Janicot because she never got so loaded that she couldn't lead him back to the house; but you can imagine that it was hard to separate Janicot from the tankard. On another occasion, when she was bothering him, he said to her, "Janette, you know who I saw yesterday: that gentleman, you know what I mean? I won't say a word about it, Janette; but let me drink; go away, my love, I'll be home as soon as you." And he went on drinking; then, when he was on his way home, — which was never before he was completely loaded, — it was easier to figure out where he was coming from than where he was going, for the street wasn't wide enough for him; he staggered, tottered, and stumbled. He always bumped into a workshop, or, when it was dark, into a cart, and he always got a bump on his forehead; but it healed before he noticed it. He often fell from the top of a stairway or through the trap door of a cellar; but he never hurt himself: God always helped him. And, if you ask me where he got the money to pay for it all, I'll tell you that there wasn't a dish or a bowl that didn't go towards it. Tablecloths, bedcovers, he sold everything; when his wife was somewhere on an errand, he sold her girdle if he could get it, her bonnets, her dress if necessary. But why wouldn't he have pawned all that when he even pawned his wife to whoever gave him money for drinking? And so he always had a payer around because what the hole above spent the one below guaranteed. As it turns out, Janicot always had his three-quart bottle, which he kept near him all night, and he took a nip every time he woke up; and even while he slept, he dreamed only of his bottle, and he was so handy at it that he grabbed it while sound asleep and picked it up to drink just as though he were awake. Since she knew this, his wife very often beat him to it and drank the wine out of his bottle; then she filled it with water, and poor Janicot drank it while sleeping. And he frequently awakened at this taste of water which made his mouth feel tasteless all over; but, with that complaint, he went back to sleep, without making much noise. And also, most of the time there was a third party in the same bed, and he danced the horizontal whoopee with his wife; but none of that did him any harm. Sometimes he took it into his head to put water in his wine; but it was with the point of a knife, which he wet in the ewer, and he let a drop fall in his glass, and no more. You'd never have found him without a ham bone in his pouch. He loved only sausages, cheese from Milan, sardines, red herrings, and all such wine teasers. He hated apples and salads like poison; when he heard custards and tarts hawked in the streets, he plugged his ears. His eyes were rimmed with bright scarlet, and, one day when they were bothering him, his wife had a freshwater doctor forbid him to drink wine; but you could have struck any other bargain with him rather than that one because he preferred to lose the windows instead of the whole house. And, when he was told that he could wash his eyes with white wine, he said, "Ah! what's the use of washing yourself with it on the outside? That's just so much wasted. Isn't it better to drink it until it comes out of your eyes and wash yourself inside and out?" When it hailed, he threw himself on his knees and, in a loud voice, pitied only the vineyards. And when he was told, "Hey, Janicot, what about the wheat?" he said, "The wheat? With a piece of bread as big as a nut, I'll drink a quart of wine: I don't care about wheat; there'll have to be very little of it for there not to be enough for me." And this was when he was in his right senses: indeed, some say that after he acquired his habit he never sobered up again; and they even maintain that all his blood turned to wine. Consequently, he spoke only of wine, and, had he been a priest, he would have sung mass only with wine, so addicted to wine was he. It's very true that he had to die in his turn. Therefore, two or three days before his death, his wine was taken away from him, and he complied with the greatest regret in the world, saying that they were killing him and that he'd die only for lack of something to drink. And, when it was time to confess, he didn't remember having done anything wrong, except that he'd drunk, and he was unable to speak to his confessor about anything but wine. He confessed how many times he'd drunk some which wasn't any good, and he was sorry about that and asked God's forgiveness. Then, when he saw that he had to go drink elsewhere, he ordered in his will that he be buried in a wine cellar, under a wine cask, and that his head be placed under the spigot so that the wine would fall into his mouth in order to quench his thirst: as a matter of fact, he'd noticed at the Holy Innocents cemetery that the dead have very dry mouths. Notice what a good philosopher he was to think that men maintain after death their taste for what they loved in life. It's wine which thus makes man think that nothing is impossible for him. Others say that he wanted to be buried at the foot of a vinestock and that since then the stock has never ceased to bear more and more fruit: in fact, when the whole vineyard was damaged by hail, they noticed that the vinestock had held out and produced as much or more than ever. I leave it up to you as to whether it's true and, if so, how.

Tale 78

OF A GENTLEMAN WHO PUT HIS TONGUE IN A YOUNG LADY'S MOUTH WHILE KISSING HER

In the city of Montpellier, a gentleman who had recently arrived there was at a party where there was dancing. Among the ladies who were in that gathering, there was a very lovely woman who was a widow and still young. I think they were dancing the Piedmontese dance, in which it's a question of kissing each other. It happened that the gentleman paired off with this young widow. When the time came to kiss, he decided to do it as they do it in Italy where he'd been: so, when he kissed her, he put his tongue in her mouth. That fashion was then very new in France and still is today, but not as much as then: in fact, the French are quickly beginning to find nothing wrong, particularly in such matters. The young woman was a little surprised by this penetrative kiss, and, although she wasn't able to take offence, nevertheless, she looked at the gentleman reprovingly and was unable to keep quiet about it; a short time later, she talked about it in a group she was in, and one person who was there and whom it concerned perhaps in some way said this: "How did you put up with that, Madam? That's something which is done in Rome and Venice while kissing courtesans." The lady was very angry because she understood by that that the gentleman took her for something she was not. As a result of this person's insistence, she decided that, if she left the matter alone, she'd greatly wrong her honor. Therefore, she thought of one means and another to seek redress from the gentleman, but she found no better expedient than to deal with him through legal means in order to call him to account and do herself credit. To make a long story short, she immediately obtained a personal summons against the man, owing to the support she had in the city, and he never suspected anything until he was summoned to appear in court. And, because he wasn't from the city, although he wasn't from far away, his friends advised him to go away for a little while, pointing out to him that he couldn't win and that, because she was related to the judges and lawyers, she could take such action against him that he'd regret it; after all, there was no denying the act, as he himself had admitted it in a few gatherings in which he'd been since. But he was rather confident and didn't take it seriously, and he answered that he wouldn't run away because of that and that he knew exactly what he had to do. When the appointed day came, he appeared in court, and there was a rather good crowd to hear the discussion over this dispute, which was well-known throughout the city. He was asked one thing and another: If on such a day he hadn't been in such a dance? He answered yes. If he didn't know the complaining lady well? He answered that he knew her only by sight and that he'd certainly like to know her better. If he wanted to say or maintain that she was other than an honorable woman? He answered no. If it were not true that on such an evening he had kissed her? He answered yes. "Yes, but you've done her a great dishonor, as she complains." And he denied it. "You put your tongue in her mouth." "Well! And what if I did?" he said. "That's only done (the judge said) to women of ill repute; you weren't supposed to do that."

When he saw himself pressed that way, he answered, "She says that I put my tongue in her mouth; as for me, I don't remember it; but why did she open her mouth, fool that she is?" As if to say: If she hadn't opened it, I wouldn't have put anything in it. But for those who understand it, it's a little more charming in the language of the country: *Et per che badave, la bestia?* That is to say: Why did she gape, the dummy? Yes, but what was said about it? They laughed about it, and the case was dismissed, on condition, however, that in the future, she would close her mouth when she let herself be kissed.

Tale 79

OF THE PICKPOCKETS AND THE PRIEST WHO HAD SOLD HIS WHEAT

There's no trade in the world which requires greater skill than that of pickpockets because these fine people have to deal with men, women, gentlemen, lawyers, merchants, and priests, whom I should have mentioned first; in short, with all sorts of people, except perhaps with Franciscans, although there are some who still carry money, notwithstanding the Franciscan prohibition. But they keep it so well hidden that the poor pickpockets can't get to it. With all the business they have with everyone mentioned above, the worst and most outrageous part of it all is that they rob you in your presence and of what you hold most dear. And then they know very well what's at stake for them; and, therefore, you can imagine how they must conceive of their estate and in how many ways. I'll tell you only two or three of their tricks, which I heard were rather subtle ones; however, I don't want to say that they don't do others that are just as good, indeed better ones when necessary. I say then that in the city of Toulouse one of these good merchants I've been talking about was caught. I don't know if he was one of the craftiest among them; but I should think not, since he let himself get caught and then hanged, which was even worse; but the pitcher goes so often to the well that at last it breaks. The fact remains that while he was in prison, he informed against his companions, tricked by the promise of immunity, and he began to reveal very many lovely tricks of the trade, of which this was one: one day the pickpockets, who were in a gang of at least ten or twelve, were at the square in Toulouse on a market day and they saw a priest receive forty or fifty francs and a fine payment for some wheat he'd sold, and he put the coins in a pouch he carried at his side (you can be sure that he didn't carry it on his head); these cunning fellows were very delighted with this, for they wouldn't have taken a penny less for it. And, because the booty was good, they began to stand near one another because that was where they had to work it out and nowhere else; and they began to crowd around the priest as close as they could; he was as careful with his pouch as a beggar with his packsack because, when he was in a crowd, he always had his hand on it suspecting mischief, and his impression was that everyone he saw was a purse and pouch snatcher. Meanwhile, these companions pressed around him, turning and whirling him about in the crowd, pretending to be in a hurry to pass in order to find a way to snatch that pouch; but, no matter what harassment they came up with, the priest didn't take his hand off his prize, and they were very angry and astonished that a priest was giving them so much trouble; and, in fact, the one who recounted it told the judge who was questioning him that he'd been in on a hundred put-up jobs, but that he'd never seen a man more determined to keep up his guard than this priest or who had less desire to lose his purse. Now, they had sworn that they would get it. What did they do while pushing him around that way in the crowd? They worked to such good purpose that they brought him near a large pile of wooden shoes, *alias* sabots, which they call clodhoppers in that region (if I remember well) and which are pointed at the tip for elegance. (You see, they even make elegant sabots!). When he saw this, one of them, as they're all quick to profit by everything, pushed one of these clodhoppers with his foot and kicked it hard against the priest's leg; he felt a great deal of pain, and he was unable to keep from putting his hand on his leg because a pain like that makes one forget everything else; but no sooner had he let go of the pouch than that skillful fellow took it away from him. The priest, with all his pain, wanted to put his hand back on what he held so dear; but he found nothing more than the strings, and he began to shout louder than he had about his leg; but the pouch was already in the hands of a third, indeed of a fourth, if necessary, because in such undertakings they help each other out marvelously well. Thus, the poor priest left as the loser of his wheat, wounded in his leg and having lost his pouch and his money. Some people are so scrupulous that they'd say it was a sin to sell the Church's goods. But I'm not saying anything about that; I prefer to tell you another tale.

Tale 80

OF THE SAME PICKPOCKETS AND PROVOST LA VOULTE

You have to understand that the best decision the pickpockets made was to keep themselves well-dressed: after all, when they were poorly dressed, they wouldn't have dared to go among people of importance, who are in places where they have the greatest business; or, if they were there, you had to stand on your guard against them because poorly dressed men, even if they are churchy people, are taken as spies everytime. It so happens that one day, when King Francis was at Blois, some of those fine merchants in question were there, and they were all dressed as gentlemen: one of them got caught plying his trade in the lower courtyard at Blois; he was immediately brought before Monsieur La Voulte,[1] a man who did away in his time with many a person's fever. I'm mistaken: he threw them into a fever, but he had the doctor with him, and he cured it. When this pickpocket was before the provost, many people gathered around him, as everyone runs to such cases as to a fire, in order to meet this handicraftsman as well as to see the provost's manner, for he was a vicious and dangerous fool with that neck wringer of his. Now, the other pickpockets also stood nearby, pretending to be honest men, in order to hear the examination the provost would make of their companion and also to put to use a good chance, if it presented itself, since in such a place people aren't particularly careful: they don't think that there might be more than one wolf in the woods, and there are perhaps more than ten. And then, who would think that there would be some so bold as to steal in the very place where a thief is on trial? But someone was taken in. Now, guess who it was; you won't figure it out straight off. Hot damn! It was the provost: while he was examining the one he had in his grasp with regard to the purse that had been stolen, there was one in the crowd who stole his from his sleeve and deftly handed it over to his companion and friend. The provost, no matter how

---

[1] François Dupatault, Lord de La Voulte, a dreadful man and a provost in 1545.

attentive he was to this prisoner, noticed all the same that someone was poking about in his sleeve. He felt for it and found that his purse was gone, and it upset him no end; and, seeing around him only honest people, or at least well-dressed people, he didn't know whom to blame. But, without a moment's warning, he seized the gentleman nearest him, saying to him, "Are you the one who took my purse?" "Not so fast! Monsieur La Voulte," the gentleman said to him, "go back to your hiding, you didn't guess right; blame somebody besides me." The provost was in despair. And the best part was that, while he was busy inquiring about his purse, the one he held got away from him and made off in the crowd. So, out of pure spite, La Voulte hanged a dozen others whom he held prisoner, and then he held their trial.

Tale 81

OF THE SAME ONES AGAIN AND THE CUTLER
WHOSE PURSE WAS SNATCHED

At Moulins, in Bourbonnais, there was a man who had the reputation of making the best knives in the whole province; attracted by this talk, one of these venerable pickpockets went to Moulins to look up this cutler in order to have a knife made, thinking that while touring that area he could pay for his trip on the highways as well as in the town. When he reached Moulins (and I'm not saying anything about what he did on the way), he went to see the cutler and said to him, "My friend, will you make me a knife exactly as I describe it to you?" The cutler answered that he could do it if any man in Moulins could. "My friend," this honest man said, "the design isn't particularly difficult; the main thing is that it cut well, and I'd like it as a sharp as a razor." "Well!" the cutler said, calling him "Sir" (for he saw that he was well-dressed), "don't worry about the cutting edge; just tell me how you want it." "My friend," he said, "I want it so long and in such a shape." And he didn't forget to sketch it all out for him just as he needed it, saying to him, "My friend (he did want to butter him up), just make it for me, and don't worry about the price; I'll pay you whatever you say." He left. The cutler set about making the knife, and it was ready at the appointed time. The other came to get it and found it to his liking and according to his requirements. He took a coin out of his pocket and gave it to the cutler; and, as such people are always on the lookout to see if luck will send them some booty, he saw that his cutler, in order to put the coin away, took his purse from his sleeve, where they kept them in those days, and it was passed through a slit in the sleeve of the jacket or doublet. As soon as the crafty fellow saw the purse in the open, he began to badger the cutler with a few ready remarks and distracted him so that he made him forget to put his purse back in his sleeve, and he let it dangle without looking out for it. Since this purse was such good game, the wily fellow kept near his prey, talking to him very familiarly and at close quarters, and already he was his cousin. From one thing to another, the cutler ventured to say to him, "But, Sir, I hope you won't be offended if I ask you what this knife is for? I've made all kinds in my life, but I never made any like this one." "My friend," he said, "if you knew what it was good for, you'd be amazed." "And for what? Tell me, please." "You won't tell?" the pickpocket said. "No," the cutler said, "I promise." The pickpocket drew near as if to tell him a secret and whispered to him, "It's for cutting off purses." And, on saying that, he brought about his knife's first masterpiece, for he didn't fail to cut off the purse which was dangling that way; then after having cut off his purse, he cut off the chitchat and went looking for business here and there throughout the city, and he performed several grand acts of his trade with the knife; but I think he became so fond of that place that during a sermon he was caught cutting off the purse of a young man from that city (as it always happens to the men in that trade, they're caught sooner or later); indeed, all foxes finally end up at the furrier's. After he'd been in prison for a few days, he was promised (according to custom) that no harm would come to him if he decided to speak freely and tell the truth as required in such a case; with this promise, he began to own up and tell all he knew. The cutler's case was included in his examination because he'd heard that this pickpocket had been caught and he'd come to take action and complain to the court; the provost (for such persons are not willingly remanded to the bishop) said to him, laughing like an innkeeper at the expense of his guest, "Come now. You were very bad to cut off this cutler's purse when he fashioned for you the tool you need to earn your living." "Hey! Sir," he said, "who wouldn't have cut it off? It was hanging down to his knees." But the provost, after all the games, sent him to the gallows to be hanged.

Tale 82

OF THE HIGHWAY ROBBER CAMBAIRE AND THE ANSWER HE GAVE THE HIGH COURT

In the judicial district of Toulouse there was a famous highway robber, who went by the name of Cambaire, and he'd formerly been in the king's service and in charge of infantrymen, and he had acquired a reputation as a brave and bold captain; but he'd been discharged with some others when the wars were over, and out of resentment and necessity he had become a bandit in the mountains and surrounding areas. He did so well at this trade that he immediately became the most famous of his companions; the High Court had him so pursued that he was finally charged and taken to prison, where he was but a short while before his case was tried and settled; he was summarily sentenced to death for the outrageous deeds he had committed and perpetrated. And, although the prosecution charged him with several crimes and offences, the least of which was enough for him to lose his life, nevertheless, the Court did not apply its usual severity, for it is said: the sternness of Toulouse, the humanity of Bordeaux, the compassion of Rouen, the justice of Paris, bloody beef, bleating mutton, and rotten pork, and none of it's worth anything if it isn't well cooked. But the Court had a certain regard for this Cambaire, and it wanted him to understand that before he died. The president sent for him and said as follows: "Cambaire, you must thank the Court for the mercy it is showing you; you deserve a very severe punishment for the deeds of which you've been accused and convicted; but, because in the past you were in the right places serving the king, the Court is satisfied to condemn you only to the loss of your head." Cambaire listened to this speech and answered immediately in his Gascon dialect, "God almighty! I'll gladly give you the rest, you prick." And, in truth, the rest couldn't be worth very much without a head, seeing that the whole wasn't worth anything. But because of this answer, he fared very badly: the Court, irritated by this arrogance, condemned him to be drawn and quartered.

Tale 83

OF THE WORTH OF MONSIEUR SALZARD

I want to tell you a good story about a worthy man whose name was Salzard. Do you know what kind of a man he was? First of all, he had a head like a butter pot, a face wrinkled like a scorched parchment, eyes as large as the eyes of an ox, a nose as watery, particularly in winter, as a fisherman's pouch, and he always went around sticking up his snout like an ironmonger; his mouth was as twisted as I don't know what, and he wore a cap dirty enough to grow a pot of cabbage, a robe which drooped so that you would've thought his shoulders were out of joint, a coat that dangled down to his calves, breeches that were torn in the crotch and weighed down as on Breton lovers. I'm mistaken: they weren't breeches, it was filth bordered with cloth; his lovely three-week old shirt was already dirty when he first put it on; his nails were long enough to make lanterns or to claw it out with the one who's under St. Michael's feet. To whom shall we marry him off, girls? Isn't there one among you who's struck by his qualities? You laugh! Now, don't laugh anymore. I grant him a wife who'll see some perfection in him; as for me, I couldn't find any in him without thinking about it. No, no; don't put off loving him; he's good-natured in compensation. When he was asked, "Sir, how do you do?" he answered in bumpkinese, "I never do it." "What's the matter, Sir?" "My head matters more than my fist." "Sir, dinner's ready." "Eat it." "Sir, it's eleven o'clock." "It will soon be twelve." "Do you want your fish fried, or boiled, or roasted, or what?" "I want it what." And who was that worthy man? Indeed, go tell him in order to set off a row! Don't inquire after him if you don't want to marry him.

Tale 84

OF TWO STUDENTS WHO TOOK THE TAILOR'S SCISSORS

In the University of Paris there were two young students who were fine rascals and always up to some mischief, especially when it came to removing things. They took books, belts, gloves; everything was suitable; they didn't wait until things were lost to find them, and they just had to grab something, even if it were only to carry off shoes. Even when they were in your room, right in front of you, if they saw a pair of slippers under a corner of the bed, one of them neatly put them on over his shoes and left with everything. And at that rate, in order to be on guard against them, you had to beware of feet and hands, even though the proverb warns us only about hands. In short, they'd sworn that no matter where they entered, they'd always come out better equipped unless they couldn't, and they worked well together: while one kept watch, the other made the grab. One day, the two of them were at a tailor's shop (for one was almost never without the other) where one of them was having himself measured for a jacket; and, as they glanced here and there to see what they could carry off, they saw nothing which was really worth their taking, except that one of them noticed a pair of scissors that was there for the taking; since his companion was closer to it, he nodded to him, saying in Latin, *Accipe*. His companion, who well understood this word and knew how to put it to use, very gently took the scissors and put them under his cloak while the tailor was busy elsewhere; of course, he heard this word *accipe*, but he didn't know what it meant, never having been to school; but, when he looked for the scissors after the two students had left, he was very astonished not to find them, and he began to think of who had come into his shop, and he could only suspect those two young people; and, in fact, recalling how they'd acted, he also remembered the word *accipe*, and he began to grow suspicious. A man soon came into his shop and he asked him, while talking about his scissors (old habits die hard), "Sir," he said, "what does *accipe* mean?" The other answered him, "My friend, it's a word women understand; *accipe* means 'take'." "Oh! by God (I believe he said the devil), if *accipe* means 'take,' my scissors are lost." And

indeed they were, no doubt about it, or at the very least they'd
certainly gone astray.

Tale 85

OF THE FRANCISCAN WHO KEPT WATER NEAR HIM AT THE TABLE AND DID NOT DRINK ANY

There was a gentleman who usually invited to dinner and supper
a Franciscan who preached the Lenten sermons in the parish; the
Franciscan was a good friar and loved good wine. When he was at
the table, he always wanted the ewer next to him, and yet he didn't
use it because he found the wine strong enough without water,
drinking *sicut terra sine aqua*; [1] the gentleman kept noticing this,
and he said to him one time, "Good Father, how come you always
ask for water and don't put any in your wine?" "Sir," he said "why
do you always have your sword at your side and don't do anything
with it?" "That's right," the gentleman said, "but it's to defend
myself in case someone attacked me." "Sir," the friar said, "water
also serves to defend me against the wine if it should attack me,
and for that reason I always keep it near me; but, seeing that it
doesn't do me any harm, I don't do it any harm either."

> A Franciscan, a belted and holy man,
> Drinks his wine like any other man.

---

[1] Psalm 142: as a thirsty land.

Tale 86

OF A LADY WHO HAD THE ROOSTERS TENDED APART FROM THE HENS

A lady from Bourbonnais had learned, through the teaching of
a gentleman who knew what it was to live deliciously, that the meat
of young roosters that hadn't been castrated was as tender and even
better than that of capons, provided they hadn't experienced hens,
and that making love with hens, as all males do with females, was

what made the roosters become so tough: no doubt about it, it was a man of some experience who said that he who does it the least deceives his companion, that apprentices are masters at it, that its greatest practitioners end up on the gallows, that men die from it and that women thrive on it, and other fine remarks pertaining to the matter. In any case, I'll let the thing speak for itself; what I have to say about it isn't to quell quarrelling. Apropos of our roosters, this lady I'm talking about had them kept apart from the hens in order to serve them for dinner instead of capons, and she was very pleased with this. One day, a great lord came to see her (her family was great and noble), and she welcomed him as splendidly as she could. She wanted to show him the features of her house one by one, and among them she didn't forget her roosters, boasting about them at length and promising to have him experience it at supper. The lord took that for a great novelty; but he took pity on those poor roosters, which he saw thus harshly punished by being deprived of the greatest pleasure nature put in this world, and he thought to himself that he'd do a merciful deed by giving them some help; so, he left the lady's side, summoned one of his servants, and secretly ordered him to get three or four live hens in a little while and, without making any noise, to be sure to put them in the coop where the roosters were, and this was immediately done. As soon as those hens were inside and the roosters all around them, the battle began; never was there such a war; as one got on, another got off. Those poor hens were worn out, for it's said that:

> Gallus gallinaceus ter quinque sufficit unus.
> Ter quinque viri non sufficiunt mulieri.[1]

But I believe that the latter is false because I heard a lady say that she was quite happy with three times a night: one on getting into bed, another between two naps, and the third at daybreak; but, if there was an extra one, she took it in her stride. As for me, I'd say this lady was rather reasonable, and that once is nothing, twice does a lot of good, three is enough, four is too much, five is the death of a gentleman, unless he was starved; more than that is up to wagoners. Indeed, there was a gentleman who boasted of

---

[1] One cock of the walk is enough for fifteen hens, but fifteen men are not enough for a woman.

seventeen times in one night, and everyone who heard him was amazed; but, in the end, when he had made the most of his story, he corrected himself by saying that he'd been wrong by fifteen; that was a good bit less. But what am I telling you? Excuse me, ladies: it was the roosters that made me lapse into this subject. Upon my soul! It's such a sweet thing that one can't help talking about it at every turn. Consequently, I didn't undertake at the beginning of my book to speak to you of the rising cost of living.

Tale 87

OF THE MAGPIE AND HER CHICKS

That's enough said about men and women: I want to tell you a story about birds. There was a magpie which led her little chicks through the fields in order to teach them how to live; but they acted foolishly and always wanted to return to the nest because they thought that their mother should always feed them; nevertheless, seeing that they were all ready to fly anywhere, she began little by little to let them eat all alone, instructing them as follows: "Children," she said, "go into the fields; you're big enough to look after yourselves; my mother left me when I was nowhere as big as you are." "Yes," they said, "but what will we do? The crossbowmen will kill us." "No, they won't," their mother said, "it takes time to take aim. When you see them raise their crossbows and put them against their cheeks in order to fire, flee." "All right! We'll do that," they said, "but if someone takes a stone to hit us, he won't have to take aim. What will we do then?" "And you'll still see," the mother said, "when he stoops to pick up the stone." "Yes," the chicks said, "but what if by chance he keeps the stone in his hand, ready to throw it?" "Ah!" the mother said, "you know so much about it! Now go ahead and take care of yourselves." And, on saying this, she left them and went off. If you don't laugh about it, I won't cry over it.

Tale 88

OF AN ABBOT'S MONKEY AND AN ITALIAN WHO UNDERTOOK
TO MAKE HIM TALK

An abbot had a monkey who was marvelously well bred: besides his capers and the funny faces he made, he knew people by their features; he recognized good and wise people by their beards, clothes, countenances, and he made much of them; but he could have picked out a page from a hundred others even if he'd been dressed as a girl: he simply recognized him by his page-ness as soon as he entered the room although he'd never seen him before. When some matter was being discussed, he listened with discernment, as if he'd understood the speakers, and he made rather definite signs to show that he understood; and, if he said nothing, rest assured that he thought all the more. In short, I believe he belonged to the same race as the Portuguese monkey who played chess so well.[1] The abbot was very proud of this monkey and often spoke of him while having dinner and supper. One day, when he had good company in his home and the Court was in that region, he began to praise his monkey. "But," he said, "isn't that a marvelous kind of animal? I believe nature wanted to make a man when it made him, and because she was busy with so many other things she forgot man had been made. As you can see, she made his face like that of a man, his fingers, hands, and even the irregular lines inside the palms, like those of a man. What do you think of it? He only needs speech to be a man; but wouldn't it be possible to make him speak? We do teach a bird to talk, and it doesn't have the intelligence or the use of reason that animal has. I'd like him to speak as well as my parrot, even if it were to cost me a year's income; and I don't believe it can't be done: after all, even when he complains or when he laughs, you'd think he was a person and that he's ready to express his thoughts; and I believe that, if someone wanted to develop that aptitude, he'd succeed." It so happened that a certain Italian was present at this conversation; when he saw that the abbot spoke

---

[1] Allusion to an anecdote related by Castiglione in Book II of his *Il Cortegiano.*

with such fervour and that he was well on the way to believing
this monkey ought to learn to talk, he boldly introduced himself
(which is typical of that nationality) and said to the abbot, without
forgetting the Reverences, Excellencies, and Graces, "Lord," he said,
"you see it as it is, and you can be sure that, since nature made
this animal so like a human, she didn't mean for it to be impossible
to finish the rest through artificial means and she has deprived him
of language in order to put man to work and to show that there's
nothing that can't be done through constant work. Doesn't one read
of elephants which have spoken and of an ass too? (In fact, more
than a hundred, I would have said readily). And I'm amazed that
there hasn't been yet a king, prince, or lord who wanted to try it
with this animal, and I say that the one who does the experiment
first will earn immortal praise." The abbot pricked up his ears at
these philosophical reasons and particularly because they were
Italic, for the French have always had that fine trait (among other
bad qualities) of granting attention and favor more willingly to
foreigners than to their own. With his large eyes, he took a closer
look at this Italian and said to him, "Truly, I'm very pleased to
have found a man who agrees with me, and I've had that idea for
a long time." To make a long story short, after a few other arguments
were alleged and discussed, the abbot decided that this Italian who
professed to be a man of understanding had the look of one and
he said to him, "Now then; would you like to undertake this task
of making him speak?" "Yes, your Lordship," the Italian said, "I'd
like to undertake it. I tackled things that were just as difficult in
the past, and I managed it." "But how long will it take?" the abbot
said. "Father," the Italian answered, "you can understand that it
can't be done in a short time. I'd like to have a good while for such
an undertaking and such an unknown one: after all, in order to
do this, I'll have to feed it at certain hours, and with rare and
precious choice meats and be with it day and night. "All right," the
abbot said, "don't speak of the expense: whatever it may be, I'll
spare nothing; speak only of time." The upshot was that he asked
for a period of six years, to which the abbot agreed, and he boarded
the monkey with him; the Italian asked for a good sum of crowns
in advance and took the monkey under his wing. And you can
imagine that the discussion they carried on provided those who
were present with laughter; however, they waited to laugh some

other time at their leisure because they didn't want to take too much notice of it in front of the abbot. But the Italians who were acquainted with this adventurer were very angry about it, for it was at the time they began to be in vogue in France, and, because of this monkey business, they were afraid of losing their reputation. For this reason, some of them strongly scolded this schoolmaster, pointing out to him that he was dishonoring all his people with this foolish undertaking and that he wasn't to deal with the abbot for the purpose of taking advantage of him and that, when it came to the attention of the king, he'd be roughly handled. After this Italian had heard them out, he answered them as follows: "You know what I think? You don't know anything about it, the whole lot of you. I've agreed to make a monkey talk in six years; the time is worth the money, and the money's worth the time. A lot of things happen in six years: before they're over, either the abbot will die, or the monkey, or perhaps myself; thus I'll be rid of it." You see what it is to be a bold adventurer! They say that it all worked out for the best for this Italian. The abbot, when he lost sight of the monkey, began to be so disturbed that he no longer took any pleasure in anything; you have to realize that the Italian took him on the understanding that he had to give him a change of atmosphere, and he also said he wanted to use certain secrets that no one was to see or know. For this reason, the abbot began to see that it was the Italian who was enjoying his monkey and not he, and he regretted his bargain and wanted his monkey back. Thus, the Italian was released from his promise, and, nevertheless, he lived well on the abbot's crowns.

Tale 89

OF THE MONKEY WHO DRANK THE MEDICINE

I don't know if it was this same monkey we were just talking about, but it's all the same; if not he, it was another. At all events, this monkey's master became ill with a very high fever, and he called the doctors; they prescribed right off an enema and bleeding in the usual fashion, then some syrups for four mornings and at the same time some medicine which the apothecary brought him early in the morning on the appointed day. But when he found his patient asleep, he decided not to awaken him, particularly since he hadn't rested for a long time. He put the medicine in a goblet on the table, covered it with a cloth, and left. When the patient woke up a little while later, he saw his medicine on the table, but there was no one to give it to him because everyone had left in order to let him rest. And by chance they'd left the door of the room open, and that's how the monkey got in to see his master. The first thing he did was to climb up on the table, and he found the silver goblet which contained the medicine. He uncovered it and began to put this liquid to his nose; he found its odor slightly unpleasant, and it made him make all sorts of new faces. Finally, he ventured to taste it, for he never would have passed it up. But, because of its sugary bitterness, he wrinkled his nose, pursed his lips, made the strangest faces in the world. Nevertheless, because it was sweetish, he went back to it one more time and then again. In short, he tasted and retasted it so much that he finally managed to drink all of it; he even licked his whiskers. Meanwhile, the patient, who was watching him, took such great pleasure in the faces he saw him make that he forgot his illness and began to laugh so hard and so heartily that he was completely cured. In fact, by means of sudden and unexpected joy, his spirits were invigorated, his blood was cleansed, his humors settled down, and the fever left him. The doctor soon arrived, and he asked the patient how he was and if the medicine had done its job. But the patient was laughing so hard that he had a difficult time speaking, and the doctor took this as a bad sign, thinking he was delirious and that it was all over for him. Nevertheless, he finally answered the doctor: "Ask the monkey," he said, "what its effect was." The doctor stayed a little while longer, but he didn't understand this comment until he noticed the monkey begin to defecate all around the room and on the tapestries: he jumped, he ran, he made a terrible mess. The doctor realized that he'd substituted for the patient, who was hardly able to tell them what had happened he was laughing so hard; they were all delighted over it, but the patient even more because he easily got out of bed and made merry, thanks to God and the monkey.

Tale 90

OF A HUSBAND'S INVENTION TO AVENGE HIMSELF ON HIS WIFE

Many people have been of the opinion that when a woman deceives her husband he should blame her rather than the one who had access, and they say that whoever wants to put an end to a disorder must remove the cause, according to the Italian proverb, *Morta la bestia, morto il veneno,* [1] and that men only do what women invite them to do and they don't readily get involved where they haven't been attracted by the lure of eyes or words, or by some other advances. As for me, if I thought I'd please women by defending them on the basis of their frailty, I'd gladly do it because I only wish to be of service to them; but I'd be afraid of being disavowed by the majority of them and by the fairest of them all, who'd all say, "It isn't fickleness which makes me do it, it's the great perfections of a man who deserves more than all the pleasure he could receive from me; I consider myself deeply honored and think myself very lucky when I see that I'm loved by such a virtuous person as he." And to be sure, that argument is a good one and, at the moment, invincible; there isn't a husband who wouldn't be hard put to answer it. It's true that, if by chance he thinks himself honest and virtuous, he has the opportunity of keeping his wife all to himself; but, if his conscience judges him to be otherwise, it would seem that he doesn't have much reason to scold or to forbid his wife from loving a more attractive man than he; otherwise, one would answer me that indeed he mustn't, nor can he prevent her from loving virtue and virtuous men. But it goes without saying that it's spiritual virtue, and not substantial and spermatic virtue, and that joining spirits together is enough without the bodies approaching one another, for

> The shepherd and the shepherdess
> Are in the shade of a tree,
> And are so near each other,
> They are difficult to see.

---

[1] The proverbial equivalents in English are *dead dogs do not bite* and *dead men tell no tales.*

To excuse women on the strength of the presents they're given would be a vile, sordid, and abject thing. Rather, women deserve severe punishment for allowing greed to triumph over their bodies and hearts, even though the heart is the strongest part in the whole battery and the one which makes the greatest breach. But on what grounds shall we then excuse them? We must find a few reasons (if not sufficient ones, at least acceptable ones for lack of a better settlement). To be sure, I'm of the opinion that there's no more worthwhile defense than to say that there's no place so strong that constant and furious bombardment won't level. Too, there's no woman's heart so firm, nor so ready to resist, which in the end isn't compelled to give in to the obstinate pursuit of a lover. Even the man who claims constancy in something which is natural and peculiar to him weakens more often than just every other day and forgets about the things which he ought to prize the most, advertising for sale what is bound by honor. Therefore, how is woman, who is by nature gentle, of compassionate heart, gracious speech, delicate constitution, feeble strength, to hold her own against a man who's persistent in his requests, obstinate in his pursuits, inventive in his ploys, subtle in words, and excessive in promises? Truly, it's a thing so difficult as to be nearly impossible; but, nevertheless, I won't settle anything here because this isn't where this dispute is to end. I'll only say that a woman's happy, more or less, according to the husband she has, for there are all kinds: some know about it and go on as if nothing had happened, and they prefer to wear horns in their hearts rather than on their foreheads; others know about it and take revenge, and they're unpleasant, foolish, and dangerous. Others know about it and endure it, and they think that patience is better than knowledge, and these are poor men; others know nothing of it, but they inquire about it, and they seek what they wouldn't like to find. Others don't know about it and don't attempt to find out, and, of all the cuckolds, they're the least unhappy, and the're even happier than those who aren't and think they are. Now that all these cases have been advanced, I'll tell you about a gentleman who was one of them; but, certainly, it wasn't at his request because he was very angry about it. But he was one of those of the first group, concealing his misfortune as much as he could until the opportunity came up to do something about it, whether by avenging himself on his wife, or on her friend, or on both if he got the chance. And, because it was handier to deal with his wife, the first lot fell upon her by means of an invention which he thought up. While the court was in recess, he went to enjoy himself on a property he had some two leagues from town, and he brought his wife there with the promise of a good time, and he treated her constantly in the usual manner the whole time they were there. When it came time to go back to town, he told one of his valets (whom he'd found to be loyal and discreet) a day or two before they were to leave that, when it was time to water the mule his wife used, he wasn't to lead it to the trough, but keep it from drinking the whole two days; also he was to put salt in its oats; however, he didn't tell him why he was having him do this; but the events that followed brought it to light. The valet did everything just as his master had ordered so that when it was time to leave the mule hadn't drunk for two whole days. The lady mounted on the mule and headed straight for the road to Toulouse, and its course almost took it to the Garonne and went along its bank for a while, and this was the first water one found along the road. When they got near the river, the mule began to smell the water from quite a distance away and headed straight for it because it was so eager to drink. Now, the spot was deep and impassable, and the mule (in order to drink) had to throw itself in the water, and the lady was quite unable to stop it, for the mule was dying of thirst. So, the lady, overcome with fear, encumbered by her gear and in rough terrain, fell right off into the water, and her husband stayed back on purpose with his valet in order to let the thing come about as he'd planned; so, way before the poor lady could have help, she drowned in the water. That's one way to avenge oneself on a wife but it's a little cruel and inhuman. But what do you expect? It angers a husband to see himself a cuckold. And so he thought that, if he dealt only with the lover, he wouldn't be able to forget his misfortune, constantly seeing at his side the animal that had done the damage; and then she'd be quite ready and prepared to take up with another lover. After all, a person who's done wrong once (if, however, that's wrongdoing) is always presumed to be guilty of that sort of wrongdoing. As for me, I can't say anything about it: there's no one who isn't at a loss when it's his turn. Therefore, I leave these thoughts and actions up to those who are involved.

*On the substance of the Novel Pastimes and
Merry Tales contained in this first book*

to his readers

Well, it's done; have you had enough of it?
But tell me now, have you heartily laughed?
At any rate, it's not due to my craft.
I compiled these gay tales for your profit.

I have mixed up new and old together:
Go to the best ones; leave me the worst part;
But reject sorrow which troubles your heart.
The more you ponder, the more you blather.

Enough, enough, the dismal years ahead
Will bring along with them sorrow and dread;
Therefore, rejoice in merry levity;

Then, when misfortune comes to do you wrong,
You can take heart. But how? Be bold and strong;
Just arm yourselves with mighty constancy.

PART TWO

(Tales attributed to Des Périers)

Tale 91

OF THE RENDEZVOUS THAT FATHER ITACE, PASTOR OF BAIGNOLET,
ARRANGED WITH A GOOD-LOOKING TURNIP VENDOR, AND
WHAT CAME OF IT

Although Father Itace, pastor of Baignolet, was a very upright
man and a doctor of theology, he was also a man, *ergo*, by means
of pertinent arguments, a natural one, *ergo* he loved natural women
like any other man; and so one day he saw a beautiful turnip
vendor who was ready and willing to do just about anything, and
he spoke to her a bit while passing by, asking her if business was
good and if her turnips were good and fresh, for he loved turnip
soup a great deal; at this juncture, he pointed out his Johnny to
her, and he told him to give her directions to his house so that
she could bring him some from then on and be well paid for it,
and *reliqua*,[1] because he was generous and especially apt to give
charity and alms where it was deserved. She promised him that
she'd go there, and Johnny bought what he needed for the time
being, paying her double at his master's request. The turnip vendor
didn't fail first thing in the morning to go by the house and ask if
they wanted some turnips; she was told to come in the evening
and speak secretly with the priest in order to receive a generous
gift; although he was giving it with the right hand, he didn't want
(in accordance with the Gospel) the left hand to know anything
about it; he appointed the following night for the occasion. The
young woman agreed. The priest awaited her very devoutly that
evening and ordered Johnny, his *famulus*,[2] to go to bed early in
the dressing room, and, if by chance he heard a noise, not to wake

---

[1] and *reliqua*: as well as for all she had left.
[2] Valet, servant; cf. tale 14, n. 2.

up, get up, or cry out. Meanwhile, the good Itace paced up and down, went downstairs, returned upstairs, looked out the window to see if that vendor was coming; in short, he experienced the same agony that Roger did while waiting for Alcina in the romance of *Orlando Furioso.*[3] Finally, tired of going up and down the stairs so much, he sat down in a chair in his room, but he left the door to his house open so that he could welcome the vendor without his neighbors' hearing it for fear of a scandal which would be worse coming from him than from others because his life was supposed to be exemplary. The woman arrived and went straight up: "Good evening, Father," she said. "You're very welcome, my dear (he answered); indeed, you're a woman who keeps her word"; and, as he drew near to squeeze and kiss her, a man caught them by surprise and yelled to the woman, "Oh, you bitch! I was sure you were going to some evil haunt when you sneaked away in the evening." And when he said this, he began to thrash her roundly with a big stick; the good Itace objected and stepped in between them, saying, "Hey! stop!" and everything else he could think of and shout, like a person who's very dismayed by a scrap. "So, Father (the man replied), you seduce married women you summon to your home at night? And you preach that whoever wants to do evil walks in darkness and flees the light!" Then, the woman said to him, "My dear husband! you don't understand the situation; this good father, who's aware of our shameful poverty, had his servants tell me that he wanted to give us a gift, but that he didn't seek any glory from it and didn't want anyone to see it or know it. And because we have a poor bed, he decided to favor our family and descendants by giving us his bed, which, as you can see, is fine and sturdy, and his only condition was that we pray to God for him; obviously, he could only do it at this hour for the reasons already stated; therefore, my husband, forget your anger and, instead of blustering, thank Father Itace." Then, the husband began to excuse himself profusely for the sin of anger against his priest and confessor, asking him for forgiveness and mercy. This fine and subtle feminine invention greatly pleased Father Itace, who was about to be beaten up by the angry husband and in danger of being the scandal of the neighborhood, which would have been a most serious thing for a man of his position.

---

[3] In canto 7. Lodovico Ariosto's immense epic was published in 1515.

With many gracious words of thanks, the husband pulled the feather mattress into the yard and didn't even forget the sheets, which were white and fresh and ready for the tumble. He went back up, undid the beautiful multicolored serge canopy, and, with many humble thanks, he picked up the heaviest load and his wife the rest. After they left, Father Itace, who wasn't too happy both because of the prey which had gotten away from him so easily and because of the loot which had been taken from him, called Johnny, who'd heard the noise and understood most of the game, and said to him angrily, "Look, *famule*, how the scoundrel has muddied my bed with his feet; at least, he could have taken off his shoes before climbing on my bed." Johnny, wishing on the one hand to console his master and on the other angry that he hadn't had his share of the booty, said to him, "*Domine*, you know the good old Latin: *Rustica progenies nescit habere modum*, which is to say, 'Stroke a nettle, and it will sting you.' If you'd called me when the scullions came in here, I would've chased them away with a stick, and now you wouldn't be angry at seeing your room stripped without the help of the law."

Tale 92

OF THE WAYS TO COLLECT MONEY IN A HURRY
THAT A JOKER GAVE HIS KING

Since Triboulet was well thought of in the best companies and his foolishness has a place in this book, it seemed a good idea to give him as a companion one of the best fed jokers in the king's court; and, because he saw that the king was perplexed as to how to raise money to finance his wars, he showed him two ways (which few others would have thought of). He said: "Sire, one is to make your office an alternating one, as you've frequently done with others in your kingdom. If you do this, you'll be able to put your hands on two million in gold and more." You can imagine how the king and his lords who were there laughed at this first means, and some of them, hoping to push this fool to his limit, asked him, "Well! Master Fool, is that all you know about appropriate means to raise money?" "No, no," the fool answered (addressing himself to the king), "I know another one as good and better: command by edict

that all monks' beds be sold in all the territories under your rule
and that the deniers be brought to the coffers of your treasury."
The king laughed and immediately asked him, "Where will the poor
monks sleep when their beds are taken away?" "With nuns." "Yes,"
the king replied, "but there are many more monks than nuns." The
fellow had his answer ready, and it was that a nun could put up
at least half a dozen of them. "And you can be sure," the fool said,
"that it was to this end that the kings and other princes who pre-
ceded you built in many cities monasteries across from nunneries."

Tale 93

OF A THIEF WHO WANTED TO STEAL HIS NEIGHBOR'S COW

A certain habitual thief, who wanted to steal his neighbor's cow,
got up early one morning before daylight, entered the cow's stable,
and led it away, pretending to run after it. When he heard the
noise, the neighbor awoke and put his head out the window: "Neighbor (the thief said), come help me catch my cow; it's gotten into
your yard because your gate wasn't properly closed." After the
neighbor had helped him do this, he persuaded him to go to market
with him (of course, had he stayed home, he would have noticed
the theft). On the way, as day was breaking, this poor man recognized his cow and said, "Neighbor, that cow looks a lot like
mine." "That's right," he said, "and that's why I'm going to sell
mine; your wife and mine argue over it every day because they
don't know which one to choose." With these remarks, they reached
the market; then the thief, for fear of being discovered, pretended
to have business in town, and he asked his neighbor to sell the
cow for as much as he could, and he promised him some wine. So,
the neighbor sold it and brought him the money. With that, they
went straight to the tavern, as agreed; but, after they had drunk
their fill, the thief found a way to disappear and left the other to
pay. From there he went to Paris; on one occasion, he was in a
market place where there were many asses tied (according to the
custom) to rings in the walls; when he saw that all the places were
filled, he chose the most beautiful one, got up on it, rode through
the market, and sold it readily to a stranger; the only place the

buyer could find for it was the one from which it had been taken, and so he tied it up again in the same spot. As a result, when the one who was the real master of the ass and from whom it had been stolen later wanted to untie it in order to lead it away, there was such a quarrel between him and the buyer that they came to blows. Now, the thief who'd sold it was in the crowd and saw this entertainment; just as the buyer was on the ground, beset by blows, the thief couldn't keep himself from saying, "Hit him, hit that ass thief hard for me!" When this poor man, who was in such a state and who asked for nothing better than to meet up with his seller, heard this, he recognized him by his speech and said, "There's the one who sold it to me." With these remarks, he was seized, and, all the above mentioned things having been confirmed by his confession, he was executed by law, as he deserved.

Tale 94

OF A POOR VILLAGER WHO FOUND THE DONKEY HE HAD LOST THROUGH AN ENEMA THAT A DOCTOR HAD GIVEN HIM

In the province of Bourbonnais (where those beautiful ears grow),[1] there once was a very famous doctor who had the habit of giving his patients only one kind of medicine, enemas, and luckily he brought about several fine cures; and, as a result, he was so esteemed that there wasn't a mother's child who didn't go to him when he was ill. It so happened that a poor villager had lost his ass in the fields, and he was very worried about it; and, as he went around looking for this ass, he met on the road an old woman who asked him why he was in such distress; he answered her that he'd lost his ass and that he was so upset about it that he'd lost his taste for food and drink. Then the old woman told him about this doctor's house and confidently sent him there, pointing out to him that the doctor always had definite news about anything that had been lost, and the man was very pleased about this, and so he set out for the doctor's house. And when he was there, he saw around

---

[1] The extraordinary size of the ears of the inhabitants of the old province of Bourbonnais was proverbial.

him so many people who prevented him from getting near that he became very annoyed, and so he began to shout, "Alas! sir, for God's sake, give me back my ass! It's my whole life; I beg of you, don't hide it. I've been told that you have it, or that you can tell me about it." And he repeated these words several times, shouting louder and louder, and it annoyed the doctor. And therefore, he looked right at him, and, thinking that he was out of his mind, he ordered his servants to give him an enema, which was soon done. Then the poor man left, hoping to find his ass at home. But when he was half-way there, he was forced to discharge the enema. He immediately withdrew into a little shack, where he performed quite well. While he was about his business, he heard his ass braying in the fields; the poor man was overjoyed, and he didn't take the time to pull up his breeches in order to run after his ass; when he recovered it, he celebrated and then climbed on it and very quickly returned to town in order to thank the doctor; and, meanwhile, along the road he publicized the great learning and wisdom of his doctor, and how, with his help, he'd found his ass; consequently, the doctor was prized even more and esteemed more than he'd ever been.

Tale 95

OF A SUPERSTITIOUS DOCTOR WHO DID NOT WANT TO MAKE MERRY WITH HIS WIFE EXCEPT WHEN IT RAINED AND THE WIFE'S GOOD FORTUNE AFTER HIS DEATH

In the city of Paris it recently happened that a doctor was so superstitious that he even relied on the occult; it was his astrological belief that to make merry and have fun with his wife in dry weather was very unfavorable for him, and so he completely abstained; and, besides, when the weather was damp, he observed the course of the moon, which hardly pleased his wife; she often begged him for sport, and, because she needed it, she endeavored to make him do it; but she rarely won, and, as his only answer, he gave her to understand that the weather wasn't favorable and that such a thing would be more harmful than profitable to him. Thus, he lulled his poor wife into doing nothing. It happened that the doctor's wife spoke privately of her problem to one of her neighbors; she advised her that, as soon as she was in bed, she was to have three or four buckets of water carried to her attic and have them poured into a lead basin which was near the attic window and which was used to catch rainwater in order to have it trickle through a pipe or lead duct down to the bottom of the courtyard (as is usually done in good houses); and the neighbor said that, as soon as she heard the noise of the water, she was to tell her husband about it. The doctor's wife gladly did just that; and although the day had been warm and dry, nevertheless, she carried out her plan. And when the two of them were in bed, the chambermaid, who was in on it, let the water drip little by little down the duct, and it made a noise; the wife awakened her doctor and invited him to make sport; the doctor performed the best he could, notwithstanding his amazement that the weather had changed so quickly. The lady continued for several days with this subtlety, and she was very happy. Later the doctor died and because the lady was a very beautiful, young, and rich woman, several men asked to marry her; but she refused to accept anyone, however rich he might be, until she'd spoken to him. She no longer cared for doctors, and she asked the others if they knew about the stars and the moon; and several of them, unaware of the facts, answered her that they'd learned all one had to know, and because of that she turned them down. It happened that a jolly fellow, who was slightly stupid, asked her if she wanted him for a husband; and as they talked gaily, she asked him if he knew about the stars; he answered that he didn't know anything about the sun, stars, or moon, and that he didn't know when it was time to go to bed, except when he could no longer see. This pleased the lady, and so she married him; he laid her well and to her heart's content, and she boasted later that she had too much of what she'd had too little of in the past.

Tale 96

OF A JOLLY DUTCH FELLOW WHO MADE A SHOEMAKER, WHO HAD MADE BUSKINS FOR HIM, RUN AFTER HIM

It won't be out of place here to tell about the skill of a jolly fellow who was walking around in a rather large city in Holland;

he went into a shoemaker's shop, and the owner asked him if there was anything that appealed to him. And because he'd seen him glance at some buskins which were hanging there, he asked him if he wanted to have a pair. When he answered and said yes, he selected for him the ones which seemed to suit his legs best, and he put them on him. When he had them, he also tried on some shoes, and he thought they fit his feet as well as the buskins fit his legs. Then, instead of bargaining and paying, he chatted with the shoemaker and asked him, "Tell me, upon your word, hasn't it ever happened to you that someone you'd outfitted so well for running fled without paying?" "Never," he said. "And if by chance it happened, what would you do?" "I'd run after him," the shoemaker said. "Are you saying this deliberately?" "I'm telling the truth, and I wouldn't do otherwise," the affable shoemaker answered. "Let's have a demonstration," the other said. "Now then, I'll start running first; you run after me." And with this he began to run as fast as he could. Then the shoemaker ran after him and shouted, "Stop, thief!" But the other one, seeing that people were coming out of their homes and fearful they'd get their hands on him, acted as one who only did this for amusement: "Don't anybody (he said) stop me; this is a large bet." So the shoemaker returned and was very angry at having lost his time, his money, and his trouble; obviously, the other had won the prize for running. Now, although the word *buskins* is used in this merry tale, you mustn't take it to mean buskins made like our modern ones, for they were worn in shoes.

Tale 97

OF THE STUDENT WHO LEAFED THROUGH ALL HIS BOOKS IN ORDER TO FIND THE MEANING OF *brush, to brush, box, gallows box*, ETC.

The naughty word *box*, very well known and extolled in peacetime France, had once upon a time frustrated a young student because he couldn't interpret it for those who asked him (although he'd asked the clerics in his village a thousand times); but the word was all Greek to them. Even more irritated than before, the student combed *Calepinus auctus et recognitus, Cornucopiae,* and *Catholicon magnum et parvum*[1] from end to end; but it was all for naught because it wasn't there. Nevertheless, after he'd mulled it over in his head a good while, he remembered that some ten years earlier, while in Paris one night, a chambermaid who said she was from Picardy (although she was from Normandy) had taught him what it was without thinking; while he was building up the firewood before going to bed, she'd rambled on that *brush* was a broom and *to brush* was to broom, as in the song:

Brush my firebox for me.

Therefore, *box* (he said), talking to himself, is the receptacle for a fagot or bundle in Paris, or what we call a package in my blessed region; therefore, I realize that when one shouts, "in the king's name, under penalty of the gallows box (box *est foeminini generis!*)," it means the same thing as "on pain of the rope," since they used to use tree branches in order to save hemp. Thus, the charming student carried out his promise; he'd read what is written in one of Clément Marot's poems to the king, that is, to smell of the gallows box is the same as to be a gallows bird:

And so he went away, a gallows bird all right,
This valet who was mounted like Saint George the knight.[2]

---

[1] Titles of Latin dictionaries in use at this time.
[2] From the poet Clément Marot's famous poem "Au roi, pour avoir été dérobé" (1531).

Tale 98

OF TRIBOULET, KING FRANCIS I'S FOOL, AND HIS FOOLISH ACTS

The late King Francis I (God rest his soul!) was a very virtuous and magnanimous prince who took care of a poor idiot in order to be frequently amused by him (after his work on the affairs of the kingdom of France), and he happily had him go before him when he travelled along the road. One day while Triboulet was in front of the king, constantly chatting and showing off his nonsense, his horse let out six or eight farts, and this angered Triboulet no end; and so he immediately got off his horse, put the saddle on his back, and said to the king, "Cousin, today you gave me the worst horse that ever was. He's a drunk; after he's drunk his fill, all he does is fart. By God! he'll go on foot. Ha! ha! he farted in front of the king." And with his club he struck his horse, and he continued to carry the saddle. Thus, he went about half a league on foot. Another time, the king entered his Sainte-Chapelle in Paris in order to hear vespers, and Triboulet followed him; and when he entered, he noticed the greatest silence possible. A little while later, the bishop began *Deus, in adjutorium* [1] (rather beautifully); and immediately thereafter all the cantors responded singing, so that you couldn't have heard thunder in there. Then Triboulet got up from his seat and went straight to the bishop, who had begun the office, and he hit him with heavy blows. When the king noticed him, he called him and asked him why he hit that worthy man, and he said, "Yes, yes, cousin, when we came in here, there was no noise, and this one began the noise. Hence, he's the one who must be punished." Another time, Triboulet sold his horse in order to get some hay; another time he sold his hay in order to get a club. And thus he lived, constantly playing the fool until his death (which was greatly regretted), for it is said that he was happier than a wise man.

---

[1] Psalm 69: Haste thee, O God, to deliver me.

Tale 99

OF TWO PLAINTIFFS WHO WERE PROPERLY PLUCKED BY THEIR LAWYERS

While eating his cabbages, a farmer, who was always about his business, took it into his head that one of his neighbors was doing him wrong; he took him to court, and, on the advice of some of his friends, he chose a lawyer, whom he asked to handle his case, and he accepted. Two hours later, the other party appeared; he was a wealthy man, and he also asked him to be his lawyer in this same case, and he accepted it too. When the day that the case was to be pleaded drew near, the farmer went to his lawyer (he was confident he wouldn't fail to do for him what he'd promised) in

order to tell him to be ready to plead the next day; he was somewhat sheepish about it, considering he'd taken his opponent's case.
Nevertheless, in order to exonerate himself even more, he said to
him, "My friend, when you came the other time, I told you nothing
because of some business I had; now, I can tell you that I can't
be your lawyer since I am your opponent's; but I'll give you a
letter of introduction to a worthy man who'll defend your case."
Then, picking up his pen, he wrote to the other lawyer as follows:
"Two fat capons have come into my hands; I've chosen the best
and the plumpest, and I'm sending you the other one." Then, on
the sly, he wrote: "Pluck on your end, and I'll pluck on mine."
When he finished the letter, the lawyer gave it to the farmer, who
(having no more confidence in the one to whom he was to take
the recommendation than in the lawyer who was sending it)
ventured to open it and read it; after having litigated for a long
time without having gotten anywhere and seeing himself deceived
by the superior influence and power of his opponent, he decided to
settle with him, as he'd often been asked to do by his own friends.

Tale 100

OF THE MERRY REMARKS OF THE MAN WHO WAS BEING LED
TO THE MONTFAUCON GALLOWS

A real good-for-nothing, who on his own merits had been sent
up a ladder backwards in order to come down a rope (as jolly
fellows say), stood there preaching marvelously. During his sermon,
the hangman, who was getting his equipment ready, passed his hand
under and around the preacher's neck so many times that he finally
looked at him and said, "Hey! chief, my friend, don't pass your
hand there anymore: I'm more ticklish around the neck than you
think. You'll make me laugh, and then what will people say? That
I'm a bad Christian and that I make fun of the law." Then, realizing
that the hour for his hanging at Montfaucon was drawing near and
because he was going past the city gate, he began to call the gatekeeper loudly several times although the gatekeeper had clearly
heard him the first time; but, because he was just as worthy of a
rope as the one who was being taken to hang, he took off instead

of going to speak to the man for fear that he might denounce him to the law (since such people usually tell more than they're asked). Thus, this poor hoarse man finally spoke to his confessor and said to him, "Father, please tell the gatekeeper not to forget to close the gate early because I don't intend going back to Paris to sleep today." And among other consolations, his confessor said, "My friend, in this world there's nothing but pain and suffering: you're lucky to be leaving such misery today." He answered, "Ha! ha! brother, I wish to God you were in my place to enjoy immediately the happiness you're preaching to me." The priest pretended not to hear that, and, going on, he said, "Take heart, my friend; no matter what wrongs you may have done, ask for God's forgiveness sincerely: all will be forgiven and today you will go up above to dine in paradise with the angels, etc." "Dine today in paradise, good father! It would be fine if I could be there for lunch tomorrow; and, because a man is easily bored when he travels alone, I beg of you, keep me company that far. Do this charitable work for me, especially since you know the way." The affable fellow told several other jokes, but they'd be too long to relate.

Tale 101

OF THE WISH MADE BY A CERTAIN ADVISOR TO KING FRANCIS I

One advisor to King Francis I was a man whose wit was naturally fertile with jokes; one day when a group was talking to the king about the means he should choose to resist the emperor, who was coming with mighty forces they said, he heard one person wish the king so many good Gascons, another so many mercenaries, the rest expressing some other fine wish. He said, "Sire, since it's a matter of wishing, I too, if you'd like, will make my wish; but I'll wish for something which won't cost you anything, whereas what they're wishing for would cost you a great deal." The king asked him what this thing was, and he quickly answered, "Sire, I'd only wish to become a devil for a quarter of an hour." "And what would you do?" the king said. "I'd go right away and break the emperor's neck." "Indeed," the king said, "you're a big fool to say that; as if there were no holy water in the emperor's hand, as in mine, to

chase away devils." He was determined to make the king laugh,
and so he replied, "Sire, you will pardon me, if you please; I'm
sure that if it were a young devil who didn't know his business
well he would run; but a devil like me wouldn't flee." He said it so
wittily that he made everyone in the group laugh because he was
so amusing in word and deed.

Tale 102

OF THE STUDENT WHO FELL IN LOVE WITH HIS LANDLADY
AND HOW THEIR LOVE TURNED OUT

In the days when people wore shoes with long pointed toes, put
pots on the table, and hid in order to lend money,[1] the faithfulness
of women towards men was inviolable, and it was no more permis-
sible for men to cheat on their virtuous wives, whether by day or
night. Thus, the custom was reciprocally observed, and one could
only marvel and wonder in praise of them; therefore, jealousy didn't
exist, except for that which is caused by illicit love and from which
cuckolds die. Because of this marvelous confidence, all the married
couples, and those to be married, slept indiscriminately in a huge
bed, built for that purpose, without fear or dread of some unwar-
ranted notions, and the men and women made love to one another
only in order to tell of their thought. However, since the world
became incontinent, everyone has wanted to have his bed apart,
and for a very good reason, namely to prevent each and every danger
that might come up. As an example, let's look at that young student
who, although not yet eighteen years old, began to long for his
landlady's favors, and, going further, to haunt merry company and
have affairs with wenches. Somewhat fired up by it all, he became
completely addicted to his landlady and so taken up with his love
that he threw away to hell and gone all reason, logic, philosophy,
and all other such triflings, besides a good part of his money, in
order to cater all the better to his passions and indulge his fantasies.
Hence, he went from being a sophist and crazy logician to being
one of the silliest lovers in the world, as he demonstrated with

---

[1] The Church prohibited loans at interest.

regard to his landlady. He wanted to show her his passion and he said, "Alas! O one and only mistress of my insides, how I wish I could anatomize them for you without dying! My liver smokes; my lungs roast, and my spine burns so ardently that my life is ruined! I'm lost if you don't choose to console me." Then he remembered the sighing poet's maxim, and he said, "Alas! my Lord, what pains for the one who falls in love! He can't satisfy his hunger without fattening his partner. Ah! ah! Love, when I think of your seat, I conclude that one must enter it pecker first, and hard and taut, because a soft one isn't worth a damn." Then, recalling the means his late uncle had bequeathed to him to beguile his sorrows, he began to make up a song; aware of this and fearing that he might broadcast the mournful anguish and nocturnal passions which she aroused in him, his love asked him to sing, saying, "Close your mouth, dear; I saw the corner of the memorial in your brain where you put it away for safekeeping." She thought she might distract him from his thoughts with these allusions. However, impassioned for too long a time, he began:

SONG

This refusal is beyond me,
And it very nearly kills me.
Woe! one must endure much dismay
To enjoy just a little lay.

Ah! you are very wrong, my dear.
I thought you were sweet and sincere;
But I did find out that, in fact,
You were making fun of my act.

I have declared to you my woe,
And why I am drawn to you so;
I am suffering way too much,
And you have no pity for such.

Now something else has to be tried
Because my love shut up inside
Will not let me peacefully lie
Until you otherwise reply.

Every time I see you laugh and play,
I would very much like to say:
Tell me, fair one, if you love me!
I adore you, do not blame me.

Your features are quite beautiful,
Like me you are big and fruitful;
Therefore, love me, Woman, love me,
And end my heart's anxiety.

If my discomfort can please you,
Will my happiness displease you?
He who enjoys another's hurt
Will be mocked when he hits the dirt.

Every day when we pray,
Let's forgive our enemies' way;
But I am not your enemy,
I'm just your languishing lackey.

If you do not wish to love me,
Then at least you can set me free
And over it utter some sighs
Or else you will cause my demise.

For living I'd not give a hoot,
Constantly pining in pursuit;
It's much better to love no one
Than to wait and not have some fun.

Since you are loved, go love as fit,
You'll be better esteemed for it;
Your demeanor, your charming way
Keep me hanging on all you say.

Sunday, my weary heart flared up,
Isn't it time I mounted up?
I've now waited a three-day span,
Too long for a practical man.

I cannot really comprehend
What joy there is to wait on end;
I'm grieved for the time lost of late,
With all due respect to your mate.

Tale 103

OF THE PRIEST WHO GOT ANGRY IN HIS PULPIT BECAUSE HIS
COLLEAGUES DID NOT CARRY OUT THEIR OBLIGATION TO PREACH
TO THEIR PARISHIONERS AS HE DID

A priest somewhere or other was rather well known because
of his funny remarks and his incompetence for the responsibility

entrusted to him. One day, while preaching to his parishioners, he began to swear, by golly, against the Lutherans of his day and, wanting to prove that they were worse than the devil, he said, "The devil would run as soon as I made the sign of the cross to him; but if I made the sign of the cross to a Lutheran, God! he'd grab me by the throat and strangle me. Therefore, I advise you, my dear parishioners, to avoid their company altogether." Then, getting all hot and bothered over the fact that several other priests didn't carry out their obligation to preach as he did, he began to exclaim in the pulpit, "And they say they aren't learned enough! Let them study, for God's sake or for the devil's! And, if they aren't, they can make themselves wise as I did." And, quickly noticing his parishioners' faces, he said to them, "Ah! you know very well, ladies and gentlemen, that only a year ago I didn't know anything and now you see how I preach!" This charming priest told his parishioners tons of other little tales in order to keep them from falling asleep during his sermons.

Tale 104

OF A KNAVISH TRICK THAT AN ITALIAN SKILLFULLY PLAYED ON A FRENCHMAN IN VENICE

It happened in the Sturgeon Inn in Venice that a Frenchman who had recently arrived was warned by an Italian, who was also staying there, that in his country it wasn't safe for people who had money to show that they had it; and, moreover, he told him that when he had some crowns to weigh or a sum to count out not to do as he usually did, but to shut himself up in his room. The Frenchman took this advice as having been given sincerely and thanked him very much for it and immediately made his acquaintance. As soon as the Italian thought he was making progress, he said to him that, if he wished to change some crowns for some pistoles, he'd change them for him. "And," he said, "instead of your crowns not being worth any more than pistoles, I'll make them worth something more." The Frenchman answered him that he'd be delighted to have him do it, but he asked him to remember what he'd told him a few days earlier. "Well," he said, "as for keeping secret the money one has, I think we should get into a gondola and bring a gold balance with us and, while riding along the long canal, we can weigh our crowns and make our exchange." The Frenchman answered that he was ready to do whatever he thought best. The next day then, they got into a gondola, and the Frenchman spread out his crowns; the Italian gathered them up, having, however, first weighed them in order to put on a good front. He put them away, and, while he pretended to look for his purse and the coins which he was to hand over in exchange, he had the boatman, who was in on it, dock and put him ashore in a part of the city where there were several small streets going in every direction. He got away so smartly that the Frenchman has yet (as you can imagine) to hear from him and his one hundred crowns, and I firmly believe that the Italian proverb, which is used in several countries, should serve him as a warning in the future not to associate with such bankers, who, to justify their fame, practice this maxim: *Zara a chi tocca*[1] while crossing themselves, letting it easily be understood that unfortunate is he who trusts them.

---

[1] Italian proverb about unlucky players; cf. Dante, *Purgatorio*, VI, 1-3: "The loser when a game of dice is done remains behind reviewing every roll sadly, and sadly wiser, and alone."

Tale 105

OF AN IRISHMAN'S MERRY ADVENTURES AND WAYS FOR MAKING A LIVING IN EVERY COUNTRY

An Irishman, who was a rather witty man, decided to learn the ways of foreign countries and their speech habits; although he travelled in several countries and kept his money hidden in the soles of his shoes, nevertheless, he didn't miss a meal because he really knew how to get along in all countries; and, since he didn't care about the honors of this world, he didn't worry over any wrongs which might be done to him, and, instead of spending his time in litigation, he preferred to follow the custom of the Myconians, a poor and starving people, who, because of their indigence and poverty, invited themselves to banquets and feasts. One day, this delightful fellow entered the king's palace at dinnertime; not wishing to miss the opportunity of gorging himself and, moreover, having seen that the table was set for the king's officers, he waited until they were seated, then sat down with them and dined very well without uttering a word; amazed, some in the group, who weren't used to seeing this strange duck dine with them, asked him where he was from and to whom he belonged, and he answered them all without losing a single bite. Then they asked him if he had some position at court: "No," he said, "but I'd certainly like to have one." Then they ordered him to get up from their table and get out, on pain of quickly receiving payment for his great temerity and boldness. "Yes, indeed, gentlemen," he said, "I'll do it after I've eaten." And he kept on eating. They watched him for quite a while, and those who were offended and had threatened him were forced to forego their anger and laugh like the others. Now, in order to get more amusement and pleasure out of him, they asked him how he could have been so bold (being a vagabond and a stranger to the country) as to enter the king's palace and pantry. "Because," he said, "I knew very well that the king was rich enough to give me my dinner." By this gaiety and ready wit, he captured more often than not the good will of those who, on merely looking at him, would have snubbed him completely.

Tale 106

OF THE MEANS A DOCTOR USED IN ORDER TO BE PAID BY A SICK ABBOT HE HAD ATTENDED

A doctor, who was highly praised by many for his good reputation and learning, was sent for by an abbot to treat him in his illness, and he accepted willingly; he performed his duty so well that in a few days he had gotten him back on his feet. Now, he realized that the abbot (in the grips of his illness) promised him the moon and stars, but, when he began to get better, he didn't look kindly upon him and made no mention of satisfying him for his troubles, and he doubted very much that he'd ever receive any money; he decided to use this means in order to get paid: he gave the abbot to understand that he greatly feared a relapse worse than the illness and that he had substantial opinions about it, but that, however, he still had to take medicine; he had it prepared for him so that two hours after having taken it he found that he'd reckoned without his man and that he needed his doctor more than ever. When he found himself in such a state, he sent one messenger after another to his doctor; but, just as he'd previously played at being forgetful about satisfying him, the doctor now played at being busy. Finally, the abbot sent him one of his servants, who greased his palm very well, telling him that his master begged him for God's sake to call on him because he didn't think he'd recover from his illness. So, using the right means to put an end to all the doctor's objections, the servant worked to such good purpose that he went to see the abbot, and he made him as happy as a lark in three days, and his palm was greased again. By this means, this fine doctor was paid by his abbot, whom, in no time at all, he'd decided to let live and die, or die and live, just like a true doctor.

Tale 107

OF THE APPRENTICE THIEF WHO WAS HANGED FOR HAVING TALKED TOO MUCH

An apprentice thief entered a house by way of the roof in order to see if he might not have some good luck; he was discovered by the people who were inside because of the noise he made on entering; this was the reason that all the neighbors around gathered to see what it was all about; but, when the thief saw that everyone shoved his way in to look for him, he went down some back stairs he'd noticed and took his place in the crowd of people who were going in to look for him, and by this means he kept from being discovered. Shortly after he saw that the commotion had subsided and that they were no longer looking for the thief—they thought he'd escaped—, he decided to leave by the door, not fearing recognition, pretending to have remained alone to look for him; but, because he failed to control his tongue, he gave himself away and put the rope around his neck: as he was on the verge of leaving, he met at the door several people who were talking about the thief and cursing him; he began to curse him too, saying that he'd made him lose his cap. Now, it's to be noted that, while this rascal was trying to get away, running this way and that, his cap had fallen off, and it had been kept in the hopes that it would give some clue to the thief. Therefore, when they heard him say that, they immediately became suspicious; so he was caught and immediately hanged for having talked too much.

Tale 108

OF THE MAN WHO LET HIMSELF BE HANGED UNDER THE PRETENSE OF DEVOTION

A certain magistrate somewhere wanted to save the life of a thief who'd fallen into his hands for the purpose of sharing in the booty (as they, in fact, had agreed); then again, he realized that he'd be reprimanded and there'd be much grumbling if justice weren't done and, moreover, he'd be in great danger and so he devised this means: he had a poor man arrested, and he told him that he'd been looking for him for a long time and that he was the one who had done such and such a thing. This man didn't fail to deny it loudly and firmly, as one whose conscience was clear of everything that was charged against him. But this magistrate, determined to go on with it, pointed out to him that he'd be much better off to confess (since he was to lose his life anyway) and that, if he did confess, the magistrate would pledge on his oath to have so many masses said for him that he could be assured of going to heaven; if he didn't confess, he'd still hang and go to hell since there would be no one who'd have a single mass said for him. When the poor man heard of being hanged and then sent to the devil, he was greatly astonished and preferred to be hanged and go to heaven. Finally, he ended up saying that he didn't remember having done what he was accused of, but that, if others remembered it better than he and were very certain of it, he'd willingly accept death, but he beseeched him to keep his promise concerning the masses. And he'd no sooner said the word than he was led to take the place of the other one who deserved to die. But, when he was on the scaffold and panic started to set in, he began to speak in a way that implied he repented, notwithstanding what he'd been promised. To remedy this, the magistrate, who feared he might expose him to the people, motioned to the executioner not to let him go on: and it was done. And thus the poor man was hanged under the pretense of devotion.

Tale 109

OF A PRIEST WHO USED ONLY THE AUTHORITY OF HIS HORSE TO CONFOUND THOSE WHO DENY PURGATORY

A priest, who wanted to show what a keen and lively mind he had (although he hadn't been exposed to learning for very long), used only the authority of his horse to confound those who deny purgatory, whereas others (to do this) have ordinarily used and still use the authority of so many good and learned scholars. So, speaking about Lutherans, who didn't believe that there was a purgatory, this good fellow said, "I'm going to tell you a tale which will show you how very wrong they are to deny purgatory. I'm the son of the late Mr. d'E ... (as you know), and we have a rather beautiful place in a village near here. Going there one day, we were caught by darkness, and my pack horse (note — he said — that I want you to know that I have a very handsome and good pack horse which is at the disposal and service of the entire company) stopped against his habit and began to huff and puff. I said to my groom, 'Spur him, spur him.' 'I'm spurring, Father (he said); but your pack horse sees something for sure.' Then I remembered hearing my mother say one day that there had once been an apparition in that spot; for this reason I began to say my *Pater* and *Ave Maria,* which she'd taught me (the good woman), and once again I told my groom to spur, which he did. But the horse, having taken two or three steps forward, stopped harder than ever and again huffed and puffed (perhaps he was too tightly girthed), and again my groom assured me that the horse saw something; so, I added my *De profundis,* [1] which my late father had taught me, and immediately my horse went on his way. But, when he stopped for the third time, I no sooner said *Avete omnes,* [2] etc., and *Requiem,* etc., than he went on briskly and, thereafter, didn't balk any more (perhaps he didn't

---

[1] Psalm 129: Out of the deep have I called unto thee, O Lord.
[2] Farewell, all men.

lead him back there after that). Now," he said to his parishioners, "let these wretches say that there's no purgatory and that one mustn't pray for the deceased! I'll send them packing to my horse, yes, to my horse, to teach them their lesson."

Tale 110

OF THE JUGGLER WHO BET A DUKE FROM FERRARA THAT IN HIS CITY
THERE WERE MORE DOCTORS THAN OTHER PEOPLE,
AND HOW HE WAS PAID FOR HIS WAGER

One day, a delightful juggler, who was very welcome among fine Italian families, called on Nicholas, marquis of Ferrara, a valiant and very merry prince; to test this good fellow, he asked him laughingly which trade and profession he thought was practiced by the greatest number of people in the city of Ferrara. The juggler, who knew the marquis's disposition, decided to lure some of his money his way under the guise of a wager, and, in answer to what he'd been asked, he said, "Ah! Who doubts that in this city the number of doctors isn't greater than that of all the other professions?" "O you poor fool!" the marquis said, "it's obvious that you haven't frequented this city much, since one would be hard put to find two doctors, native or foreign." The juggler replied and said, "Oh! How occupied with great and urgent affairs must a prince be that he hasn't visited his towns and doesn't know what subjects and vassals he has!" Then the marquis said to the juggler, "What do you want to pay if what you've assured me is found to be untrue?" "But," the juggler said, "what will you give me if it so turns out that it is true?" Then and there, the marquis and the juggler agreed on what the loser would give the winner. Therefore, the next morning, the juggler, dressed in skins and opening his mouth and coughing as hard as he could, went to the door of the city's main church and pretended to be very sick. And, as each one who entered the church noticed him, several asked him what illness tormented him, and he told them it was a toothache; many gave him remedies to cure it, and he took their names and remedies and wrote them on a little pad, and, in order to be more certain of his wager, he dragged himself through the city and begged the people he met on his way to tell him about a remedy for his pain; and, by this means, he noted more than three hundred people who'd given him remedies, and he wrote them and their names on his pad. When he'd accomplished this, he entered the marquis's house and he saw him at the table, dining, and he went to him muffled up as he was, and, pretending to be wracked by illness, he told him his teeth were beginning to hurt him a little. When the marquis looked him over, he didn't guess that it was his juggler, and he said to him, "Take the medicine I'm prescribing for you and pray to Saint Nicholas, and you'll be cured immediately." The juggler, having heard this recipe, returned home, took a sheet of paper and wrote each and every remedy and name of the people who'd given them to him, and he put the marquis at the top and, in order, the others by rank. Three days later, pretending to be partly cured, he wrapped his throat and muffled himself up as before and went to see the marquis; he showed him the sheet of paper on which he'd written all the remedies he'd been given, and he asked him to pay off on his wager. When the marquis read what was written on the sheet of paper and noticed that he held first place among the doctors, he began to laugh with his entire company, which knew about this bet, and he admitted that he'd been bested by the juggler, and he ordered that he be given what he'd been promised.

Tale 111

OF THE CAPERS PULLED BY TWO FELLOW THIEVES WHO HAVE SINCE BEEN HANGED AND STRANGLED

A fine rascal, who was a native of the city of Issoudun in Berry and who had commited an indefinite number of thefts and had often been threatened, was finally condemned to be hanged and strangled; but, just as he was being taken out to be hanged, it happened that a lord passed by, and through him he obtained the king's pardon, and all for having spouted a few words of dog Latin which, although they weren't understood, gave the impression that he was a man for hire; and, in fact, once he got his pardon, the king sent him as just that to the New World with Roberval; this trip bore out what Horace asserts:

Coelum, non animum, mutant qui trans mare currunt.

That is to say:

> Those who cross the oceans wide
> Change the sky, but not their hide.

In fact, upon his return, he pursued his thieve's trade even more than before; so, when he was caught for the second time, he went up the steps he'd not taken before. Now, to tell the truth, I believe that our second thief wouldn't have gotten off any more lightly, inasmuch as it's very likely that he had been caught many other times since it wasn't possible to undertake thefts by the dozens and pull off each one of them skillfully; indeed, if there ever was a man who could be considered as having a natural inclination for thievery, this one was a perfect example of it. In order to reward one of his friends for the trouble he'd taken to save his life on several occasions, he took his brand-new mantle and several other things; he was caught wearing the mantle, and over it another one which he'd similarly stolen elsewhere. He was also found wearing three shirts one on top of the other; and, not long before that, he'd done the same thing with a velvet jacket belonging to someone who had been good enough to put him up. But his most notorious theft in the matter of dress was when he stole all the clothes which had been made for a certain man and wife; they seemed worth the taking because most of them were made of silk; and what was even more astonishing about this theft was that, in order to carry it all off (as he had done), he had had to make six or seven trips. Now, he had taken them to a room which he'd been given at the monastery of the Sisters of the Holy Cross of Poitiers; he was there when they came to make him account for those garments, since he was the only one under suspicion. But, when he saw through the window that they were coming for him, he didn't wait for them, but locked the door and fled. Nevertheless, they found a way to get into the room, and (besides the garments they were seeking) they found what they weren't looking for, that is, about forty pairs of shoes of all sorts and shapes and several pairs of breeches as well as several pieces of cloth wrapped around some books he'd stolen from students. But this crafty fellow was worse on the sisters than on his friends because, while he'd only taken a few garments from them, he stole the sisters' most beautiful relics for the fun of it. However, the most notable trick this subtle thief played was the one he pulled in the prison's pound where he was being held for his crimes; he couldn't even wait to get out of there before he returned to his trade, and in that very place he snatched the jailer's cloak and sold it on the spot by passing it through the prison bars facing the street. Nevertheless, for all his subtlety, he wasn't able to avoid being packed on a mule and then hanged and strangled.

Tale 112

OF A GENTLEMAN WHO WHIPPED TWO GREY FRIARS FOR THE FUN OF IT

A gentleman from Savoy, who practiced his thievery in and around his home, had a particular quirk: although he was a bandit of greater repute than anyone else in the trade, nevertheless, he was most often satisfied to share with the people he robbed when they gave up promptly without waiting for him to get angry. But, on the contrary, what they held against him most at the time was that he really had it in for monks and nuns, and he amused himself by playing on them many tricks which were (as the proverb goes) fit for a king, that is, tricks which please those who play them: among them, I'll describe one of his schemes, or rather one which is divided into two parts, by which he made two grey friars very happy at first (so he thought) and then very sorry. He received these two friars in his castle and fed them well, and then he told them that in order to put the finishing touch on their entertainment he wanted to give each one of them his own wench; when they refused, he told them to make themselves at home where he was concerned inasmuch as he considered them to be just like all other men, and he locked them up by force in a room with the wenches; when he went back to see them an hour or so later, he asked them how they'd been getting along in their new setup; he wanted to delude them into believing that they'd done it, so he forced them to admit it in spite of themselves and, frightening them, he said, "What! You miserable hypocrites! Is that how you overcome temptation?" And, then and there, the two poor friars were stripped as naked as when they came from their mothers' wombs; the gentleman and his servants whipped them as much as their arms could bear, and then he sent them on their way in the nude. Now, as to whether that was well done or not, I leave the decision up to their learned judges.

Tale 113

OF THE PRIEST FROM ONZAIN, NEAR AMBOISE, WHO WAS PERSUADED BY HIS LANDLADY TO HAVE HIMSELF CASTRATED

A priest from Onzain, near Amboise, was persuaded by his landlady (with whom he was carrying on) to pretend to do away, so she said, with all of her husband's suspicions; he agreed to have himself castrated (more discreetly referred to as emasculated) and put himself in the hands of a man by the name of Peter des Serpents, a native of Vil-Antrois in Berry, and this princely priest sent for all his relatives and friends; and, after he'd told them that he had never dared let them know his condition but that he was finally reduced to such a state that he was forced to go through with it, he made his will. And, to put on an even better show, he told this Master Peter (whom he'd told, however, just to pretend and, accordingly, had given him four crowns) that he'd willingly forgive him for his death if, by chance, he happened to die from it. He put himself in his hands, let himself be tied up, and all set up like someone who was really going to be castrated. Now, you have to know that, just as this priest had told Master Peter to pretend only, the mistress' husband, for his part (after having seen through this farce), told him to do it in earnest with the promise of giving him double what he'd received from the priest for pretending. So, persuaded by the husband and holding the poor priest in his power, Master Peter tied him hand and foot and, in fact, actually performed his duty and then explained to him that he wasn't used to treating his trade lightly and that, if he ever did, his trade would make fun of him. And that's how this woman's scheme affected the poor priest and how, instead of his getting ready to deceive the husband more than ever with this ruse, he himself was deceived by a subterfuge far more detrimental to his being.

Tale 114

OF A TRICK A YOUNG WOMAN FROM ORLEANS USED IN ORDER TO LURE INTO HER NET A YOUNG STUDENT SHE LIKED

A young woman from Orleans, who saw no way of letting a young student know that she liked him more than anybody else, used the good nature of her father confessor in order to attain her goal, which was to lure him into her net. She went to the church where the young student usually went, and, pretending to be distressed, she told (under the pretext of confession) the priest that there was a young student who was constantly after her dishonor by exposing them both to grave danger; he happened to be in the same place (fortuitously), but not thinking about her, and she pointed him out; she movingly asked the priest to admonish him as he saw fit in such a case. And, immediately making all of it up in order to lure the one she falsely accused of having pursued her, she told this father confessor then and there (in detail) about all the ploys the student used, saying that he was in the habit of climbing over a certain wall at a certain time of night because he knew that her husband wasn't there then and that he climbed a tree in order to get in through the window; in short, he did this and that and he used such means that she had a difficult time defending herself. The priest spoke to the student and admonished him as he thought best. The student, who knew in his heart that there was no truth in what this woman said and that he'd never thought about her, pretended, nevertheless, to accept these reproaches as though he needed them and thanked the priest for them; but, as the heart of man is inclined to evil, he had sense enough to realize that this woman had accused him of what she wanted him to do in view of the fact that she'd given him all the ways and means that he was to use. With this opportunity, the young man, going from bad to worse, didn't fail to follow the road he'd been shown; so, in a little while, the poor priest (who had acted in good faith) realized that he'd been tricked by the woman's ruse, and he couldn't help shouting from the pulpit: "I see the one who made a pimp out of me"; and, since she'd been found out, she didn't dare go back to confession to him from then on.

Tale 115

THE WAY TO MAKE WOMEN SHUT UP AND DANCE WHEN THEY START NAGGING

A rather quiet and sedate man married a woman who was such a bitch that, although he ran the house and did the cooking, he couldn't get away from constantly having her torment and nag him, even at the table with company, and, no matter how much he warned or sweet-talked her, she didn't heed him, even though she was usually fondled with a stick. The husband was very astonished at this, and he decided to use another means: every time she took a notion to annoy and nag him he'd start to play a flute he had and which he no more knew how to play than to make love. Nevertheless, for all that, his wife didn't stop nagging him until she noticed and got indignant that he didn't bother with her as much as before, and so she began to dance around angrily and, completely fed up with the sound of the flute, she grabbed it from his hands. But, the husband didn't want to lose the means with which he whiled his cares away, and he grabbed her around the neck in order to get his flute back, and then he began to toot and play more than ever. So, this miserable woman, offended at how the flute annoyed her, left the house and promised herself not to put up with such behavior in the future, and, the next day, as soon as she returned, she went back to nagging better than ever. Nevertheless, the husband did as he pleased and went on playing his flute, and, when she saw this, his wife was defeated and promised him that in the future she'd be more than obedient in all proper things, provided that he put the flute away and not play it any more because, she said, the sound deafened her. In this way, the husband subdued his wife and realized that it wasn't a bad proverb which says that there are many ways to humble women's pride and make them shut up without striking a blow.

Tale 116

OF THE MAN WHO OFFERED TO SERVE AS INTERPRETER FOR THE AMBASSADORS OF THE KING OF ENGLAND, HOW HE CARRIED IT OUT, AND HOW HE WAS DISGRACED

A gentleman, who was rather well known because of the great honors he held in France, did indeed show that he had some knowledge in his head (but no more than was absolutely necessary): when he read the letter that the king of England, Henry VIII, had written to King Francis I and saw that it contained among other things, *Mitto tibi duodecim molossos,* that is to say, "I am sending you a dozen mastiffs," he interpreted it as, "I am sending you a dozen mules." And, sure of this interpretation, he and another lord went to see the king to ask him to give them the present the king of England was sending him. The king hadn't yet heard about this, and he was amazed that he was being sent mules from England and said that it was a great novelty, and so he wanted to see them. Now, because he also wanted to see the letter and have others see it too, they read *duodecim molossos,* that is "twelve mastiffs." When this lord realized that he was being laughed at (and you can just imagine how), he looked for a way out, and it only made him look worse because he said that he'd misread and taken *molossos* for *muletos.* Nevertheless, for all that, those who were with the king couldn't help laughing because they were unable to accept his brand of Latin.

Tale 117

OF THE SMALL TALK THAT A PRIEST CARRIED ON WITH THE KING OF FRANCE, HENRY II

A certain priest, who was delivering a sermon to his parishioners, heard several small children shouting, which kept him from saying and explaining what he had in mind, and this made him angry; he remembered that some other children went through the city singing dirty songs, and so he said, "A bunch of little sons-of-bitches

go around singing that song *I'm Going to Bang You!* etc. I wish
I were their father: God knows how I'd bang them! " He was just
as funny on another occasion when he spoke to King Henry II, who
had summoned him to amuse him: when the king asked him for
news of his parishioners, he told him that he didn't care to preach
to them unless they were upright people. And when the king asked
him if they did conduct themselves well, he said, "In my presence,
they put on a good front and play a bad game, and they're ready
to do everything I tell them; but, as soon as I turn my rear around,
it's all air, Sire." The king took this in good part because there was
no malice in it any more than in the slips which were usually a part
of his sermons: indeed, if it had been thought that he was deliberately playing on the word *air* (which, in addition to its primary
meaning, is used in the language of the common people for what
is also expressed by "fiddlesticks," that is, "that's a lot of hot air"),
he would have been taught to air his opinions differently. And now
play it up, drummer!

Tale 118

OF THE MAN WHO LOANED MONEY ON HIS OWN COLLATERAL AND HOW HE WAS MADE TO LOOK RIDICULOUS

A fine rascal had invited to dinner two of his friends whom he'd
run into in town and, when he returned, he saw that the coldest
thing in his house was the fireplace and that there wasn't a single
crown in his purse. He immediately decided upon this expedient in
order to keep his promise to those he'd invited. He went to the house
of a certain fellow he knew, and, in the absence of the cook, he took
a copper pot that had meat cooking in it, put it under his cloak, and
took it home. When he got back, he ordered his servant to pour the
stew into an earthen pot, and, after the copper pot had been emptied
(he had it scoured very well), he sent a boy to the owner in order to
ask him to lend him some money, using this pot as collateral. The
boy brought his master a favorable reply, that is, some money, which
came in the nick of time to supply the table with everything else
that was needed, and he also brought back a receipt in which this
creditor admitted he'd received the copper pot as collateral for the

money. When the creditor decided to eat, he discovered that one of his pots which had been placed on the fire was missing, and then did he scream. The cook asserted that, since she'd last seen it, only this rascal had been there; but they hesitated to suspect him of such an act. Nevertheless, they finally went to see if they might not catch sight of it in his house, and, because they didn't see it at all, they asked him about it. He answered that he didn't know anything about it, and, when he began to feel pressured (inasmuch as they maintained that no one else had been there around the time it was taken), he said, "It's quite true that I borrowed a pot; but I sent it back to the man from whom I'd borrowed it." When the creditor denied it, this rascal said, "Look, gentlemen, how wise it is to trust people today without a proper receipt! He'd immediately like to accuse me of theft if I didn't have a receipt written and signed by him." Then, he showed the receipt the boy had brought him: so, for payment, the creditor was laughed at throughout the city, the word having spread immediately that So-and-So (calling him by name) had loaned money on collateral which belonged to him.

Tale 119

OF THE TRICK THAT A YOUNG BOY USED TO DRIVE OUT SEVERAL MONKS WHO LODGED IN AN INN

In the diocese of Anjou, there was a good woman who was a widow and innkeeper and who, out of piety, was in the habit of lodging grey friars and treating them as best she could. One of her sons was unhappy about this because they depended a great deal on his mother's charity, and, since there was no hope for compensation, he decided to drive them out. It so happened that, three or four days later, two grey friars went there for lodging, and the son didn't show any ill will for fear of offending his mother. But, when each one had retired to his room, the son led a three-week or month-old calf to the friars' room in the middle of the night without being seen. Now, as soon as the calf realized that it didn't have its nurse nearby, it wandered all around the room, looking for nourishment, and by chance it got under the bed in which the friars were sound asleep. And as this poor calf was foraging about, it ran into the youngest one's head, which was hanging over the side of the bed, and the calf began to lick the poor monk, who was sweating like a pig: he woke up with a start and called to his fellow friar for help, and he told him that there were spirits there which had touched his face, and he begged him to comfort him. And, while saying these words, he trembled so much that he amazed his companion, who ordered him, on pain of disobedience, to get up and light a fire, which the poor monk refused to do, fearing the spirit. Nevertheless, notwithstanding the pleas he made, he got out of bed and went towards the fireplace to light a candle. When the calf heard steps, it thought it was its mother, and it went over and put its muzzle between the friar's legs and grabbed him by his genitals (friars are scantily clad under their long cassocks). Then, the poor friar began to shout loudly, "Mercy! " and he immediately went back to bed, imploring God's mercy and saying his seven Psalms and other prayers. The calf, fretful over having lost its nurse's teat, ran around the room and finally shrieked its head off (as you can imagine), which astonished the monks even more. The next morning, before four o'clock, the son went back as secretly as before and took his calf away. When the poor friars got up, they told the widow what they'd heard that night and gave her to understand that it was a ghost who was doing his penance there, and, as a result, they so criticized the inn, while talking about it to all the monks they met, that no friar or monk has ever stayed there since.

Tale 120

OF THE THIEF WHO WAS SEEN RUMMAGING IN THE POUCH OF THE LATE CARDINAL OF LORRAINE AND HOW HE ESCAPED

It happened in the days of King Francis I that a thief, dressed as a gentleman, was rummaging in the pouch of the late cardinal of Lorraine when he was noticed by the king, who was at mass opposite the cardinal. The thief realized he'd been seen and he began to motion to the king that he not say a word and he'd see something funny. The king was delighted that something funny was being concocted for him, and he let him go on; a little while later he went to speak to the cardinal and gave him reason to go into his pouch. When he was unable to find what he'd put there, he was puzzled and began to amuse the king, who had watched this farce performed. Nevertheless, after having laughed heartily, the lord asked that he be given back what had been taken from him, as he too thought that the taker's intention had been just that; but, while the king thought he was an honest gentleman, and rightly so since he was so sure of himself and kept such a straight face, experience showed that he was a very expert thief, disguised as a gentleman, who had had no desire to fool around, but who, pretending to do so, had acted in earnest. And then the cardinal turned all the laughter on the king, who, using his usual oath, swore on the word of a gentleman that it was the first time a thief had wanted to make him his accomplice.

Tale 121

OF THE MEANS AN ITALIAN GENTLEMAN USED IN ORDER TO AVOID
FIGHTING A DUEL AND THE COMPARISON THAT A MAN FROM
PICARDY MADE BETWEEN FRENCHMEN AND ITALIANS

An Italian gentleman realized that he couldn't honestly avoid a duel that he'd agreed to with one of his own kind without coming up with an irrefutable reason, and so he accepted it; but, having later regretted it, he advanced no other reason (when the time for the duel came) except to tell his enemy that he was ready to fight and was anxiously awaiting him, and he said, "You're desperate; I'm not; and yet, I'll take care not to fight you." It's quite true that someone might say that you cannot judge everyone on the basis of one example and that, if it were the case, one could (and rightly so) hold all Frenchmen responsible for what one man from Picardy said in testifying to his prowess: he was boasting of having been at war for several years without drawing his sword and when he was asked why, he said, "Because I never get angry. But," he continued, "every time the truth is really told, it will have to be said loud and clear that Italians have borne the marks of angry Frenchmen more often than the French have borne the marks of desperate Italians and that, even if there weren't a single man from Picardy who could get angry, at least the Gascons get angry enough, indeed they've gotten angry enough at times to make the Italians tremble ten feet deep in their stomachs if they had them that big."

So, the seven or eight inept and foolish war terms that we've borrowed from them put both the Gascons and all the other areas of France in danger of having a different reputation than they had before.

Tale 122

Of the man who paid his innkeeper in songs

A man who was travelling through the country got hungry and went into a tavern, where he glutted himself so well for dinner that he could easily wait for supper, provided it came very soon. Now, when his host, the tavern keeper, was making the rounds of his tables, he asked him to pay for what he'd had and to make room for others; he explained to him that he had no money, but that, if it was agreeable to him, he'd pay him so well in songs that he'd be satisfied. The tavern keeper was very surprised at this answer and told him that he didn't need any songs, but that he wanted to be paid in ready cash and that he'd better see to it and leave. "What!" the traveller said to the tavern keeper, "if I sing you a song which pleases you, won't you be satisfied?" "Yes, of course," the tavern keeper said. Then and there, the traveller began to sing all sorts of songs, except one which he was keeping back in order to save the best for last; and, catching his breath, he asked his innkeeper if he was satisfied. "No," he said, "because none of those you've sung can satisfy me." "Well then," the traveller said, "I'm going to sing you another one which I'm sure will please you." In order to make him more attentive to this new song, he took a bag full of money from his sleeve and began to sing this rather good song which is more than familiar to those who travel: *Mitt' la mano all' bursa, et paga l'hoste,* which means, "Put Your Hand in Your Purse and Pay the Innkeeper." When he finished the song, he asked his innkeeper if it pleased him and if he was satisfied. "Yes," he said, "that one pleases me a lot." "Now then," the traveller said, "since you're satisfied and I've kept my promise, I'm leaving." And he immediately left without paying and without his innkeeper asking him to.

Tale 123

OF THE SUIT A MOTHER-IN-LAW BROUGHT AGAINST HER SON-IN-LAW
FOR NOT HAVING DEFLOWERED HER DAUGHTER
ON THEIR WEDDING NIGHT

In the province of Limousin, a young girl about eighteen years
old and a fine country boy who was very well hung were married.
Now, it happened that the young man, on their very first night, set
about consummating his marriage, and in order to gratify his tender
bride, he first gave her his organ to handle so as to make her want
to help him do his business. But, when the poor girl held it and
saw how big it was, she steadfastly refused to let her husband put
it in her box for fear he might hurt her; she kept on fearing the
tussle, which greatly annoyed the husband, and, no matter what he
did, he couldn't persuade his bride to play with him; hence, he was
forced to do without for the night. And, when day came, the mother
went to her daughter to find out how she'd gotten along with her
husband and what he'd done to her. She answered her that they'd
done nothing. "What!" the mother said, "so your husband is castrated!" Then, furious, she went to the tribunal of the Officiality in
order to have her daughter unmarried, letting everybody know that
her son-in-law was unable to beget. In her anger, she had him summoned so that she could obtain permission to marry her daughter
off to someone else, and this made the poor groom very unhappy,
considering he'd given neither offense nor occasion to be dishonored
this way. Now, once they were all before the church official and the
plaintiff had asked for the separation of her daughter and son-in-law,
giving as her reasons that her son-in-law, on their wedding night,
had not wanted or had been utterly unable to consummate the
marriage with her daughter and that he was castrated, then the son-
in-law contradicted her and defended himself, saying that he had
just as big a rod as his wife had tail and that he was all for having
a go at it, but that his wife had refused to have anything to do with
it and had been so scared that he'd been unable to do anything.
Then, the official asked the young bride if she'd refused him, and she
told him she had because he had such a big one that she feared, and
still did, that he'd hurt her, and she expected to die afterwards rather

than live. When the mother heard this confession and realized that because of it she was going to lose, she begged the judge to order her daughter to pay the costs since she'd been the cause of this suit. Nevertheless, as a sentence, the official condemned the poor girl to give her lovely and pretty instrument to her husband so that he could get to work on it and do what he was supposed to have done the previous night, and there were no costs, considering the relationship of the parties involved.

Tale 124

How a Scot was cured of a stomach ailment
with the means his landlady gave him

Not long ago, a Scot, who had already served in the guard of the king of France and who had, in his youth, obtained a little learning, realized that the king favored learned persons; and so, since he saw that he could go about studying while he was out of the service and unemployed, he chose to lodge with a widow, and he stayed there for some time. He had trouble making himself understood and one day when he wasn't feeling very well (he sought his landlady's advice because she understood him), he said to her, "Madam, my pudding hurts a great deal." His landlady readily understood that he meant he had a stomachache and that, in order to get prompt relief, he was asking her advice; so she told him he had to pray to Saint Eutropius, who, they say, cures such ailments. The Scot listened to her and, because he felt his stomach going from bad to worse, he didn't want to scorn his landlady's advice: so, he took it and went to the first church he came to, and he prayed so much that it seemed to those who heard him that the saint had to come promptly to his aid. By chance, while he was meditating that way, there happened to be a fine rascal hidden behind the statue of Saint Eutropius, and he was studying the faces of those who came and went; and when he noticed the expressions this Scot made, he began to shout, "To hell with John of Scotland and his nonsense!" The Scot heard these words which were yelled rather rudely and thought it was some knave who wanted to keep him from his devotions; for this reason, after he'd made out the spot from which the voice he'd heard could have come from, he picked up his bow and arrow and shot right at the saint's statue. The thief, who was behind it, feared that the Scot might let another one go, and he began to go down the wooden stairs he'd climbed; but he was unable to get away so quietly that he didn't make a noise which frightened the Scot so much that he thought it was the saint who was coming after him to punish him for having offended him; he was so frightened that his ailment immediately disappeared, and from then on he lived as happy as a lark.

Tale 125

OF THE EPITAPHS OF ARETINO, CALLED THE DIVINE, AND HIS FRIEND MAGDALENE

Aretino, not the One and Only,[1] but the one who usurped the appellation of the Divine, also gave himself the arrogant title of *scourge of princes* because he was completely given over to excoriation. And so, as the well-known proverb goes, he spared neither king nor thing, and he wrote in a preface to one of his Italian comedies that the very Christian King Francis I had sent him a gold chain in the shape of tongues in order to gag him so that he wouldn't write about him the way he had about several other lords. Likewise, in one of the dialogues he wrote, he introduced two courtesans who tell one another how they acquired their riches and how, because of their good behavior and respectful deportment, they were kept by noble company; therefore, when one of them died, he composed for her the following epitaph, which has since been widely publicized:

---

[1] Bernardo Accolti (1465-1536), called Unico Aretino because of his birth in Arezzo and his unequaled facility in impromptu poetry and music. The subject of the tale is the famous Pietro Aretino (1492-1566); it was Ariosto, in the 1532 edition of his *Orlando furioso*, who gave Aretino his titles: *Ecco il flagello / De' principi, il divin Pietro Aretino*; "Behold the Scourge of Princes, the divine Pietro Aretino."

Epitaph

The remains of Magdalene lie here.
In her lifetime, she found pricks so dear
That after her death I ask each fine sir
To piss on her grave and so to bless her.

Now, this grand Aretino died not long ago, and his compatriots, the
Florentines, made up this epitaph, which is worthy of him and his
atheism.

Aretino's Epitaph

Qui giace l'Aretino, amaro tosco
Del seme humano, di cui la lingua trafisse
E vivi e morti, di Dio mal' non dice
E si scuso con dir': No lo conosco.

Translation

Here lies Aretino, the bitter draught
Of all mankind; his tongue did sting a lot
The quick and the dead; as for God, his thought
Did not attack because he knew Him not.

Tale 126

OF THE SPEECH THAT A YOUNG MAN SET OUT TO MAKE WHEN HE WAS
INSTALLED AS A COUNSELOR AND HOW HE WAS REBUFFED

A young man, who had been sent to universities to learn common law and how to use it in due course at his father's will and
pleasure, was rather nicely and pleasantly treated there. Because
he basked in his comforts and delights, it chanced that he forgot
all about his law codes and digests in order to impress on his
brain the idea of a sweetheart, and, feeding on such a thought, he
converted his studies into the reading of Petrarch and other such
famous prodigals. In the meantime, his father died. When they
were told, the relatives and friends of the young man, thinking that
he was a learned scholar and that he'd reasonably benefited from

his law studies, sent him word of his father's death and advised him that it was time he chose the occupation and profession he wanted to pursue and they would help him in this endeavor. The young man, yielding to their advice and counsel (although he hadn't yet studied law), set out for his late father's home. After he had visited his friends and made certain of the assets his father had left him, he took a notion to buy a counselor's position in the judicial court. His friends concurred with this; and, because of the friendship they'd had with his father, they promised him to request it of King Francis I, who reciprocated their affection because they were very faithful servants. One day when they were with the king, they asked him for this counselor's position; he granted it, and they were issued letters patent. Delighted with this, they notified the young man about it and told him how he was to conduct himself when he went before the court. The young man followed their advice in every respect and paid his assessment and made ready. In short, he submitted his credentials; they were read in open chamber. Soon thereafter, the court established the petitioner's deficiencies and sent him back to his studies. He was very astonished at this, and he returned to his relatives and friends and implored them to let the king know the judicial court had refused him. The king was told about it. He immediately sent word to the gentlemen of the court that they were to appear before His Majesty. The court delegated two of its counselors and instructed them to give whatever reasons were called for. After they'd appeared before the king in order to hear his will, he asked them why they refused to receive this young man into their group, seeing that he'd granted him this counselor's position. The delegates told him, as they'd been instructed, that the court was rather well informed of his inability and, for that reason, could not honestly admit him. The king accepted this explanation as sound and reasonable, thanked the gentlemen of the court, and gave it no further thought. A few days later, the young man took up his case again and urged his friends so much that they were persuaded to ask the king again to order the court to receive him and submit him to the examination required in such cases; moreover, they pointed out to him that he was a man who could be of service to him in the future, besides which the young man's father had been one of his officers for a long time and had acquired a good reputation during his lifetime. The king heard these reasons too, and, not forgetting those that the gentlemen of the court had given him on this matter, he ordered again that he be received. The court opposed it and gave its reasons a second time. Nevertheless, the king wanted him to be received. And, as the gentlemen of the court argued that the young man was flighty and foolish, he said to them, "Well, then! Since they're such a large number of wise and learned persons, can't they put up with one fool among them?" With this remark, the delegates left and assured the court of the king's will. The young man, certain that he'd been successful and that he'd now be received, went before the court once again and asked to be examined according to the rule. The court ordered one of the ushers to bring him in and lead him to a rostrum that had been prepared for this purpose. After he'd climbed it and thoroughly pondered what he wanted to say, he began his speech with a verse from Psalm 118 and said:

Lapidem quem reprobaverunt aedificantes, hic factus est in caput anguli, that is:

> The stone rejected by those who
> Have charge of the building and all
> Has been set down and installed too
> In the central part of the hall,

thereby insinuating to the court that it shouldn't have scorned him as it had. When he heard this, one of the older members of the court, who was hardly pleased by the young man's boldness, got up, and, formulating a reply worthy of such arrogance, answered as follows:

A domino factum est istud, et est mirabile in oculis nostris, that is:

> That's a heavenly creation
> Made by the God of gods, 'tis true,
> And a marvelous formation
> Who is presented to our view.

With this answer, he put down the young man's audacity to such an extent that he never spoke again in that manner in such an august assembly.

Tale 127

OF AN ELDERLY KNIGHT WHO GOT HIS WIFE'S FANTASIES OUT OF HER
HEAD WITH A BLOOD LETTING, AND HOW PREVIOUSLY HE HAD
BEEN UNABLE TO RESTRAIN HER FROM PLAYING OVERLY WILD
AND LUSTY TRICKS ON HIM

It's a great asset in marriage to know one another's imperfections
and to find remedies to avoid the many quarrels and disputes which
normally occur in most households, as in the case of a very fine
knight from Tuscany; after having spent the flower of his youth in
the feat of arms as well as in hunting and studying, he decided
rather late to enter the bonds of matrimony, but he finally did with
a young and beautiful maiden whom he treated very kindly in all
things except when it came to making love at which he was rather
poor because of his age. But the new bride wasn't aware of this
deficiency until she overheard the conversation of other fine wives
whom she frequented and who were talking about the steady delights
they got from their young husbands. This incited her to want to
experience the same thing as the others. But, in order to accomplish
this and with her honor intact, she complained about it to her own
mother; she advised her against it (conscience condemned her
course), but she was plainly unable to dissuade her from her announced intention, and so she told her, in an attempt to divert her
from this scheme, "My daughter, since I see no other balm to di-
minish your pain, I'll tell you this. There are men of various tempera-
ments and dispositions who cut off and get rid of their horns with
knives or poison; some wear them patiently, and, because they have
stronger stomachs, they swallow cuckoldry easily without saying
a word. Therefore, you must test your husband's patience with a
few harmless and relatively unimportant tricks." To these remarks,
the daughter replied that she didn't want to rely in any way on the
cunning required in such cases, but that rather she wanted to lure
into her net a man of lusty disposition and good name who would
keep their reputation as good as that of her chaplain. The mother
instructed her to try the knight's good will and, accordingly, work
out the rest. The daughter promised her not to delay in doing this.
While her gentleman husband was out hunting, she picked up an

ax and went into his garden, and she began to cut down a beautiful laurel tree which had been planted by her husband's own hand, and, for this reason, he was possessive about it, and in its shade he gladly passed the time away, waiting for the meats he'd ordered to be seasoned as a treat for his friends. To make it short, down went the tree and home came the husband; she built a fire with the branches, and he immediately recognized them. Nevertheless, before raising a ruckus over it, he put his cloak back on his shoulders and went to the spot in order to be more certain about it. You needn't ask if he was very upset when he saw the fresh hole: he returned full of threats and asked his wife who had played this trick on him, and she answered that she'd done it in order to warm him up on his return from hunting and because she understood that this tree comforted old age. This time she appeased him and thought that she'd made him swallow his anger as easily as sugar. The next morning, she told her mother what she'd done, and she told her that it was a good beginning, but that she had to try even more, such as killing the little dog he loved so much, and she set out to do it. She did it when this little dog, on coming back from the city with its master, was covered with mud and jumped on the bed where the lady had put a fine spread on purpose; and, when the dog was chased off, it jumped on the lady's dress, and, pretending that her beautiful clothes had been ruined, she picked up a knife and, in front of her husband, cut the dog's throat. According to her mother, this was still not enough if, after the tree and the dead dog, she did not, in addition, offend her husband in the presence of some of his dearest friends, and she did this too: she turned over (at a banquet he was giving for his best friends) the table, which was laden with meats, and, excusing herself, she said that she had inadvertently done this, wanting to tend to the service. As a result of these indignities, the gentleman decided that night to keep her from getting out of bed; he kept her there whether she liked it or not and told her that she had to stay there for a few remedies he'd prepared in order to cure her. She defended herself and said that she was in good health and that her mind was alert. He said, "I believe it, and a little too much so, and it must be remedied immediately." Then, remembering the three fine tricks she'd played on him one after the other, notwithstanding the reproaches and threats he'd made to her each time and justly fearing a fourth one worse than all the previous ones, he sent for a barber, and he told him what he wanted him to do: to wit, for certain reasons which he kept from him, his pleasure and intention was that, as soon as he introduced his wife to him, he not fail to perform his duty if he wanted to please him. The barber listened to these remarks and ventured to ask the gentleman what he wanted, and he was immediately reassured. The gentleman lit a large fire in a room in his house where the barber was waiting, and then he went to his wife's room and found her completely dressed (pretending to go see her mother, to whom, a few days earlier, she'd disclosed her husband's impotence, asking her, moreover, to help her in an amorous contest which she'd entered into with a champion of her own age). Aware of this, the gentleman redoubled his rancor and anger (which he disguised as best he could) and said to her, "My dear, your blood is much too hot, and its ebullience causes all these vagaries and inconsiderate tricks you play every day. The doctors I've consulted about it are of the opinion that you need a little bloodletting, and they say that for your health." The lady heard her husband speak that way, but she didn't yet perceive his intention, and she let herself be led where he wanted. He led her into the room where the barber was waiting for her, and he ordered her to sit down with her face towards the fire; he motioned to the barber to take her right arm and open her vein, which he did. While the blood was flowing from the lady's arm, her husband noticed her fantasies weakening and ordered this vein closed and the one in the left opened, which was also done. As a result, the poor lady was half dead. The gentleman was very happy to have reached the end of his undertaking and had her carried to a bed, where she had time to learn not to anger her husband anymore. As soon as she recovered from having fainted, she sent one of her servants to her mother, and the messenger told her all about the nasty tricks she'd played on her husband; she suspected (the good woman!) that by this means her daughter wanted to hold her to the promise (against her will) she'd made, and she went to see her in bed and said to her, "Well! my daughter, how are you? Don't be angry; your wish with regard to what you requested of me will soon come about." "Ah! Mother," she answered, "I'm dead; such passions no longer consume me; my husband has operated so well that I'm even more grateful to him today for having put me back on the

had Lady Isabel not encouraged him with the promise of the reward that she'd arranged for him with her friend and the fact that her husband slept soundly and wouldn't wake up until daylight. Now, all she wanted Alessio to do this for was so that, when her husband moved in bed, he'd feel his leg, or some other human part, and think it was she. "What! Will I have to do it very long?" Alessio, persuaded first by one then the other, undressed, not without great fear, and, hanging on to Isabel by her dress, quietly went to bed on his side, being careful not to cough and spit near his bedmate. Meanwhile, Lucio and Isabel played their game peacefully in another room in the house. Poor Alessio, seeing himself near the knight, didn't dare move while he trembled and thought about all sorts of things; at times he thought the lady was betraying them both, throwing him first to the lion's mouth; at times he thought that, although she might be dealing with them sincerely, she was carrying on in his friend's arms, leaving him in this great and imminent danger until daybreak; and, at that very hour, he was very surprised to see them come in the room and slam the door shut: they approached the bed and asked him how he'd spent the night. Immediately, Lady Isabel raised the bed cover, and Alessio saw his lady friend in bed next to him instead of the enemy, and she (sweet thing!) had no more stirred nor batted an eye than he. The two lovers were highly praised for this, to wit, Alessio for the danger in which he put himself in order to advance his friend's undertaking, and his lady friend because she had so virtuously contained herself while in bed next to him. Therefore, they were allowed to have half an ounce or so of pleasure in amorous tussle. They say that these four lovers kept their affair going while the husbands were away in the service of their king.

Tale 129

OF A YOUNG GIRL NICKNAMED ASS HIDE AND HOW SHE GOT MARRIED WITH THE HELP OF LITTLE ANTS

In an Italian town, there was a merchant who, when he saw that he was reasonably rich, decided to retire and spend the rest of his life enjoying his wife and children, and for this reason he

withdrew to a small farm he had in the country. Now, because he
was a man of considerable good cheer who loved a witty conversation, many fine persons visited him, and among others a gentleman
from an old family, who was his neighbor and who wanted to join
several pieces of the merchant's land to his; he made him believe
that he very much wanted his son to marry the youngest of his
daughters, who was named Pernette, provided he improved his lot
somehow. The merchant, who understood very well what the gentleman was driving at and that he was making fun of him, thanked
him graciously as one who would never have hoped that such a
boon might come his way. Nevertheless, these remarks reached the
ears of the gentleman's son and the merchant's daughter; they
ventured to sound out one another's heart and affections, and
they did it so skillfully that, in intimate conversation, they promised
to marry and decided to tell their parents about it. A little while
later, the gentleman's son spoke to Pernette's father and confronted
him with reasons that were so sweetened with promises to further
his interests that he finally agreed to let her become his wife, provided her mother consented. Now, you have to understand that
Pernette's sisters were jealous of her happiness and of her being
first; as a result, in order to divert their father from his promise,
they told him one thing and another. On the other hand, the mother,
who regretted ever having carried her in her womb, refused to
agree to this marriage unless Pernette first picked up off the ground,
and with her tongue, a bushel full of barley, grain by grain, which
she would have scattered around for this purpose. Furthermore,
seeing that this marriage didn't please his wife and heeding what
his other daughters had told him, the merchant insisted that Pernette from then on wear no other clothes but an ass hide that he
bought for her, thinking that by this means he'd drive her to despair
and disgust her friend with her. But, on the contrary, because of
the severity with which she was treated, Pernette redoubled her love
and frequently took walks dressed in this hide. When her sweetheart
heard about this, he went to the merchant, who put on a good
front and played a worse game; he told him that he wanted to
keep his promise to him but that his wife wanted such and such
a thing (which he told him about) done. When she heard this,
Pernette went to her father and asked him when he wanted her
to start. Honestly unable to break his promise, her father set a

date. She didn't fail to show up. While she was after the grains of barley, her father and mother watched carefully to see if she'd pick up two at a time, thereby releasing them from their promise; but, since constancy has its rewards, along came a number of ants which crawled to where the barley was, and they worked so diligently with Pernette (and without anyone noticing them) that the place was soon empty. In this way, Pernette was able to marry her sweetheart, who caressed and loved her as she well deserved. And so, for as long as she lived, the nickname *Ass Hide* stuck to her.

SELECTED BIBLIOGRAPHY

Editions

Contes ou Nouvelles Récréations et Joyeux Devis suivis du Cymbalum Mundi. Ed. P. L. Jacob. New edition. Paris: Garnier, n.d. (1872). Particularly useful for its annotation.

Conteurs français du XVIe siècle. Ed. Pierre Jourda. Paris: Gallimard, 1965, pp. 359-594. Best available edition of complete text of *Nouvelles Récréations et Joyeux Devis* and the one followed in our translation.

Cymbalum Mundi. Ed. Peter H. Nurse. Manchester: University Press, 1958. Essential edition; excellent discussion of work's meaning.

Nouvelles Récréations et Joyeux Devis, suivis du Cymbalum Mundi. Ed. Louis Lacour. 2 vols. Paris: Librairie des Bibliophiles, 1874. Additional annotation; good supplement to 1856 edition.

Œuvres françoises. Ed. Louis Lacour. 2 vols. Paris: P. Jannet, 1856. Old, but still very useful.

Three Sixteenth-Century Conteurs. Ed. Alban J. Krailsheimer. New York and Oxford: Oxford University Press, 1966, pp. 75-90. Contains very fine and judicious introduction to Des Périers's life and works, particularly the tales.

Translations

Cymbalum Mundi. Trans. Bettina L. Knapp. New York: Bookman Associates, Inc., 1965. Incisive preface by Donald M. Frame.

The Mirrour of Mirth and Pleasant Conceits. Ed. James Woodrow Hassell, Jr. Columbia: The University of South Carolina Press, 1959. Fair, but elliptical, Elizabethan translation of thirty-nine of Des Périers's tales.

Critical Studies

Becker, Ph. A. *Bonaventure des Périers als Dichter und Erzähler.* Vienna and Leipzig: Hölder-Pichler-Tempski, 1924. Sound general study.

Charpentier, Françoise. "Une Page rabelaisienne de Des Périers: la première nouvelle en forme de préambule." *Revue d'Histoire Littéraire de la France,* 67 (1967), 601-5. A study of likenesses in Rabelais and Des Périers.

Chenevière, Adolphe. *Bonaventure des Périers, sa vie, ses poésies.* Paris: Plon, 1886. Solid and still useful.

Delaruelle, Louis. "Etude sur le problème du *Cymbalum Mundi.*" *Revue d'Histoire Littéraire de la France,* 32 (1925), 1-23. Refutation of the atheistic thrust of the *Cymbalum Mundi.*

Febvre, Lucien. *Origène et Des Périers ou L'Enigme du "Cymbalum Mundi."* Paris: Droz, 1942. Good study, but minimizes excessively Des Périers's originality.

Frank, Félix and Chenevière, Adolphe. *Lexique de la langue de Bonaventure des Périers.* Paris: Léopold Cerf, 1888. Good glossary of Des Périers's language although there are errors and omissions.

Hassell, James Woodrow, Jr. *Sources and Analogues of the Nouvelles Récréations et Joyeux Devis of Bonaventure des Périers.* I, Chapel Hill: University of North Carolina Press, 1957. II, Athens: University of Georgia Press, 1969. Useful schematization of tales by source and analogue.

Haubold, Rudolf H. *Les Nouvelles Récréations et Joyeux Devis des Bonaventure des Périers in literarhistorischer und stilistischer Beziehung.* Reudnitz-Leipzig: Hoffmann, 1888. Good study of tales, but superseded by Sozzi's work.

Lefranc, Abel. "Rabelais et les Estienne; le procès du *Cymbalum* de Bonaventure des Périers." *Revue du Seizième Siècle,* 15 (1928), 356-66. Detailed examination of condemnation proceedings.

Mayer, Charles A. "The Lucianism of Des Périers." *Bibliothèque d'Humanisme et Renaissance,* 12 (1950), 190-207. Sound discussion of Lucian's influence on Des Périers.

Neidhart, Dorothea. *Das "Cymbalum Mundi" des Bonaventure des Périers. Forschungslage und Deutung.* Geneva, Droz; Paris, Minard, 1959. Useful critical survey of studies up to 1957.

Nodier, Charles. *Bonaventure des Périers, Cyrano de Bergerac.* Paris: J. Téchener, 1841. Spirited rehabilitation of Des Périers after long eclipse; still worth reading for its disarming presentation and engaging style.

Nurse, Peter H. "Erasme et Des Périers." *Bibliothèque d'Humanisme et Renaissance,* 30 (1968), 53-64. Stresses Love as principal idea of both the *Cymbalum Mundi* and the *Praise of Folly.*

Pabst, W. *Novellentheorie und Novellendichtung zur Geschichte ihrer Antinomie in den romanischen Literaturen.* Hamburg: De Gruyter & Co., 1953. Contains penetrating analysis of *Nouvelles Récréations et Joyeux Devis* as well as Marguerite of Navarre's *Heptaméron.*

Reynier, Gustave. *Les Origines du roman réaliste.* Paris: Hachette, 1912, pp. 197-204. Emphasis on lack of reproduction of reality in Des Périers's tales; not very useful.

Rodax, Yvonne. *The Real and the Ideal in the Novella of Italy, France, and England.* Chapel Hill: University of North Carolina Press, 1968, pp. 48-61. Diffuse, speculative, but a few perceptive remarks.

Saínéan, Lazare. *Problèmes littéraires du seizième siècle.* Paris: De Boccard, 1927, pp. 275-82. Deals with authorship of the *Nouvelles Récréations et Joyeux Devis*: forceful presentation attributes them to Des Périers.

————. "Les Provincialismes de des Périers." *Revue du Seizième Siècle,* 3 (1915), 28-59. Linguistic study of regionalism in Des Périers's work.

Saulnier, Verdun-L. "Recherches sur diverses poésies de Bonaventure des Périers." *Bulletin du Bibliophile et du Bibliothécaire* (1950), 225-51. Best discussion of Des Périers's poetry.

Saulnier, Verdun-L. "Le Sens de *Cymbalum Mundi*." *Bibliothèque d'Humanisme et Renaissance*, 12 (1951), 42-69, 137-71. Lucid reexamination of Des Périers's so-called atheism.

Screech, Michael A. "The Meaning of the Title *Cymbalum Mundi*." *Bibliothèque d'Humanisme et Renaissance*, 31 (1969), 343-45. Compelling refutation of Pauline source of title.

Sozzi, Lionello. *Les Contes de Bonaventure des Périers. Contribution à l'étude de la nouvelle française de la Renaissance*. Turin: Giappichelli, 1964. Methodical and comprehensive; best study of Des Périers's tales.

Spitzer, Wolfgang. "The Meaning of Bonaventure des Périers's *Cymbalum Mundi*." *PMLA*, 66 (1951), 795-819. Emphasis on man's presumption and love of gossip as the butt of Des Périers's attack.

INDEX

The index consists of two parts. Part I is an index of the proper names and topics found in the Introduction, the first 90 tales, and corresponding notes. Part II is a similar index for the last 39 tales.

PART I

PART II